An
Enchanting
Case of
Spirits

An
Enchanting
Case of
Spirits

Melissa Holtz

Berkley
New York

BERKLEY
An imprint of Penguin Random House LLC
penguinrandomhouse.com

Copyright © 2024 by Melissa Saneholtz
Penguin Random House supports copyright. Copyright fuels creativity,
encourages diverse voices, promotes free speech, and creates a vibrant culture.
Thank you for buying an authorized edition of this book and for complying with copyright
laws by not reproducing, scanning, or distributing any part of it in any form without
permission. You are supporting writers and allowing Penguin Random House
to continue to publish books for every reader.

BERKLEY and the BERKLEY & B colophon are registered trademarks of
Penguin Random House LLC.

Library of Congress Cataloging-in-Publication Data

Names: Holtz, Melissa, author.
Title: An enchanting case of spirits / Melissa Holtz.
Description: First edition. | New York : Berkley, 2024.
Identifiers: LCCN 2023035165 (print) | LCCN 2023035166 (ebook) |
ISBN 9780593640043 (trade paperback) | ISBN 9780593640050 (ebook)
Subjects: LCGFT: Cozy mysteries. | Paranormal fiction. | Romance fiction. | Novels.
Classification: LCC PS3608.O49443447 E53 2024 (print) |
LCC PS3608.O49443447 (ebook) | DDC 813/.6—dc23/eng/20231003
LC record available at https://lccn.loc.gov/2023035165
LC ebook record available at https://lccn.loc.gov/2023035166

First Edition: April 2024

Printed in the United States of America
1st Printing

Interior art: Tarot cards © Bigmouse 108 / Shutterstock

Book design by Alison Cnockaert

For Z, A, G, and #14
Thank you for brightening my world every day;
I love you all in this life and the next.

An
Enchanting
Case *of*
Spirits

Five of Cups

ANOTHER SPOONFUL WILL dull the painful truth.

My youth is gone.

A carton of ice cream is gripped between my legs like my life depends on it not slipping from my clutches. A cool autumn breeze flits through the open window next to my whitewashed sleigh bed, and I shiver as it races up my exposed arms.

I consider closing said window but refrain, too comfy to move from under the heavy down comforter and matching gray sheets I'm currently curled beneath.

My lips wrap around a tarnished silver spoon—a wedding present from my mother—and a chill settles over me. Whether from the draft or cold dessert, I'm not sure, and I couldn't care less either way.

Less than nine hours remain of my fortieth birthday, and I'm alone, eating my ice cream as though it's my last supper.

My eyes are fixed on the harvest-yellow walls, a color I adored once upon a time but now resent because I'm no longer the carefree wife and mother who chose that cheerful shade.

Birthdays come and go, and the next may not be promised, but it's just a day. Tomorrow, all the calls and messages will stop. I'll be one year closer to my own death, with nothing but wrinkles and cellulite to keep me company.

Dramatic much?

My phone chimes from the nightstand and I ignore it. It's been going off all day with messages commemorating a day I'd rather skip from family and friends who know this yet refuse to oblige me.

Almost immediately the phone rings, and I know that either I answer or risk a wellness check from the police, courtesy of my well-meaning friends. There's no doubt it's Lanie or Nina on the other end of this call. Both of my best friends are dogs with a bone, and neither will stop until I shut off the phone or scream down the line that I'm alive.

Sighing, I grab the black smartphone and push accept.

"I'm breathing. You can stop calling," I drone, sounding pathetic even to my own ears.

"Well, that's a relief." Lanie's dry tone just barely hides the irritation she works so hard to conceal. "I thought you'd managed to drown yourself in Chocolate Salted Fudge Truffle or that nasty riesling you adore." I hear Lanie's deep breath before she continues. "Alyssa, you can't hide from your birthday."

"But I'm going to give it my best try," I say, eyeing the now-empty ice cream container with contempt, sending a thanks up to the gods that she didn't attempt a video chat. If Lanie Anderson saw my current condition, she'd stage a full-on intervention.

All traces of irritation and worry vanish when she says, "Ava called."

I groan, silently cursing my far-too-perceptive daughter for calling my overprotective best friend. This wouldn't be the first time. In fact, it seems to be happening far more often than reasonable.

I know Ava doesn't want me to be alone today, but I don't want her worrying when she should be focusing on studying for her exams. She's a little over an hour away at a prestigious boarding school for the arts, and if it were her choice, she'd give up her dreams and come back home.

"She shouldn't have done that. I told her I was fine."

"She doesn't think you are, Ally. You haven't left your house for more than a grocery run this week. It's your fortieth birthday and you aren't celebrating, when we all know that birthdays are a big production with you."

"I left my house," I say indignantly, blowing a wayward piece of hair out of my eyes.

"Don't be cranky. It's unbecoming of a woman in her prime." Her teasing lilt is meant to make me laugh, but I don't.

"I'm not cranky and I'm not in my prime."

"Sure you are!" she says far too cheerfully when moments ago it was all doom and gloom. "Forty is a prime number."

"It's not."

"It isn't? Hmm . . ." she murmurs, and I can see her clearly in my head, full lips pursed and one perfectly microbladed eyebrow cocked in contemplation. "Well, I guess you're right. Nothing prime about forty."

"I hate you."

"You don't," she practically purrs.

She's right. I cherish our friendship. Even more for her part in picking me up off the floor on numerous occasions over the last two years. Lanie has been a constant friend. One who hasn't allowed all of me to break into the million tiny pieces it wants to. A fate my poor heart didn't escape.

Two years ago, my soul was crushed, and it wasn't with one hard knock to my front door.

The harsh reality is that I was sitting next to my husband Garrett the day he died. My head hit the side window, and the last thing I remember is a bright light and the color red. For over a year, I relived the accident nightly. I didn't have dreams; it was always the same nightmare. One I couldn't wake up from.

Garrett died. I survived. And that truth has haunted me for a long time.

My eyes catch on Garrett's ashes, which sit in a generic, unmarked container on top of my dresser. Too cliché for a life as beautiful as ours had been.

A tear slips down my cheeks unbidden, and I swipe it away.

Not today, Satan.

My current grief is brought to you by my birth. I only have room for one trauma at a time.

"Earth to Ally," Lanie sings through the phone.

I shake my head, clearing my mind. "What did you say?"

"It's your birthday, and it's Thursday wine night. I know you said you didn't want to celebrate, but you must. Nina and I are headed out, and you're coming."

I chance a glance into the floor-length mirror resting against my wall and grimace. My wavy strawberry-blond hair is matted at the crown of my head, and I have dark circles underneath my bloodshot eyes. The entirety of my face is blotchy and swollen, a byproduct of crying.

I'm a hideous beast today.

"No, thank you."

My spoon scrapes the bottom of the empty ice cream carton, and the tears stream briskly down my cheeks.

It's been two years and I know this breakdown isn't about him. It's about a number. Forty always sounded ancient and here I am living it and feeling every ache and pain that decided to start on this very day.

How convenient.

"I . . . I'll be . . . fine," I cry. "I'm just so . . . ugly." The wail that accompanies that last part resembles that of a dying animal, and I'm sure Lanie is beyond concerned about my mental state.

"You're not, babe. You need us." The tenderness she uses is so unlike her.

She's my bossy, no-nonsense friend, who's more likely to slap the sense back into me than to allow the moping.

"As much as I don't want to be the overbearing friend on your day, this isn't a situation that I'm going to back down from. I'm coming to you."

"No, I—"

It's no use. The line is dead, and I know without a doubt that Lanie and Nina will be here at some point regardless of any protest on my part.

Forty wasn't supposed to look like this. I'd had every intention of marching out of my thirties with my head held high, ass tight and no lines to be found from the corners of my eyes to my hairline, seventeen years into a blissful marriage.

Exactly none of those things are my reality.

I have tracks deeper than an off-road path lining my forehead and a scar that runs from my temple to the corner of my right eye, a permanent reminder of all I've lost.

Lanie is right. I'm wasting away in this room.

If Garrett were here, he'd tell me to pull myself together, get dressed, and plan on a headache in the morning. But he's not here, so I'll eat my ice cream and feel sorry for myself until the birthday hijackers I call friends arrive.

✦ ✦ ✦

AT FIVE O'CLOCK on the dot, I hear the key turning in the lock in the door. I gave spares to both Lanie and Nina in case of emergencies. Apparently, my breakdown earlier constitutes an emergency.

Seated in a dark corner of the living room, with a clear view of the front door, I watch Lanie pop her head inside. The sun has long set, and darkness blankets the room, shielding me from her view.

"Alyssa?" she calls out, as though she cares about my privacy. "We're coming in."

Lanie flips a switch, and the overhead lights beam down around us. Lanie's brown eyes are wide, one black-and-white-Converse-covered foot still in the door as if she fears what she'll find. I'd laugh if I wasn't having too much fun watching these two tiptoe around like some ghost is about to pop out at them.

Nina's head peeks around Lanie's body, her blond hair hanging loosely over one shoulder, and our eyes lock. My lips tip up in amusement.

"Hi, love," Nina says, pushing Lanie through the door when she sees me sitting in my comfy chair.

I raise my hand and wave, not wanting to speak for fear I'll start laughing and pee myself, which has been a danger ever since giving birth. Yet another less-than-sexy problem I deal with on the regular.

"I'm glad to see you're not in your bed," she says, sitting down on the arm of my chair and pulling me into a hug.

Nina is a high school counselor and very adept at handling grief, which is a real pain in the ass for someone who's trying to avoid talking about her feelings. "How you doing?" she asks, backing up and looking me over, her gaze lingering a little too long.

If they see that I've managed to pull myself together, they'll insist on birthday shenanigans, and I'm not quite fond of that idea.

I showered, hoping to wash away the remnants of my earlier wallowing, but it was no use. My pale complexion can't hide the stubborn splotches of distress, even with a Sephora's worth of makeup plastered over my face.

"I'm struggling."

A complete exaggeration.

My head lowers, shaking back and forth, playing up the misery card. Based on how her eyes are narrowed in on mine, she knows better. I've managed to fake it till I make it before, but tonight, I'm failing.

"We know better, Ally," Lanie cuts in, walking toward her typical spot on the outdated ottoman, complete with a gaudy floral print. It's a hand-me-down from my mother, which is about the only thing that woman has ever given up to me. "You're trying to avoid a celebration for the big four-oh, and we are not here for it. You and I both know you'll regret it eventually."

Lanie gets comfortable, stretching her long, lean legs out on the couch as Nina takes a seat on the floor at my feet.

"She's right, Alyssa. This happened on your thirtieth and you still to this day whine about not throwing a party."

"We promised we'd never let you do that again. So pull up your big girl panties and embrace your midlife hotness," Lanie says, earning a stern glare from Nina.

Nina springs back up, putting her arm around my shoulder. She pulls me into her embrace again. "Don't listen to her. We all know she's about as comforting as sitting on a cactus."

The most unladylike snort rips through me.

Lanie's mouth opens and then closes like a fish out of water. "I didn't say anything *bad*."

Nina rolls her eyes, turning her focus back on me.

"I know you're struggling, love. We won't push you into going out if that's not what you want," Nina coos, hand running down my untamed hair soothingly.

I look up into Nina's ice-blue eyes, framed by the longest non-manufactured eyelashes I've ever seen, determined to change the subject.

"Have I gained weight?"

She nods and Lanie gasps.

"Nina Joy Dunbar, what the hell's the matter with you?" Lanie's high-pitched squeal is enough to pull a smile from me. I try to smash my lips together to contain my laughter, but it's no use. A fit of preteen giggles escapes me.

Nina's eyes widen as her head bounces back and forth between us. "Huh? What did I say?"

Lanie rolls her eyes this time. "Pay attention. You're not typically the space cadet."

Nina ignores her, gaze settling on me. "I'm sorry, love. I'm . . . distracted."

I want to ask her why, but she forges ahead, beating me to the punch.

"My mother called. She wants to come to town for the holidays."

Nina isn't distracted, she's distressed, and I can't blame her. Samantha Woods is equal parts obnoxious and terrifying.

"Why?" Lanie says, parroting my thoughts.

"I'm sure she needs more money." Nina sighs, picking at her fingernails. "She had a botched cosmetic surgery and is tapped out of funds to fix it."

"Oh, please. The woman is fake from her head to her toes. What more can she need?" Lanie practically spits the words. None of us are fond of Nina's mother, but Lanie in particular despises the woman.

"This time it's true. I heard it myself via an unwanted video call."

My eyes narrow. "You heard it? What, pray tell, does that mean?"

Nina's lip tips up. "She went back to get bigger implants and now her boobs squeak." She waggles her eyebrows, grinning so widely her brilliant white teeth are on full display.

"Squeak?" Lanie asks. "Like a rubber duck?"

Nina's head bobs. "Let's just say that the neighborhood dogs follow her around. And I am not exaggerating."

We all burst into laughter. Of all the people for something like that to happen to, the universe got it right this time.

Lanie wipes under her eyes. "Don't you dare help her fix that. Let her suffer in squeaking until she finds Husband Number Six to pay for it."

I take a good hard look at my friends, recognizing how lucky I truly am, despite the hardships I've endured. Having Lanie and Nina by my side today is something I've rejected, but, man, am I glad they didn't listen.

"I needed this. You two being here," I explain, and Nina offers me a wide smile. "No matter what I said, I'm glad you ignored it."

"If I'd known my stories would make you laugh like this, I would've been here sooner." Nina frowns as she rubs her chest. "I'm sorry I waited so long to barge in, Alyssa."

I wipe under my nose, grunting. "I ate a carton of ice cream and chugged half a bottle of wine. I was fine. Wonderful, even."

"Ally, why didn't you call us?" Lanie's irritated voice draws my attention to the couch. "I would've gladly taken one for the team and drank the other half of that bottle."

"Then you would've tried to force me out of this house. Which was something I was avoiding."

Lanie sighs. "What a shame. I had so many things ready to go."

"And that is precisely why I didn't call."

My hand runs down my face, stopping over my mouth. A cold draft floats through the room and I shiver. It's the one downside to owning an old home. This part of town is the historic district. It's a beautiful area full of charm and ornate buildings, but it's also expensive to maintain.

Neither one of them speaks their thoughts on the matter,

allowing me my choices. What's there to say anyway? It's my birthday. My decision. The best thing about our friendship is that we all know when to speak and when to remain quiet.

After several long moments of silence, Lanie changes the subject.

"Ava really wanted to come home."

I wish she were here, but it wouldn't have been good for either of us. I would've made sure to put on a happy face for her, but she would've seen through it. No matter how hard I try, Ava knows how hard forty has hit me, and it likely would've been the last straw. She would insist on pulling out of school and moving home.

"I know, but she's where she needs to be. She doesn't need to be worrying after her middle-aged mother."

Nina nods her head. "You might be right, but Ava isn't like other girls her age, Alyssa. She hates that you're alone. She's struggling. You need each other," she says, giving away that Ava calls her more than I know.

I fake a yawn, done with this conversation. Thinking about Ava only makes matters worse. "I want her to enjoy school. She's living her dream, and that's what I want for her. It's what Garrett wanted."

Lanie smiles sadly. "We all know that girl was made for greatness. She's probably got her nose stuck in a book as we speak."

I smile, picturing Ava curled into her purple bean bag chair, sitting in the corner of her room, nose pressed into the book I bought her last time she was home. "Anything is better than sitting by her phone waiting for my calls."

"What would you like to talk about?" Nina asks, steering the conversation away from Ava. She knows it's a touchy subject. Ava and I have very different ideas of what needs to happen. I want her to focus on her passion, and she wants to move home to babysit me.

When I don't speak, Nina presses on. "Want a drink? I brought wine."

Lanie's phone beeps, and she removes it from her overly large bag, frowning at the screen.

"Everything okay?" I ask.

She looks at Nina and then me. "Yeah. All good. I just need to cancel a reservation I made for tonight."

"Oh, shoot. I completely forgot about that," Nina says, fidgeting.

My eyes volley back and forth between my friends.

"Thursday wine night," Lanie explains, avoiding my eyes, while she types a message into her phone.

Thursday wine night is something the three of us held as a standing date for years. Sometimes we'd see a movie. Other times, we'd just do a wine tasting and dinner. The only consistent part? Wine. Since the accident, we haven't kept our weekly date.

I told Lanie over a week ago I wasn't up for a birthday dinner, but it doesn't surprise me she made reservations just in case. Inspecting my friends closely, it's obvious they planned on something.

On a typical night in with the girls, yoga pants and oversized sweatshirts is the preferred dress code. But tonight, Lanie, the brown-haired beauty of our group, has on a pair of black Spanx leggings and a gray off-the-shoulder sweater. Not over the top, but nothing she'd typically wear to hang out here. Nina is still wearing the gray slacks and black V-neck shirt that she likely wore to school.

"Don't cancel," I say, picking at invisible lint. "You two can go."

Nina shakes her head. "We're not going to El Picante without you."

They made reservations at my and Garrett's favorite Mexican restaurant. It's the one place sure to get me out of any slump by simply placing bottomless tortilla chips, queso, and the largest mango margarita possible in front of me.

My lips form a thin line as I war with my yo-yo feelings. One part of me wants to remain in my pajamas, on this chair, sulking. The other part wants to live a little on the wild side, venturing out to do more damage to my waistline via shrimp fajitas—something I haven't indulged in since the accident.

"I'm in." I hardly get the words out before Lanie is popping up from the couch, as though she always knew this would be the outcome. She pulls something from her bag, chucking it at my head. I duck out of instinct.

"About time you come to your senses. You said you didn't want to celebrate, but I brought this for you just in case."

She turns away without another word and saunters through the arched doorway toward my kitchen with a bottle of wine she also pulled from her Mary Poppins bag.

I hold up what I now see is a white T-shirt that reads *Forty-licious* in sparkly fuchsia.

"Forty-licious? She's got to be kidding."

"You are," she bellows from the kitchen.

The woman has catlike reflexes, hawk eyes, and the hearing of a moth—expert-level senses that I didn't possess even in the height of my youth. Heck, I'm not sure anyone possesses such acute senses.

"You might as well put it on. We all know that you'll wear it because you're too nice," Nina whispers, taking a seat on the arm of my chair and peering at the offending shirt with me.

We simultaneously tilt our heads and sigh. Nina speaks the truth.

"I poured the wine," Lanie says, walking in with a stainless-steel tray carrying three wine glasses and the remainder of the bottle I didn't finish earlier.

Lanie's the youngest of our group, and the newest addition.

Nina moved to the Midwest her freshman year and ended up attending my high school. I was one year older, but we met and bonded through cheerleading. She was quiet and always seemed a bit sad, mirroring me in ways that hurt my soul.

She was the family I never quite had. Being the only child of two workaholic attorneys, I was always an afterthought. Nina and I saved each other from toxic family dynamics.

After high school, we both went to the East Coast to attend the same college. Lanie joined our group much later, after we'd settled down in the quaint town of Knox Harbor.

She was the barista at our favorite mom-and-pop coffee shop and the yoga instructor at the only exercise facility in our small town. She's the wild child of our little threesome and the one who's always able to test boundaries.

"Drink up, witches. We ride at six." She raises her glass, filled midway with red wine.

"Wait. That's your birthday speech?" Nina glares into the side of Lanie's head, annoyed. "We need a toast worthy of our best friend." She raises her glass into the air. "To you, Alyssa. May your forties be full of health, happiness, laughter, and love. You deserve it."

"Unlike Nina, I've never been good with words," Lanie adds. "But I can't agree with her more. You deserve every ounce of happiness this world possesses. And the largest damn margarita this side of Knox Harbor."

I smile at my dear friends, grateful that they haven't given up on me.

"Happy birthday," they both say in unison.

We clink our glasses together and throw back the wine. Something tells me I'm going to need it to get through this night.

The Tower

I LIFT A finger into the air, waving down our waitress. "I'll have another one, please," I say, pointing to my nearly empty margarita.

The tiny woman nods, rushing off to fulfill my request.

"Get after it." Lanie whoops, smiling like a loon. "I haven't seen you suck one of those down that fast in ages."

One shoulder lifts before I bring the enormous glass to my lips and take another sip. "I guess forty is turning me into a lush."

"Wanna talk about a lush? You should've seen Lanie last week during wine and woo," Nina says, chuckling into her napkin.

I suck on my teeth, pulling my hair at the ends. "Wine and what?"

"You know . . . woo." Nina repeats the word, as though it means something to me.

I shake my head, signaling she's lost me with the *woo*.

"You didn't tell her?" Nina has an edge to her voice that catches me off guard. When Lanie winces, I know I'm about to hear something I won't love.

"Tell me what exactly?" I stare straight ahead, waiting for one of them to elaborate.

"I forgot to talk to you about modernizing Thursday nights, and Nina here is reminding me of my epic faux pas. We tested it out last week." Lanie grimaces.

A twinge of hurt passes over me at the knowledge my friends reprised our Thursday girls' night without me. Not that I can blame them. It was my decision to put it on hold, and I haven't given either one of them any indication I was ready to start again.

"We didn't think you were ready, love. Last Thursday was a very last-minute thing," Nina says, leaning forward, looking uncomfortable.

Completely ignoring Nina, I turn toward Lanie. "Why does Thursday night need 'modernizing'?" I ask, air quoting the word with both hands. "What does that entail?"

"We're just trying to spice it up with some woo-woo intermixed with the wine." Her eyes widen animatedly. "Spirits all around," she says, waggling her eyebrows. "Get it? Spirits as in ghosts and spirits as in . . . well . . ."

"Yeah, I got it." I grab the saltshaker, inspecting it for no other reason but to avoid eye contact with my friends.

"Alyssa," Nina draws out my name. "Don't do that. We didn't intentionally leave you out."

I cluck my tongue, raising my chin to meet her eyes. "I know. It's all good," I say, hoping to cut the tension off. "Enlighten me about this woo business."

Nina frowns, not one to allow something serious to go unspoken.

"Let's just forget about it and maybe order some food?" Lanie attempts to change the subject, but I'm not going to let her this time.

"Nope. I want to hear it. Tell me what I'm missing."

Lanie pushes her chest forward, raising a hand, palm up. "Woo as in woo-woo. Tarot cards. A medium. Speaking with the dead. What do you think? Cool and modern, right?"

My back straightens, and Lanie's face pales.

Her eyes close and she gulps before offering an apology. "I didn't mean to say the last part. I'm so sorry, Ally."

My head moves back and forth, and one hand comes up to stop Lanie. I'm tired of being treated like a fragile child.

Heart pounding and palms sweating, I try and fail to formulate words. Not for the reasons either of them would think. My mind is swimming with possibilities.

"It was a horrible idea," Nina says. "We're both sorry." Her head ping-pongs from me to Lanie, eyes wide and mouth smashed into a thin line.

Rubbing at my temples, I bring myself back to center. It was the last thing I expected Lanie to say, but the more it settles over me, the more intrigued I am.

"Speaking with the dead? Is that a real thing?"

Nina and Lanie share an uneasy glance, likely debating whether to answer at all.

"Umm . . . yes?" Lanie drones.

"Yes or no? You don't sound so sure," I press, my whole body leaning forward.

She blows out a breath. "Madame Corinne claims she can tap into the spirit world. *I* believe her."

I consider this for several minutes. Do I believe that's possible?

I've never given it too much thought because I've never personally experienced anything otherworldly. I've been known to watch shows about hauntings, and I never question the people who give their accounts. If they say it happened, who am I to say differently? I've even had my tarot cards read in the past. But is a lack of skepticism enough to warrant shelling out money for a medium who claims to speak to the dead?

"It was just something new to do," Nina jumps in, sounding almost frantic. "You know I think that stuff is all a hoax. Just phony men and women trying to bamboozle people out of their hard-earned money."

Lanie's nose scrunches up as though she's smelled something foul. "Bamboozle? Who's the forty-year-old in this room?"

Nina shoots her an irritated scowl. "You know what I mean." She turns her head back to me. "That stuff isn't real. It's all in good fun."

My eyes meet hers and I offer a smile, but I don't miss Lanie stewing out of the corner of my eye. Her arms are crossed over her chest, and the glare she has aimed at the side of Nina's head could burn a hole right through if she stares long enough.

These two unlikely friends couldn't be more different. Their stances on woo-woo aside, they rarely agree on anything. Nina's the practical—bordering on cynical, analytical, show me proof or I won't believe—girl. Meanwhile, Lanie feels the wind blow and believes it's the universe sending her signs that the vision board she spent weeks creating is manifesting well.

Me? I'm of the belief that there are unexplainable things all around us. Is it the universe speaking to us? Or is it something that science will one day be able to explain? I don't know, and truthfully, I don't care at the moment. I'm just ready to bust out of my comfort zone for a few hours and forget that I've climbed that dreaded hill and I'm teetering on the decline down the other, less preferred, side.

"We should do it. Tonight."

"Whoa, whoa, whoa," Nina says, raising her open hands. "That isn't a good idea." She looks to Lanie for support. "She might not even have availability on such short notice. Besides, nothing is guaranteed, Ally."

I scoff. "You won't know unless you try, right?"

Nina reaches across the table, grabbing my hand in hers.

"I'm just not sure that trying to communicate with the dead will be helpful right now . . . considering . . ." Her words trail off and my head swivels between my friends.

"Considering what?"

Lanie bats her eyelashes, glancing at Nina, likely hoping she'll finish her thought and spare her from the task. When Nina doesn't jump to it, Lanie sighs. "Considering I found *several* empty ice cream cartons in your trash, I'm not sure you're in the right head space to conjure spirits."

I shrug, unwilling to make excuses for my dairy binge. "Why not? It's all in good fun. What's the worst that could happen?"

Lanie and Nina share another look.

"Come on, guys. If—and that's a very big *if*—this medium is actually legit, maybe I can summon Garrett."

Nina's eyes close. "And therein lies the problem." When her lids lift, her crystalline eyes are filled with tears. "I don't want you to think that's going to happen. If you don't make contact with him, where will you be then?"

She's chewing on her bottom lip as her chin quivers. She's scared that this will set me back, and I don't blame her. We've done this dance. One step forward, four steps back, several times. It's been two years, and I'm ready to try to get back to living. So, I mentally roll up my sleeves and put on the most contrived optimism I can manage.

"Please," I scoff, making a point to roll my eyes while grinning playfully. "Garrett will obviously be waiting at whatever portal he needs to in order to connect with this Madame Cora. If that's even possible, of course."

"Corinne," Lanie corrects, and Nina shoots her a glare that practically screams *Shut your trap.* "What?" Lanie scrunches her nose. "She's very particular. Wouldn't appreciate anyone confusing her with her competitor; Cora has been stealing Corinne's clients for years."

I tilt my head to the side, pursing my lips. "What?"

"Ignore her," Nina bites, and Lanie's mouth snaps shut. "This isn't a good idea."

"Nina is right," Lanie says, staring over my head at nothing. "I only see Corinne for my card readings. That's what we had scheduled with her last week. I'm not so sure she's the real deal where mediumship is concerned."

I rub my hands together. "That's okay. It's just something fun and different to do."

Lanie crosses her arms over her chest once more. "Who are you and what have you done with my friend?"

I smile. "This *is* me, Lanie. I've just been gone for a while."

She returns the smile, but it doesn't reach her eyes, as she likely recalls the last two years, and just how gone I was for a large portion of it.

"Call her," I try again, lifting my head. I meet Nina's gaze head-on, because of my two friends, she's the one who needs the most convincing. "For fun. For something different. Tarot seems harmless, and I want to celebrate in a big way."

Her lips form a thin line as she glances at Lanie. "What time does she close?"

"Ten. She has late hours." Lanie's eyes brighten. "We have time for another drink."

My hands come together like I'm praying. "Please. I want to revive Thursday wine night and I want to see Madame Corinne. I only turn forty once."

Nina's shoulders droop and her eyes close in resignation.

"Fine. Make the call." She sighs heavily. "But I'm going to need about three more drinks."

"Nope. You're driving," Lanie singsongs. "Someone has to be responsible, and you have to work tomorrow."

"Since when are you the voice of reason?" Her tone is terse, but her eyes are sparkling as she pulls Lanie into a side hug.

At that moment, our waitress reappears with my margarita. "Here you go. Cheers." She places the large salt-rimmed rocks glass down in front of me.

Smiling up at her, I take the drink and bring it to my lips, sucking it down faster than the one before.

+ + +

AFTER DRIVING TWENTY-FIVE minutes to the next town, Nina pulls into a shopping center, stopping right in front of a store-front labeled *Cori's Nail Spa.*

"We're here. Time to be one with the spirit world."

Nina has a white-knuckled grip on the steering wheel. "Don't promise that," she scolds Lanie. "We all discussed that this might simply be a night of tarot."

My head turns to the back, where Lanie's leaning forward, both hands on the backs of our seats.

"You forced me to lie. If Corinne can't summon a spirit, I'll eat crow."

I smirk, knowing that these two are about to argue. They're more like sisters than friends, and of our threesome, they're the two that squabble the most.

Opening my door, I step out of the car to inspect the plaza. It's your run-of-the-mill strip mall, complete with a T.J. Maxx and HomeGoods on one end, and the nail spa, a Subway, and a kick-boxing studio on the other.

My eyes are glued to the tawdry storefront that is Cori's Nail Spa.

"This can't be it," I say, pointing to the dark building, as both of my friends exit the car.

The red neon sign next to the door flashes *Closed*, and my shoulders relax, hoping that Lanie managed to give Nina the wrong address. Wouldn't be the first time.

"Where is this place?" I ask, head turning to look at all the options.

"That's it," Lanie says, slamming her car door and pointing to Cori's. "Corinne uses the back room every night after they close."

I blink several times, waiting for her to say she's just kidding. No genius medium rents space in a dingy nail spa. However, after several seconds of zero response from Lanie, I know she's not joking.

"Oh my god, I thought you were messing with me. What kind of medium is this woman?"

My head turns in time to see Lanie's head loll back on her shoulders. "I am deeply offended on Corinne's behalf."

My whole face screws up in pure bewilderment at Lanie's obvious irritation.

"You seem surprised," Nina says, walking up behind me and placing one hand on my shoulder. She leans down to my ear. "This is Lanie we're talking about."

"But this?" I motion toward the darkened storefront, peering at it suspiciously. "You were on board with this place?"

Nina laughs. "Are you really shocked that her medium sets up in the back of a massage parlor masquerading as a nail salon?" She winks, letting me in on the fact she's trying to get a rise out of Lanie.

"It's not a massage parlor, and it's not that bad," Lanie drawls, looking to me for backup.

My eyes widen. "The windows are *tinted*."

"Traitor," she mutters, moving toward the door and ignoring any further appeals to leave.

My eyes scan the area, and across the street there's a Victorian house with a large, illuminated sign that reads *Cora: Her Mediumship*. It's written in lovely cursive and looks professional. Unlike the dingy nail spa's red-light-special vibe.

"Huh. I guess that explains the whole Cora-Corinne feud." I nod to Cora's. "Why couldn't we be going there?"

Lanie scoffs. "Cora advertises on Kiss FM. *She's* the phony, operating under a fancy facade paid for by her daddy. I'm positive you've heard her name before and that's why you confused Corinne with her to begin with. Everyone does. It's Cora's tactic." She grunts. "Her real name is Margaret."

Nina and I share a look. There's so much to uncover in that tirade, but both of us remain quiet, eager to move past Lanie's clear disdain of Corinne's competition.

"Looks like Corinne can't afford rent, let alone marketing," I whisper for Nina's ears only as I survey the sketchy part-time home of Madame Corinne's operation. I shake my head, trying to talk myself into this. It's supposed to be a night of fun. I can do this.

"It's really not that bad. I promise," Nina says, with a smirk that belies her words.

"Let's go before I lose my nerve," I say, walking toward the door with Nina hot on my heels. "Have your cell phones ready in case we have to call 9-1-1; this looks like a potential sex trafficking situation," I call over my shoulder to Nina.

Lanie turns to me, nose scrunched and eyes squinted in something like disgust. "We'd be a bit past their target."

My mouth drops open. "How do you figure?"

"We're old," Lanie deadpans.

The most unladylike snort rips through Nina's throat as she

attempts to smother her laughter behind her fist. It doesn't work, and soon she's full-on belly laughing, all while Lanie stares at her as though she's lost her mind.

"Are you done?" she snaps, clearly annoyed.

"Yes," Nina squeaks out, smothering her mouth with her fist.

"Good. We need to hurry."

The bell above chimes as Lanie pushes it open and we step into the dark nail salon. Shadows dance off the walls, making the place far more eerie than it ought to be. The only light in the entire place flickers ahead from under what appears to be heavy drapery.

The high-backed chairs look occupied in the dark, and if I wasn't spooked before, I am now. I scoot close to Nina, linking our arms together. "Don't you dare leave my side."

We follow Lanie straight to the back, where a red velvet curtain separates Madame Corinne's makeshift den from the rest of Cori's.

Nina bumps my hip. "You sure about this?"

I raise my eyebrows in a *what the heck do you think* expression.

"Come in," a deep, throaty voice calls from the other side. "Move it."

We push past the curtain into the small candlelit room that boasts one large oval table, covered by more red velvet. The walls are stark white, and the only other furniture in this oversized supply room is a metal shelf full of various tchotchkes that I can't quite make out in the dim light and a vending machine full of a copious number of snacks. Directly to the right is a white door that blends in with the walls. I'm assuming this space functions as an employee lounge during the day, but it's the most mundane space ever. I wonder what's behind the door. A restroom? A supply closet? Bodies?

Good grief.

A throat clears, drawing my attention back to the table.

I immediately notice there's nothing on top of the tablecloth, which surprises me. No deck of tarot cards or crystal ball in sight. Not that I expected that.

Okay . . . I did. I totally thought there'd be something kitschy.

"Are you done perusing?" A bored, sensual voice pulls my eyes to where Corinne sits at the head of the table, looking far too normal to be a genuine medium. I was expecting a red robe and bedazzled flapper headband, staples of every tarot reader I've ever encountered. Each tried harder than the next to look authentic, and they missed the mark every time.

Her dark brown hair is piled on top of her head in a messy bun, and her green eyes glow with irritation. She's slouched back, looking much younger than me and my friends, which sparks a bit of jealousy.

Here I am on my fortieth birthday, getting a stare down from a wrinkle-free diva with cheekbones to die for. Not fair.

Her eyes seem to narrow further, likely from my staring, but I don't take it upon myself to stop. She's wearing a red sweatshirt with white letters that spell out *I hate people* across her chest.

Lovely.

"You're the medium?" I ask, not even attempting to keep my skepticism out of the question.

"Duh," she says, unaffected by my doubt. "Take a seat," she orders, sweeping one hand out and motioning to the empty chairs. "We need to get started, since you're a last-minute addition to my schedule. Communication with the spirit world can take time."

"We're just here for readings," Nina says, looking to me with wide eyes.

"You're not. Lanie specifically asked for communication with the spirit world." She drums her fingers on top of the table.

"I don't think that's such a great idea," Nina presses. "We shouldn't . . ."

"I'm well aware of the events and I'm more than capable of protecting her." Corinne's eyes meet mine and I wonder what exactly she knows.

"What were you t—"

Corinne raises her hand, cutting Nina off. "Never mind that. The channel has been changed, and I was tipped off about your circumstances."

My head snaps to Lanie, who is already sitting in the chair directly across from Corinne, head bowed as she appears to meditate. I turn to Nina, who offers her signature shrug, but sits slowly into her own chair, to Lanie's left. This leaves me to sit between Lanie and Corinne.

I have questions. *So* many questions. But Corinne dives right in, leaving me no choice but to go along with whatever is about to happen.

"Join hands," Corinne commands.

I eye her outstretched palm for a moment, wondering if I'm making a huge mistake. I jumped feet first into this with the expectation of letting loose and having fun. Now that we're here, my stomach is in knots.

I'm not sure whether my unease is due to this place, Corinne's less-than-friendly demeanor, or the thought of actually connecting to spirits.

Corinne clears her throat, and without another thought, I place my hand in hers.

When my palm connects with Corinne's, electricity stronger than any static I've ever experienced jolts through me, and my eyes slam shut.

Visions of *that* night assault me.

Bright lights.

A flash of red streaking past.

Garrett hovering over my supine body, smoothing my blood-soaked hair from my face.

The scene disappears, and I rip my hand from Corinne's grasp. "What the hell was that?" I pant, blood pumping in my ears.

Corinne's pink lips are agape as she stares into my eyes, looking equal parts shocked and awed.

"Did you feel that too?" I ask her. Her brows draw together, and she continues to gawk at me, seemingly stupefied.

That vision, though.

It was similar to my dream, but more, and not entirely from *my* perspective. The differences make me question if Corinne unlocked some part of my memory by touching me. How was I able to see the scene from multiple viewpoints? Have I seen red in every dream? Yes. A red streak? No. I had always assumed the red was blood, but from this vision, I question whether it was a red vehicle all along. The way it zoomed past gave the impression that it was an object.

Then I remember Garrett hovering over me, and I know it can't be a memory. He died on impact, according to the coroner.

"What was . . ." Corinne's words trail off, and I widen my eyes in an *out with it* expression. But she doesn't continue her train of thought. Instead, she shakes her shoulders, takes a deep breath, and stands. "Does anyone need gin? I need gin," she mutters, walking to the shelf and pulling down a decanter. She pops the top and takes a deep pull.

"What is going on?" Nina asks, looking between Corinne and me.

"Why is she chugging gin like it's juice?" Lanie asks, scrunching her nose in bewilderment. "Are we missing something?" She motions between her and Nina.

I can't form the words to answer their questions, and Corinne doesn't seem in a hurry to come to my aid. She takes one longer gulp, not even making a face at the burn I know she must be feeling.

Corinne blows out a harsh breath and places the gin back on

the shelf before taking a seat. "Shall we try again?" she asks, ignoring my friends and avoiding my gaze altogether.

She wiggles her fingers atop the table, signaling me to place my hand in hers once again. Finally, I find the will to speak.

"No, we are not going to try again." I'm on my feet, staring down at everyone. "Am I the only one who felt that? I can't be. It was so strong. So freaking eerie."

"Ally—" Nina tries, but I shake my head.

"You felt it. I know you did."

My eyes bounce from one woman to the next, none of them saying a word. They each wear various expressions. Nina appears sad, likely thinking this has broken me completely. Lanie looks confused, which isn't surprising. Corinne seems bored, and that pisses me off, because I know from her reaction that she felt what I did.

Nobody in their right mind chugs gin for the hell of it.

"Tell them," I bite through my teeth, hoping she realizes I might strangle her if she doesn't.

"Sit down, please." She points toward my seat, meeting my glare with one of her own. "I know you want answers, but that's not how it works," Corinne snips. "You won't get answers throwing a temper tantrum."

I don't have a chance to react to Corinne's crankiness because Lanie raises her hand as though we're in school again. "Isn't that the entire freaking reason we're here? For answers from the other-world?"

I've never wanted to kiss my friend more. "Thank you," I say, a little haughtier than I intended.

Corinne smacks her lips together, really honing that mask of boredom, and turns to Lanie. "Yes, and in order to see exactly what happened, which I don't know at this point, it's best we try again. Okay?" She directs the last part to me.

I contemplate what she's saying. Do I want answers at this point? Am I willing to experience whatever the heck just happened again?

The answer is yes. No matter what, I'm not leaving here until I understand what exactly happened moments ago.

Begrudgingly, I sit and nod, lowering my eyes to the red table-cloth. "Fine, but if I feel that again, I'm out."

"Can someone explain what the hell you all felt?" Nina's voice pitches, signaling she's scared.

Not a surprise. Nina is the resident scaredy-cat. Always has been. She doesn't watch horror movies, doesn't particularly love Halloween, and ultimately isn't for anything that sneaks up on her.

"It was me," Lanie admits. "My phone buzzed and . . ."

My head drops back and I groan, growing agitated by the constant interruptions. "It was not a *phone* vibration, idiot."

"Alyssa," Nina chastises, while Lanie looks on in shock.

I'm lashing out because I'm off kilter and it isn't fair to Lanie. I mouth the word *sorry* and she nods her acknowledgment.

Corinne claps her hands together, garnering our attention. "All right, calm down. Let's all take hands so that we can all *hopefully* get answers."

Lanie doesn't waste time, grabbing my and Nina's hands in hers. Nina is more hesitant, looking at me for verification that we're really going to do this again. She mouths, *Are you sure?*

I shrug both shoulders in a *what the hell, why not* gesture and tentatively join hands with Lanie and Corinne.

There isn't static this time, but warmth cascades over my hands and up my arms. The tiny hairs along my arms and on the back of my neck stand at attention. I'm a live wire, with energy rushing through every synapse. At any moment, I'm going to look down and find I've caught fire.

What is happening?

I've been here for less than five minutes, and I'm ready to bolt. "Breathe," Corinne instructs. In between deep breaths and skeptical glances, my nerves begin to calm, and the heat and other foreign feelings dissipate. "Good, Alyssa," she praises, turning away and addressing my friends. "Let us pray," she says, closing her eyes and bowing her head.

What happens next borders on bizarre and truly outrageous. It's worse than the strange sensations and possible fire. Her voice shifts into something straight out of a B-rated horror movie, and I am instantly shooketh.

"God. Goddess. Universe. Maiden, Mother, Crone." Each word is drawn out and overexaggerated.

My eyes spring open at Corinne's shift in demeanor. Lanie and Nina both seem unaffected by the animated quality of her tone. It's as though a different person is seated where Corinne once was. Someone older. More experienced in the ways of woo-woo. She sways back and forth, gyrating her chest and shoulders. My eyeballs bulge and I have to refrain from breaking into a fit of giggles.

Am I imagining this?

We're moments away from needing to call the Catholic church for an exorcism, and neither one of my friends appears to recognize it.

Their heads are still bowed, eyes closed. I'm alarmed, fearing that we're dealing with a crazy person, who obviously hates people according to her shirt, and these two haven't so much as flinched. Their apparent trance has me questioning what sort of hex Corinne has placed over my friends.

Calm down, crazy.

I've been to psychics before. They're generally over the top, but Corinne takes the cake. She's next-level loony, and I'm two seconds away from pulling Nina out of here and leaving Lanie to fend for herself. *She* got us into this mess.

Corinne's throat clears. "Eyes shut, please."

I slam them closed despite my concerns, bowing my head and praying to whatever god is listening to deliver me from this evil.

Corinne continues her bellowing. "We ask you to come to us. Flow through us. Help us connect to you so that we may achieve our greatest and highest good. Amen."

"Amen," the girls say in unison, with me following suit a moment after to complete the chaotic opening of what's sure to be a truly peculiar night.

My head swivels from Lanie to Nina and back again, and still these two are oblivious.

"Now. Who am I channeling?" Corinne asks the collective.

Lanie looks to me, her brow furrowing when she gets a good look at my untamed panic. Meanwhile, Nina remains heavily rooted in her world of complete unawareness, fidgeting with her fingers. I pull my hands into my lap and wait for one of them to speak. Neither does.

I'd like to jump up from this table and run out before the place ignites in hellfire, but I don't. I came all this way, and something *did* happen a moment ago. Maybe this is my chance for answers. Maybe I could get some closure if I don't squander the opportunity.

Inhaling deeply to calm my nerves, I finally state my request. "I'd like you to connect with my late husband, Garrett."

Corinne takes a deep breath, nodding once before lowering her head and murmuring unintelligible words.

My eyes land on a clock hanging on the wall behind Corinne's head, counting down the minutes until this hour is done and the jig is up. She may have some real spooky stuff going on in here, but all I care about is whether she'll really be able to get through to Garrett. I focus on the large hand, trying to block out whatever it is Corinne is up to now.

"Give me your hands," Corinne says, grabbing my attention away from the clock. "I need to draw from your energy."

"My energy?"

She glowers in irritation. "Do you want to connect with your husband or sit here and ask me to repeat myself all night?"

I place my hand back in hers, and this time the severe jolt and heated touch are absent. I focus on the softness of her skin, wondering what hand cream she uses and completely shutting out the fact that she's supposedly attempting to contact Garrett.

Corinne's eyes are closed as she appears to concentrate. After several minutes, her brows knit, and she opens one eye. "Do you believe that contacting your husband is possible?"

"Yesss?" I nod slowly, averting my eyes from her intense gaze.

She pulls out of my grip, folding her hands on top of the velvet tablecloth.

"Something is blocking me. Does one of you doubt this is possible?"

My head jerks back, looking to both my friends to uncover the culprit. Both look equally mystified. My hand comes to my chest. "I believe," I stress to Lanie first, who nods her head in solidarity. "I'm open!" I reiterate to Nina, who smiles sadly. "Don't you believe me?"

"I don't doubt you, Alyssa. It's her ability I doubt." Madame Corinne balks at the slight, but Nina doesn't apologize. "We should go."

She stands to leave, and I yell out, "No," shaking my head vehemently. "I want to do this. We came all this way, and something happened." I hold Nina's stare, hoping to convey that although I'm nervous about what's to come, I don't want to throw in the towel. "I need you to trust that Corinne can do this."

Desperation to contact Garrett clings to me like lint, forcing me to come to terms with the fact that I mean what I say. My stance has shifted, and I believe—for the time being—it's possible.

Nina's eyes close. It's written clearly all over her face—she wishes we hadn't come—but I don't dwell on that for long.

I throw my shoulders back, close my eyes, and do the first thing that comes to mind.

Beg.

"Garrett, if you can hear me, I'm open. I. Am. Open!"

"What's wrong with you?" Lanie asks Nina, but I don't pay attention to them, keeping my eyes shut tight and conjuring an image of him in my head.

I'm hyperfocused on willing Garrett to this room. I bite my lip, concentrating hard. My hands ball into fists and my foot taps the ground, creating a vibration I feel work its way through me. The table trembles, and I don't stop to consider why or what it means.

Come on, Garrett. Please.

My eyes open in time to see the candlelight flicker, scattering shadows that resemble wayward spirits flitting around the room. Lanie chokes, Nina screeches, and Corinne remains utterly silent. Still, I persist, centered on this one lofty goal.

I'm open. Come to me.

The table halts its quaking, and the lights stop flickering. The three women in the room are deathly silent, but I feel their eyes fixed on me. A heavy breath rushes through my chest as every last iota of energy abates and I slam my back into the chair, falling limply into it.

Corinne drops my hand and Nina and Lanie spring to action, coming to my side.

"Alyssa! Are you all right? What the hell was that?"

My head moves slowly back and forth. I'm bone-tired and unable to speak. I can't focus my eyes on any one person or object.

The room vibrates in waves of energy that somehow I *can* see. My ears ring and my entire body tingles.

I can just barely make out the swarm of questions and accusations being flung around the room until the noise stops and my vision focuses.

Three sets of eyes peer at me as though I've sprouted a third eye right in the middle of my forehead.

And maybe I have.

"Alyssa . . ." Nina whispers my name, drawing close. "Talk to me, love."

I blink several times, attempting to swallow, but my mouth is desert-dry.

"Water," I manage to croak out, and Lanie jumps into action, rushing toward the shelf.

"Not gin," Nina chastises. "Corinne, do you have a bottle of water?"

I don't see or hear Corinne's answer, because Nina is all up in my personal space, clamoring on about god knows what. Moments later, a bottle of water is shoved against my mouth.

"Drink," Nina commands and I don't argue, sipping down every last drop. I lick my parched lips, ready for more water.

I take a deep breath, ready to ask for it when Corinne states firmly, "You all need to leave. Now."

Nina's head jerks in the direction of Corinne. "Excuse me?" Nina sounds ready to attack, which is so unlike my docile friend. "You did this," she says, waving a hand in my direction.

Corinne wears a mask of boredom, but I don't miss the way her hands tremble. She's freaked but doing her best to hide it.

"I did nothing. There's clearly something wrong with her."

She knows damn well that the only thing wrong with me is this place. I'm not sure how she managed to make me feel the way I did, but this is all her.

"I'm closed and you need to leave before I call the police," she says, with an edge of irritation.

"Corinne, you've got to be kidding me," Lanie says, finally joining the conversation. "We're friends and this is how you're treating my people?"

Corinne huffs a laugh. "We aren't friends. I don't have friends. Get them out and don't bother coming back."

With that, Corinne turns on her heels and stalks out of the room toward the front of the shop, leaving the three of us to exchange glances.

"What the f—"

I raise my hands. "Doesn't matter. She wants us out and I'm more than happy to follow directions. This room is swimming with bad vibes."

Nina nods, holding her hand out to me. "Let's get you out of here."

That's something she does not have to say twice.

3

Seven of Wands

A GUST OF wind tosses my hair into my face, but I don't have the energy to bat it away. I take a swig straight from the wine bottle I have a tight grip on, and I can practically feel Nina's intense stare drilling into the side of my head.

After replaying what happened tonight, I need the wine. Even if this particular bottle has notes of licorice and something akin to wet gravel, two flavors I would be perfectly content to never taste again. My lips curl after swallowing the less-than-delicious cabernet, and I have to stop myself from scraping my tongue to remove the foul aftertaste.

"Come on," Nina drawls. "It's not that bad."

If not for the mostly full moon overhead, I wouldn't be able to see her lips tilted up into a playful grin.

"It's no riesling."

Lanie snorts from the next step up. Her hand lands on my shoulder. "Hate to break it to you, girlfriend, but riesling is shit wine."

Mock gasping, my hand flies to my heart. "How dare you."

The three of us laugh, breaking the tense air that's been surrounding us since we began discussing the night. All of us are on edge from whatever that spectacle was at Cori's Nail Spa.

I may not have connected with Garrett, but something happened, and I don't know what to make of it. None of us do.

We've been going over the night's events for the past hour and a half on the steps of my front porch. I needed the fresh air to discuss the subject.

"What do you think it could mean?" Nina asks, grabbing the bottle from my hands and placing it between her legs like a mother hen protecting her egg.

"The electrical sensations?" I ask, thinking back to the currents that ran through my body at Corinne's touch.

Nina shakes her head. "No. I mean the visions you saw when you touched her," she clarifies.

I chew on my bottom lip, considering her question for a moment. "I'm not sure what it means. They weren't my memories. I was seeing it through someone else's eyes."

Multiple someones.

A strident noise grates through Lanie's clenched lips. "This is spooky. I'm not trying to sound like a baby, but I can't shake the chills I've had since you told us what happened."

"Same," Nina says, rubbing her arms.

A gust of wind picks up, rattling the trees that line the side of my property. In the dark, the branches look like ghostly arms reaching out toward us. Mix the creep factor of the darkness with the conversation we've just had and chills start rushing over me too. The sensation brings me back to the moment my palm touched the medium's.

"I can't believe that neither of you felt the peculiar sensations I felt whenever I touched Corinne." I turn my head away from the swaying branches and focus on the street ahead.

"Are you sure you didn't imagine it because you really wanted her to be the real deal?" Nina asks in a placating tone. "Because I know how badly you need closure. I just don't want this to eat at you."

I went into the night with an open mind, and though I really hoped Garrett might show up, it figures that he didn't. Those kinds of moments might happen for others, but not me. Closure is something I'm unlikely to get in this lifetime. But the events that occurred were real. I didn't imagine them. Corinne's reaction only validates that truth for me.

"There's no way I imagined it. You saw Corinne's face. She felt it too."

"Which has me questioning things even further," Nina admits. "I believe you, but I wouldn't put anything past Corinne. She could've been messing with you."

Nina's gaze cuts back to Lanie for support, or possibly for confirmation that Corinne isn't above staging things, but Lanie just stares forward, lost in thought.

The wind settles as I say, "It was real. I know it."

My eyes close and the vision I saw comes to me easily.

Bright lights.

A streak of red.

Garrett hovering over me.

I inhale sharply, my eyes flying open.

Nina pulls her bottom lip into her mouth and remains quiet. I know she's preventing herself from saying any more. She doesn't want to push me, but it's too late.

My body shakes with laughter and an edge of hysteria. All I wanted for the rest of tonight was to have fun with my friends after a nearly two-year-long hiatus.

But the night went to shit, and here we are, still contemplating the likelihood of a nail salon medium being authentic, and whether

I imagined being practically electrocuted by her touch. And worst of all? The cabernet is—gag me—awful.

Nina's hands raise, likely misunderstanding my pinched expression and feeling the need to make things better.

"I'm sorry. Please look at me," she begs. "I'm just struggling because I touched her too and I felt nothing. No visions. No memories. Nothing. This is a me issue, Alyssa."

I shake my head, trying to signal for her to stop, but Lanie chimes in.

"Maybe it's because Alyssa was the one who asked for the connection," she offers as an explanation.

"Possible. What do I know about this stuff?" Nina says, head bouncing. "I'm the skeptic."

I can't be upset if either of them doubts what I experienced. They didn't feel the shocks or see the visions, and when it comes to unexplainable things, people tend to want to concoct reasons why the supernatural can't be real. I'd probably be doing the same if the roles were reversed. But it *did* happen, and I alone can unravel the aftereffects.

"I'm still not over the fact that neither of you seemed to find her eccentric behavior batshit crazy," I say, trying to get us back on solid ground and onto a lighter topic.

Nina snorts. "I just figured it was part of the act."

"I don't think she was acting," I say mostly to myself.

I grab the bottle from between Nina's legs, bring it to my mouth, and chug. My throat bobs as the liquid slides down, heating my insides.

"Okay. That's enough," Nina scolds, prying the bottle from my tight grip. "You've had enough for one night."

"I don't need you to mother me, Nina. I'm fine," I snip.

Nina looks to Lanie, and when neither of them say what they're thinking, I crack.

"What *is* that?" I say, motioning between them. "You two have done that all night. I'm not gonna break." My voice rises, and I have to ball my hands into fists to calm myself. Taking two deep breaths and willing my racing heart to slow, I start again. "I'm not fragile. You can say what you want. I can handle it."

"Okay," Lanie says, folding her hands and leaning forward. "You're *not* all right. No one who relives a tragic accident on their birthday, in which the love of their life was killed, is all right," she emphasizes. "It's not healthy, Ally, and there has to be something that Dr. Lara, or some other psychiatrist, can do to help. You're never going to move on if you keep reliving that night."

Nina's hand rests on top of my knee. "She's right, love. Chasing after closure when there's likely none to be found isn't healthy, and I take responsibility for that. We never should've encouraged you."

"I didn't go chasing closure, Nina. I went because it actually sounded like fun. I was trying to force myself back out into the world."

Her head snaps forward, eyes narrowed on something between the houses across the street. There's nothing there except more trees, swaying in the breeze.

"Still . . . we should've done something else. Something less . . . triggering."

A bitter laugh escapes me. "You're probably right, but I can't promise I won't seek Corinne out again."

The more I think about what happened, the more I need to get to the bottom of Kooky Corinne's antics.

Nina sighs. "I know, love. I know."

My shoulders deflate and my head falls forward. "Maybe he didn't show tonight because this is meant to be my penance."

Nina's and Lanie's heads turn to me.

"For what?" Lanie asks. "You didn't cause that accident. Neither one of you did."

My eyes focus on my black leggings, not wanting to see the looks on their faces as I admit one of my greatest fears out loud. "We don't know that. I don't remember everything that happened."

"Sounds to me like—" Lanie's words are drowned out by a sudden gust of wind that has us all shielding our faces from flying leaves and dirt.

"Ugh," I call out, a second away from jumping up and rushing inside to get out of this mini whirlwind that sprang up on us. But as quick as it started, it's over, and the eerie silence that follows is a tad disquieting.

"You can stop punishing yourself. Garrett wouldn't want this for you," Nina says, placing a hand on my shoulder and breaking up my momentary alarm.

"You weren't behind the wheel. Some asshole probably caused that accident," Lanie bites.

"She might be right. Maybe that was Garrett's way of communicating," Nina suggests.

My head lifts and I meet Nina's gaze. "You believe it was another vehicle?"

It's a total one-eighty from moments ago, and I can't help feeling like they're just placating me because it's easier to allow me to believe what I saw than to continue watching me beat myself up over the accident.

"Why not? Stranger things have happened. You felt something, right?" Lanie prompts.

Nina nods vigorously. "Lanie's words of wisdom."

Lanie harrumphs. "I'm very smart."

I feel myself start to slump. Between the alcohol and the conversation, every bit of energy I possess is drained. I don't have it in me to talk about the accident or Corinne anymore tonight.

"I hate to be the party pooper, but I'm exhausted," I say, yawning into my fist. "My bed is calling me."

"Me too," Nina says, standing. "I have an early morning tomorrow."

"I'm a little bummed we didn't get a single glimpse of Hot Cop," Lanie says, stretching out her legs.

"Hot Cop? You mean Detective Douche?" I quip. "He's the most infuriating man I've ever met."

"What? Why?" Lanie practically whines.

My head turns toward my neighbor's house, dark and quiet. He's likely asleep, or maybe still on the job. In truth, I know very little about him.

"The man has hardly said two words to me the entire time he's lived next door. But now he insists on taking down my trash every Monday morning and bringing the cans back in at night," I prattle on, growing more agitated by the minute. "Now he's grabbing my mail and leaving it inside of my screen door."

"I'm failing to see the problem here." Lanie deadpans.

Nina's lips purse, showcasing a set of slight dimples on each cheek. "Am I to believe that you're holding a grudge because he's a gentleman?"

"Ugh! He's a pest." I raise my hands to my head, massaging my temples.

"A very good-looking and courteous pest," Nina says under her breath.

"He just wants to help."

Headlights shine on us as a car pulls into the detective's drive. "Looks like you'll get your peek," I groan, determined to remain bitter about his unwanted chivalry.

The detective steps from his car, looking in our direction. "Ladies," he drawls.

Nick West is a god among men. According to the local gossip, that is. Every woman in town is fascinated by the single loner badass who lives next door. Their words.

Even I can admit that he's handsome. Strong jawline lined with salt-and-pepper scruff that matches his unruly hair, which looks like someone ran their hands through it recently, chiseled cheekbones, straight nose, all sitting atop a carved-from-stone body. I've seen it out my kitchen window in the summers. It's awe-inspiring, if you like well-defined abs and a V that disappears into a man's shorts.

"Everything okay?" His smooth, throaty timbre washes over me, and my eyes narrow in response.

A hand raised in acknowledgment of our presence I expected, but the man uttered actual words.

"Yes," Lanie and Nina say in unison.

"Just having a girls' night, officer," Nina offers, ever the calm one.

His husky chuckle irritates me. Is he flirting with them?

"It's Nick after hours."

Oh dear lord. He is.

Nina giggles, and I pull a face, looking at her out of the corner of my eye.

"Alyssa?"

Lanie pokes my back, and I twist around to glare at her.

"What?"

"He asked how you've been."

I take a deep breath, turning back to face him. "Better." It's all I offer, because what else is there to say?

Nick smiles, probably not believing a damn thing I said. "Better is good."

It's the most he's ever said to me, and I'm caught off guard. I'm two seconds from bolting inside the house so I don't say something rude and look like an ass. I shrug, because after the day I've had, that's the best I've got. "Well, I'm sure tomorrow will bring a new set of feelings."

"That means we're alive."

"I guess that's the issue; not all of us are." As soon as the words are out of my mouth, I hate myself. Both girls gasp, Nick grimaces, and I snap my mouth shut so hard, my teeth hurt.

"I'm so sorry. I had a rough day. I really do appreciate you asking, and I agree, better is good."

He bites the inside of his cheek, rocking back on his heels, likely weighing what to say next. "You know I'm always here if you need anything."

I nod. "Thanks. Well, we should be going in."

If he says anything more, I don't hear it. My back is already to him.

As soon as the front door is closed and the light turned on, the girls practically jump me.

"Oh my god, Alyssa. What was that?" Nina's shrill voice is almost comical.

"I know," I moan. "It just came out. And now you know why I stay inside and away from people."

"You're awful quiet," Nina says to Lanie, whose eyes are wide.

"What's there to say? Alyssa was savage."

"Oookayy. As fun as tonight has been, we've established that we all have early mornings. I need to go to bed for fear I might burn down the neighborhood with my dragon tongue."

Lanie rolls her eyes, leaning in and laying her head on my shoulder. "I love you."

"Love you most." I sigh.

Nina places a kiss on my cheek on her way past me.

"Get some sleep, love."

"I will. You too," I say, plastering on a smile.

I shut the door behind them, turning to slide my back down the wall. My butt thumps against the hard ground, but I welcome the sting. It's a sign that I am alive.

A heavy breath rushes through me as my eyes roam the empty space around me. It's too quiet. It leaves too much room to think, and thinking is the last thing I want to do right now.

The events of tonight with Corinne weigh heavily on me.

Garrett didn't speak directly to me, and that fact is heaviest of all.

Judgment

TAP. TAP. TAP.

My hand swats at the air, attempting to bat away whatever nuisance is messing with my forehead. My alarm hasn't gone off, which means there's still time for sleep. And sleep is what I need.

Thunder rolls overhead, shaking the house, and I snap up to a seated position. A flash of lightning bursts through the room, and my heart slams against my chest in response. Something streaks across the end of my bed, and the hairs on my neck stand at attention.

More lightning shines through the window, causing shadows to dance around the dark space. It's only shadows from the trees outside my room. Nobody is here.

My eyes land on the alarm clock next to my bed. Three thirty. Plenty more sleep to be had.

I sigh in blissful relief, curling back into my fluffy pillow and pulling the blanket up to my chin. It's not long before my eyelids lower and my breathing slows.

The bed shakes and I spring up again, fear slinking its way under my skin. The storm wasn't behind that.

My hand fumbles with the lamp on my end table until I find the small round knob and twist, illuminating the room. Blinking to adjust to the light, I lose a few vital seconds of awareness. Seconds that could doom me.

A scream bursts through my chest, rocking my small frame as I yank the blankets to my chin. There's a man at the end of my bed, wide-eyed and pale as milk.

I should jump up. I should fight. Instead, I sit here like a damsel waiting for some prince to come to my rescue. Pathetic.

My eyes dart around the room looking for something that could be used as a weapon, eventually landing on the lamp.

"What are you doing?" His hoarse voice has my teeth chattering and hands shaking.

Not wasting another second, my hand darts out, and I manage to pull the lamp into my hands, only to detach the cord from the electrical outlet and plunge myself back into darkness with a strange man.

"Help," I scream at the top of my lungs. "Help!"

There's a noise that sounds like the snapping of fingers, and the overhead lights turn on. The man is still in the same position at the end of my bed. His face is shielded by the gray hooded sweatshirt he's wearing.

Had he moved? If so, how did I not hear him? The floorboards of this old home creak when you tiptoe.

"How . . . how did you do that? You didn't move."

"What?" he asks, a little too smug for my liking. "The lights? That's easy—"

"Who are you and why are you in my bedroom?" I cut him off, no longer caring about the hows. I'm more interested in the why.

The corner of his mouth tips up. It should terrify me, but it doesn't. There's nothing sinister in his smile. Irritating, but not sinister. "Billy Garet, ma'am. I'm here because you called for me."

"I what?"

"You know," he says, lifting his right arm, palm up. "You said . . . 'Garrett, I'm open.'"

I gasp, recalling those very words from Cori's. "You've been stalking me?" My voice is high and shrill, panic rushing through me. "Ohmygodohmygod . . ."

"What are you babbling about? Are you having a mental break?"

"Are you going to kill me? Or . . . worse," I screech.

The man's head jerks back as though I slapped him. "Whoa, lady. I'm here because *you* summoned me, not the other way around. There will be none of any of *that*. Yuck," he says, shaking his head and shoulders simultaneously. "Besides, even if I wanted to kill you—which I don't—" he supplies quickly, "I couldn't. I haven't even mastered moving objects."

"Stay where you are. Do not move, or I will hit you with this," I say, wielding the lamp like some deadly weapon as my eyes scan the room for options for escape.

The door to the hallway is directly across from the bed, but he'd be able to get to me before I could make it out of this room.

The door is still closed . . . and locked. I twist to the windows, and they're all shut.

My head snaps back to the intruder. "How did you get in here?"

Billy crosses his arms over his chest. "You really need to get your shit together. I'm trying to communicate with you because there's something you need from me. Either you wanna talk or you don't."

"I don't," I snap. "I don't want you in my room. I don't want you anywhere near me. I don't need a damn thing from you."

I no more than say the words and Billy Garet vanishes.

"What the . . ."

I leap out of bed, falling to my knees and peering underneath it. He's not there. I rush to the window to find that it's locked. He couldn't have escaped that way. I spin in circles, inspecting every cranny from my current spot. There is no obvious way he entered or exited this room.

He disappeared. Like a ghost.

I rush from the room, down the stairs, and out the front door as soon as I can get it unlocked. Gnarly lightning streaks across the sky, followed quickly by a crash of thunder. I jump, but don't stop, running across the lawn in the pouring rain.

Fists raised, I pound on my neighbor's door.

I'm not sure how long I've been outside, yelling and causing a scene, but I'm soaked from head to toe and shaking like a leaf.

I'm about to go to the next house when the lights inside flip on and Nick's sleep-husky voice calls out, "Damn it. I'm coming."

When the door swings open, Nick's eyes lift into his hairline. "Alyssa. What the—"

I push past him, inviting myself into his home. The adrenaline coursing through me begins to dissipate and the shaking commences. My knees buckle under my body, and I collapse.

Nick's arms fly out, wrapping around me, pulling me flush to his firm, bare chest. He's the only reason I'm not a crumpled mess on the hardwood floor.

"What's wrong, Alyssa? You're freezing."

Nick's gruff voice brings me back to my senses, and I practically crawl out of my skin at the way I melted in his arms.

I slink out of his grasp, and his eyes widen when he gets a good look at what I'm wearing. I'm in a white T-shirt that's currently see-through from the rainstorm. The smallest pair of plaid shorts I own barely covers my rear. My hair is drenched and sticking to my cheeks, and whatever leftover makeup I went to bed in is surely running down my face. Based on the way he's looking at me, I'm a mess.

"Alyssa, talk to me. What happened?"

"There's a ghost in my house. He was in my room at the end of my bed," I blurt. "He . . . talked to me. Said he wasn't there to hurt me." The words spill out as my body continues to tremble.

Nick's demeanor shifts from confused to deadly in a split second. "Stay here," he commands, rushing down a hall. He's gone for less than a minute, and I stand in the entrance of his home, eyes shifting around warily as I shake from the cold seeping in. When he returns, I start breathing again, grateful to no longer be alone.

"Here. You're shivering." He holds out a sweatshirt, averting his eyes.

I'm grateful to see that he's covered his torso with a sweatshirt too. I take the offered clothing, pulling it over my head. It's huge, falling to the middle of my thighs, but I appreciate the cover it provides.

Nick moves to a small table and pulls out a gun from a drawer.

"Whoa. What are you doing with that?" I ask, voice pitching in horror.

"I need to go check your house," he says, inspecting the gun—for what, I have no idea. "Lock the door behind me and don't answer it for anyone but me. I'll be back soon."

I leap forward, eyes wide in fright. "But why do you need that?" I jab my finger at the weapon.

"I don't know what I'm walking into. If a man is in your house, he could be armed, and I need to protect myself so I can help you." His voice is calm and reassuring, helping me to relax marginally.

"That isn't gonna work with a ghost. You need to call someone." My voice is shrill.

Nick puts the gun back on the table and turns toward me,

placing both hands on my shoulders. "Alyssa, listen to me. I know you're scared and half-asleep, but this isn't a ghost situation. If a man spoke to you in your house, he's very real and could be very dangerous. I need to search your place." His eyes roam my face. "Okay?"

"No. Please. I . . . I can't be alone. I'm freaked out."

He leans down so we're at eye level. "I don't want to leave you alone, but I have to. It's not safe for you to go back to your house until I've cleared it. I promise, as soon as I'm done, I'll come right back here." He searches my face again. "Will you be okay for a few minutes?"

"I-I don't know. I don't feel comfortable."

He places a large hand on my shoulder. "You'll be safe here," he assures me. "There's a blanket next to the couch." He tilts his head toward a small black leather sofa in front of a bay window. "Curl up and get warm. I'll be back before you know it."

I take a deep breath and nod, not knowing what else to do. He must see something that makes him feel better about leaving me alone because he mimics the nod, turns, and heads through his front door. "Lock it," he reminds me, before rushing off toward my house.

Jumping into action, I lock the dead bolt on his door, taking a few deep breaths to compose myself. When I turn around, the spacious, dark room before me only manages to kick my imagination into overdrive.

In a corner of the room, a dark presence looms, and my legs begin to shake again.

I flip a switch on the wall and an overhead light shines down, brightening the expansive room. The looming figure that I was sure was preparing to murder me is a whitewashed hutch.

My hand lands over my racing heart. "Holy mother. Pull yourself together, Alyssa."

My shoulders move as I shake off the fear and walk around in search of more warmth.

I grab the blanket that was just where Nick said it would be and wrap it around myself before slumping down into the couch. My head swivels, taking in the home. For a bachelor pad, it's rather homey, and that surprises me.

The one-story ranch is one of the smaller homes in the neighborhood, but its open floor plan is spectacular. The vaulted ceilings showcase beams that run the length of the home, from this end all the way to the walled-off section that separates the open space from the hallway that surely leads to the bedrooms.

I have a perfect view of the majority of the place from my perch in the smaller seating area at the front of the house. The walls throughout aren't simply white. They're light gray, a shade that favors blue tones and matches perfectly with the gray hardwood. The entire back wall is a darker shade, almost navy in color. It's hard to tell, as the only lights that are on provide little light to the back of the house.

A two-story stone fireplace takes up the middle of the wall, where a large television hangs just above the bare white mantel.

In the center is a large sectional and two matching chairs that are identical to the leather furniture in this part of the house.

A small dining nook is at the far right corner, where a set of French doors lead to the backyard. There's a small four-person table, where a laptop currently sits open. A large, framed picture hangs above the table on the side wall, where the kitchen is positioned. I'm too far away to make out what the picture is.

A long island runs parallel to floor-to-ceiling white bookshelves, situated along the wall shielding the bedrooms. A small part of me wants to walk to the shelves and see what treasures it houses. But the bigger, chickenshit part of me remains rooted to this seat.

I know little about Nick West, but this isn't what I expected. For the first time ever, I wonder what his story is.

I've put in little—okay, no—effort to get to know the guy. Garrett had a good camaraderie going with him, but I never cared to ask what he knew about our neighbor. What did I care? I was happily married and busy raising Ava. My single neighbor was low on my list of priorities.

Considering he's currently putting his life on the line for me, I should probably change that and give the guy a chance.

Maybe he's not as infuriating as he seems.

Strength

Nick

THERE ARE VERY few things in this world that surprise me, but Alyssa Mann pounding on my door in the middle of the night, soaked through and scared as hell, was something I didn't see coming.

We've hardly spoken to each other in the four years that I've lived next door. I've never gotten the impression that she cares much for me. Whenever I'm around, the woman dashes off like her ass is on fire, and I have absolutely no clue why.

I considered asking her once but thought better of it. Garrett was a great guy, and I respected him too much to interrogate his wife about shit that doesn't matter. Her opinion of me is none of my business.

The fact it was my door she knocked on tells me how damn scared she must've been.

Maybe after tonight things will change? *Doubtful.*

I've canvassed the entire first floor and I'm making my way through the second. I take one last look around what must be her daughter Ava's room, based on the girlie pink-and-purple flower decor. I searched the closets, looked underneath the gray four-poster bed, and managed to get myself tangled up with white drape netting. It was set up like a tent, and in my hurry, I damn near pulled it down. Seeing it for the hazard it was, I pulled the fabric together, attaching it at the corners, with ties tied into matching white bows.

I'm helpful like that.

The room is secure, so I close the door behind me and make my way down the poorly lit hallway to the next door. This one's narrow, indicating it's likely a closet.

With one hand on my holster, I rip it open to find nothing but towels in the same shade of blue on the first three shelves and two bins with labeled cleaning supplies on the bottom.

This place is next-level organized. I didn't think it was possible for someone to be more anal than my sister, Jackie, but I think I found a contender. Outside of the office space, which was bedlam, the house is immaculate.

The light above flickers, indicating the bulb is burning out. No wonder Alyssa was scared. The flickering alone gives me *Amityville Horror* vibes. I make a mental note to offer to replace it for her. Along with the yellowed smoke detector attached to the ceiling, the color a clear indicator it's old.

Something crashes, and my head snaps toward the sound coming from the closed door at the end of the hall. I grab my phone from my back pocket and fire off a quick text to my partner, Eric.

> **NICK**
> Need your assistance at the house next
> door to mine.
> The standoffish widow. Possible intruder.

I wince at the description I've given of Alyssa. Unfortunately, that's the only detail I've given Eric about my neighbor, and it's the easiest way to ensure he finds himself at the right place. If he went busting into Mrs. Fields's house at this hour, he'd likely scare her to death.

Literally.

At eighty years old, she's had more than her share of frights through the years, and I've been called for every one of them since I've lived next door. Not that I mind. It's what I live for. The chance to help and have my adrenaline spike. It's a thrill that only people in my line of work would get.

I shove the phone back into my pocket and check my gun once more to ensure it's ready to go in the off chance it's needed. Typically, an intruder can be apprehended without the use of a deadly weapon. Let's hope tonight proves to be typical.

With my gun raised, I throw open the door, popping my head around the white frame, doing a quick sweep with my eyes. My hand feels around the wall, locating the switch for the overhead light and flipping it on.

The yellow room with white furnishings suits Alyssa. There's a busted bulb from a fallen lamp, but no additional signs of an intruder as far as I can tell. I take a few tentative steps into the room, keeping my back to the wall and eyes on any and all places where someone could be hiding out.

I make my way to the windows to ensure they're all locked, and they are. Not that anyone would chance a fall from this height. They wouldn't escape without broken bones or worse.

Making my way back toward the door, I search the bathroom and ready myself to open the closet, but right before I do, I catch a glimpse of a man's profile in a floor-length mirror, trip, and land flat on my back. The hardwood floor is unforgiving, and pain shoots up my spine.

"What the . . ." I groan, rubbing at the back of my neck. I don't move, taking this time to internally berate myself because it was me. I was startled by my own damn reflection.

I don't scare easily, so why the hell am I so jumpy? I'm a detective for crying out loud. This is just embarrassing. "Get yourself together, West."

Rolling onto my side, I come face-to-face with a pair of lacy pink underwear peeking out from under the bed. I leap up off the floor, head swiveling as though I've done something wrong.

I've got to get out of here.

I run my hands down my face, concentrating on breathing. Anything to slow down my racing heart, so that I can finish this job and crawl back into bed. My current state is brought to you by exhaustion. That must be the issue. I'm naturally cool, calm, and collected. Right now, I'm a jump scare away from disaster.

It's the lack of sleep that has me on edge.

When I've managed to shake it off, I continue my perusal, searching every crevice of the second floor.

I find nothing.

At this point, I have to assume that (1) the lamp fell because it was too close to the edge of the nightstand, likely a byproduct of Alyssa thinking she saw a man in her room and hurrying out; (2) the house is old and drafty, causing it to fall and subsequently break; or (3) Alyssa was seeing things due to the storm and possible sleep deprivation.

There's no one here, and every window and door is locked save the front door, which is most definitely the exit Alyssa used. Someone could've potentially fled the house through that door, but it's unlikely. All the homes in the area have cameras on the front door, making it hard to go undetected. Not to mention there hasn't been a crime in this part of town since I've lived here and well before that from what I've been told.

I'll post to the neighborhood forum, asking everyone to check their cameras for anyone aside from Alyssa or me coming or going, but I doubt anyone will pop up.

I run my hand back through my hair, tugging a bit at the roots. As the adrenaline wears off, my knees buckle slightly, and I have to grab hold of the end of her sleigh bed to right myself. "Shit."

Thank god nobody is here to witness this play out. I've been bested by bed netting, scared by my own reflection, accosted by pink panties, and if I can't get these tremors on a tight rein, I'm going down for the second time tonight.

I sway a bit, but eventually I'm able to get myself under control enough to head back downstairs. I'll feel better if I can manage one more sweep.

My phone rings—probably Eric checking in on his way over.

"Sorry, man. It's all good here. No need to come out." I spit the words out fast, feeling shitty for involving him instead of patrol, like I should've.

He yawns on the other end. "Thank Christ, because I'm still in bed. I forgot to turn my ringer on."

Wouldn't be the first time. I've saved his ass on numerous occasions from Captain's wrath for that very thing. Detectives are always on the clock. Time of the day doesn't prevent a murder and subsequent investigation from happening.

"Go back to sleep. See you in the morning." Even to my own ears, I sound gruff and moody. The events of the night are taking a toll.

"Night, West."

I'm just rounding the corner heading back to the kitchen when the front door creaks, putting me on high alert.

I'm not alone.

I pull my gun from the holster and lean around the wall. There in the doorway, illuminated by the lightning streaking across the sky, is Alyssa looking like a disheveled specter.

Five of Wands . . . Reversed

AFTER SITTING IN Nick's house for over thirty minutes, listening to the house settle, I began to calm down, but a noise down the back hallway had terror kicking back in.

"It's just the house shifting," I tell myself, hoping that if I utter the words out loud, it would make them true.

My eyes scan the area. Was I just being hypersensitive because of the man in my room? Or was someone actually there with me?

"Hello," I call out, like every idiot from the horror movies I watched as a kid.

But when something crashed in response, I didn't think twice. Jumping from the couch, I unlock the door in record time, and sprint toward my house in pursuit of my armed neighbor.

It vaguely occurred to me that I was running from a noise directly toward a confirmed break-in, but at least that direction included a detective and a gun. Back at his place, I was a sitting duck with a lamp as a weapon. And I'd been in that predicament once tonight already.

Not that any of this was going to help with a ghost.

I rush through my front door as Nick leans around the corner leading to my kitchen. He must've heard me because he peeked around the wall, gun raised.

"Don't shoot!" I cry, covering my head as though that's going to save me from a bullet. I manage to trip over my own feet in the process, grabbing for air to save me from falling over and making a complete ass of myself. I give full credit to forty years of klutziness and learning how to cope with it.

As soon as Nick realizes it's me, the gun lowers, and he heaves a breath, stepping into the hallway. "What are you doing?"

"Thank you for not shooting," I say, teeth chattering at the cold coming from the open door behind me. I turn and shut it quietly, as if it matters at this point. I just screamed, alerting any intruder—ghost or otherwise—to our presence and likely foiling Nick's sweep.

His lips smash together like he's lost for words.

"There was a noise at your house," I say, pointing over my shoulder. "I ran."

He nods.

"I'm not going back there alone."

He nods again, sucking in his cheek in thought. He looks like he might argue with me, but he doesn't. "Okay, but stay behind me. You'll need to be as quiet as you can."

"Too late for that."

He tilts his head with a *true story* expression. "I still need to do one more quick sweep, to be sure I didn't miss anything."

I nod like a bobblehead, likely looking ridiculous, but Nick doesn't seem to notice. He's a professional, and it's the only truth holding my sanity together at the moment.

We walk through my entire house. Nick checks every closet, window, and door. No nook goes unsearched. The entire time, I remain behind him, vigilant and, most importantly, quiet. As promised.

When the search is concluded, Nick turns to me and says, "Nobody's here."

I take one giant step back, frowning up at him. "Someone *was* here, Nick."

He holsters his gun. "I believe you, Alyssa. I'm just stating that I didn't find anything out of place, aside from the lamp. I'm not discounting what you went through. I can tell you're terrified. I want to help." He takes a step toward me, and I take another step back.

"Of course you didn't find anything. Ghosts are sneaky."

He purses his lips and blinks several times.

"Why do I get the feeling that you think I'm crazy?"

"Not at all. Someone could've been here; I just didn't find any evidence of it. That's all."

There's nothing smug about him while he delivers his account, but I'm growing more embarrassed with every second that goes by. It's clear he's not a believer in the supernatural. Not that I can blame him. Before last night, I wasn't much of one myself.

"Do you have a pen and paper? I need to get your account of the events. I'll have to call this in."

"You just said that there were no signs of entry, so why make a report?" I cross my arms over my chest, sounding like a brat, which is my typical go-to response when I'm humiliated.

I know this, yet I can't bring myself to stop.

His eyes narrow in on my crossed arms and stiff posture. "I need to involve the station so they can keep an eye on the place. I'll be on alert, but an extra patrol in the area wouldn't hurt either."

I want to argue that his extra patrol isn't going to stop a ghost, but I refrain, knowing it won't help my case. If I want to get through this night without digging myself a hole I can't crawl out of, I need to allow him to do his job, despite my suspicion that he's on the wrong path.

I'm tired, mortified at my current state, and still very scared, but he doesn't deserve my attitude. He's been nothing but kind since I practically knocked his door down in the middle of the night, and I owe him an apology, or a thank-you at the very least.

"I'm sorry, Nick. I'm just—"

His hand comes up to stop me. "There's nothing to apologize for. It's been a traumatic night. Don't worry about me."

I want to argue, but that would only drag this night out more. Tomorrow, I'll make him a casserole and deliver it with a sincere apology.

"Follow me," I say, moving through my dark house, flipping on every switch as I go.

My stark white kitchen is at the back of my cookie-cutter house. After having been in Nick's, I'm less than thrilled with my layout. There's nothing open about it, with the exception of the great room that we built on five years ago.

I pull a pen and paper out of my one and only junk drawer and hand them to him, motioning for him to take a seat at the white granite-topped island. He nods, taking the closest barstool while I lean against the opposite countertop.

"Tell me what happened, from the beginning."

I bite on my lower lip, trying to recall the events in my room. "I don't remember word for word. Something about him being there because I called him."

His eyes raise to meet mine. "Did you call someone? Anyone?"

My nose scrunches. "No. It's the middle of the night, Nick. Why on earth would I call a strange man?"

I'm not about to admit that I kinda, sorta did call out to a man tonight, but he's not alive, and also that might be the reason I'm in this mess.

Out of habit, I lift myself up to sit on the countertop, a position I often took while watching Garrett cook.

Nick's eyes stray, and his cheeks redden. I'm not sure if it's from my tone or something else entirely. The more I focus on his reaction, the deeper down the well my thoughts fall.

"Out with it," I demand, knowing there is something he doesn't want to say.

He blows out a breath. "Listen, it's none of my business. It's just—you were out tonight with your friends and, well, I'm just doing my job, asking all the questions I'd normally ask."

"What is it you're asking me exactly?" I rub at my temples, trying to stave off the building headache.

"Well . . . I—"

"Oh, just say it! Did I make a booty call to a random guy?" My hands fly up. "No. Not to a man or woman or anyone. No calls were made. I'm forty! I'm not doing . . . that."

His eyes widen and his hand flies up, motioning for me to calm down. "I-I wasn't insinuating that."

"It sure seemed like it."

His head shakes back and forth and his eyes close as he appears to be composing himself. "I'm sorry. I just . . . never mind. There was no call. Moving on," he says, shuffling the papers as though he'd love to hide behind them. *So would I, buddy.* "What else did he say?"

My arms cross over my chest and my head falls back into the white cabinet behind me. "He said he wasn't there to kill me or . . . ravish." My eyes avert from Nick's, and the words stumble out of my mouth before I have a chance to rephrase the stranger's less-than-kind rebuttal.

Nick coughs, fist coming to his mouth, and I roll my eyes, jumping down from the counter, feeling fidgety.

"He said that . . . exactly?"

"Well . . . no. Just that he wasn't there to hurt me. It was implied. Apparently forty-year-olds are not, in fact, worthy of being ravished."

"The intruder implied that Mrs. Mann would not be ravished," Nick says under his breath as he scribbles on his sheet of paper.

"Are you quite done?" I ask, a little too prickly.

"For what it's worth, I wholly disagree," he offers, and I shoot him a look of annoyance.

Not quite sure what comes over me, I decide to mess with the detective, placing my elbows on the island and leaning over it, head tilting to the side.

"So you're saying you'd ravish me?"

He chokes on air. "I'm simply saying I don't agree that forty-year-olds are not ravishable."

I raise an eyebrow. "Is that even a word?"

His head shakes in surrender. "Doesn't matter. I will be ravishing no one."

I smirk, straightening away from the island. "Continue," I say, trying to move the conversation away from ravishing.

He sweeps his hand out in a gesture to remind me that I'm the one who needs to continue.

"The perp was wearing a gray hoodie, faded jeans, and had a brown leather bracelet on his left wrist. He looked to be in his late twenties."

"What else can you tell me about the perp?" His smile tells me he's amused.

"What? I watch *Law and Order*."

He chuckles. "Anything you want to add?"

I stare at the stainless-steel refrigerator, trying to focus on what was said, and then it hits me.

"He told me his name," I offer, turning back toward Nick.

His eyes fly to mine. "Why didn't you lead with that?" His words aren't harsh, but he's surprised by this revelation.

I shrug. "I forgot."

"Do you remember what he said?" Nick chews on his bottom lip, gaze trained on my face.

"Yes," I say, raising my finger into the air. "Billy Garet."

Something shifts in Nick's expression, but I can't read it. "Billy Garet?"

I nod tersely.

His eyes narrow before he turns on his toes and walks from the kitchen toward my formal dining room. I'm hot on his heels, wondering what he's up to. He sits at the six-person table, pulling my laptop toward him.

"I remembered seeing this while I was searching the place," he explains, eyes focused on the screen. "Is there a password for this?"

My cheeks heat, and I turn my head to avoid looking at Nick.

"What's wrong?" he asks, leaning to the side as if to see my face more clearly.

"I'd rather not share. Scoot the thing over here, and I'll enter it."

His eyes narrow. "I'm not going to steal your internet. I have my own."

My shoulders straighten and I meet his stare. Why do I care what he thinks of me? "Boobs fourteen. Capital *B*."

His lips form a thin line, but he thankfully doesn't press for the story behind my less-than-appropriate password, choosing wisely to continue on with the task at hand. A few long minutes go by as he clicks through whatever he's looking at, then he swings the computer toward me.

"This him?"

I take a couple steps toward the table, bending down to get a good look at the Mac. When I see the picture, a grin spreads across my face.

"That's him," I confirm.

Nick shakes his head. "That's impossible, Alyssa."

"I just told you that's the guy. You win; it wasn't a ghost. Go arrest him."

"Listen, I worked his case until I was called off, and this isn't your guy."

My fists rest on my hips. "What are you talking about?"

Nick points to the text under the picture, and the smile of triumph drops off my face.

Deceased.

"Billy Garet is dead."

Huh.

No shit.

7

Page of Cups

"THAT . . . CAN'T BE right."

I read and reread the small text. Billy Garet, whose picture shows the same guy from my room, is in fact a ghost. Guess I was right after all.

"What does that mean?" I exhibit faux concern like a seasoned Oscar nominee.

Nick blinks, appearing to contemplate his next words as though he's afraid whatever he says might throw me into a spiral.

"I saw Billy Garet's body. He's dead." Nick's eyes hold mine. "Are you sure that the man you saw wasn't someone else? Maybe someone who looks similar enough to claim he's Billy?"

My eyes narrow in on the picture. "Maybe?"

Nope.

"Can you tell me one more time what he said to you?" Nick asks, looking down at his notes.

"That's it. Aside from telling me his name is Billy Garet and then disappearing, there isn't anything else to say."

Nick's brows scrunch together. "Disappearing? What do you mean?"

"Just what I said. One minute he was there and the next . . . poof. He was gone."

He sets down the pen, folding his hands in front of him. "I'm going to need you to describe what 'poof' entails."

I glare at Nick. "Really?"

"I'm just trying to work out all the details. Like I said, I want to help keep you safe. And details are important."

"I told him I didn't want him here, and he literally vanished. I thought maybe he dropped to the floor and crawled under my bed, but he didn't. He was gone. Like, poof," I repeat.

As the words leave my mouth, I hear the absolute absurdity of what I'm implying.

I haven't once doubted that the man at the end of my bed is a ghost, but I haven't had an opportunity to consider what that means and how it concerns me. Believing in the possibility of the supernatural is one thing; having it confirmed is quite another.

The triumph of being right bleeds away and fear creeps back into me.

Nick blinks several times, chewing on his cheek. "Could you have dreamed the situation?" he asks, keeping his eyes on the computer screen.

"What? No, I didn't dream it," I spit out, fear turning to fury. "I'm a grown-ass woman. I know the difference between a dream and reality. I'm not losing my mind."

His hands rise in surrender. "Okay. You didn't dream it. I'm just being thorough."

"No. You're being mean. Have I not been tormented enough tonight? Now you have to humiliate me?"

"No, that's not what's happening," Nick says, eyes wide.

He crosses over to me and pulls me into a hug. "I'm sorry if I've upset you. It wasn't my intention. You've had a horrible couple years, and with you having lived the trauma firsthand, well . . . I can only imagine how hard it's been. I would never purposely embarrass you."

I want to scream. Want to pound his rock-hard chest with my fists and tell him I wasn't dreaming, and that ghosts are real. I don't need his patrol; I need ghostbusters. But I don't do or say any of that. Men like Nick deal in facts. The facts here are that a dead man vanished into thin air from my room.

"I . . . I'm sorry Nick. I don't know what to say. Maybe I *did* dream it?"

"Shh. It's not important right now. All that matters is that you're safe."

But I'm not.

"Thanks for checking things out," I say, backing out of his embrace. "I appreciate you humoring me."

"No humoring was involved. If you ever need help, I'm right next door."

I try to smile, but it falls flat.

"Maybe for the rest of the night you shouldn't be alone? Is there anyone you could call to stay with you?"

I shake my head. "I'm good. I'll likely not sleep anyway."

He frowns. "You sure? I can stick around if that'll help you sleep."

That is the absolute last thing that's happening. The sooner I get him out of my house, the better.

"Not necessary. But thank you. You've been great."

He inhales harshly, pursing his lips like he might debate my decision, but in the end, he exhales and nods. "I'll leave my number here," he says, pulling the pad of paper toward him and jotting down his digits. "If you need anything, call. I don't care what time."

"I will. Thank you."

I won't, and we both know it.

He heads to the door, looking back once more and offering a small smile. "Try to get some rest."

My lips lift at the corners in the fakest smile I can muster as I shut the door on Nick and this disaster of a night.

✦ ✦ ✦

SUNLIGHT STREAMS IN through the window and I sigh in relief, knowing a new day is here and I wasn't murdered by a ghost in my sleep. Somehow, the exhaustion pulled me under, and if the clock is correct, I've slept half the day away.

I think I dreamed Ava's voice too until she calls out again.

"Mom!"

"I'm up here," I yell out, trying to pull myself together and muster the energy to sit up.

My door flies open and Ava bursts in, looking confused.

I'm sure she is, considering the only times I've ever slept until noon, I was fighting a virus from hell or depression from the accident.

"What's wrong?" she asks, coming to the side of the bed and taking a seat.

"The better question is, What are you doing here?" I say, voice full of sleep. "How did you get home?"

Her hand comes to my forehead, and I bat it away.

"I wanted to come yesterday, but I had exams. Aunt Lanie arranged to pick me up early this morning."

"She what?" I spring up, nearly knocking her off the edge.

Ava's large hazel eyes, which match her father's, go wide as she grabs hold of the comforter. "Calm down, Mom. She has the clearance. You gave it to her."

And I'm currently regretting giving Lanie Anderson any modicum of control where Ava is concerned.

When Garrett died, I needed help and Lanie and Nina stepped up. With both of Garrett's parents gone, and his sister and my parents halfway across the US, I made both of my friends emergency contacts for the school and got clearance for them to act on my behalf in all matters pertaining to Ava and her education.

"What about your classes?" I ask, finally managing to sit up.

"Nothing important was happening today. Exams finished up last night, or else I would've been here to celebrate your birthday."

I purse my lips, and she rolls her eyes.

"I'm on the dean's list, Mom. I can afford to miss a day of classes."

She doesn't have to remind me. Ava is my pride and joy. Always has been. She's a good girl. Studious, empathetic, and protective, like me. She's also funny, passionate, and has a penchant for excitement, just like her father. Ava's the best parts of us both.

"I wasn't going to allow more time to go by without spending time with you for your birthday," she says. "We're going to celebrate."

My hand lands on top of hers and I squeeze. "I'm not really up for celebrating. It was a long night."

Her eyes narrow. "Are you sick?"

"Maybe?"

One brow lifts in question. "Maybe?" she repeats. "What's going on, Mom? Is this about your milestone birthday?"

I pull a pillow up to cover my face, groaning into it. "Can't we just pretend I'm sick and stay in bed all day?"

The pillow is removed from my face and Ava frowns at me.

"Nope. No more pity parties about turning forty. We're going to get through this together."

"It's not a pity party," I whine, but I don't elaborate on what has me still in bed at noon.

When Ava finds out the events that led me to Nick's in the middle of the night, she'll harp on how I shouldn't be alone and how she could transfer to the local public high school. I won't allow that, because we both know she'd only be doing it for me. It's a fight I don't want to have.

She wraps her arms around me, and I squeeze back, thrilled that she's here and that she's not going to press the subject.

I've missed her so much, and today, I just want to enjoy my time with her. "I'm glad you're here, kiddo."

"Me too."

"Now, let's get you up and showered." She pulls away, her nose scrunching in mock disgust. "And make plans."

"Nothing too big. I'd like to just spend time with you. Maybe order food in and binge-watch some terrible TV?" My hands come together as if in prayer.

Ava smiles. "Sure. But tomorrow, we're going to try venturing out." She lifts her brows like this is some sort of treat for her, and I can't help but laugh.

"I'll be fast. Go get things ready downstairs," I suggest.

"We are going to talk about whatever happened last night," Ava calls over her shoulder as she retreats to the door.

I don't say a word, content to put off that conversation for as long as possible.

What would I say anyway? A dead man visited me last night, and I involved the detective next door?

The reminder of that isn't any less humiliating in the light of day.

One thing's for certain. I will now avoid Nick West at all costs, for as long as humanly possible.

When Ava's out of sight, I throw off the heavy duvet and swing my legs over the side. Lowering my feet onto the cold hardwood floor, I mentally note that I need to purchase a large rug for this very reason.

I pad toward the ensuite bathroom that we had redone at the same time we added the bonus room. Garrett thought we should spring for heated floors, but I'd objected, being the cost-conscious one in our partnership. Today, I regret not splurging as the cold seeps into me.

For the shower, however, I did take the upgrade. I didn't want glass doors to keep clean, so we opted for a walk-in stone sanctuary with jets jutting out from every wall. I turn the knob to what I refer to as *hot as hellfire*, and as soon as it's warm enough, I plunge myself into the spray, hoping that somehow it scrubs all of it away.

Taking my time, I wash off the remnants of last night and watch as it swirls down the drain. I allow the lavender soap to clear my head and calm my fragile nerves. It only lasts so long before my mind sifts through every moment from last night.

I shake off the unease curling its way around my middle and grab the towel hanging over the shower door. I'm not going to waste any more time on last night when Ava is downstairs.

Dressed in my comfiest navy-and-cream-striped pajamas, I go in search of her.

She's parked in front of the TV, armed with snacks and drinks, our typical setup for a night in together. From the day this two-story bonus room was built, it became our favorite part of the house. Ava, Garrett, and I spent many Saturday and Sunday afternoons curled on that oversized gray cloth sectional, watching movies and laughing until we cried.

"Hey, Mom." She smiles when she notices me. "I ordered a pizza from Angelo's. Should be here in about thirty minutes."

I return the smile. "Pizza sounds good."

She pats the couch next to her and I take a seat, cuddling up under the blanket she set out.

"What should we watch?" I ask, grabbing the remote.

She shakes her head. "Nope. You have some explaining to do."

"You're not gonna let this go, are you?" I mumble, avoiding her eyes by keeping mine trained on the maroon blanket and pretending to pick lint.

"Not a chance," she answers with a smirk. But that quickly fades with her next words.

"What happened? I sent a text to Aunt Lanie and Aunt Nina to ensure they were with you, and neither one of them responded. When I asked Aunt Lanie today, she danced around the subject." She nibbles on her full bottom lip, a giveaway that she's nervous. "You and I both know that's never a good sign. Are you fighting?"

Those two only ever ignore her when they're trying to hide something. They couldn't be any more obvious if they showed up with detailed sticky notes from last night taped to their heads.

I groan because there is no way of getting around this without leaving Ava to worry about her aunts and me.

"Nothing like that. They showed up here and we had a night out and then . . . ended up going to see a psychic."

Ava's eyebrows shoot up into her hairline. "A psychic?" She laughs, sounding even more nervous. "Oh boy . . . Do I even want to know what happened from there?"

I widen my eyes in a *probably not* expression, but fill her in on everything anyway. I don't spare a detail about what occurred at Cori's Nail Spa with Corinne. When I'm done, Ava's worrying her bottom lip, and her eyes are narrowed in thought.

"Do you think that was a good idea?" Here we go. Mother Ava

clawing her way to the surface. "It's just that—" Her words stop, and she shakes her head.

"It's just what, Aves?"

Her head lifts and our eyes meet. "I don't want to ruin our night by talking about this."

I force a smile. "It won't."

She takes a deep breath and continues. "That stuff isn't real, Mom, and it isn't healthy for you to think otherwise."

I pull a face, not loving her tone. She must notice because she rushes on.

"It's been two years and you're *barely* living life," she stresses. "Trying to chase down Dad's ghost isn't a healthy coping mechanism." Her head shakes. "Dad wouldn't want this. He wouldn't want you suffering like this, Momma." Her voice hitches and that lump in my throat intensifies.

Momma.

It's been so long since she's called me that.

Tears stream down her cheeks, and my hand lifts to wipe them away. I pull her in to my chest, running my hands down her back soothingly.

"I'm doing better, Aves." I whisper the promise into the top of her head. "You don't have to worry about me."

She pulls out of my grip. "But I do."

Inhaling deeply, I close my eyes and swallow down the tightness building at the base of my throat.

"What should we watch?" I ask, trying to turn this day around.

She frowns, obviously not ready to be done with this subject, but ultimately, she relents, leaning forward to grab the remote from the leather ottoman.

"Something funny." She points the remote toward the eighty-six-inch smart TV mounted to the wall.

I smile and nod. We could both use a little laughter.

We snuggle in close and spend the rest of the day watching romantic comedies and laughing until happy tears stream down our faces.

The events of the night before fade, and all is right with the world again.

8

The Empress

THE FALL SEASON in Knox Harbor is as close to heaven as you can get. The enchanting New England town boasts a covered bridge that welcomes visitors into downtown as they cross over a pristine stream that empties into the bay.

As soon as you exit the cover of the red-roofed passage, you're greeted with cobblestone sidewalks and Victorian-style storefronts straight out of a fairy tale.

I take it all in, realizing how lucky I am to call this place home.

I lift my face to the warm sun and inhale a deep, calming breath, savoring the peacefulness of this moment. The crisp air coming off the bay is tempered by the full sun overhead, making it a perfect day for a stroll along the tree-lined streets.

Having Ava by my side only heightens the perfection, and I don't want to think about how that all ends tomorrow when she heads back to school.

We've spent the day browsing through the specialty shops that dot the charming Main Street. My hands are full of bags from two boutiques that Ava insisted we visit. I have no need for more clothes, yet somehow I was talked into three new outfits, all in the name of the birthday that never ends.

We walk past the antique shop, Marmalade and Rye, and Ava squeals.

"Mom, look," she says, pointing toward the beautiful window display.

A storefront is like the cover of a book, luring you in to discover the treasures hidden in its depths. The perfect cover will guarantee a browse, even if the interior doesn't match the excellence.

Marmalade and Rye does it right with the nearly full-sized picture window decorated for the season, pairing perfectly with the red facade of the building. But it's when you step inside that you find the pretty packaging is only the beginning of the true magic. The beautiful building and display are offset by the most wonderful antiques.

Turquoise Turkish dishes in varying shapes and sizes have me stopping to gape. I've never been a collector of anything apart from handcrafted Turkish treasures. It was my one indulgence that I never felt bad about.

"For your birthday. Time to splurge." Ava grabs my arm, ushering me through the door.

"You said the same thing about the pantsuit I'll never wear." I groan.

"Alyssa!" the elderly Mrs. Hampson exclaims, clapping her hands as she hurries toward us on shaky legs. "I haven't seen you in here in ages. How are you, darling?"

Mrs. Hampson is a petite woman. Her white hair, streaked with gray, is pulled into a French twist like it is every day, and she's wearing her signature blue pantsuit that matches her cornflower eyes.

She grabs my shoulders, and I bend down so that she can kiss both cheeks.

"Let me guess," she says, backing away, eyes smiling. "You saw my display."

I chuckle. "You know me too well, Mrs. Hampson."

She bats her hands at me. "None of that. Matilda will work just fine. Come." She motions for us to follow her to the window.

"Wow," I breathe, taking in the vast collection. "I've never seen so many together."

Matilda's head bobs. "Poor Mrs. Craft had to sell off her collections to pay for her son's funeral." She mumbles under her breath, but I don't miss her words. "That fool Ollie didn't deserve the beautiful wake she gave him." She scowls, shaking her head and looking back to me, plastering a smile across her face. "Her loss is your gain, if I do say so."

Eyeing the dishes, I wonder how much this collection costs, if she was able to pay for a wake with the profits.

"Too expensive for me," I murmur. "Can I purchase one dish?"

Mrs. Hampson shakes her head. "It's a set. I really can't sell one piece separately."

"That's really sad," Ava says, looking to me.

I nod. "I'm not about to spend thousands for a simple birthday."

She pulls a face. "No, I meant it's sad that Mrs. Craft's son died?"

My mouth forms an O and I'm about to agree when Matilda cuts in.

"Thousands?" Her nose scrunches.

I turn my head toward her. "You said this sale paid for her son's wake," I answer.

"No, dear. Mrs. Craft sold off multiple collections. She was practically a hoarder of fine pieces. This is only one of fifteen sets of antique dishes she sold. The least expensive of the lot."

Mrs. Hampson's eyes narrow in on me. "Alyssa Mann, which birthday are you celebrating?"

"It's over," I say, shooting Ava a look I hope conveys that she's going to pay if she spills any details.

Ava smirks, turning toward Mrs. Hampson. "The big four-oh."

Mrs. Hampson's eyes light up. "Happy birthday, dear. You must splurge, then."

I blow out a breath. "How much?" I ask, shooting Ava another look as she laughs.

"For the set?" she asks, picking at something under her nail. "Six hundred."

I purse my lips. "It does seem unfair that Gloria should have to part with these for such a meager amount. First her son, then one of her prized collections? It feels wrong."

"Didn't she lose a daughter a few years back?" Ava asks, and I rack my brain, unable to recall.

Mrs. Hampson frowns. "The cornered rat will lick the balls of the cat," she says, tilting her head in thought. "Or maybe it's the cat who licks the balls?" She shrugs both shoulders. "Either way, Mrs. Craft did what she had to."

"Huh?" I ask, looking to Ava, who's practically choking on her laughter.

"Turkish proverb, dear. I became very interested in the culture while researching the worth of the collection." Her eyes practically glow with delight—whether from shocking me or from simply recalling her research, I'm unsure.

My eyebrows lift into my hairline. "Interesting." It's all I can manage. Those words coming out of little ol' Mrs. Hampson are too much to unpack. "Can you wrap it all up?" I ask, trying to steer her back to safer topics.

"Of course." She beams, rushing off toward the back room.

I turn to Ava, who's bent over laughing.

"Ava Marie, pull yourself together." My smile gives away the mock scold.

"I can't," she wheezes. "Your face when she said 'balls.'" Her voice cracks and my eyes roll.

"And here I thought you were the mature one."

She snorts and I turn toward the window.

My hands run across the dishes, taking in all the pieces. Two large and two small platters, a set of three large bowls, a decanter, four hand-painted stemmed glasses, and something I can't identify. All in various shades of turquoise with a deep blue color creating the flower motif etched into the dishes.

Mrs. Hampson returns with bubble wrap and boxes, setting to work.

"What's that piece?" I ask, pointing to the unidentified dish.

She doesn't meet my eyes when she says, "That's an urn."

"An urn?" My bottom lip pops out. "With dishes?"

She continues wrapping the bowls in the bubble wrap and sighs. "That's what my research found. But don't worry, dear. When I spoke to Gloria, she assured me that it was only ever used as a cookie jar."

Ava snickers. "She used an urn as a cookie jar?"

"That's what she said. Not that she would've had any use for it. Gloria doesn't believe in cremation. Her loved ones were buried in Wintersgate Cemetery." Mrs. Hampson's eyes fly to mine. "Not that there's anything wrong with cremation, dear. Gloria's just an old soul, is all."

I smile to assure her that I'm not offended. There was never a chance I was being lowered into the ground. It was one of the many things that Garrett and I wholeheartedly agreed on. It was also a source of contention with his Catholic mother, but not even she could sway us.

"Well, I think this will be used for its intended purpose," I say, looking to Ava. "It's time to move your dad out of that plain container and into a home that's more suitable."

She smiles, but it doesn't reach her sad eyes. "Yeah. It is time."

The door to the shop flies open and a group of local women come barreling in, chirping about town gossip.

"The cock that crows at the wrong time is killed," Mrs. Hampson calls out, and one of the women, Mrs. Jenkins, splutters.

"What on earth are you talking about, Tilda? It's near time for our Red Hatter meeting. We're right on time."

Matilda glances at her watch and frowns. "Damn it. She's right," she whispers to us. "I hate when Nan Jenkins bests me."

She closes up the last box and stands, turning toward her company. "Turn that sign to *Closed*. I'm just finishing up. Hats on, ladies. We have a festival to finish planning."

They each pull a red hat from their bags, situating them onto their heads. They're in an assortment of styles, each more elaborate than the next. Nan Jenkins's takes the cake.

Its wide bill looks like something an old-time baseball player would wear, more pink than red, with feathers of various colors splayed across the crown of her head, making her look like a deranged peacock. Add to that her burgundy pantsuit, and it makes quite the ensemble.

"One day soon, you'll join us, Alyssa." Nan smiles and I wince.

Today of all days, I don't need the reminder of how I'm moving closer to the ranks of the Red Hatters.

I head in the direction of the cash register.

When I've settled my bill, I rush Ava toward the door, calling out a farewell to Mrs. Hampson and thanking her for the incredible dishes. I balance the box and bags in my hands, trying to clear my view so that I don't walk into the street or into a person. As I shift the box, two men walk out of Milly's Diner.

Nick West and a handsome stranger with black hair and deep brown eyes walk toward us dressed in street clothes, jeans, and long-sleeved Henley shirts. I try my best to hide behind the box, but it's no use.

"Alyssa?" Nick says, and I stop walking, peeking around the box.

"Hey, Nick," I say, nodding at them both in turn. "And . . ." My words trail off as I settle on the younger man with him.

His hand juts out and he takes a step toward me. I lift the box slightly to indicate I can't shake his hand, and his arm drops back to his side. "Eric Malone. This grump's partner." He tilts his head toward Nick, offering a charming smile, complete with deep dimples on both cheeks. "And you are?"

"This is my neighbor Alyssa Mann, and her daughter, Ava." Nick jumps in to make the introduction.

Eric smirks at Nick, who quickly turns his gaze away. I wonder for a moment what that was about but quickly push it away. What do I care what he's saying about me?

"Do you need help with that?" Nick moves forward, not waiting for my reply.

"No, I . . ." He lifts the box from my hands. "Thanks," I grumble, just barely able to contain my annoyance at his continued chivalry. It's even worse considering he witnessed me in all my glorious mess the other night.

"Where's your car?"

I raise my arm, pointing toward the white Volvo parked at the end of the block. Eric takes the box Ava's carrying and follows Nick toward the vehicle. I rush forward, hoping to get the car unlocked, boxes situated, and Ava and me out of here before anything is said about the other night.

No such luck.

"How are you?" Nick asks, after he's placed the box into the back seat. "I meant to stop by, but I saw Ava backing her car out of the garage." He smiles over at Ava. "It's good to see you, Ava."

"You too, Mr. West. How's life?"

Nick chuckles. "Life is busy, but I can't complain. How's art school?"

Her eyes light up. "It's awesome. I'm taking several graphic design classes this semester. I'm loving it."

He smiles wide, showcasing straight, white teeth. "I'm sure you'll excel at whatever you do."

Ava offers her most dazzling smile in return. I don't miss how her eyes stray to the younger of the two, cheeks turning a shade of pink that implies a crush.

"Well . . . thanks again, Nick," I say, pushing a gawking Ava toward her door.

"I meant to ask if you've remembered anything else about last night. Anything at all that could be added to the report."

I grind my teeth, pushing Ava down into her seat and turning toward Nick. "I thought we were skipping the report, considering . . ." I let my words trail off, hoping to convey that I don't want to discuss the events of that night with Ava present.

His eyes narrow slightly, and I see the light bulb moment as he looks to Ava out of the corner of his eye. "Right. Well, I'll let you two get going. We can talk about it another time."

"Wait. What report? What happened?" Ava's head peeks over the car door, bouncing between Nick and me.

I close my eyes as I inhale deeply, opening them with a huff that blows a wayward hair away from my face.

"There was an incident, and I recruited Mr. West to help me." Ava's lips form a thin line and I know she's growing frustrated with me. The jig's up. "We can discuss it at home," I say. "Thanks again, Nick. I'll be in touch if I think of anything else."

His chin tilts down. "Have a good day, Alyssa," he says, turning and walking away.

"You have some explaining to do," Ava cuts into my thoughts as I slide behind the wheel.

"Can't it wait?" I groan.

She shakes her head. "Spill it, Mom."

I speed through the events that occurred after my friends left, and when I'm done, Ava is speechless for several moments.

"Let me get this straight. You ran through the rain . . . in your pajamas . . . next door to Mr. West's house?" She doubles over, holding her belly as she laughs. "I would've paid money to see that." Her voice cracks through her laughter.

"It's not funny, Ava! I was petrified." I cry. "And of all the things I just told you, that's what you're focusing on?" I stare at her, puzzled. "I told you I'm being haunted."

She raises a finger. "One . . . based on what you said, it sounds more likely that you drank too much wine."

My head jerks back. "Too much wine?"

"Mom . . . think about it. You went to a psychic, who also happens to be a medium, and asked to connect with Dad. You claim to have seen visions that couldn't be your own, and you begged Dad to come to you." She pauses, allowing that to sink in. When I continue to stare at her uncomprehending, she continues. "The same night, some strange man whom you find out is *actually* dead shows up in your room and vanishes into thin air."

"And you jump straight to too much wine?"

She sighs. "I think you had a very vivid dream."

I massage my temple as I prepare myself to lie through my teeth to the one person I swore never to lie to. "You're probably right. Thanks for setting me straight."

She purses her lips, seemingly contemplating my words. "You don't mean that," she says, seeing right through me.

I'm about to insist I agree with her and that ghosts don't exist, but she speaks.

"What did you say his name was?"

"Who?" I ask, bewildered by the shift in questioning.

She smacks her lips together as though she's annoyed. "The man in your dream."

I have to school my features so that I don't show my annoyance. Blowing out a breath, I answer. "Billy Garet."

I question whether continuing to talk about my night from hell is healthy for either of us.

"You don't find it at all strange that the man's last name is Garet? The exact name you supposedly opened yourself to connect with?"

This stops me short. I'd never even considered the similarity. The intuitive part of my brain that's never steered me wrong is practically beeping in the back of my mind to pay attention. That has to be how Billy came to be in my room. A mix-up due to my lack of experience where the mystical is concerned.

My beautiful, intelligent daughter is unknowingly putting together the pieces I was missing.

"I mean, Mom . . . it makes sense. Your mind concocted one heck of a dream from the experience at the medium."

"You are so right, Ava. Well done."

Her one eye narrows while the eyebrow on the opposite side of her face lifts to her hairline. "You don't mean it," she says. "You actually believe there's a ghost in your house."

I shake my head back and forth a little too quickly.

"Am I in the twilight zone?" She laughs. "Aunt Lanie? Yes. You? I never would've seen this coming."

"Why do you doubt me? Nina's the cynic of the group."

I've hit rock bottom. Here I am arguing about who's more likely to believe in the spirit world with my teenage daughter, who is currently looking at me like I've lost it.

"Dear god, you truly think you see the dead."

Every part of me is screaming *Abort!* I don't want to freak out Ava. She might be sixteen, but she's still a kid. A kid who lives alone in a dorm room at an old and spooky school for the arts.

I need to steer this conversation to safer ideas. Otherwise, she may well and truly think I've lost my marbles.

"I started taking some new meds, and I think they might be the cause."

"New meds?" Ava's eyes narrow in on me, but I don't react, sticking to something she can make sense of. It's true. I did change medications, and one of the side effects is hallucinations.

Ava eventually shrugs.

"You should probably call your doctor then. Or at the very least, stop drinking wine while you're on them." I nod my head, but she doesn't see it. She's staring out the windshield. I follow her gaze to where Nick West is getting into his Trailblazer. "Seems dangerous if you're having dreams that lead to having guns pointed at you," she says, finally turning toward me.

I nod again, agreeing wholeheartedly. "You're right."

Her worry melts away and she grins. "Let's go home and get ready for dinner. Aunt Lanie and Aunt Nina are going to meet us."

Internally I sigh, happy to be done with this conversation, but reluctant to share Ava. I plaster on my best smile. "As long as we're not going to Marina Grille."

She grins. "I told them anywhere but Marina."

We make our way home, chatting about school and all things non-ghost, but a small part of me continues to circle back to Ava's words about Billy Garet. I send a silent prayer of thanks up to whoever's listening that I won't have to sleep alone tonight, and an extra prayer that Billy stays away.

9

The Moon

AVA PLACES HER bag in the back seat of her maroon Corolla and slams the door. Sunday came far too quickly.

"I wish I didn't have to go," she says, jutting out her bottom lip.

"Me too."

I'm trying to hold back tears because I don't want her to worry. No amount of time is ever enough with Ava, but I don't want to make her feel guilty about living her life. Going back to school is what's best for her.

I pull her into my chest, squeezing a little harder than necessary.

"Can't . . . breathe," she wheezes through chuckles, and I step back, cringing.

"Sorry. Can't help it." My voice betrays me, cracking on the last part. So much for playing strong.

Her features contort in concern, and I bite my cheek, knowing whatever's coming next will either make me sad or prickly. "Please call your doctor and get to the bottom of your medication."

I lift my hand, moving a piece of hair that escaped her messy bun behind her ear. A large part of me wishes I didn't have to lie to Ava, but the mother in me whispers, *It's for the best.* Nothing good could come from me convincing my teenage daughter that I'm being haunted.

"When did you become the parent in this relationship?"

She smirks. "If you want me to stop, start taking better care of yourself."

I grimace at all the ways I've allowed myself to go downhill, and the fact that Ava's noticed makes it even worse. My eyes lower to my slipper-clad feet and shabby gray pajama pants. It's nearly eleven in the morning and I'm still not dressed, which is sadly not uncommon for me these days.

"I know, Aves. I'll call Dr. Lara as soon as you pull away."

She gives me a tight-lipped smile, searching my face for falsehoods. When she's satisfied, she opens the driver's side door and takes a seat behind the wheel. "I'll call you when I get back to my dorm."

"Did you grab your parking pass?" I ask, worrying at my bottom lip.

She hasn't been allowed to take her car to school because I didn't want her having an excuse to constantly come home. With the holidays approaching and a hefty amount of begging on Ava's part, I gave in—with the stipulations that she doesn't speed and doesn't attempt another visit until the annual fall harvest festival.

"Got it. All set, Mom."

I nod, shutting the door behind her.

With one last smile and a wave, she backs out and drives away.

Taking a deep breath, I make my way back to the house. I don't stand around to torture myself any longer.

Once the front door is shut, I lock it, a habit I've always had. When I turn around, I screech, hands flying to my mouth.

Less than ten feet from me is Billy Garet, looking alive and well, wearing the same gray hoodie from before. Yet one more sign that he might look alive, but he's not.

My hands slide down my face in hopes that when my eyes open, he'll be gone. Otherwise, I'm paying a visit to Corinne. Pronto.

"Oooo. Who's this Corinne?"

The man's voice has my eyes flying open.

"You're supposed to be dead." I lift my finger, pointing at him accusingly, completely ignoring the fact that he read my mind, because I did *not* say that out loud.

"No shit. Kinda guessed that a while back."

"Stay away from me," I say, back bumping into the door. "Go to the light."

His eyes roll. "Haven't we already been over this? Not gonna hurt you." He wiggles his outstretched fingers like some deranged cheerleader doing spirit fingers.

"Why are you here? What do you want?" The words rush from my lips, anxiety building low in my belly.

He puckers his lips and looks around the room. "I can't answer that. Haven't uncovered why exactly I got stuck with you, of all people." His eyebrows rise animatedly. "No offense, lady, but you're not exactly living your best life." His hands motion toward my getup.

My arms cross over my chest. "You're in my house for the second time, so clearly something has you coming back."

"I never really left," he says, examining his fingers and sounding bored.

My head jerks back. "What do you mean you never really left?"

"Just what I said." He shrugs one shoulder. "I made myself scarce because I could tell you were freaked out. And if there's one thing I've learned about women, it's that you'll get nothing from them when they're freaked."

"Y-you've been in my home this whole time?"

"More or less."

My thoughts float to Ava. She'd been here, and he was just hiding out? What if he'd hurt her? What if he'd been watching her get dressed?

"Whatever is going on in that head of yours, stop it," he scolds. "I've been minding my own business, waiting for her to leave so we can get to business."

I grab the long black umbrella that sits beside the door and lurch forward, jutting it toward the man. His hands fly up and he laughs.

"There's no need for that. It won't do you any good, anyway."

"Not another word," I warn. "You move, you get poked."

He shrugs. "I could use a good poking. Do your worst."

"Ugh!" I scream, waving the umbrella around like a lunatic. "Get out!"

He smacks his lips together. "Like I said, I can't. There's something keeping me trapped here, and until I figure out what, it's you and me, Karen."

"Who's keeping you here?" My eyes scan the room, looking for signs of another intruder.

"God? Satan? One can only guess, but at this rate, if there is a heaven, *this* has to be purgatory."

I slink my back down the door until my ass hits the ground. Pulling my knees up to my chest, I curl into myself and wait for him to go away. Surely, he'll leave at some point.

He clears his throat, but I don't dare open my eyes. "Not leaving. Sure you want to continue to act like a child?" The humor in his voice is annoying. The last thing I need him doing is making me second-guess myself.

"Helloooo . . . Karen . . . Whatcha doin' down there?"

I peek my eyes open, and Billy is perched right in front of me, squatting so he's at my eye level. He's solid, not an apparition. My hand shoots out to punch him in the face, but my fist goes right through.

"Told you," he says smugly.

I scream at the top of my lungs and jump to my feet. Grabbing my car keys from the hook, I unlock the front door and bolt from the house. I already believed he was a ghost, but further confirmation isn't any less terrifying. Pulling my phone from my back pocket, I dial Lanie's number.

She doesn't answer. So I leave her a frantic message.

"It's eleven. Call me as soon as you get this. I'm having a mental break and I need you to take me to the hospital. Or get me an exorcist. I'm seeing ghosts."

✦ ✦ ✦

AN HOUR LATER, I arrive at Cori's Nail Spa on two wheels, screeching my tires as I pull into the last remaining spot. In the light of day, it's not so sketchy. The simple glass storefront matches every other business on this side of the plaza.

Stepping from my car, I feel the blazing sun on my back. It beams directly into the place, explaining why tinted glass was chosen.

I burst through the front door, ignoring all the gawking women watching me stalk toward the back room.

"Excuse me, ma'am. Where are you going?" I keep moving, ignoring the insistent questioning. "Ma'am, *where* are you going?!"

I spin on my heels, coming face-to-face with a man who's several inches taller than me, with jet-black hair that parts on an intense widow's peak. He's handsome. Chiseled features and a straight nose somehow make him more striking the longer I stare. His dark eyes are narrowed in on me.

"Care to explain that entrance?" His eyes do a quick scan of my attire, and I glare in return. "Or maybe you can tell me what led to this." He smirks, motioning to my outfit.

I huff, ignoring his second question. "I'm looking for Madame Corinne."

He harrumphs. "Of course you are. Cori, you have a visitor."

I turn to see Corinne, bent over, filing a woman's nails.

"Oh, for shit's sake. She's a nail tech too?"

He grunts. "She's a lot of things."

She's much more put together today. Her brown, almost black hair hangs over one shoulder. Gone is the offensive sweatshirt. In its place is a black smock over a white blouse with sleeves pushed up to her elbows.

I have so many questions about this woman. How she came to be a supposed medium and why today she seems almost normal. That is, compared to the voice-changing, body-convulsing buffoon from the other night.

"Cori," he barks, and she flings one hand into the air, gesturing for him to go away. Her focus is on her current customer and whatever the ginger-haired woman is saying.

The woman's blatant staring gives away the fact that it's likely about me.

"Unreal," I hiss under my breath.

He places a hand under my elbow. "Follow me. You can wait in the back until *Madame Corinne* deigns to pay attention." The sarcastic way he says her name tells of his lack of belief in any psychic abilities she may claim.

Facing the stares of the room full of curious clients, I don't argue. The last thing I want is an audience for my impending showdown with the woman who broke me.

As we make our way to the back, I take in the space. In the light of day, it's your typical nail salon. The Grecian decor, complete with white columns throughout, and the tranquil spa music add a perfect ambiance.

"Can I get you something to drink?" the man asks, as I choose the closest seat at the table of horrors.

"I'll take some of that gin," I say, nodding toward the bottle Corinne drank from the other night.

He lifts a brow. "I was thinking along the lines of water." He lifts his hands to mimic a scale. "Maybe a Coke. Something that won't aid and abet you in the murder of my sister."

I side-eye him. "Your sister?"

"Mmhmm," he drawls, almost sounding reluctant. "Twin sister."

Scanning him from head to toe, I guess I see it. While he's taller and appears to have a charming disposition, compared to his petite, supercilious twin, I do see the resemblance.

"You good?" he asks.

I count to ten in my head, to calm my nerves. "I'm only here for answers. She did something to me the other night, and I need her to fix it."

His eyes widen. "You," he says, with something that sounds an awful lot like awe.

What did Corinne tell him? The idea that she said anything about that night at all raises a host of questions. If she's talking about it, it must've been just as surreal to her as it was to me.

Medium indeed.

"Me what?" I bark at the man.

He points at me. "You're part of the freak fest from the other night."

My hands shoot into the air. "Wonderful. Now I have an insane medium-slash-nail-tech's brother calling me a freak. Want to kick a puppy while you're at it?"

"Why the hell—"

I lower my arms, hands splayed out, to make him stop. A headache builds between my eyes, and I groan. "Can I get some Advil?"

He eyes me warily, but walks from the room, hopefully in search of the requested meds.

The freak fest.

That's exactly what I'd call it. Except she's the freak . . . not me. Not my friends.

When he returns, his outstretched hand holds two white pills that, upon examination, are exactly what I asked for.

"I'm not going to drug you," he says, grinning.

"That's . . . reassuring."

The man holds out a bottled water, offering a tentative smile. I take the proffered drink and swallow the pills down in one gulp.

"Thank you," I say, and he nods.

"Now. Care to tell me what you mean when you say Corinne needs to fix you?"

Taking another sip, I consider the question and whether I wish to answer it. I don't know this guy or his motives. I'm still trying to get to the bottom of what Corinne did, and although this twin seems a bit easier to talk to, I think I'll keep my secrets close for now.

"Why don't you start with what she told you about that night?"

His heavy sigh sounds more tired as his hand runs back through his dark hair. "Listen, she's under a lot of stress." My eyes nearly bug out of their sockets.

"She's *stressed?* You should be concerned about what I'm going to do to her when she finally brings her butt back here. Her actions have led to pandemonium in my life."

His hands run down his jean-covered thighs. "Our family puts a lot of pressure on her to fulfill certain . . . expectations. Until that night you showed up, she was only doing what was demanded of her."

"Meaning?" I snap.

"Go gentle on her. Please." His voice is soft. Pleading.

"What are you, her agent?"

"Darian, run along," Corinne says, sashaying through the doorway, not once looking at me. "Don't you have some checks to sign?"

His hands land on his hips as he bears down on the woman who dwarfs him. "Since when do I take orders from you?"

Gone is the man who was worried for her well-being only moments ago. Right now, he looks ready to throttle her.

Get in line, buddy.

She scoffs. "The day you came to work as my assistant."

He laughs without humor. "Quit calling me your assistant. I own this place."

"Semantics." She waves him off and he stalks from the room, mumbling about kicking her highness out on her ass.

"You came back," she says, taking a seat directly across from me.

"There was hardly a choice. You broke me. Now fix me."

Her hazel eyes—more green than blue—lift into her hairline. "Broke you how, exactly?" She places her hands on top of the table, looking more like a shrink than a medium in this moment.

"Don't play coy with me. We touched. You zapped me. And now I see ghosts."

Her eyes widen and her mouth drops open, but she quickly snaps her lips together and plasters on a feigned expression of boredom.

"Ghosts?"

"Well, ghost," I correct. "Just one very annoying man-child who has an affinity for insulting me."

"Riiight," she drawls. "Look. I don't know why you're hallucinating—"

"I'm not," I say, cutting her off. "And something tells me you already know that."

"As I was about to say . . . I can try to tap into your energy to see if I can uncover what's happening with you."

My eyelids close to near slits as I inspect Corinne. She's up to something. I have no idea what, but I know it. Every hair on the back of my neck is standing on end, and that pesky voice inside my head whispers not to trust her.

"What are you up to?"

She stands, heading toward the vending machine. She taps a code into the pad before selecting her snack of choice—Peanut M&M's, which might be the only thing the two of us have in common.

"I offered to help," she says over her shoulder.

"No. You don't do anything that doesn't benefit you. I know your type." I stand and make for the door. "I'm out of here."

I'm bluffing, hoping that whatever she wants is worth her showing a modicum of candidness.

"Wait!" she calls to my back, and I smile in momentary triumph.

Schooling my face back to neutral, I turn and wait for her to speak.

For several seconds, she appears to weigh her words. I cross my arms over my chest and tap my foot, signaling she's running out of time and trying my patience.

She sighs. "Please sit." Corinne motions toward the chair as she takes her own seat.

The red tablecloth is noticeably absent today.

"I don't like people eating on it," she explains, as though she can read my mind. "Sit."

I take a seat, but I don't say a word. This is one of those scenarios in which the first to speak loses, and I plan on coming out on top.

"That night, when we touched, I saw your memories."

I shake my head. "Those weren't mine."

She takes a deep breath and I have a sudden feeling I am going to regret coming here. "No . . . No, they weren't," she agrees. "They were those of your husband's soul."

My breath hitches and a chill seeps into my bones. "How do you know?"

She bites her bottom lip and closes her eyes when she says, "Garrett spoke to me."

Two of Swords

"NO, HE DIDN'T."

I jump up from my chair, annoyed that I allowed this phony to play on my emotions.

"How do I know his name?" she asks, a little too calm for someone who's desperate to keep me here.

"That's easy. Social media. White pages. There are any number of ways for you to get that information. Knowing his name means nothing."

I grab my keys and turn to walk away. "He said you'd fight me." My hand lifts to silence her, implying she should give it up. I don't care to hear anything more she has to say.

"He said you'll always have Barbados."

My feet skid to a stop. "What?" The word slips from my lips.

"He showed me your first time."

I whip around with a look of horror.

She lifts her hands. "Not *that* part. Good god. If that were the case, I'd be blind from bleaching my eyes."

My face twists into a glower, but quickly melts as I consider the possibility. "He showed you that night?"

She nods. "The whole setup. You had some fascination with Barbados, so he put together a date to bring the country to you. It's the night Ava was conceived."

I gulp, because she's right. We were the only two who knew about the specifics, as far as I know. A night under the stars, next to his parents' in-ground pool while they were away in Florida, complete with Bajan cuisine, rum cake, and rum punch. We stayed up until the sun rose above the horizon, wrapped in each other's arms under a bed of blankets that Garrett had set up himself.

We never actually made it to Barbados, because I became pregnant and then life took over.

"Why are you just now telling me this?"

"He asked me not to." She pops an M&M into her mouth.

I want to rage against her words, because there's no way that Garrett would speak to her and not me. Not unless . . .

"He doesn't believe I could handle seeing him, does he?"

She smiles sadly. She doesn't have to say the words. I know it. It's such a Garrett thing to do, worrying about my well-being even after death.

I blow out a breath and concentrate on slowing my heart rate. Resolved, I straighten in my seat and meet her gaze.

"What did he say?"

She crumples up the M&M's wrapper in her palm and tosses it across the table. "Not much, honestly. Just that you weren't ready for him to communicate with you." She chews on her cheek. "And something about me needing to help you remember."

I narrow my eyes. "Remember what?"

She shrugs. "Beats me. He wasn't exactly clear with his message."

"Why didn't you press him for more information?"

Corinne stalls, pulling her hair into a high ponytail and taking her sweet time answering me. "I'm going to be honest with you."

"That's a first," I quip, earning a stern glower from the gremlin pixie.

"Before that night, I'd never made contact with a spirit."

"I could've guessed that," I deadpan. "No medium worth their name conjures in the back of a nail salon."

She bares her teeth at me. "I own the place. It's a cost-saving measure."

"According to your brother, he owns it."

She gnashes her teeth together like she wants to yell at me, but she must decide against it. Her eyes close and she appears to breathe in and out several times before she says, "Are you going to fight with me all day, or are we gonna get to the bottom of what was unlocked that night?"

Her words bring me up short. "Unlocked?"

She nods. "After you left, I did a lot of research." She clears her throat, averting her gaze. "I might not be the medium I represent myself as, but I come from a long line of very gifted psychic mediums," she gloats, raising her chin as though this information should make me humbled in her presence. "I'm the first of my lineage to not have the innate gift by my age." Her eyes meet mine and hold. "Until you showed up in this room."

I squint, trying to work out what she's implying.

"When we touched, a bit of your latent power transferred into me, and now I'm able to do things I wasn't able to do before."

I shake my head. "I'm not following. What are you trying to say?"

She groans. "*You're* a medium."

My head jerks back. "What?" I shout. "Of all the ludicrous sh—"

"Listen to me, Alyssa," she orders, cutting me off. "I consulted with some family, and they all agree. Whether you knew it or not, you have the ability, and that night, it was unlocked."

"How is that even possible? I don't come from a long line of mediums. I might've been curious about this stuff, but that's where it starts and ends."

"Sometimes, curiosity is all it takes to unlock Pandora's box."

She rises, heading to the shelf that's lacking the tchotchkes from the other night. From the top shelf, she pulls a thick leather-bound book, heading back toward me.

"A lot of people have abilities that they never uncover," she explains. "We're conditioned to forget how powerful our minds are. The world shelters us from this knowledge, and unless we go seeking it out and become open to those abilities, they stay dormant." She levels me with a stern look, placing the book in front of me. "You came in here ready to make contact, and because of that, you unlocked your gift."

I slink back in my chair, suddenly exhausted.

I have no idea if I believe a word coming out of her mouth, but with the events that have occurred over the past few days since I left this place, I can't argue that something is different with me.

"What do I do?" The words come out dejected, and Corinne clucks her tongue.

"What all mediums have to do."

I scrunch my nose, open my mouth, and shake my head in what is sure to be a very unattractive face that I hope reads as follows: *Get to the damn point.*

She smacks her lips together but continues. "You need to study." She nods her head toward the book. "At some point, you need to learn to harness your abilities and block out unwanted spirits."

"That sounds like a lot of work. Something that'll take far too long. I need this ghost gone, like yesterday."

She shrugs. "I wouldn't know how long it takes. I've been begging the universe to bestow these powers on me my entire life. *I'm* not trying to block out anything."

I eye her warily. "If you had this mouthy bastard stalking you, you'd be doing everything in your power to block him out."

She ponders this. "Most spirits that haunt a particular person do it for a reason. Sometimes they don't even know what that reason is. He's stuck in a sort of limbo," she explains. "If he continues to come back to you, even when you've asked him to leave, you're the only person that can help him cross over."

I scoff. "How the hell am I supposed to do that? I didn't even know the guy."

"That's the question you need to answer," she says.

"I can't even be in the same room as the man without shrieking in terror or wanting to bodily harm him. Which I can't, by the way."

She shrugs one petite shoulder. "Why don't you try having a conversation with him? Ask him how he died. Ask him what unfinished business he has."

"What if he doesn't go away?" I counter, not at all convinced that having a conversation with Billy Garet will result in my peaceful pre-mediumship world returning.

"We can always purify your house. Sage his ass out."

I bob my head. "I like that. Let's go with that."

She rolls her eyes. "Try helping him first. Can you imagine being stuck here?"

I consider her words. I can't. I'd probably be just as snarky as he is. When death comes for me, I want to head straight to that promised beam of light and be whisked off to the land of wine and chocolate.

"If you want, I'll help you communicate with him."

My head snaps to Corinne. The thought of having someone next to me is much more comforting than going about this alone.

"Can you bring whatever clarifying things you have, so if he gets unruly, we can just snuff him out?"

She smirks. "I'll bring the sage."

I nod. "Let's go," I say, jumping to my feet and grabbing the book. "I'm assuming you're letting me borrow this?"

"Yes on the book, but no to the leaving. I still have clients."

"Cancel them. This is important," I grind out, waving my free hand in the air to signal for her to hurry up. "You caused this. You're going to fix it."

"I didn't cause anything," she bites, tugging on her flowy black skirt that's caught on something. "You did, with your overeager openness."

"You make me sound like some sort of psychic hussy."

She yanks once more and the skirt rips, causing Corinne to stomp her foot in annoyance.

She tilts her head and raises one hand palm up. "Next time, think before you go opening yourself up to other dimensions. You could've lived blissfully in denial the rest of your life if you'd been more careful."

"This all would've been great information to have before I touched you," I snarl through clenched teeth, spinning on my heels and making my way out of the small room.

"What is meant to be, will be, and it seems you were destined to unlock your potential. Lucky for me, you helped unlock mine as well," she calls to my back.

"Sounds like you owe me. *Big* time." I stress the word *big*, hoping she realizes that she's not going to be filing nails the rest of today. I'm prepared to drag her out kicking and screaming if she resists.

I turn to confirm she's still following me.

"We close early on Sundays, so you can wait until I've finished my last few clients. I'll help you, but then *you* owe *me*."

I don't bother asking her what more she could possibly want from me. I'm too eager to get the ghostbusting underway. If I'm lucky, Billy Garet will be well on his way to the pearly gates, or land of fire, by nightfall.

+ + +

THE FRONT DOOR creeps open, and I pop my head inside. Corinne's chest presses against my back as she peers over my shoulder.

"Can I help you?" I drawl, looking back at her and pursing my lips at her invasion of my personal space.

"Sorry." She takes a step back. "Is he here?"

"I haven't even made it in the door yet. I have no clue if he's lurking."

I push down the building anxiety and rush into the foyer, searching for any signs of Billy. Corinne follows, closing the door a little too loudly.

The stairs leading to the second floor are directly in front of me, and I'm happy to find the area free of Billy.

To the left is the living room that bleeds into the dining room, which circles into the kitchen. To the right is a hallway that also circles around to the kitchen. Garrett's office is to my immediate right. It's been converted into a junk room. Boxes of papers and books, clothes, and shoes are stacked against the walls, hiding his personal belongings that I couldn't stand to see. I close the double glass doors, closing off that room. I don't want to think anymore about the contents of those boxes. It's not my current problem.

"Where is he?" Corinne hisses.

"Shh," I scold, tiptoeing toward the back of the house, with Corinne hot on my heels.

Nothing seems out of place. It's quiet, but not abnormally so.

Maybe because it's the middle of the day and the sun is shining brightly through the windows, but the uneasy feeling I've gotten every time Billy Garet is near is absent.

"I don't think he's here," I whisper. "At least, it doesn't feel like it."

When we make it to the back, the kitchen is empty. Off to the right is the addition, and that too is clear.

We've walked through the entirety of the first floor, and every room is Billy-free.

"What should I do?" I ask.

I turn toward Corinne, who appears to be taking in the place.

"What have you done every other time?"

I think back over all the moments that Billy appeared, and nothing stands out.

"He just pops in whenever the hell he wants. Which is half of the reason I'm on edge in my own damn house."

"Would a warning really be any better?" She lifts an eyebrow.

She's not wrong. A flick of the lights or a noise would have me screaming like a banshee.

"Why don't you try calling out his name?" she suggests.

I breathe in and out slowly, preparing myself for what might come.

"Billy," I say, just above a whisper.

"Really?" Corinne levels me with a look of exasperation. "Come on, Alyssa. Put a little more oomph into it."

I glare in return but do as she advises. "Billy," I yell.

"You rang?"

I jump, twisting around and crouching into a fighting stance. "Dammit, Billy! Don't sneak up on me like that."

He slaps his lips together. "What are you doing? You look ridiculous."

I stop holding my breath, straightening out of my warrior pose. "Preparing to attack."

He scrunches his nose, and Corinne snorts behind me.

"You tried that once. Didn't work so well, now did it?" His condescending tone and punchable face are enough to make me feel violent.

"Ugh." I throw my hands up. "Just . . . don't scare me."

"Listen lady, it doesn't matter what I do; you're the definition of chickenshit. Whether I pop up or slowly glide into existence, you're going to freak."

I fold my arms over my chest like a petulant child. "You don't know me."

"And I really don't want to, but here we are."

"Ugh!" I shout again, entirely absent of adult vocabulary at the moment.

"He's here?" Corinne says, and I turn to find her eyes narrowed, sitting at the kitchen island, reading through my grocery list.

"Yeah. He's right there." I motion toward Billy. "You don't see him?"

Her eyes lift from the notepad. "No. I don't see anything."

"You said I unlocked your powers too?"

She bats her lashes, mouth smashed together. "I've only really connected with Garrett."

"But you heard Billy . . . That's why you snorted."

She raises a brow. "I snorted because of your attack position. It was either that or cry, because we're dying if our lives depend on you saving us." She stands from the stool, looking around. "Why can't I see him?"

I shrug in response.

"It might've been an exaggeration to say I gained my powers too."

I bite my cheek, trying to control my mounting irritation. "So basically, you're siphoning off me. Great. Glad I brought you here." I turn to Billy for guidance.

"Don't ask me," he responds. "I don't control this show." Billy lets out an annoyed breath. "What did you call me for? I have stuff to do."

"You're dead. What could you possibly have to do?" I snap.

He's positioned by the back sliding door, blocking my only quick exit.

He lifts his top lip, baring his teeth. "You just interrupted a meeting with Harry. It seemed important, but I guess we'll never know, because you summoned me."

"Harry? Who the hell is Harry?"

"My guide. Apparently, all spirits stuck in limbo have one. He's not very happy with you, by the way."

My head jerks back. "What have *I* done?"

"You're taking too long, and we're stuck here until my unfinished business is resolved." He lowers himself to the floor, sitting with his legs crossed. "You really need to get a rug for this room."

"What?" Corinne asks, but I shake my head and continue to address Billy.

"So, you do have unfinished business? What is it?"

"Obviously, if I knew, I'd be taking care of it to get the hell away from you and this dusty house." He pushes away a dust ball to prove his point.

I huff. "There's literally no reason for you to be so hostile with me. I don't want you here any more than you want to be here. Let's work together, figure out what's connecting you to me, and get you on the other side. Wherever that might be."

He nods. "Good call." His head tilts to the side, looking beyond me. "What's she doing?"

I glance back and find Corinne wielding a bundle of rosemary.

Her hands shake, and her eyes dart around wildly.

"Corinne, what are you doing?"

She steps toward me. "I saw that move." She's pointing to the dust ball. "He's really here."

"Obviously," I deadpan. "But what are you doing with that?"

A billow of smoke wafts from the bundle, the smell not at all appealing.

"Getting prepared. He sounds nefarious."

Billy snorts. "I'm already dead. What's a burning weed going to do to me?"

"It was *supposed* to be sage," I drawl, looking to Corinne with a level of annoyance I didn't think possible. "We were gonna smoke you out if we had to."

"Oh yes, I've heard all about this from Harry. Could you please inform the hot newcomer that sage only works if you truly want me gone? The rosemary won't do a damn thing but give you all a headache."

"I *do* want you gone."

"Not true. You're curious about the unfinished business. We're stuck. I'm not going anywhere."

He's right, I am curious. Who wouldn't be? This entire situation is not of this world, and I'd be a liar if I said the knowledge that I have the ability to commune with the dead wasn't a little mind-blowing.

As ridiculous as it is, I'm awestruck with myself for having such an amazing gift. I'm special and that's something I'm going to hold on to for a bit longer.

I groan. "Put that down," I call over my shoulder to Corinne. "Billy and I are going to take a stab at communication. So, Billy, you can see her, but she can't see you?"

He shrugs. "Seems so. She looks like she'd be more fun than you. I've always been a fan of brunettes. And I'm digging that skirt."

With Billy the Killjoy running around constantly offending me, I'm even more sure that he's not leaving until I solve this mystery of why he's linked to me.

And, if he keeps up his attitude, I might just go ahead and draw it out to make his afterlife as miserable as I can for as long as I can.

Corinne nods like a bobblehead, running the rosemary under water from the kitchen sink. "I'd like to know why I'm blocked," she says, in response to the question I posed to Billy.

A loud crash from the second floor draws the attention of all three of us.

"What was that?" Corinne asks.

"I . . . don't know. Billy?"

His eyes are trained on the floor above. "Something's here."

"A person?" I whisper, and he shakes his head.

"Another spirit."

His dark eyes meet mine.

"Run."

He doesn't have to tell me twice. Without another thought, I grab Corinne and get the hell out of my house.

11

Ace of Cups

BRILLIANT SUNLIGHT STREAMS in through floor-to-ceiling windows, enveloping me in a warm caress. I snuggle into the cozy terra-cotta sherpa blanket I pulled over top of me last night before dozing off on Lanie's cream L-shaped couch. The very last thing I want to do is move from this spot.

Despite the craziness that is my life, here in my best friend's bohemian space, I feel safe.

Lanie's two-story studio apartment is located in the heart of downtown Knox Harbor, situated directly above her yoga studio, ZenFlow, and the local coffee shop, Java Hut.

The smell of roasted coffee beans wafts up through the vents and weaves its magic, doing its best to convince me it's time to rise. The aroma of burnt sugar is my own personal siren in the morning, but still, sleep sounds better today.

"Rise and shine, sleepyhead. I come bearing gifts." Lanie is bent over me, holding a cup of my favorite roast right under my nose.

"You're evil," I moan, pushing her hand away while I stretch out my arms. "I don't wanna get up."

She clucks her tongue twice, and that noise has never sounded so loud in all my years. Lanie's industrial open-floor-plan space bounces any sound around the room, intensifying it tenfold. I'm surprised the music from her class this morning didn't jar me awake. Just goes to show how soundly I slept.

"I should've made you come to my first class. You'd feel like a new woman." She slumps down next to me on the couch, kicking her feet up and into my face.

"Seriously?" I say, pulling the blanket up to my nose, creating a barrier between me and her narrow size nines. "I'd be broken and in pain."

A slight exaggeration, but the last time I took one of Lanie's classes, I didn't walk for two days. I enjoyed the experience and the atmosphere, but the sauna-level temperatures had me swaying on my feet and seeing stars. If the class hadn't ended when it did, I would've ended up face first on the mat.

I sit up, glancing around the brightly lit room, marveling at Lanie's ability to make the most modern of spaces cozy. Her apartment is one large area with the kitchen opposite the front door. On the same wall as the entrance is an office, positioned directly below a loft that separates her bedroom from everything else. The sitting area rests in the middle, allowing me views of the whole apartment. Exposed brick is painted white, but specks of red peek through, giving it character. Her furniture and accents are all various shades of cream and tan, offset by the greenery of her live plants. They're scattered throughout her home in pots and hanging baskets of varying sizes. Across from the couch, in a corner next to the kitchen, is a macramé egg chair suspended from the ceiling, a new addition since I was last here.

I close my eyes, sighing in blissful contentment. Lanie has perfected Zen in all aspects of life, and I'm going to bask in it for a little while longer.

"You'll be broken if you don't figure out what's in your house."

The memory of yesterday and the noise I ran from hits me square in the chest. The air had shifted, growing uncomfortably warm and stale, which can't be good. Corinne and I bolted, not bothering to shut off lights or lock the door. I'm not sure what I'm more afraid of—the living or the dead busting into my house uninvited.

"We have research to do before my eight o'clock class."

Lanie pulls a large leather-bound book from her coffee table into her lap. I recognize it immediately. It's the one Corinne had pulled from the top shelf at her nail spa.

"What is it? And how do you have it?" I never had a chance to ask, or get a good look at it, because fixing my ghost problem was my highest priority at the time.

"The Moradi family grimoire." Lanie perfects a seasoned narrator voice while delivering the description, and I can't help but smile despite the array of questions I have.

"Corinne practically clubbed me with the thing last night when she plopped you on my doorstep." I don't recall any of this. My adrenaline had been working overtime and I was a sweaty, shaky mess when we arrived. Everything that happened after we left my place is a haze.

"Moradi grimoire?"

Lanie doesn't look up at me as she flips through the pages. "Moradi is Corinne's last name. It's essentially her family's book of spells." I never thought the day would come when I wouldn't react to talk of witches and spells by breaking into a fit of laughter or rolling my eyes. Less than a week ago, I would've mocked Lanie.

These days, it's becoming the norm and I'm not sure how I feel about it.

My heart thumps in my chest, telling me precisely how I feel. I've gone from finding the subject humorous to finding it downright petrifying.

If ghosts and spells are real, what else is out there?

"Corinne said we needed to read the sections on how to block unwanted spirits."

My ears perk up at the idea of blocking ghosts and my heart rate slows. "Give me that," I say, extending my arms and wiggling my fingers like an impatient preschooler begging for a cupcake.

She reluctantly places the heavy book into my outstretched hands, scooting closer to me so we can both read the text.

I flip through the ancient book, noting additional chapters of interest: "How to Cleanse Your Space from Negative Energy" and "Setting Boundaries." Toward the middle, I find the chapter Corinne suggested.

Skimming through the yellowed pages, I can't help but wonder how old the thing is. There isn't any indication of who the original writer was or a date to confirm its age. It reads more like a journal than a book of spells, and that is most interesting to me.

"I was expecting recipes with mugworm and verbane."

Lanie's face screws up like she's tasted something sour. "Mug-wort and vervain," she corrects me. I shake my head to say *I don't care if I botched the words*, which is met with an exasperated huff. "Both are extremely useful for various things."

"I'm sure they are." I bite my lip to hide my smile when Lanie crosses her arms over her chest, appearing to pout. The last thing I need to do is encourage Lanie to begin a lesson on the benefits of plants. We'd be here for hours, having read not a single page of this book.

"My point is, this is nothing like what I expected. It reads like a diary." I continue running my finger down the page as I skim through the words.

"Out loud," Lanie orders. "You never know when this could come in handy for me too."

I lick my bottom lip to prevent an unnecessary retort and then dive in.

"I've come to find that mindful meditation is a medium's best friend. It has aided in the ability to block spirits when I do not desire to converse. Close your eyes and focus on something that makes you smile. For me, it will always be my children playing in the creek behind my mother's home. Focus on whatever image or memory makes you most happy. Now, visualize a warm light surrounding you on all sides, creating a bubble around your entire being. When you feel safe inside this cocoon of light, say to the spirit, 'Go away.'"

Go away?

My nose screws up and I read and reread the passage, waiting for the punch line. I turn my head to Lanie, assuming she'll be on the same page as me.

"Totally," she says, bobbing her head as though it makes perfect sense.

"Totally what? Uninspiring?" I motion toward the offending book. "Come on, Lanie. This is *total* crap."

She smacks her lips together, further irritating me. "I can see you're disappointed."

"Disappointed? That hardly cuts it. I don't think these people have a clue what they're talking about, and now I'm stuck with Billy the Idiot for life."

I close the book, falling back into the cushions with a huff. For one short minute, I thought that book might've been the answer to all my problems. Instead, it was an epic letdown.

Lanie leans forward, getting into my personal space. "No. We won't let that happen."

"How, Lane? How the hell am I going to do this?"

She taps her chin, while I wait with bated breath for whatever is about to come out of her full lips.

Lanie's watch chimes, and she lifts her wrist to read something on the screen. "More on that later. It's time. Class starts in ten minutes. Get dressed."

I groan. "I'm not going. I already told you I'll die. Besides, this is all I have." I gesture toward my ratty clothes that I've been wearing for two days now.

"You won't die, and according to that book, yoga will be good for you. I'll give extra time for guided meditation. You can practice."

"I thought we already discussed that the book is useless."

Ignoring me, she jumps up from the couch, jogging toward her bedroom loft while I continue to sit and mope about my spiraling circumstances.

Thirty minutes later, I'm dressed in a too-tight pair of leggings and a sports bra from Lanie's closet, an outfit I wouldn't be caught dead in if we were anywhere but this yoga studio.

I've been standing in Warrior 2 for the past minute because I'm afraid Goddess will result in Lanie's Lulus splitting right in the crotchal region.

"Vinyasa," Lanie calls out, in the most soothing voice she can muster.

I move through the motion, following it up with Downward Dog, because I can't achieve Dolphin quite yet.

"Somehow, you manage to make yoga look awkward."

I yelp, falling right through Billy as I slam down into the mat.

I pop up to my feet, head swiveling around the room, looking for the asshat.

"Everything okay?" Lanie asks, one brow lifted as she takes in my current state.

Ladies around me stifle their giggles while my cheeks warm to an uncomfortable level.

"Fine. Sorry, slipped on my own sweat." I grimace at the way the twenty-something next to me gags at the mention of my sweat. "Come on, you're sweating too."

She snaps her head forward, back straight with obvious indignation. Lanie gives me a look that says *behave*.

I shrug, taking the next pose she calls out. Cat is something I can do all day.

"You sure know how to disgust . . . everyone," Billy says, lying on the ground next to me, but I do my best to ignore him, determined to finish this class and not bring unwanted attention my way.

He glides to standing, walking around my mat, inspecting me like I'm up for prize heifer at the state fair.

"You should be working to solve the mystery behind my death. Not attempting to cause your own."

I twist my head away from him, doing my best to maintain calm. He manages to find his way back into my view and I catch him inspecting the ass of the girl next to me like a perve.

I glare at the pest. "Go away, moron."

The glistening girl next to me gasps, cornflower eyes wide and hand tapping over her heart like my words might have spurred a heart attack. Oh, the drama.

"I wasn't talking to you," I offer, as a last-ditch attempt to save face. She rolls up her mat and stalks out of the room, bleach blond ponytail bouncing behind her.

Lanie marches toward me while everyone else stares from their Cat pose. "What's wrong with you?" she whispers, glancing around the room. "Savasana," she snaps a little too loud in the small space.

Everyone moves into their final pose of the class, and I breathe a sigh of relief it's almost over.

"Billy's here," I whisper. "He's being his typical self."

"Tell him to go away," she says through her teeth.

I nod, just wanting her to go back to her class and get it over with. Plopping to the ground, I stare at the ceiling and am not at all surprised when Billy hovers over me, bent at the waist and fists on his hips.

"I'm not even surprised you'd choose Corpse." He shakes his head. "I bet your husband had a lot of late nights at the office."

"Ugh. Go away."

My outburst pulls all eyes on me yet again, and nobody can contain their irritation. I feel like the outcast on the playground as everyone whispers behind their hands, not even bothering to make it seem like they're not discussing me.

Mortification sets in, and I don't even waste time rolling up my mat. I spring from the floor and rush out of the studio, right onto the sidewalk on Main Street.

With my hands behind my head, I concentrate on breathing in for ten and out for ten. If I could strangle Billy Garet, I would. No question. I'm not a violent person, but for him, I'd make all the exceptions.

A car horn blares, pulling my attention to the street. A lime-green Mazda cruises by with two teenage boys hanging out the windows, catcalling to someone. "Nice tits, lady."

"Language," I shout back, but there's no way they heard me over the purr of the souped-up car.

I glance around and find I'm the only person currently on the sidewalk.

Oh my god.

They were hollering at *me*.

Despite the crass words, and the fact they're kids, I can't help but feel some semblance of vindication. I refuse to dissect all that is wrong with this scenario, determined to bask in my momentary win.

"Ha. Take that, Billy. I still got it," I taunt to the air, fist pumping with glee.

A woman in her late seventies, if I had to guess, walks by at that very moment side-eying me and moving to the farthest edge of the sidewalk as she passes by. I drop my hand to my side, and that's when I realize I'm standing on Main Street wearing pants that are too small and a bra that just barely contains my floppy size Cs, celebrating the fact that children noticed me.

Oh, how far I've fallen.

12

Five of Swords

Nick

"ARE YOU SEEING this?" My partner Eric chuckles, pointing out the window that takes up the entire front of Milly's.

Across the street, outside of ZenFlow, a half-dressed woman wearing black leggings and a pink sports bra appears to be interpretive dancing. I've seen some things in my day, but this woman is a truly shit dancer.

"Do you think she's high on something?"

I shrug, taking a bite of my scrambled eggs. "Not our problem."

He shakes his head, shoulders shaking slightly. "Good call."

My gaze wanders back to the woman, who's just stopped middance, glancing down at herself. There's something oddly familiar about her, but I can't quite place what.

Lanie Anderson joins her on the sidewalk, and they appear to be in an intense conversation. The way the woman's back straightens and hands ball into fists, it isn't hard to tell she's angry. She shifts her body away from Lanie, and her face comes into full view. I lean forward, squinting my eyes. My fork falls from my grip, clanking against my plate.

"Jesus." I breathe, eyes sweeping the woman from head to toe, to be sure. "That's Alyssa Mann."

"Who?" Eric asks, leaning forward too, trying to get a closer look like I'd been doing.

"My neighbor." I don't turn my head, watching the scene unfold. Alyssa's hands fly up into the air and Lanie plops her hands on her hips, watching her friend have what appears to be a meltdown. Curiosity is eating at me. What is going on over there and why does Alyssa look two seconds away from jumping into traffic? I consider getting up and going to intervene but think better of it. They're close friends. I'm sure whatever is happening, they'll work it out. I'd only make things worse.

"You gonna eat that?" Eric gestures to the bacon I've been pushing around my plate for the past few minutes.

I stare down at my half-eaten breakfast and shake my head. "Nah. Go for it."

He doesn't ask twice, grabbing it with a stab of his fork and shoving it whole into his mouth.

"For the love, Malone, chew. You're gonna choke on that, and I'm in no mood to play savior today."

He smirks around a mouthful, taking his time to gnaw his way through the leathery bacon. His brown eyes alight with mirth.

"Idiot." I chuckle, watching him attempting to swallow and half choking.

He'll be fine. The kid's got eight more lives.

Eric Malone might very well be the luckiest son of a bitch I've ever encountered. He's been my partner for the last three years, and he's skated by death more times than I have in my whole career. He chases danger and manages to drag me along with him.

He's the youngest in our unit at twenty-eight, having joined the academy right after high school graduation. Being the former chief's son, it's in his blood. Nepotism runs rampant in these parts. Hard not to, when Knox Harbor rarely sees newcomers.

Either way, Malone has more than proven himself. I'm damn lucky to have him at my side.

"What's your deal? You've been sulking over there for the better half of an hour. Break's almost over, and you've barely touched your food."

He isn't wrong. I've been distracted, and now that I've seen Alyssa, it's even worse.

It's been three days since she showed up on my doorstep, soaking wet and scared as hell. In that time, I haven't gotten any closer to making sense of the situation. I didn't find any indication that a break-in occurred, but she was insistent a man was in her room. A seasoned criminal could have escaped without trace, but it's unlikely. My search was thorough.

The report was filed and it's in the hands of patrol, but there's a level of responsibility I carry to offer some explanation of the events to Alyssa. With her being in that house alone, I won't sleep until I have concrete proof that she's safe.

"Earth to West. What gives, man?"

"Nothing. I'm fucking tired."

It's not a lie. I've barely slept this week.

Between worrying about the woman next door and the intrusive calls from Jackie with her mental health check-ins, my mind is working overtime.

Eric doesn't press, already sidetracked by Christine, the pretty blonde working the diner. She bats her unnaturally long eyelashes at him, earning the Malone smolder in return.

My only complaint about Eric is that he's a charmer. The guy can't walk down the street without flirting with some random woman, attracting too much attention our way. It can be a hazard at times for a plethora of reasons relating to the job, but mostly, I'm not one for socializing. Eric makes it damn near impossible to have a simple meal without drawing a crowd.

The bell above the red door chimes, and I glance up in time to see Lanie strut in, still in her tight black leggings and neon green tank top, with her dark hair twisted in a messy bun on top of her head. She doesn't look upset at all, which is good. Hopefully that means she and Alyssa have settled their issue.

Malone whistles low, earning an eye roll from me.

"Not a chance. She's a bit old for you."

He guffaws, playing at being offended. "I like my girls a little bit older."

"Did I mention she's also out of your league?"

He scowls at me, mumbling a series of curses under his breath, turning back to his plate. I grin, lifting my hand to wave back at Lanie, who's spotted us.

The day that woman stepped into Knox Harbor, every eligible bachelor in town made their move. A former Kansas City beauty queen, she definitely turns heads. Not that I paid too much attention. Lanie's beautiful, but not my type. She doesn't hold a candle to the likes of Alyssa Mann.

Not that I'd ever admit that shit out loud.

"Boys," Lanie coos, stepping up to our table with a take-out bag in hand. "Fancy seeing you two here."

"Lanie," I drawl. "Pretty sure I just saw you in here last week."

She chuckles. "Appears this is the local hangout."

Milly's Diner is a local hotspot and for good reason. The food is incredible, and the owners are lifetime residents who are revered among the locals for the money they put back into the community.

"Not today, it would appear," Eric says, glancing around the sparsely filled room.

It's a ghost town for this time of day. The locals are off preparing for the annual fall harvest festival, which is a bigger deal than Christmas around here.

"All the Red Hatters are busy asserting their dominance by pushing their antiquated ideas onto the younger members of the council." Lanie frowns, parroting my thoughts. "We need to step up and demand some new ideas for the festival. It's bullshit the same people have their way every year."

Lanie has never been one to remain quiet when she feels passionate about a subject. She's taken on the Red Hatters on multiple occasions. She's even won a time or two, which rarely happens.

In my days on patrol, I was called to several meetings that got out of hand. Those Hatters are a feisty group that don't shy away from stirring up a good debate, mostly among themselves.

"What was going on across the street earlier?" Eric asks, earning a stern glare from me.

"None of your business, Malone. That's what."

Lanie chuckles. "Just a little misunderstanding." She turns her attention to me. "Any news on the issue at Alyssa's? I really don't like how slow this investigation is moving." Her dainty hands are perched on her curvy hips, and her full lips are pursed. "She needs to feel safe in her home, Nick."

I swallow, recalling the events of a few minutes ago. Was all that because she's scared?

"Not our jurisdiction, sweetheart," Eric practically purrs, sounding like the Casanova he attempts to be.

"Fine. Point me in the direction of who is. I'll start harassing them." Lanie clucks her tongue and for a moment, I think she's got more to say on the topic, but the bell on the door chimes again, drawing her attention just long enough to save us from Lanie Anderson's wrath.

Mayor Dunbar strolls in with his obnoxiously contrived

swagger and pompous grin, staring far too long at Christine for a happily married man.

Lanie bares her teeth when she sees who it is and where his eyes are currently trained. "Ugh. Douche alert," she calls out, not even trying to be quiet.

"I see the most irritating of the Gilded Glindas is present," the mayor grits through his teeth, earning something close to a growl from Lanie. "Boys," the condescending asshole calls to us, and I have to physically restrain myself from getting out of this chair and showing him what a real man looks like.

The guy's ten years older, but due to the massive amounts of cosmetic surgery and cheap hair dye he uses, he could pass as my age.

"I have no idea how Nina puts up with that asshole," I mutter under my breath.

Lanie widens her eyes as if to say, *You and me both.*

"I've gotta run. The place suddenly reeks of herpes," she says, meeting his eyes with a challenge I'd love to see play out, but like the coward he is, he turns on his heels and stalks away, slumping into a booth at the far end of the diner. "Nick, promise me you'll keep an eye on Alyssa's place. If something seems off, break down the damn door."

I nod. "Will do."

It's not an empty promise. If I think Alyssa is in trouble, I won't hesitate to act.

She offers her signature saccharine smile, showcasing teeth whiter than I thought possible. "Good seeing you two," Lanie says, pulling her glare away from Mayor Dunbar's back and smiling down at us. Her gaze lingers on Eric a little longer than necessary.

His goofy grin says it all. She's ensnared him. My leg kicks out, hitting him square in the shin.

"Oof," he says, glaring across the table at me.

I shrug, hoping it hurts like hell. He needs a good kick in the ass if he thinks pursuing Lanie is a good idea. She'd chew him up and spit him out. He'd never recover, and it's my duty as his partner to ensure that doesn't happen.

She grins, likely knowing her effect on the poor kid. When she's out of earshot and walking through the door, Eric attempts to kick me back.

I'm too quick for the idiot. Saw that coming a mile away.

"What?" I say, playing dumb.

"You made me look stupid. She likes me."

My head lolls back on my shoulders as I groan. "She likes toying with you."

"So the hell what? Maybe I want to play toy to that woman."

My head shakes and mouth forms a thin line. "She's made it clear she isn't interested in long term."

"Who said anything about long term? I want a go—" I kick him again. "Christ, West. What the heck's your deal?"

"Be respectful," I scold, knowing what was about to come out of his mouth was anything but. "Lanie's a nice woman, and she doesn't deserve the shit this town gives her for enjoying what all *you* assholes get to without judgment."

If there's one thing I despise, it's hypocrisy, and the residents of Knox Harbor have it in spades.

Eric nods briskly. "I agree. It's hot as hell. You won't hear me say otherwise."

"I'd better not."

He blows out a breath, averting his gaze. Malone is a brave guy, but he knows when to back down from me.

"Anyway." He drags the word out. "What exactly went down at your neighbor's? You mentioned something about her thinking it was a ghost at one point."

"It's . . . a long story." I run my hands through my hair, thinking about that night and the fact that I could use a haircut.

I trust Eric with my life, but I probably shouldn't have told him the bit about Alyssa claiming it was a ghost. I'm not sure why, but I feel guilty about that.

"She losing it?"

"She's had a rough go, Malone."

His hands rise. "Got it. Don't speak badly about the standoffish, crazy, hot neighbor. Who you don't have the slightest thing for."

"Have you lost your mind? I don't have a thing for her. I'm simply worried about her safety. Until I can assure there wasn't a break-in, I'm going to be on alert."

"Sure . . . that's all your snippiness is about."

I take a deep breath. "I will be the first to admit that she's attractive." He narrows his eyes in on me. "Okay, fine. She's *very* attractive. But that's not why I'm concerned for her." I rub my jaw, contemplating how exactly to frame this. "I know firsthand what she's been through and that makes me feel bonded to her in some fucked up way."

Eric's features soften and he clears his throat. "It's not fucked up, man. You two have something massive in common. That sort of thing brings people together all the time." He shrugs one shoulder, sucking on his teeth. "You should make a move."

"That's exactly the opposite of what I should do. She needs space, not someone to trade grief stories with."

He shrugs. "Someone needs to protect her from bad guys or ghosts."

I'm about to kick him again when it occurs to me, he was a close acquaintance of Billy. Maybe he knows details from the family that I don't. Something that could at the very least check the Garets off my list.

I fill him in on what occurred that night and how every neighbor checked their cameras and found nothing suspect. He knew there was a reported possible break-in, but since it's not in our division, I never gave him Alyssa's full account.

"What's your take?" he asks, seemingly invested in the details.

"My best—and only—guess is if someone was in Alyssa's house, they used Billy's name as a decoy, knowing it would send us down a dead end."

He appears to mull this over for a few minutes. "Criminals do all sorts of dumb shit. They don't think twice about throwing family and friends under the bus. Wouldn't think twice about claiming to be a dead guy."

I nod. "Exactly. If someone were trying to pass himself off as a dead man, it was to stall the investigation."

"Wouldn't be the first time," he agrees. "But that'd be hard to prove. Besides, you said nobody entered through the one and only entrance and exit that was unlocked."

He's right.

In my twenty-two years in law enforcement, I've seen it all, but this one is turning into a head scratcher.

"She described Billy to a tee. Oddly, she even claimed he was wearing the exact clothes and accessories he was wearing the night he died. How would she have conjured that description out of thin air?"

"Billy was wearing pretty basic shit. A hoodie is something a lot of burglars wear. It's not too inconceivable that she'd describe those clothes."

"True, and between you and me, her account of what occurred has holes the size of Texas."

He bobs his head. "Men don't disappear from a secured room. It seems more likely she dreamed the incident."

I huff a humorless laugh. "That's not something I'll suggest again. Made that mistake once, and I almost paid dearly for it."

His eyes widen. "Oh yeah? How so?"

"By way of a glare that could incinerate if it's aimed at you for too long."

He throws his head back and laughs. "Who would've thought a woman could scare the alpha of the homicide unit?"

"Funny, asshole." I give him a few moments to pull himself together before starting my inquisition. "What do you know about Billy Garet?"

He sputters a few more laughs before taking a drink of his water and seeming to launch into detective mode. "He was a rich asshole who lived off his daddy's money," he says, placing the glass on the table. "He was an acquired taste. Dry sense of humor. People either loved him or hated him. I happened to love the guy."

"What have you heard about his accident?"

"The basics. Two years ago, his Jeep was headed southwest on Spooky Hollow Road."

You don't live in Knox Harbor and not know that road. It's hilly and curvy, with blind spots galore. It's a dangerous road that leads to many casualties every year.

"Billy's Jeep was found in a ravine on its top the next morning. The coroner's notes said his death was caused by internal bleeding. It seemed like a standard case, but the family insisted it was suspicious." He takes a sip of his overly creamed coffee, and my leg starts to bounce under the table. Our break is nearing its end, and I need information I can use to help Alyssa. I'm about to press when he continues.

"The night of his death, he was playing pool at Clementine's, and witnesses told his dad he got into a heated argument with a known pool shark, Jackson Moore."

"Moore had an alibi," I cut in, remembering that the family hired a PI and went digging themselves. They didn't feel like the police were taking their claims seriously.

"Right, but the family was insistent that the eleven witnesses that provided the proof of alibi were all in cahoots together—Theresa Garet's words."

So far, I already knew all that he's shared. The family is friends with Mayor Dunbar, so he called in a favor and the file ended up on my desk for about five days until the family withdrew their request and claimed they found a note that led them to believe he took his own life.

"If it was Moore, justice was served," he mused. "He died in a motorcycle accident eighteen months ago, and the only thing that learning he was involved would provide at this point is closure." He plays with his straw, looking at something over my shoulder. "I can understand the family needing that. As Billy's friend, I'd like some." He bites on his lower lip. "It wasn't Jackson though, and no amount of pointing fingers and wishing will change that. He's on camera leaving the bar at close, well after the accident was determined to have happened."

Again, all things I already know. I decide to bring up the one thing that was likely kept from Eric—the part about his apparent suicide. The family did their best to keep that hush-hush by sealing the records.

I lean in so I'm not overheard. "You know why they called off the investigation?"

His head moves to indicate he doesn't.

"They say they found a note."

His eyes narrow. "A note?"

I nod once. There's no need to elaborate. He knows what a note represents.

Eric's face contorts, cheeks blazing red. "Bullshit." He thumps his fist onto the table, drawing the attention of the few people in Milly's.

"Keep it down," I snap.

"That's complete shit, Nick," Eric hisses. "He wouldn't. I

knew him, and the last thing he'd ever have done was take his own life. I can assure you of that." He blows out a harsh breath. "He had plans. Big ones. Told me so a few days before the accident."

Something had always felt off about that claim to me. A guy like Billy Garet has the world at his fingertips. Wealthy family, graduated with honors from Knox Harbor High, headed to Boston for college, good-looking according to the local ladies . . . he had options.

"I believe you," I offer, hoping to quell Eric's anger. "The question is, If it wasn't suicide, what did happen?"

We stare at each other for several minutes, each contemplating what could've gone wrong on his drive home. In the end, I look away, because it doesn't matter. My gut is telling me something is off with the Garet accident, but it's not my circus, and his death has nothing to do with Alyssa's break-in.

"Anyway," I say, trying to steer the conversation into safer waters. "The storm likely played games with her head." I lift one shoulder, pushing my plate away with my opposite hand. "Either way, it's not my department, so I have an excuse to keep me out of trouble with her."

"Which is all you care about, right? Because you're neighbors . . ."

Something about the way he says this, coupled with the irritating grin spreading across his tanned face, annoys me. He isn't going to let this idea of me going after Alyssa drop.

"Exactly. We're neighbors."

He full-on smiles, pointing a finger at me. "You'll eventually cave. I know that look."

My head jerks back, and the urge to punch him in his nose rears its ugly head. "Screw you."

He chuckles. "Whatever, man. Your secret is safe with me."

I roll my eyes, shaking my head. "You've got it *all* wrong. It's purely her safety I'm interested in. Nothing else."

Eric's staring down at his phone, brows furrowed. "We have to head to Silverton. A car was found covered by brush in a wooded area. Car is registered to a Knox Harbor local."

"Why would we get called out to an abandoned car? Is there a body?"

"No clue. Guess we'll find out when we get there."

13

Death . . . Reversed

IT'S A BEAUTIFUL New England fall day, and I'm about to ruin it by chasing ghosts. The sun shines brightly overhead, helping to make what I'm about to do a little less chilling.

For the moment.

"Remind me why we have to go back in there?" Corinne says, picking at her black yoga pants as we walk up the steps of my front porch.

She showed up sans makeup, with wet hair and clothes that indicate she likely worked out and showered right before coming over. Corinne is a natural beauty. It's annoying, considering I actually attempted to do something with myself, and she manages to shine without even trying.

"You know I can do a tarot reading anywhere, right?" she asks, breaking into my moment of self-pity.

It's never a good sign that the one who came to crack the code about the ghosts appears to be the biggest scaredy-cat of them all. Her fingers twist around each other in a move I recognize as the jitters.

Wednesday is her day off, so I've been biding my time, waiting for her help. She thinks reading my cards and the energy in the house might help us determine any other presence as well as why Billy's stuck with me. I'll do anything to get rid of him, including enter my home that may or may not be overrun by something truly scary.

My hand runs down my temple, over my scar. Whenever I'm fearful, I find myself feeling my battle wound, a reminder that I'm stronger than I give myself credit for.

"I can't keep staying at Lanie's. This is my home, and I won't be frightened off." I throw open the front door and take a step inside. "Besides, it can't hurt to do the reading inside the place they seem to keep popping up."

She grunts. "From what you've said, they pop up anywhere. At least Billy does. And we've yet to determine if there are any additional spirits."

My mind goes right to yoga the other day and I'm immediately pissed, which isn't a bad thing. Far better to go into a potentially dangerous situation angry as opposed to terrified.

The house is quiet, void of the otherworldly presence and feeling of dread that was thick in the air last time we were here. Thankfully, nothing seems out of the ordinary.

"Maybe we imagined it?"

Corinne glances my way, nose scrunched up like *I'm* insane. "You're right. We were probably having a shared hallucination."

I shrug. "Could be possible. Your rosemary was probably laced."

Her mouth opens, but she quickly shuts it, opting to take the mature route and flip me the bird.

"Classy."

Her finger remains in the air as she stalks past me, head swiveling from side to side as she makes her way to the back of the house. I follow, ready to get this done and over with.

Corinne makes herself at home, plopping down into a chair at the head of my dining room table while I clear a space for her reading. She pulls several tarot decks from her bag, removing them from their boxes and shuffling each pile meticulously.

I watch as she absently cuts the decks and recuts, over and over, head bowed as she mumbles words I can't make out. I don't disrupt her process, knowing that it will only prolong things from getting started. When she's ready, she motions for me to take a seat.

"I'm going to start with this deck asking Spirit to enlighten us on your situation and then use this one to clarify if I need it. After that, we'll ask about the other presence that was here. Does that work?"

She's practically speaking a foreign language. I know nothing about this stuff. I bob my head just to get the ball rolling.

"Spirit, tell us what Alyssa needs to know to rid herself of these ghosts."

Speak of the devil and he shall appear. Billy materializes right over Corinne's shoulder, pulling one card, then two, from her pile.

Corinne tilts her head, watching the scene play out. "What's happening? Is it Billy?"

"Mmhmm," I say, taking a deep breath and slumping back into my chair. "He's your problem today. I don't have the energy."

Corinne looks up into the air as if he's flying overhead. "I will find a way to unalive you a second time if you touch my cards again, dipshit."

Billy howls. "I like this one. She's feisty."

"And she's serious. Somehow, I believe she could arrange a second death for you."

Corinne pulls her thick hair into a high ponytail, rolls up her sleeves, and scoots her chair in.

"Okay, ghost and Alyssa, can we get back to this? Billy," she calls out, speaking directly to him. "If you want out of here, you need to allow me to work. Got it?"

He licks his lips, eyelids lowering to slits. "Can she really figure this out with those?"

I shrug, inspecting the bold-colored cards. "It's worth a try."

He raises his hands and steps back, not fighting me for a change.

"We're ready," I say, giving Corinne the go-ahead.

She repeats her question to Spirit and begins to shuffle the cards quickly between her two hands. I'm in a trance, watching as she continues until one, two, three cards fly from the deck, landing on the table. "One more, please, Spirit," she calls out, and moments later, one additional card falls.

She flips the cards over one by one, placing them in a line. When she has them in position, she turns the rest of the deck face up, next to the four drawn cards.

"The bottom of the deck is . . . the lovers?"

She scans the other four cards, her face increasingly pinching with every second that goes by.

I lean forward, attempting to get a better look at them. "Umm . . . why are there so many knives?"

"They're not knives." She shoos me away with her hands, continuing to inspect the cards as though she's trying to solve some impossible riddle.

"Two of Cups, Seven of Swords, Two of Swords in reverse, and Five of Wands." She taps each card as she explains what I'm looking at. "Interesting."

"What?" I say, throwing my hands into the air. "What does it mean?"

Tapping her chin, she says, "This reads more like a love reading than anything. I'm a little baffled."

"Me too," Billy chimes in. "Not like she has *any* potential love interests."

"Shut up, Billy," I snap. "Can you elaborate? I've literally no clue what's happening."

"This is a four-card spread. The first card represents you and your energy. In this case, the way I'm reading it, you are wanting a connection with someone. Or at the very least, to partner with someone."

"Yeah. I want to partner with you to rid my house of spooky beings. And in his case," I say, motioning to the air where Billy is, "jackass removal."

Billy doesn't even react, too focused on the cards in front of Corinne.

"I mean . . . maybe," she says. "But I have to be honest, my intuition says it's about a guy."

"Yes . . . he is a guy. An annoying dead guy, who I want gone."

She rolls her eyes. "The Two of Cups typically refers to union. A combining of energy in a partnership. Like I said, it's most often pertaining to love readings."

A vision of me curled into Nick West's chest, him placing chaste kisses on my forehead, pops into my mind uninvited, and I want to crawl in a hole even if I'm the only one privy to it. Why the hell is my mind putting these asinine thoughts in my head? Since when do I have thoughts of *him* like that?

"Moving on from love," I snap, ready to get on to something that makes sense.

The picture of two naked people, looking skyward toward an angel with flaming hair, mocks me. Love isn't in the cards for me, tarot or otherwise. I'll be a lonely old spinster with nothing but my wine and ghosts to keep me company.

You could always give Nick a chance.

That vexatious voice whispering in my ear needs to die off

quickly. It's not helpful. And if I were to open myself up to love again, the hot detective next door would not be on the list of candidates.

Nope.

He might be sexy, but it's a no. The last thing I'm setting myself up for is more embarrassment where my neighbor is concerned.

"The second card is the unknown, which speaks of people or events you are not aware of or refuse to accept as true. The Seven of Swords tells of betrayal and trickery. Someone who is attempting to get away with something and your need to look at the evidence from all angles."

"Could it be the ghosts that are trying to get away with something?"

Maybe they don't want to move on? They're using this mystery as a way to stay rooted on earth.

"Unlikely," Corinne says. "Tarot doesn't necessarily read the dead, since most of their energy has moved on."

My head nods toward Billy. "He's clearly not moved on."

She shakes her head, biting her lower lip. "I'd have to consult with my mother on that. I'm not sure. But what would be his motive? Nobody wants to stay in limbo if they can't live life with the people they loved."

"And nobody wants to be stuck with you, Karen," Billy says, sticking his tongue out like the child he is.

I stick my tongue out, earning a brow raise from Corinne. "Mature."

"What does that card mean?" I say, moving us along.

"The third card is the known, which is what *you* are aware of." She shakes her head, chuckling. "Ha . . . very funny, Spirit. Tell us something we don't know." She makes a noise like she's clearing her nose. "This card reversed says you're confused and on information overload."

"Sounds pretty accurate to me. Tarot is something you actually *do* have talent with. Good to know."

She guffaws, hand rising to her heart. "You wound the only person who can help you."

"We've yet to determine that. Moving on." I motion toward the last card.

She makes a face, rubbing at her throat. "The final card is the action Spirit is encouraging you to take." She studies the card closely, and I can see the moment the light bulb flicks on. "Now this one is helpful. Essentially, Spirit is recognizing that you are currently fighting a losing battle, one that's preventing you from moving forward. So, what Spirit is saying is knock it off and work together, or else this mystery will never be solved."

Billy and I share a look, but quickly turn our heads in opposite directions. Neither is willing to be the first to extend an olive branch.

"See. That right there will get us nowhere. The cards have spoken on Spirit's behalf, and either you two grow up and listen, or you'll be stuck together forever." She chews on her bottom lip, continuing to mull over the cards. "Perhaps the Two of Cups is encouraging you to partner with Billy. Have you two even attempted to brainstorm why he could be connected to you?"

I avert my eyes, not really wanting to admit that I've not remotely attempted to communicate with him. He's just too . . . obnoxious.

"Why don't you *try* getting to know each other? Maybe something will click," she suggests.

It's not preferable, but I did say I was willing to do anything to make him go away. Maybe I should take Corinne's advice and get to know about his life.

"What's your story, Billy?"

"Seriously? We're going to do this?"

I purse my lips and shrug while he makes himself comfortable, sitting on the edge of the table.

How is it he's unable to pick up items, but he can manage to not fall through solid objects? This whole ghost world stuff is confusing.

"I was twenty-eight, single, and just got back into town. I'd been living on the West Coast, studying for the Series 63. I failed, and my dad made me come back home."

I bite my tongue, deciding now isn't the moment to make cutting remarks. Not while he's opening up.

"You'd just gotten back into town when you died?"

"Yeah. I'd been here for about two weeks. Dad and I weren't seeing eye to eye because I was spending a lot of time over at Clementine's running the pool tables. He'd also found out that I planned to head back to California to join a band."

The more he says, the less irritating I find him. There's a childlike innocence to Billy in this moment. One that tells of a struggle to be good enough but never quite measuring up. A willingness to throw everything behind to chase a dream. One that was never reached but somehow still manages to bring a smile to his face.

"Tell me how you died," I say, curious how someone so young lost their life. I'm assuming it was foul play; otherwise, why would Nick have worked the case?

"Harry's been trying to help me uncover the details. Apparently, when you die, things get a bit fuzzy for a while. At least for some spirits."

I had forgotten all about this Harry guy. It occurs to me that I have a dead man following me around—someone tied to the afterlife and what happens after you leave earth—and I've never asked questions. For months after Garrett's death, I cried over where he could be and if he was okay. I have knowledge right in front of me, and I've been too caught up in my ego to tap into it.

Stupid.

"I was fighting with this biker dude, who wanted to throttle me because I'd hustled him. Dad refused to pay my way any longer, so I decided to trick people out of money."

Ah, yes. This is why I haven't attempted to talk to the guy. He's a dirtbag.

"All I remember is leaving the bar that night and taking Spooky Hollow Road."

My neck aches and I attempt to rub it out, listening to Billy's account of the night he died. I'm not sure if it's that fact alone or something else that has me on edge, but my gut twists and my hands tingle.

That voice inside of me whispers to pay attention.

"I vaguely remember looking down to change the song on the radio, and bam—I was hit."

It sounds fairly standard. Curvy road at night, distracted by the radio, impact as the accident occurs . . . so why did the homicide unit get involved?

"My neighbor is a homicide detective, and your death hit his desk. Why?"

He blows out a breath, lips flapping as the air expels. "It was suspicious. Or at least, my mother fought for the police to treat it as such, according to Harry."

"Do you remember anything else about how you died, Billy? What did you hit?"

"It wasn't what I hit, but who hit me. I was run off the road."

The recount of his death sparks multiple emotions at once. Anger. Fear. Sadness. That's when it hits me. Spooky Hollow Road, accidents . . .

"We're connected by our shared accidents on the same road."

"Now we're getting somewhere," Corinne says, sounding more excited than she should, considering people died in both cases.

"Let's pull some cards to determine what or who else is present in this house."

She grabs a different deck and begins to shuffle them quickly, and one card flies out, but that's not abnormal. What is, is the other decks shuffling themselves in midair and additional cards flying out.

"Corinne?" I say, backing away from the table.

She quickly scoops up all the cards that flew from the decks and flips them over.

Corinne looks up at me, gripping the table with white knuckles. "They're all Death."

The house begins to shake, pictures falling off the walls. "Get under the table," I yell, dashing underneath, pulling Corinne down with me.

"What's happening?" Corinne bellows, as the walls tremble and groan in a chilling, otherworldly show.

"Earthquake?" I scream above the noise.

There's no doubt in my mind this is something else, but I don't want to admit it out loud.

Billy bends down, looking under the table at Corinne and me. "This is no earthquake. Something's here again."

"A ghost?"

He shrugs, and if a ghost's face is able to pale, Billy's does. "This isn't looking good for you," he murmurs. "Nothing like this happened when I arrived. This has to be a demon."

"Seriously?" My voice pitches. I don't know if he's serious or messing with me, but my body trembles. "Get your sage. Where's your bag?" Corinne apparently doesn't hear me over the chattering of her own teeth.

I can only hope she managed to grab sage this time. It seems more likely the only thing she carries is rosemary, and we're well and truly screwed.

A piercing scream that doesn't belong to me or Corinne rattles the house. My hands fly to my ears to prevent my eardrums from bursting. In a far corner, a woman blinks in and out, more transparent than solid, wholly unlike Billy. Her face is contorted in a scream. Her dark hair is caked to her face, and there's dirt or something like it all over her clothes. She looks like something straight out of a horror movie.

After several minutes of the house sounding like it's going to cave in, everything stills into a deafening silence. We all seem to hold our breaths, waiting for what's to come.

The woman appears to be gone. Thank god.

"What the—" a deep male voice booms from the foyer.

Corinne and I share a look before inching our way out from under the table and toward the disembodied voice. When we round the corner arm in arm, Corinne grinds to a halt.

A tall, slovenly man built like a linebacker twists in circles, taking in his surroundings. Greasy dark curls poke out from underneath a basic black stocking cap. A punk rock T-shirt that appears to be at least one size too small just barely covers his flabby gut. There's something familiar about him, but I can't place it at the moment.

When he stops turning in circles, his eyes lock with Corinne's.

"You," they say in unison.

My head turns slowly toward Corinne. "You can see him?"

"Yeah, she can, and that's good because she has a debt to settle." He spits.

Not like he spits the words, but he literally spits on my floor.

My top lip curls in disgust. "Excuse me," I bark.

He takes a threatening step forward, and my mouth snaps shut. Every insult and threat I'd planned to hurl dies on my lips. Thankfully, he loses interest in me, walking toward the wall of windows, peering out.

"She's the narc who nearly got me locked in the pen."

Corinne's hands fly to her hips. "You almost got yourself locked up." She turns to me. "This moron was selling drugs in front of the spa. Some of my older clients were none too pleased. So I called the cops." She shrugs her shoulders. "I'd do it again."

The man turns to growl at her like a rabid dog, and not for the first time since I've known the woman, I fear for her.

"Can't you do something?" I ask Billy, who's been entirely too quiet through this whole exchange.

"I . . . can't even see him. This is your fight, lady." He poofs out of sight and appears in the living room, seated on my sofa, looking far too content, given the newcomer.

"If I die at the hands of a deranged poltergeist, you won't be getting your ticket stamped to the afterlife, idiot."

His eyes widen. "I literally can't see him. How the heck am I supposed to help you?"

"Yo, blondie. Who you talkin' to?" The new ghost looks right past me into the living room, searching.

"Myself?" I'm not even sure why I lie. Maybe to give Billy the benefit of surprise in the event he pulls himself together and deigns to help us.

I have to admit that I'm less frightened with the sunlight streaming in through the windows. The white walls and dark blue wainscoting always made this one of my favorite rooms. That, and the antiques that line the shelves of my whitewashed hutch.

But when my eyes fall on the new guy, that fear creepy-crawls its way to the front and my legs shake a little.

His eyes narrow in on me. "Are you mental?"

I laugh manically. "I'm seeing ghosts, so that's a very real possibility." Corinne jabs me in the side with her elbow and I grunt. "What?"

"On'tday isspay offyay ethay ostghay," she whispers.

"What does that even mean?"

She groans. "Don't piss off the ghost."

I huff, shaking my head in exasperation. "Listen, whoever you are. I'm not sure why you're here, but I've recently learned that ghosts can communicate with me." I motion toward the wooden bench and chairs situated around the formal table. "Why don't you sit, and we can talk."

One bushy eyebrow raises in response. "You're a ghost whisperer?"

"I'm not exactly positive what that means, but sure. I can speak to you and maybe help you cross over."

His head shakes. "Nope. No interest. I'm liking the new digs," he says, looking around with a smile plastered on his face. "Not keen on the whole idea of hellfire."

"You don't know you're going there for sure," I say, hoping to change his mind. I want him here less than I do Billy, and that's saying something.

"It's inevitable." He shrugs. "Hey! Those look like my momma's dishes."

He points to the open box of Turkish platters I bought from Marmalade and Rye, sitting on the end of the table.

"She collected all sorts of stuff. Well . . . she called it collecting. Others called it hoarding."

My breath hitches as I recall the words that Mrs. Hampson had said about Mrs. Craft.

"Are you Ollie Craft?"

His eyes close to mere slits as he watches me. "Who's askin'?"

My eyes dart from him to Corinne. She shakes her head slightly. "Me. I'm asking." His features turn hard, and I fear the wrathful spirit from earlier is about to return, so I rush on. "I know Mrs. Craft, and you look a lot like her son who recently passed."

He lifts his chin in answer. The harsh snarl from moments ago evaporates into something closer to sadness. "She's a good woman. Don't judge her based on my actions."

I shake my head. "I wouldn't. She's always been very kind."

"Were those her dishes?" Corinne asks, finally speaking for the first time in a bit. She sits in the chair closest to her.

I nod. "The owner of the store I bought them from said so."

"Hmm . . ."

"Hmm . . . what?"

I'm growing so tired of hearing my own voice speak that word. If she'd only just be straightforward, we'd waste a lot less time.

"He's connected to those platters," she muses. "Incredible."

She might be on to something. Could he be in limbo because his actions caused his mom to have to part with her favorite collection? Mrs. Hampson said she had to sell them to pay for his wake.

"Do you know why she sold them?" I ask, turning toward the dirty ghost.

He shakes his head. "No clue. But I know it had to be the most difficult thing she's ever done. Those were an early wedding present for my sister. She died."

A lump forms in my throat, and now I truly feel awful about the purchase. I might not have known, but the need to right this terrible wrong is intense.

I might not have known Oliver Craft, but I have dishes that link me to him. If I return them, could it be the key to getting this particular ghost to move on?

Could something in this house be tied to Billy too? Something from the scene of both our accidents? Can it possibly be that simple?

"What's with the creepy smile?" Ollie directs to me.

I wipe whatever goofy grin I was sporting from my face, not

wanting to tip him off to my plan. He made it clear he doesn't want to go. I have to hope that he won't have a choice once Mrs. Craft's dishes are returned.

One ghost potentially down.

However, one thing lingers in my mind. Who was the ghostly woman, and what happened to her?

14

King of Pentacles

SUNDAY MORNING ROLLS around and for the first time in weeks, I feel rested. I've managed to actually get dressed, opting for a pair of black leggings and an oversized gray sweater. I spent some time applying a bit of makeup and curling my hair too.

Not that my attempts hide my split ends, darkened roots, and bags under my eyes. It doesn't matter. The only thing on my agenda today is a quick visit with Gloria Craft.

We'd decided that the dishes would be returned, but with some quick detective work on Corinne's part, we found that Mrs. Craft spends most weekdays at a community senior center two towns over and has in-home care most evenings. Sunday is her only free day.

I just finished loading the first box, taking my time, unwilling to risk breaking them and ruining this whole experiment, while Corinne reads cards to see if anything has changed.

"Alyssa?"

Nick West's husky timbre has all heads turning toward the front of the house.

The sultry way he calls my name makes my stomach tumble over itself, not unlike those first butterflies adolescents feel when they experience their first taste of love.

What is wrong with me?

"Who's here now?" Corinne asks, looking up from her tarot spread. "And why is your face all flushed?"

Sending a glare in her direction, I head toward the foyer, where I find Nick standing just inside the door, one hand on the holster of his gun. He's wearing a pair of jeans and a black Henley, a shirt that appears to be a Nick West staple.

My eyes widen as I take in his defensive stance.

His hand drops to his side. "I just got home from a call, and your front door was wide open. I wanted to check to make sure you were okay."

The fact that he's watching out for me makes me feel warm all over.

"Oh, yeah . . . sorry. I was carrying boxes out and left it open," I say, ignoring the heat racing over my skin.

"I should be the one apologizing. I just charged into your house."

He runs his hand back through his hair and bites down on his bottom lip. I don't know what to fixate on. It's a bit disarming. My belly flops again and if I could slap myself and not look certifiable, I would. Instead, I shake off the indecent perusal my wayward eyes took for a moment and bring myself back to center.

"All good, considering last week. I appreciate you checking in."

He nods his head, eyes narrowing and a half grin appearing. "What do we have here?" he asks, head tilting to the side.

I turn to look over my shoulder where Corinne stands, arm stretched out with the previously soaked rosemary in hand.

My eyes close as I count to ten, trying to think of a way to explain the snowballing oddities that keep occurring here.

"Don't mind her," I say, shaking off the building headache.

"*Her* name is Corinne, and you are?" She bats her lashes, laying the flirtation on rather thick.

Nick takes a step forward, reaching out his hand to Corinne. "Nick West. I'm Alyssa's neighbor."

Corinne lifts the rosemary to signal she won't be shaking his hand. He nods, dropping his arm to his side.

"That was very kind of you to check on your spinster neighbor," Corinne says, puckering her red-painted lips like a loon.

Who is this Chatty Cathy? She's not been this nice since I met her.

I pull a face, and Nick smothers a chuckle.

"Well, since everything is all right here, I'd better get going."

"He's got a gun and a badge, but no uniform," Billy mumbles. "What is he, a mall cop?"

"He's the detective," I say, turning my head just slightly.

"What was that?" Nick asks, brows tilted inward.

I straighten, realizing my error. "She asked what was with the gun," I say in explanation, trying to cover up my misstep.

Nick looks between Corinne and me, nodding. "Part of the job." He smiles at her.

"I didn't—"

I jab my elbow into her side, and she grunts.

"Well . . . thanks again for checking in."

"Actually," Corinne jumps in, and I beg the gods she doesn't say something that'll force me to pack up and move to effectively avoid the man. "Could you help us carry a couple boxes? We're in a bit of a hurry."

"He doesn't have time for that. The man just said he had to get going."

"I could spare a few minutes," he says, taking a few steps forward, glancing down at me.

I'm not a short woman. At five feet seven inches, I'm usually one of the tallest women in any room in Knox Harbor. Right now, I feel small.

"Care to show me the way?" His buttery, smooth, raspy drawl makes my legs a little weak, and that thought alone prompts another internal face slap.

My back straightens and I twist around, hoping he didn't witness my face redden, because my cheeks are currently burning worse than they were a minute ago.

"This way," I say, head remaining forward.

I haul ass down the hall to the dining room, trying to put distance between Nick and me. When I flip on the overhead light that for some reason was off, Ollie is inspecting a dish, somehow managing to hold it in his hand—a feat Billy hasn't seemed to master.

"Floating dishes won't go over well," Corinne hisses through her teeth.

"Crap," I say, diving forward and grabbing the plate just as Nick enters.

Ollie has been absent since Wednesday, and of all times for him to reappear, it would have to be now. He took one look at Nick, though, and blinks out before I can tell him to get lost. Maybe it was the sight of a badge and gun that spooked him, even though the police can't touch him now.

"Everything okay?" Nick says, and I don't turn around to look at him.

"Alyssa's just struggling with the fact she needs to part with the dishes." Thank god for Corinne's quick thinking. Otherwise, I just look like an idiot, holding a saucer in the air, with one foot raised behind me.

"I am," I say, turning around. "But they belong back in the hands of the poor lady who was forced to sell them."

Nick's eyes narrow in on the plate, and something in his demeanor shifts. "May I?" he asks, hand jutting out toward the plate.

"Uh . . . sure."

I hand it to him and watch as he inspects it, face paling with every second that goes by. "Who did these belong to?" he asks, looking up at me with suspicious eyes.

"Her name's Mrs. Craft. I bought them at Marmalade and Rye, and when I found out why she sold them, I decided I couldn't keep them."

He swallows. "Are you heading there now?"

"That was the plan." I look to Corinne, who shrugs her shoulders.

He takes a breath and hands it back to me. "Strange. I was actually heading that way too. Do you want me to take them to her?"

My lips press together, and I rock back on my heels, trying to uncover the mystery that is Nick West. "You know her?"

"I do. Very well. Today's my day to cook her dinner."

I have so many questions. The man checks in on his neighbor he barely knows, makes dinner for elderly women who live alone . . . what else do I not know about Nick West?

Answering his question, I say, "No, I should take them myself." I have no idea if this gambit will work, but I have a feeling that I need to do the handoff myself for the best chance of success.

A flash in the corner catches my attention, and my breath hitches. It's the same woman from before, still looking like she was dragged through the mud and unable to fully form, popping in and out of existence. The only difference is that she's not screaming this time and neither am I. Her shaky hand lifts, and I follow the direction her finger points.

Nick? She's pointing at Nick.

"Everything all right?" Corinne pulls my gaze away from the ghostly vision. Her stare bores into me, a silent question in her eyes. She knows something's off.

I shake off the tremors from seeing that woman. She's more

unnerving than anything I've encountered yet. "Yeah. I got a little dizzy."

"You should sit," Nick suggests. "Are these the last two boxes?"

"Yes. If you want to grab that one, I'll follow behind you with this smaller one," Corinne suggests, likely trying to get him out of here so she can interrogate me.

He nods at her before turning his attention to me. "I'll put these in your car and head to Gloria's. See you there?"

I smile. "Thanks, Nick."

He offers a brief smile in return, picks up the larger box, and leaves Corinne and me alone.

As soon as he's out of sight, Corinne turns on me. "What did you see?"

"A woman. I saw her before too, just before Ollie appeared."

"A woman? What did she look like?"

I shake my head, trying to formulate a description. "She was different. Not solid like Billy or Ollie. Translucent, flickering."

Corinne swallows. "Oh, crap."

"What?" My voice rises before trailing off.

"That sounds like a poltergeist, and that's not something you want to deal with."

"Aren't they all?" I grow more confused by the day with all the various types of spirits. The otherworld is more diverse than earth.

"No. Poltergeists are something else entirely. We'll need to involve my mom."

"Where's Ollie? Maybe he can shed some light." I glance around, finding the room empty save for the two of us.

Corinne makes a face, staring at me a little longer than comfortable.

"Do you have a thing for the hot detective?" Corinne asks, gliding alongside me. "You kinda eye-violated him back there."

"No, I didn't. Shut up."

I grab the last box and head out, not wanting to risk any more questions.

+ + +

"WHY EXACTLY ARE you driving like a bat outta hell?" Corinne asks from the passenger seat of my Volvo S60.

"I wanna get this over with," I say, staring straight ahead.

"Hmm," she muses. "You sure it doesn't have anything to do with the sexy detective? I mean, I wouldn't blame you if you were driving like Lewis Hamilton to get to him."

Corinne looks over at me out of the corner of her eye when I don't answer.

"It has nothing to do with him."

Although I must admit, knowing he's there isn't as unappealing as it would've been weeks ago. But I won't tell her or anyone else that. She's likely to blab that confession to Nick, first chance she gets.

"Don't you want to see the outcome of my theory?" I say, hoping to steer her back to our mission.

"That the dirty ghoul is linked to those platters?" she asks, and I nod in response. "Wasn't that *my* theory?"

"Whatever. I don't care whose it was if it gets one spirit out of my house. If I return these, he better be coaxed over to the other side."

"I'm not sure that's how it works. He needs to want to cross over. Ollie the Idiot sounds perfectly content to crash at your pad for good."

I groan. She's right. He made it pretty clear he has no interest in finding out where his afterlife is to be held.

"What the heck did he do in his life that has him so convinced he'll be burning for eternity?"

"He was a drug dealer, for one," Corinne says with a thick layer of disgust.

"I did it for her."

Corinne and I both scream at the deep rumble that is Oliver Craft coming from the back seat. The car swerves into the left lane and an oncoming car blares its horn, veering out of my way.

"Ohmygod," I yelp, pulling the car back into the correct lane, trying and failing to get my heart to stop galloping in my chest. "I can't breathe."

"Get your shit together," Corinne snaps, eyes wide and mouth open. "You almost got us killed back there."

Her legs bounce with leftover adrenaline. Not that I'm faring any better. I'm white-knuckling the steering wheel, attempting to keep the tremors at bay myself.

"Me?" I shout. "He did it," I say, motioning to the back seat, where Ollie sits unaffected by our almost death. "When did you even get here?"

"Been here the whole time. Had nothing to say. Until I did."

I let out an irritated breath. "Well next time, a fair warning would be appreciated."

"We all know that would not have changed anything." This time, it's Billy chiming in. He's appeared sitting right next to Ollie, who still doesn't seem to know of his existence.

"Great. You're here too," I mutter.

"Who are you talking to?" Ollie asks, looking around the car for signs of someone else.

"Never mind. You can't see him, and he can't see you. Just pretend he's not here."

"Lady, you're losing it," Ollie says, drawing a chuckle from Corinne, who's remained quiet since the near head-on collision.

"Clearly," I mumble.

We're quiet for several moments as I reflect on the past few minutes, veer off the highway, and head toward the Crafts' home. I'm thinking about all that's been said when something niggles at the back of my mind.

"Ollie, what did you mean when you said you did it for her?" I ask, recalling what set off this entire freak-out.

"I dealt drugs to help pay for her chemo." He says it so nonchalantly. As if I should've known all along that's what he meant.

"I didn't realize she was sick," I admit, peering at him through the rearview mirror.

"She was, and we were going to lose everything. It was the only thing I could do to help."

"Damnit," Corinne says next to me.

"What?" I say, looking at her out of the corner of my eye.

"Of course the drug dealer would end up having a motive that makes *me* feel guilty." Her hands fly up in the air. "I don't need this kind of karma."

My head shakes at Corinne's dramatics as I pull up to a one-story house with chipped blue paint and a rotting front porch. The grass is overgrown and mostly covered in leaves from the tall red oak tree in the side yard.

Half of the branches stretch across the border into the neighbor's yard, which is well trimmed and free of leaves. I can imagine they aren't happy with the extra work they have to do to maintain their space due to a tree that isn't even theirs.

Not my problem.

"Things have gone to hell since I died." Ollie's voice is full of concern with a bit of an edge when he says, "I didn't deal to see my home fall apart."

Glancing in the rearview mirror, I find Ollie's face contorted in anger mixed with a lot of dread. I can tell he truly cared about this place and, most importantly, his mom. Knowing that makes me question if Ollie's crimes are really worth an eternity in limbo.

"You ready for this?" I ask whomever is paying attention.

"Been ready my whole life," Corinne grumbles, making her way out of the car and slamming the door shut a little too forcefully.

There's no need to ask what her problem is; I just know. Her sour grapes stem from the fact that she's wished for these abilities her whole life, and here I am complaining about them at every turn.

I follow closely behind her, taking it all in. The closer I get to the house, the more concerned I become. When I step onto the porch, I find that the place really is crumbling beneath my feet. The concrete steps are cracked, and pieces fall away from the edges with every step I take. This is very unsafe for Mrs. Craft to walk on.

"What a sh—"

My hand darts out, covering Corinne's mouth to stop that thought. Ollie doesn't need to hear her less-than-tactful opinion and get worked into a rage. I already felt the tremors he's capable of producing back at my house. If he pulled that stunt here, we'd likely be crushed under a collapsing roof.

I lift my free hand and knock with my fist twice.

"She won't hear that," Ollie says from beside me. "You gotta really pound at it. She's hard of hearing."

I do as he suggests, and before long, a throaty voice belonging to Mrs. Craft calls out on the other side, "Coming."

When the door swings open, Mrs. Craft's fragile frame has my chest tightening. She's hunched over a walker, wearing a long pink nightgown that looks like it hasn't been washed in some time. Mind you, it's the middle of the afternoon.

"Can I help you?" she asks, head bouncing between Corinne and me.

"Mrs. Craft, I'm Alyssa Mann. I'm not sure if you remember me, but we met years ago."

Recognition dawns as her eyes widen and a smile spreads across her face.

Nick practically jogs up behind her. "Gloria, I told you to sit. Do you ever take my advice?"

"No. I'm perfectly capable of opening a door, Nicholas. Run along and continue your business."

He closes his eyes momentarily. "Could you at least humor me and head on back to your chair? I'll show Alyssa and her friend into the living room."

She huffs. "You always coddle me."

"Because you're my favorite, and I don't want you to get hurt."

She slowly backs up, turning her walker slowly and moving away, mumbling something under her breath, but I don't miss the fondness shining in her eyes as she smirks up at Nick.

So many questions.

"Why is he here?" Ollie bites. "If he allowed this place to fall apart, I'll kill him."

I ignore Ollie's grumbling, not wanting to consider whether he'd make good on that promise.

"Come in," Nick says, motioning for us to walk past him.

We follow him toward the back, entering a large room with a sofa, recliner, and television that you can just barely see over the chaos of everything else.

My eyes scan the cluttered area. Mrs. Hampson wasn't exaggerating when she said Mrs. Craft was a hoarder. There are paths wide enough for two people to walk side by side, but every remaining square inch is covered in junk. It's not trash—thank god—but thousands of various trinkets and collectibles that others have likely been thrilled to be rid of.

"Do you like my collections? I've spent my lifetime finding each of these pieces. They're my pride and joy now that I'm a lonely old spinster." She chuckles.

"I'm feeling claustrophobic," Corinne whispers into my ear. "This place is a junkyard for unwanted goods."

"Shh," I hiss, bringing my focus back to Mrs. Craft.

"That's . . . why I'm here."

I turn to Nick, and he offers a small smile, giving me the courage to admit that I have one of her favorite collections.

"I'll be outside. There's a lot of work to do. If you need me, call," he says, winking. My eyes follow him out of the room, a tightness in my chest forcing me to rub it out.

"You were saying, dear?" Mrs. Craft brings me back to why I'm here.

"I recently purchased a set of Turkish dishes from Marmalade and Rye, and it's been brought to my attention that it belonged to you."

Mrs. Crafts's eyes lower to the floor, and she twists her fingers.

"I wanted to return them to you."

Her head snaps up. "W-what? You bought them fair and square. They're yours now."

My head shakes. "Mrs. Craft, please forgive me for being so candid, but I learned of your circumstances and all you've been through, and I just don't feel right keeping something that should've never left your possession."

"She also has a pesky guest that won't leave her alone because of it." I elbow Corinne in the side and she harrumphs, shooting a glare into the side of my head.

Tears well in her eyes, and I have a strong desire to console her. She wipes away a wayward drop and straightens her shoulders. "That's . . . very kind of you, Alyssa."

I raise a hand to stop her. "Please don't thank me for doing the right thing. I want you to have them back."

"Corinne," I say, turning toward her. "Can you please bring in the boxes?"

Her nose scrunches, signaling she isn't happy. "I didn't come along to play assistant."

"Yes, you did," I say through my teeth, maintaining a smile that probably looks deranged.

She huffs and stamps her foot like a child, but eventually heads toward the door, mumbling curses under her breath.

"Would you like something to drink?" Mrs. Craft asks.

Based on the state of the place, I won't be eating or drinking anything offered here.

"I'm fi—Ouch!" I rub at my arm, raising my eyes to Ollie's smug smile. Somehow he managed to pinch me. "How . . ."

I want to ask how the hell he accomplished that, but based on the look I'm getting from Mrs. Craft, I think better of it.

"Something wrong, dear?"

"No." I shake my head. "Just a bite. Nothing of concern."

"Accept the drink," Ollie grits through his teeth. "It's important to her that she can repay the gesture in some way."

I pull a face at thin air and Mrs. Craft clears her throat.

"Umm . . . water please? Thank you."

She smiles before shuffling off to the kitchen.

I swing around toward Ollie. "Don't pinch me again, asshole. I didn't want her to get me a glass and fall. If you can't tell, she's not exactly agile."

"Don't offend my mother," he snaps back. "This place might be cluttered, but it's clean."

I grimace, continuing to rub my arm. "It wasn't my intention to offend." I narrow my eyes at the surly spirit. "How did you pinch me, anyway? I was told that's impossible."

He shrugs. "I got pissed enough, and it happened."

I've read of accounts where ghosts have moved objects and in-flicted wounds on people, but I hoped that was all crap when Billy assured me he couldn't hurt me. I make a mental note to check the book or research ways to protect myself from bodily harm. Until I'm armed with that knowledge, I'll keep some distance between Ollie and me.

Across the room and through towers of books and newspapers is a rectangular wooden end table with several framed photos. I zigzag my way through the maze of collectibles and bend down to take a closer look. They're pictures of Mrs. Craft, Ollie, and a beautiful girl with flowing red hair that I've never seen.

"That's my Isla," Mrs. Craft says from behind me.

I jump about ten feet in the air, wondering how she snuck up on me without being heard.

"Sorry about that. I didn't mean to scare you."

With my hand over my racing heart, I choke out, "All good."

Mrs. Craft leans in, taking a look at the picture I hold. "She died six years ago."

"Who?" I ask, trying to get my breathing under control.

I'm not sure why I'm so jumpy. Maybe it's from the realization that Ollie can get physical or the serial killer vibes I'm getting from this house. Either way, I want out.

"Isla. The girl in the picture. She's my daughter."

I turn to look at her. "She's very pretty." Mrs. Craft smiles, but it quickly fades. "If you don't mind me asking, what happened to her?"

"Ehlers-Danlos syndrome. Doctors believe it caused her aneurysm."

I swallow, thinking about all this woman has endured. The death of her daughter and son . . . cancer. It's too much.

"I'm so sorry." It's a paltry phrase, but one I mean wholeheartedly.

"She's in a better place. They all are," she says, holding out a stemmed glass of water.

My mouth dries, considering that Ollie is, in fact, not in a better place. He's right here, currently glowering at me for no apparent reason.

I snap my gaze forward, focusing on the photos. Anything to avoid Ollie. I stop up short when I get to the last one. I bend down, taking in the ornate gold frame.

"Is that Nick?"

"Yes," she says, and that same fondness I witnessed in the way she looked at him is evident. "He was Isla's fiancé."

That . . . I did not see coming.

15

Six of Swords

"SUCH A GOOD guy, that Nick. He comes here every Sunday to check up on me. Tries to fix things around here, but as you can see, I don't need the help."

My hands shake, water spilling out over the top of the glass I have strangled in between my palms.

Ollie grunts and I wonder if his apparent disapproval has anything to do with the fact that Nick is in law enforcement.

"He sweet-talked his way into cleaning up my yard today, but I didn't need him to do that. The leaves will turn into compost eventually."

"Tell her she needs to stop fighting Nick and let him help her," Ollie orders, seemingly changing his earlier stance on the detective.

I want to rebuff his request based on his attitude, but he's right. She does need the encouragement.

"You should really allow Nick to help, Mrs. Craft."

"Where should I put this, master?" Corinne drawls, box in hand.

"Could you put them in here?" Mrs. Craft says, making her way into the next room.

A large hutch sits on the center wall of the formal dining room. Its empty shelves tell of the price this woman has had to pay to survive.

This room is in a little better shape, save for the water spots on the ceiling, which lead me to believe there's a leak somewhere.

"You wanna get that looked at," Corinne says, pointing to the stain. "I had that same problem, and it turned out the toilet was leaking. The whole ceiling almost caved in."

"Why on earth would I want to fix it? I need the place to fall down so I can get a new one."

Ollie groans from behind me.

"I'm . . . not sure that's how it works."

"It is," she says, bobbing her head. "My Ollie told me so."

Corinne and I both look toward the aforementioned blockhead responsible for this misguided belief.

"You're an idiot," Corinne mutters.

"Excuse me, dear? I have trouble hearing."

I turn back to Mrs. Craft. "You might want to speak to your insurance company. I'm not sure that's accurate information. Nick could probably help you with that too."

She sighs. "I know it's a struggle for him to be around me. The man took Isla's death as hard as I did. I don't want to make things any more painful on him."

I reach out and touch her shoulder.

All I've learned in the past few minutes has me reevaluating my relationship with Nick. There are so many reasons why he could've chosen to help me out, including a silent camaraderie I didn't even realize existed. I've been a jerk to snub his gestures, but in my defense, I had no idea that he'd gone through something similar.

We're more alike than I ever thought possible. Shared pain creates an invisible thread to others who carry the scars of heartbreak.

I set to work placing the dishes back on the glass shelves, while

Corinne complains about needing to get the last box. I've been trying to decide how best to bring up Ollie and start the process of sending him onward and hopefully upward, but nothing jumps out. Unsure what the right move is, I just spit out the first thing that comes to mind.

"Mrs. Craft, what happened to your son?"

Her face falls at the mention of Ollie, and for a moment I wish I could take the question back.

"He fell in with the wrong crowd, and it cost him his life. Drugs will do that." She slumps into a chair that reminds me of the handcrafted Amish furniture my mother had back in the day.

"He overdosed?" I ask for clarification, realizing for the first time that I never thought to ask him.

Her green eyes darken. "He was poisoned. Ollie didn't do drugs." Her words lack conviction. Mrs. Craft knows what truly happened but refuses to accept it.

When my eyes meet Ollie's, I see that truth and the regret he carries.

"It was all my fault," Mrs. Craft continues. "He did it for me. To save this place," she says, looking around at the rickety room.

Ollie moves toward his mother, trying and failing to make physical contact this time. "Why can't I touch her?" His voice breaks, and my heart aches for him.

What happens next feels out of my control. My feet move forward, and I lower myself onto my knees so that I'm eye level with her. My mouth moves without thought.

"Mrs. Craft, Ollie's here. He's with you."

"I know, dear. He's always with me," she says, brushing me off.

My head shakes. "No. I mean . . . he's literally here. He showed up in my house and I need you to help me send him to the afterlife."

Her brows pull inward, but only for a moment, before her entire face contorts. The apples of her cheeks turn a vivid shade of red, and despite her brittle appearance, she manages to jump to her feet, nearly knocking me back on my rear. I quickly stand, preparing for her wrath. She waves a clenched fist in the air, right in front of my nose.

"How dare you come into my home and tell such lies." She takes a step back, jutting her hand toward the front of the house. "Get out."

Now I've gone and done it. This woman in front of me isn't the Mrs. Craft from moments ago. The fragile woman is gone, and in her place is a mama bear, none too happy with me. Alive or dead, you don't mess with her when it comes to her kid.

Suddenly, the house creaks and moans. I watch on in wonder as the copper chandelier hanging above the dining table begins to sway and the floor beneath our feet shakes.

"What did you do?" Corinne yells over the ruckus, but I ignore her. "Why is Ollie raging?"

Ollie.

My head swivels around the room, seeking out the unpredictable spirit. He's doing this to help prove my case. I know it.

"Tell her to look in my closet for a Nike shoebox. She'll find a note I wrote to her and all the cash I saved."

The words aren't spoken out loud, but I hear them plain as day in my mind.

"You'll need to quiet this down for her to hear." As soon as I say it, he obliges.

The house settles and the place grows deathly quiet.

"What the hell's going on in here?" Nick says, rushing into the room, eyes hard. "I heard yelling."

Swallowing, I turn back to Mrs. Craft, ignoring Nick because I need to get this out. I don't want to lose my nerve.

Her eyes are bugged out and her slight frame wobbles on unsteady feet. "Here," I say, taking her by the elbow and helping her back onto the chair. "I understand this is . . . a lot, but I need you to listen to me. Ollie wants you to look for a shoebox in his closet . . ."

"Nike," Corinne chimes in, as though I wasn't going to get specific.

"Someone tell me what's going on," Nick booms, but again, I ignore him, focusing on Gloria.

"He left you a note and money."

She doesn't look convinced.

"Did you not feel that? Ollie was trying to get your attention?"

She bites the inside of her cheek.

"Don't believe me, but please look for the box."

Nick grabs hold of my elbow, not roughly, but enough to get my attention. "What are you talking about, Alyssa? Can't you see you're scaring her?"

Mrs. Craft blinks several times, but eventually stands. "I'm okay, Nicholas. Stay here with them." She walks off as quickly as her aging body will allow. Her pink nightgown hangs to her heels, and I hope she doesn't trip on it. I won't follow her. This is something that requires privacy.

Corinne pulls up a chair and makes herself at home. "What?"

I shake my head. "I didn't say anything."

"You had that look. I've been working while you've been trying to bring down the house. I deserve a break."

I close my eyes and seek patience, choosing not to argue with her. Instead, I take a seat next to her while we wait.

Exhaustion is taking root, but it doesn't help quell my nerves. What if this doesn't work? What if she doesn't find the box? Then where will we be? Stuck with a disruptive spirit who's pissed that I failed him?

Fantastic.

Nick takes the seat next to me. "What did I miss?"

"Alyssa came into some knowledge that Ollie left a note for his mother. She felt obligated to tell her."

I can feel his eyes bore into the side of my head. "How did you come into this information?"

Ever the detective.

"I can't reveal my source."

He huffs a humorless laugh. "Come on, Alyssa. You expect me to believe you know anything about Ollie Craft? You know he was a dealer. Right?"

I turn toward him, leveling him with a stare I hope makes it clear I'm in no mood to be questioned. "He might've been a dealer, Nick, but it was to keep this place for his mother. To ensure she didn't lose everything."

Nick's breath hitches, and I see something like remorse wash over his features.

Several silent minutes go by before a throat clears.

"H-how did you know about this?"

I look over my shoulder to find Mrs. Craft, shoebox in hand.

I breathe a sigh of relief. "I have my sources." I don't repeat the part about Ollie being present. That wouldn't go over well with the surly detective seated next to me.

Her head swivels, searching the area, but she won't find what she's looking for. If it were possible, Ollie would've made it so.

"O-Oliver," she calls, voice trembling. "P-please stop worrying about m-me." She inhales for five long seconds, blowing it out for ten. I count every second, focused on her. "I'm going to be fine as long as I know you're with your sister."

My throat closes and I have to tamp down the emotion bubbling up as I witness this playing out.

I can't help but think about what my own reunion with Garrett would be like. Would I spend my time crying or blurting out all the things I never said? I'd like to think I'd be composed, but it's doubtful. After this experience with the Crafts, I'm not sure I want that reunion after all. Not if it means that Garrett has unfinished business and is stuck wandering around some random house, looking for his own way to the afterlife.

That's not what I want for him. Peace is what these spirits deserve. Even Ollie.

"Would you suck it up?" Corinne scolds. "You're supposed to be helping move him to Summerland, not sitting around moping."

My head snaps to Corinne and my nose scrunches. "Summerwhat?"

She rolls her eyes. "This level of mediumship is wasted on people like you."

Out of the corner of my eye, I see Nick's posture shift. His back is straight, and his hands are balled into fists on top of the table.

Great. He's probably piecing together the conversation and making a case for my involuntary commitment.

Ollie appears behind Corinne, and for the first time, I don't jump or screech in fear.

"Will you please tell my mom that I'm sorry I wasn't stronger. That I couldn't cope with Isla's death and the fact our father bailed when we needed him most." The words are rushed out, as if he's on borrowed time and needs to spit it all out before he misses his chance.

Mrs. Craft covers her mouth with her palms. "I . . . I heard him." Her voice wobbles, but she forges ahead, pleading with her son. "Ollie, you listen to me. Your dad leaving was the best thing that happened to us. He was a varmint."

Ollie snickers, looking young and carefree for a change.

"We were better for his absence. I want you to stop blaming yourself. Go on and be with Isla. Tell her that you two are my greatest joy."

Ollie walks toward his mother and wraps her in a ghostly

embrace. I would think she can't feel it, but her breath hitches and I wonder. When the moment is done, Ollie makes his way to me.

"Thank you. That's what I needed." He takes one more look at his mom. "I'm ready now."

I smile, nodding in acknowledgment. The elation I thought would come doesn't. I find no joy in this family's heartache.

"Before I go, I have a message for you."

I bite my bottom lip, feeling uneasy.

"Work with Nick. Share with him what you know about . . ." He makes a face at the ceiling before shrugging. "Some dude named Billy."

My eyes widen and mouth gapes.

"Who told you to give her this message?" Corinne asks, sounding rather suspicious.

For the first time since Ollie has stormed into my life, he smiles. "She already knows the answer."

With that, he disappears, leaving me standing shaken in his mother's dining room.

Garrett was here.

+ + +

"DO YOU PLAN to invade my space all night?"

Corinne has her Nike-covered feet propped up on my coffee table, and she's lying back on the space typically reserved for Ava.

She makes some noise that sounds like something between a grunt and a groan, but doesn't use her words, which might be a first.

"If you insist on staying, want something to eat?" I ask.

She nods.

"What do you want?"

She shrugs.

"Have you lost your voice?"

"I'm tired," she snaps, and I have to refrain from chucking my throw pillow at her head.

"You carried some boxes and you're acting like you ran a marathon."

Her head flops toward me like a broken bobblehead. "They were heavy, and that's not what's happening here."

"Please . . . enlighten me."

Before she has a chance to explain what *is* happening, the doorbell rings. I don't move, because I'm not sure my legs work at this point.

"You gonna get that?" Corinne whines after the third chime.

"Nope."

If my past few weeks is any indication that luck has left me in the dust, it's likely Nick, coming with a host of doctors to carry me away.

After Ollie went on to the afterlife, Corinne and I hightailed it to the door, with Nick on our heels asking an assortment of questions. Thankfully, Mrs. Craft came to our aid and shooed him back to his yard work, allowing us to make our escape. It's only a matter of time before Nick comes knocking, demanding answers.

"It's a little late for a salesman."

I glance up at the wall clock and realize it's ten after eight. It is a bit late on a Sunday, but that wouldn't deter someone like Nick West.

A disheveled-looking Lanie rushes into the room, blowing out a labored breath when she sees me. "Call off the squad. She's here," she says into her cell phone, before hitting End and throwing it into her oversized knock-off Louis.

"I should've known it was you," I say.

"Nina and I have been worried sick." Her steps falter when she gets a look at my unwanted guest. "Corinne? What are you doing here?" She looks back and forth between us, waiting for someone to explain.

I sigh. "That, my friend, is a long story."

She crosses her arms over her chest, signaling she expects me to spill every last detail.

"Good thing I have all night."

I take a deep breath and turn to Corinne. "You wanna tell her?"

"Nope."

"Take a seat. I'm ordering food first."

An hour later, I've told Lanie everything and she has barely said two words through it all. I'm not sure if she's ready to laugh or bolt. Either is a possibility with my less-than-predictable best friend.

"Say something," I encourage, hoping to get her take.

She blinks several times, full lips pressed into a line.

"Wait . . . do you not believe me?" I ask incredulously. "Because that would be some twist, considering you're the one who introduced this crazy into my life."

She places her hand over her heart, mouth agape in an overexaggerated fashion. "I didn't do anything."

"Oh, stop playing innocent. You've been coming to me for over a year." Corinne waltzes back in the room just in time to come to my aid. For once. "It was you who scheduled the appointment," Corinne says, making herself comfy on my couch once more.

I bob my head in solidarity.

Lanie's hands lift, palms out. "Moving on. Where's this ghost now?"

"He's been oddly absent since Ollie left." I rub at my chin. "Do you think he could've moved on too?" I can't contain the hope welling in my chest at the thought.

Corinne frowns. "Unlikely."

We all sit in silence for a few minutes, Corinne and I likely running through the events of the night, while Lanie determines whether we need psychiatric evaluations.

"I spent three nights at your house because of this. You went through that book with me. I told you Billy was messing with me at yoga. How are you acting surprised?"

"I thought we were having fun." Her voice pitches up, wobbling slightly.

"You're right. My fear was all for fun," I say, growing more annoyed by the minute. "Being made to look crazy at your studio was *so* much fun."

"That part was not fun. I told you to get your shit together. Remember that?" She throws her hands in the air.

"Oh, I remember. You berated me on the sidewalk in the middle of town. And right before I broke into tears, you changed the subject to food. A typical Lanie move, by the way."

"I thought you were having a breakdown. I was trying to be supportive." She huffs. "One ghost I could deal with, but now it's multiple ghosts? How am I supposed to handle that?" She turns her attention to Corinne, who's glued to her phone, not seeming to care about our argument.

My head shakes back and forth, exhaustion slinking in. "You're supposed to be the supportive friend in this department. I'd expect this reaction from Nina, but you?" I let the thought trail off. I'm too tired to fight. Besides, I can't blame her for being skeptical.

How can I expect someone who hasn't experienced the things I have to blindly trust me? Would I?

Unlikely.

After several minutes, Lanie breaks the silence.

"Okay, let's say I believe all of it. What's your next move?"

Not a confirmation she believes, but a step in the right direction. If only Billy would make an appearance and prove I'm sane.

"I'll answer that." Corinne leans forward, catching my eye. "We have an appointment with my mother. Wednesday at nine."

My eyebrows lift into my hairline. "Wednesday? Why so long?"

"Trust me when I say you shouldn't be in a hurry to meet with her."

"Umm . . . should I be worried?"

She ignores my trepidation. "I'll meet you after I close up shop."

"Can I come?" Lanie asks, looking way too excited by the possibility.

"No. Mother does not like a crowd. Besides, I just listened to you snub your best friend over the idea of ghosts. You don't get to poo-poo the woo, and join in when it suits you." Corinne turns to me and winks.

I'm not even sure how to react. I didn't think I'd see the day when Corinne came to my defense. I wasn't even sure she liked me.

Lanie harrumphs, falling back onto the couch.

"Why exactly are we meeting with your mother?" I ask, not sure I'm on board.

"She'll know how to handle the situation with the poltergeist, and how to help you protect yourself from future spirits."

That all sounds important, but my gut tells me it's going to be an epic shit show.

"Look," Lanie says, pointing to the television that's on mute.

We all turn to see breaking news lighting up the screen.

"Turn it up," Corinne barks, and I leap for the remote.

"Authorities are searching for a local woman whose car was found in a remote part of Olt Forest, just off Thistlehill Road. Friends and family say Jenna Cruz has been missing for two months. They became worried after she failed to show up for a shift at Clementine's in Knox Harbor, where she's worked as a bartender for many years."

The interview shifts to a woman who must be in her eighties, holding on to the bar likely to steady her fragile frame. "Jenna wouldn't do this. She was like family." The woman's raspy voice warbles with emotion. "Even if she wanted to leave town, she never would've done it like this. She vanished without a trace."

A picture of a young woman with large hazel eyes and long brown hair flashes onto the screen. My stomach plummets and a whimper breaks through my closed lips.

It's her. The woman who keeps appearing.

I feel Corinne and Lanie staring at me, but my eyes remain forward, needing to hear the rest.

"Nobody has been able to get in contact with her since she was last seen on the night of August tenth. Silverton police got the tip about the stranded car from a local hunter who stumbled across it. The man, who wishes to remain anonymous, says it was obvious someone was trying to hide it based on the location and how it was covered. Police are asking the public to come forward with any leads on Ms. Cruz's whereabouts. Family and friends say this is unlike Jenna, who loved her job and was happy.

I stare at the woman's picture until the news switches to a story about a local dog shelter. I can't speak. Can't move. This is all too surreal.

"She's dead."

16

Nine of Swords . . . Reversed

"PLEASE TELL ME you didn't drag me out *here* to go in *there*." Nina points as though I don't see the house right out of a horror flick. "I refuse."

There was no way I was coming to meet Corinne's mom without a safety net. If the woman is even half as batty as her daughter, it's sure to be another bizarre night.

I intertwine our arms and lean into her. "Stop being a chickenshit."

"You can't tell me you're not at least on edge."

Chewing on my bottom lip, I mull over our current situation and find that Nina is not wrong. Who wouldn't be teetering on the brink of madness with everything spiraling in my life? It doesn't help that Corinne's mother only seems to deal with the dead at night.

"Can you please explain why this must occur so late? Are you people nocturnal?"

"You people? As in mediums?" Corinne huffs. "Include yourself in your generalizations; you've joined the ranks." She mumbles something under her breath about how unfair it is, but I'm too distracted by the dark and creepy funeral home in front of me to pay much attention to her ramblings. If the foreboding building wasn't enough, the light mist that hovers across the yard has me ready to abandon the mission and deal with the ghosts myself. A shiver runs up my spine and my limbs jiggle in response.

"Seriously?" I shake my head in utter bewilderment. "How can this situation just get increasingly odder?"

Corinne shrugs her shoulders, and one side of her oversized black sweater falls down her arm, revealing a tattoo I can't make out in the dark. I turn my attention back to the Addams Family mansion, not letting go of Nina's arm for a second.

"Are you going to explain to me what is going on?" Nina whispers into my shoulder.

I haven't had a chance to fill Nina in on all the happenings of late. My assumption was that Lanie had already done that for me. Apparently not. And there definitely wasn't enough time to get into it now.

"You'll see soon enough."

In the light of day, the place is probably gorgeous. The three-story Queen Anne Victorian is right out of a magazine of old restored homes. A porch wraps around the entire front, save for the turreted area at the far right of the stately white house.

I could probably get on board with calling this place home, but the wooden sign that reads *Moradi Mortuary* is a deal breaker.

I do not sleep under the same roof as the dead.

That is, until recently.

"I take it the nail salon isn't a family business," I mutter.

"Nope." Corinne pops the *p* for emphasis. "I went through this phase several years back where I took a stab at normalcy."

"I see it didn't work out."

Nina snickers and Corinne's lips pucker, her hands raising to her hips. "If you haven't already put it together, I was the weird girl whose family dealt in death, and my mom proclaims to anyone who will listen that she communes with spirits." She barks out a humorless laugh. "I practically had a neon sign around my neck that said *freak*."

The snark that usually accompanies anything that leaves Corinne's mouth is absent, bringing to light that there's more to this girl than meets the eye. This life must've truly been rough for her.

Nina's hand squeezes my arm. She recognized it too.

"I paid my way through cosmetology school and roped my savvier twin into branching out with me."

"How did the 'rents take that?" I ask, running my free arm down my jeans to remove the building perspiration on my palms.

"What do you think?" She pulls her shirt back in place, covering her shoulder, while staring at her childhood home. It makes me wonder how often Corinne comes here.

I can imagine a family of mortician psychics would be none too pleased to add nail tech to their manifest.

"And ''rents'?" she continues. "Please refrain from attempting to be cool. Nobody has said that since 2010."

I press my lips into a thin line, refraining from engaging with her barbs. It will only delay the inevitable and I just want to get this night over with.

"She isn't wrong," Nina chimes in, earning a pinch in response. "Ouch."

"We need to hurry. My mother does not abide tardiness."

The three of us scurry up the concrete stairs leading to the front porch. The door swings open, and I don't even have time to process that there doesn't appear to be anyone around to have opened it. Corinne is shuffling us through the main parlor to a door that leads to the basement.

"No way. Not going there," I say, halting my steps. "I do not plan to see dead people."

She rolls her eyes. "You see dead people all day. Grow up."

"I'm with Alyssa on this one. Nothing good ever comes from following strangers into a dark funeral home basement."

Corinne blinks. "Is that a situation you've found yourself in before?"

"Well, no—"

Corinne cuts Nina off, staring her down. "You're not even supposed to be here, and we need to get a move on." She steps aside, motioning for us to go first.

Nina shakes her head slowly, mouthing *Danger*. I roll my eyes and head down the stairs, practically pulling Nina behind me.

"How do you even get bodies down here?" I whisper, for reasons unknown to me. Do I fear waking the dead? Possibly. Who can rationalize my actions these days? Certainly not me.

Corinne doesn't oblige me with explanations, pulling us further into the bowels of death and decay.

"You're so damn dramatic," Corinne says, reading my thoughts.

"How are you doing that?" I slam to a stop and Corinne runs into my back.

"Jeez. Walk much?"

I swing around, scowling down at her.

"Well . . . I *was* touching you. Seems to be a new superpower I've obtained."

"W-what? She can seriously read minds?" Nina's teeth chatter, whether from the drafty basement or fear, I'm unsure.

"So far, I seem to be the only one plagued by this *gift*."

My eyes narrow in on the petite beauty. I will be steering clear of Little Miss Mind Reader's touch if that's the case. The last thing I need is her flipping through my thoughts and taking whatever she deems useful for whatever wicked plans she has. Her motives in helping me are still unclear, and that has me on edge as much as this dungeon of doom.

"Can we go now?" she grinds through her teeth.

My hand swings out, gesturing for her to take the lead. She brushes past me, not even trying to avoid bumping into my shoulder.

We only take about ten steps before she stops at a closed wooden door, rapping three times before someone on the other side says, "It's open."

The room is shrouded in darkness, save for a single candle in the middle of a round table. The only thing that's missing is the crystal ball, and they would've nailed the stereotype perfectly. On the opposite side sits a woman who is undoubtedly Corinne's mother.

The woman watches me keenly, her stare so intense that I have to avert my eyes. My knees wobble a bit, and my hands won't stop moving.

"Mother, this is—"

"Quiet," she hisses. "I must concentrate."

Corinne's eyes close and her hands ball into fists. Nina grabs my arm again, squeezing even tighter this time.

"Take a seat," she says after several tense minutes.

I jump to it, choosing the farthest seat possible and pushing Nina into the chair next to me. Corinne chooses to stand. My eyes widen in a *get your ass over here* expression, but she doesn't get the hint. Or ignores it. Likely the latter.

"So . . . you're the one with powers, huh?"

She has a slight accent, and I struggle to place it. Her long brown hair falls over both shoulders, and she wears a thick headband in bold shades of pink, orange, and teal. Her black ribbed turtleneck somehow looks chic on her.

She clears her throat.

"Oh . . . um . . . I don't know if I'd call it a power. More like a curse."

Nina makes a choking sound, but I ignore it, my focus on the strange woman across the table.

"Hmm," she says, inspecting me and clearly finding me lacking. "You don't understand how special it is for the universe to bestow an ability to tap into these gifts so easily. Most work their entire lives to master the art of communicating with the dead, only to never experience the fruits of their life's work." She purses her lips and glances at Corinne for a beat before turning back to me. "You're ungrateful."

Corinne snorts and I snap my glare toward her. She shrugs at me.

The woman flicks her hand in the air. "Go. Do not waste my time."

My head swings back and forth between mother and daughter, while Nina jumps to her feet.

"We'll be going now."

My hand darts out, stopping Nina from moving another foot. "Sit," I demand. She exhales loudly but places her butt back in the chair.

Anger rises to the surface and I'm not sure why. I should be more than happy to escape this place, but there's a niggling in my belly that tells me I need this woman.

"Mother, give her a moment. This is all new to her. She wasn't part of this world when her powers were unlocked."

Corinne's mom launches into breathing exercises. The entire time, she makes little mewling noises and whispers to thin air. If I thought my session with Corinne was bizarre, her mother might prove more so.

"Are you seeing it *this* time?" I whisper to Nina. She bobs her head.

"She came to you for a reading, did she not? She must've been somewhat familiar with this *world*." Her haughty behavior is raising my hackles, but I tamp them down, hoping to get something out of this disaster of a meet and greet.

She takes another deep breath, closes her eyes, and folds her hands on top of the table. When she's done meditating or whatever it is she's doing, she looks back at me with a softer disposition.

"My spirit guides have strongly encouraged me to help you."

"Thank you?"

I'm not sure who I'm thanking—her or these guides she speaks of. Either way, my chest fills with air, and I can breathe easier.

"There's another spirit here who wants your permission to manifest."

I chew the inside of my cheek, waiting for someone—anyone— to clarify. They don't.

"*Another* spirit?" Nina pipes up, coming to the rescue when I'm at a loss for words.

The older woman nods. "When you arrived, a young, rather handsome man accompanied you."

My eyes narrow, knowing full well who she's referencing, but hoping maybe another—actually attractive and less assholish— ghost is now following me. "What does this young man look like?"

She purses her lips.

"Beyond the handsome part, I mean."

She sighs. "He's wearing a hooded sweatshirt."

Billy.

"Ugh. Please don't stroke his ego. The man is intolerable."

"I'm also right here," he says from behind me, and my butt lifts about two inches off the chair. A rather pathetic-sounding squeal bounces off the dark walls. I've grown accustomed to him popping up out of the blue, but in this place, with my nerves on edge, he manages to catch me off guard.

"Who is it?" Nina squeaks, head between her shoulders, hands cupping her eyes.

"See what I mean, Natalia?" he says, motioning toward me. "She's a stick in the mud, and her friends aren't much better."

Natalia, is it? Go figure—the ghost got her name before I did.

She chuckles. "They're human. Mundane. Give them a break."

"Thank you." I bob my head. "Wait . . ."

I'm not sure that was a compliment, but at this point, I'll take any help with shutting Billy the hell up.

"Who is she talking to?" Nina asks, voice pitching. "Is there someone here I can't see?"

I turn my head to Nina. "Yeah. An asshat named Billy Garet."

Her eyes widen, head swinging back and forth, trying to find him. She won't.

"Billy Garet? As in Neda and Jase Garet's son?"

I pull a face. "No idea."

"How does she know my parents?" Billy asks, pointing at Nina.

I straighten my shoulders, determined to get the rest of *my* questions answered. There will be time later for me to enlighten Billy on how Nina and Richard are friends with the Garet family.

"You said another spirit was here asking for my permission? That's a thing?"

She smiles, showcasing brilliant white teeth that glow in the candlelit room. "Of course. Spirits have the ability to soft communicate."

My head shakes and my hand lifts to halt her words. "You lost me back at permission."

She blinks persistently, taking in a lungful of air and expelling it forcefully. This woman clearly has no patience where I'm concerned.

"Soft communication is when the spirit gives subtle hints they're there, giving you the ability to invite them to commune with you." She grins. "It's a term I created."

"Very inventive." I turn toward Billy. "Where was your soft communication?"

"Absent. Kinda like your youth."

Natalia chokes on her laughter. "Billy . . . play nice," she manages to say between chortles.

I close my eyes and count to ten. It's impossible to murder someone who is already dead. I'll just sit here and picture the scenario in my head.

"How is he able to follow me everywhere? Aren't ghosts supposed to be stuck?"

"To you. He's not attached to an item or place. He's stuck with you."

"You're telling me that *everywhere* I go, he follows?"

My mind races, thinking of all the places he could've been and what he saw.

"Yuck, lady. If you think I'm following you to the bathroom, you're out of your damn mind. You might be the last woman in the world that I'd take a peek at, and it has everything to do with your personality."

My face heats and my teeth clench. Screw it. I'm going to attempt to harm the ghost. I stand, but Nina's hand darts out.

"Sit down. We came here for a reason, and I have school tomorrow," she snaps.

I count to ten, working to calm my racing heart and block thoughts of Billy the Bastard from my mind.

"The other spirit would like to speak with you now, if that's all right," Natalia says, breaking up the movie I have on replay in my mind of me getting revenge on Billy. He appears behind Natalia, arms crossed, looking smug and annoying as ever.

"Sure," I say. "I'm happy to communicate with a ghost that's not an ass." Billy rolls his eyes. "I'm ready. Connect us."

She nods briskly. "Jackson, meet Alyssa. Alyssa, this is—"

"Jackson Moore?" Billy interrupts.

A tall, burly man, wearing riding leathers and a red bandana on his head, blinks into existence. His arms are covered in tattoos, and he has a small hoop earring in his right ear.

"You can see him?" I say to Billy.

He wasn't able to see or communicate with Ollie. Why this guy?

"You two know each other?" I ask both the men.

"This dipshit stole my money before he knocked off," Jackson says.

I like this guy already. Seems we both have a disdain for Billy.

"Interesting," Natalia muses. "These spirits are tied together just as you two are."

"Meaning?" I drawl.

"Whatever is keeping Billy here with you, he factors in," she explains, motioning toward Jackson.

"What do you know about my death?" Billy snarls, losing the calm and cool attitude he tries to project. "It was you, wasn't it?"

The guy shrugs. "What's it to ya? You're dead now. What's it matter?"

Billy's eyebrows pull together as he appears to consider Jackson's questions. "It might be the only thing that matters anymore." He turns toward me. "Get this ape to spill the details. It might be what finally sends me on."

I consider all that I know. It's been said that those spirits that stick around have unfinished business. It was also said that the spirits I can communicate with are somehow tied to me.

"Tell me what's happened since the manifestation of your abilities," Natalia commands, breaking into my train of thought.

I run through all the sordid details in order, and she listens raptly, jotting things down on a notepad she pulled from under the table. She nods, frowns, chews on her lip, but never interrupts. When I'm done, we sit in silence for several moments. My eyes scan the room, looking from one person to the next. Billy remains standing behind Natalia like her very own—worthless—protector. The newcomer Jackson sits with his back against the wall and one leg bent, picking at something on his leather pants. Nina remains seated next to me, wide-eyed, and Corinne has been texting through it all.

"Let me ensure I have this all correct," Natalia says, breaking up the silence. "You and your husband Garrett were in an accident. You don't remember what happened, but through your contact with Corinne, you saw a flash of red." She stops, looking to me. "Do I have that right so far?"

"Yes."

She nods to Billy. "He claims he was run off the road by a red truck. See where I'm going with this?"

I shake my head slowly.

Her eyes cross. "You were both in accidents where people died by being run off the road by someone in a red truck."

My eyes widen and shoot to Billy, who looks equally surprised.

"I never said my accident was caused by a red truck."

She shrugs. "Flash of red, red truck. Could you consider the possibility for one moment?"

I rub at my temples, thinking over the events of my accident, concentrating on the moment I remember seeing red. The sensation of spiders crawling across my skin is an indicator that she might be right. The red I saw could've very well been a red vehicle. Based on the size of my vehicle and the height at which I saw the

red flash, it was likely something larger than my own car. A truck.
A red truck.

Holy. Shit.

"This isn't just about your accidents. Whoever was responsible
for Billy's was likely responsible for yours too."

I slump back into my chair, reeling from this revelation.

"Why? I mean . . . does it have something to do with their
name? Garrett?" I'm grasping at straws here.

"No. That's just stupid," Natalia says, picking at her nails.
"That's merely a coincidence."

"A rather uncanny one," I say, taking a deep breath. "What
about Ollie Craft?"

"He was probably tied to the dishes. Not you. He appeared
because they were in your possession. Once they were returned, he
left."

"What about the new guy? And the woman?" Corinne asks,
joining the party.

"Woman? You didn't mention a woman." She glances around.
"There are no other spirits here."

I'm not ready to tell Natalia that I know the missing woman
from the news is dead. But even thinking about Jenna seems to
conjure her. She manifests right next to Natalia and the gifted medium appears none the wiser.

That is, until the scream once again blasts through the room,
forcing us all to protect our ears. My eyes slam shut, and that's
when things get even weirder.

A scene plays out like a movie reel in my head.

Jenna walking to her car. Someone grabs her from behind. A
dark, remote location. Someone hitting her over the head repeat-
edly. Another location in the country where two men dig up the
earth, throwing her body inside and covering her.

My eyes fly open, and everyone is staring at me. I don't say a word.

"Whatever that was, I'm unable to connect with it." Natalia muses, mostly to herself. "This is a very rare poltergeist situation."

I bob my head. "Corinne alluded to that possibility, but what's the difference between these spirits"—I motion toward the guys—"and the woman?"

She purses her lips. "Poltergeists manifest out of pure anger. Their spirits can't move on because only love and joy can ascend." She taps her chin. "This woman had to have died in a horrible way."

I swallow. Having just witnessed her death, I know that Natalia has hit the nail on the head.

"How do I help her?"

"Restless spirits need justice more than the average ghost. Uncover what happened, and she should move on."

"Do I need to be worried for my safety? Ollie was able to make physical contact. Can she?"

That thought is more terrifying than anything.

"These spirits want your attention. Give it to them, and there shouldn't be anything for you to worry about."

I tap my fingers excessively on my leg, overwhelmed by all the pressure on my shoulders.

"What about him?" I ask, turning the focus back to the two in the room.

Natalia and I look to Jackson, waiting on him to shed some light on why he's here. "After I left Clementine's, I was murdered by someone in a red truck."

Chills spread all over me as the truth sinks in. We're all connected by a red truck. Their deaths and my accident were all due in part to someone driving a red truck. The same one? That's to be determined. Regardless, it's become increasingly clear tonight that I'm stuck with these spirits until I find the answers and bring them justice.

"If he was murdered, why isn't he a poltergeist?"

Natalia half rolls her eyes. "I'm not all-knowing, girl." She tsks, picking at her fingers. "But I'd suspect the woman knew her killer intimately."

A raging ghost who's seeking revenge on a past lover?

Freaking fantastic.

Three of Cups

"IT'S A LITTLE disconcerting watching you talk to air," Nina says, kneading the pizza dough a bit harder than necessary.

Thursday wine night looks a little different at the present moment. I'm in no mood to socialize outside these walls. Not with the events that have occurred over the last two weeks. Even with Billy and Jackson hovering about, my home feels like my only sanctuary.

Even if it's a sanctuary I no longer choose to sleep in alone. Lanie moved in last night. I called her immediately after leaving the Moradi Mortuary and begged her to stay with me. She'll be sleeping right next to me every night, until I can get my unease under control. It wasn't even enough to have her down the hall. We have to spoon for me to sleep. Pathetic, but reality these days.

The image of Jenna Cruz truly haunts me. The way the woman died, and the fact that she was potentially killed by someone she was close to, is tragic.

"It's a *lot* distressing that I have a pesky ghost that won't leave me the hell alone," I snap in Billy's direction.

It's been two weeks since he sent me streaking into the night, right next door to a man who could never understand what I was experiencing. The same man that Billy is now trying to convince me is our only hope of salvation.

"You need to go to West. Tell him what you know."

I level Jackson with a scowl.

"Since when do you agree with him?" I jab my finger in Billy's direction.

Jackson shrugs.

"Natalia said *I* needed to solve this. Not Nick." I pop a grape into my mouth, done explaining this to the thickheaded ghouls.

"You couldn't solve a Rubik's Cube with a step-by-step guidebook. I'm not leaving my fate in your incapable hands." Billy's arrogant voice has the effect of nails on a chalkboard.

"Have I told you I hate you?"

"Have I told you that you look like a troll doll these days?" Billy retorts, crossing his arms over his puffed-out chest.

I'm not sure who he's trying to kid. The guy has chicken legs and the physique of a teenage boy. I bet he was still getting carded up to the day he died.

"Kiss my a—"

"Altogether scrawny ass? No thanks."

His eyes narrow and Jackson howls in laughter, but I'm too focused on what he said about me.

My hand lifts to my hair, patting it down like that will make a difference. I can't even remember the last time I ran a brush through it.

Good god, he's right.

The image of Jenna covered in mud and blood resurfaces, and I immediately regret being so shallow. That poor girl will never enjoy the simple things in life again. It was all stolen from her, and here I am complaining about my appearance.

"He might be right," Corinne says. "The cards were clear that you need to partner with someone. The more I think about it, the more I think it's Nick."

"Hate who? Need to solve what? Why are we partnering with Nick?" Lanie is struggling to catch up on the details. It took her a minute to grasp that I was truly seeing spirits, but now, she's into it. Too much. "Who's talking? The punk or the biker?"

"Both," I groan. "And I'm done listening." I swat my hands at the air like I'm batting away a fly. "Go. Let me enjoy one night with my friends."

"You need a shower," Billy mumbles. "Wash that face and get yourself together to enlist the detective. Or else—"

"Or else what?" I bite out through my teeth. "You gonna flip the lights on and off? You and I both know you aren't Ollie Craft. Your afterlife abilities are those of a toddler." He narrows his eyes at me, trying to look menacing but missing the mark.

"Since when do you fight back?" he says, arms crossed over his chest.

"I've always sparred with you, Billy. I'm just less inclined to allow you to think I give two shits what *you* think about me." I swat at the air. "Go. Away. Pester Henry for a while."

"Harry," he barks.

"Don't care. Get lost."

I don't have to say it again. Both ghosts finally disappear, leaving me alone with my friends. I reach for my gin and tonic and practically down it in one gulp.

"Whoa there," Nina scolds. "What's with the booze?"

"Wine wasn't cutting it. Gin is what I need. Gin is good."

"Good god, she's lost it," Corinne deadpans, seeming truly concerned.

"Am I losing it?" I ask Lanie, ignoring Corinne completely.

Lanie looks away. "What time is it?" she asks, pretending to search for a clock that's right in front of her.

Nina gets aggressive with the dough that's been beaten to death at this point.

"Guys," I moan. "Stop lying and give it to me straight."

Nina stops turning the dough and looks me in the eyes. "If I'm being honest . . . you've . . . seen better days."

"What is that supposed to mean?" My voice pitches. I'm losing my grip on my emotions. Corinne's words are getting to me more than I'd like to admit.

"You need a life makeover. That's what it means."

Leave it to Lanie to rip off the Band-Aid with absolutely zero tact. It's not like I wasn't thinking the exact thing moments ago. But it's never fun to hear it from friends.

My bottom lip trembles and tears well in my eyes. I'm not sure if it's because my life has truly gone to hell in a handbasket or because of the lack of sleep I'm getting.

"Alyssa," Lanie coos, walking around the island to my side. Her hand lands on my shoulder and I shrug it off.

"Don't even," I snap. "No backpedaling because you hurt my feelings."

She runs her hand down my hair and talks to me in a tone I haven't heard since Garrett died. She's preparing to handle me with kid gloves, and I resent it already.

"You haven't been taking care of yourself lately. You're beautiful inside and out. Don't let a grumpy wannabe medium and a fright of ghosts keep you down." She whispers the words, but clearly not quietly enough.

"Do you mean *a fraid*?" Nina asks, with one eyebrow raised. "The term is *a fraid of ghosts*."

Lanie rolls her eyes. "Whatever. Nobody cares, Nagging Nina."

I have to smother my laugh, because I'm not quite ready to forgive her.

"Fight for yourself. Join the living," Lanie says. I squirm at the idea of walking among the likes of Billy Garet. "You're forty and should be thriving. Make it happen."

"How do I do that?" I whisper the words, sounding insecure and hopeless.

She takes a deep breath, and I just know I'm not going to like whatever comes out of her mouth. "Allow Nick to help you help them."

I groan. "Who says he even will?"

"You won't know unless you try," Nina chimes in.

"Great. Now you two are siding with the ghosts."

"We're Team Alyssa. And Team Alyssa wants a spirit-free home for you."

Lanie nods. "So you can get back to normal."

I think about what normal has looked like for me since the accident, and I internally cringe. There was nothing normal about my life. I've given up a career I loved to live off my husband's life insurance. I've stopped playing tennis—a sport I excelled at—with a team of women who were uplifting and fun. I pushed aside everything that made me *me*, and I'm still doing it two years later.

I sniff. "I don't want normal. At least not the normal I've been living these past two years." My head moves back and forth between my friends. "I want a fresh start."

The smiles I get in response to my declaration are nothing short of encouraging. They are smiles I haven't seen in far too long. It gives me hope that my words aren't just empty platitudes. They're a spoken promise of that new beginning. I'm sharing it with the world, or at least with my friends, so that it can manifest into being.

Yuck . . . I sound like Corinne.

"I can always talk to Richard. He can get the police to

investigate. Billy is his best friend's kid. He'll do whatever he can to help."

For as smart as Nina is, she's so very naive.

"Are you insane? Richard would finally have a reason to have you committed if you breathed a word of this," Lanie practically shouts.

"She's not wrong," I agree. "We'd be the Gilded Glindas no more."

Lanie grunts. "That might be the only witty thing Dick Dunbar has ever said."

Nina's nose crinkles and I snort in response.

"Good one, Lane. Dick Dunbar." I wipe at a stray tear. "I hate that man."

We don't typically disparage spouses, but Nina's ran away with the award for the worst years ago. He's a smooth talker who managed to dupe her into thinking he was a stand-up—single—guy. Next thing you know, she's put up in a swanky condo in town, believing she hit the lotto of boyfriends. Fast-forward to three months later, and wife number two—whom nobody knew about—shows up serving divorce papers.

Nina didn't manage to escape him. His reputation was on the line right as he was up for reelection. He blackmailed her into staying and made her wife number three. It kills Lanie and me.

We don't keep secrets from each other. Lanie and Nina know everything about me and vice versa. The only exception is what Richard is holding over Nina's head. Every time it gets brought up, she changes the subject. We don't push because she's made it clear that it's the one thing she has no intention of sharing and she won't budge. She claims it's in our best interest not to know, which has always been my biggest concern. So, we do what we can to help her make him as miserable as he's made her. One day we will help her find a way out.

Nina shrugs and sighs. "Is it terrible if I admit I'm just glad he's gone for a few days?"

"I can make him gone permanently. I know people," Lanie whispers, as if the walls will talk.

The wrinkles around Nina's eyes and lining her forehead all move back into place, and her delicate features soften. "That's a convo for another day."

"Tomorrow perhaps?" Lanie singsongs and I chuckle.

"I don't even know what to do with you two." Nina shakes her head, concentrating on the dough ball in front of her.

"And you don't need to, because the last person we're involving is Richard," Lanie bites out.

"She's right. I'm going to talk to Nick." I stand from the chair, and I'm met with wide eyes.

"No!" Nina and Lanie yell at the same time.

"Please sit," Nina begs.

My lips slam together as I place my butt back in my seat.

"I thought that's what everyone thinks I should do," I say, looking around in utter confusion.

Nina's panic abates and she offers a small smile. "Yes. You should . . . but not like this." She gestures toward me.

"What?"

"You look like something that crawled out of a well, and she doesn't want you embarrassing yourself." Lanie doesn't even try to sugarcoat it and I guess I'm grateful.

"You want him to take you seriously, right?"

I bob my head. "Obviously."

"You're going to him about information you've received from ghosts. How do you think he's going to receive that?"

"He isn't. I'd never admit that part."

"Right, but he witnessed the events at Gloria's. He's likely already super suspicious about your motives."

She isn't wrong. I've been shocked to not find Nick on my doorstep inquiring about what went down at Mrs. Craft's. Especially considering the way Mrs. Craft spoke to the air and stumbled across a shoebox with a note and money that she hadn't known about before.

"Add to that your disheveled appearance, and he really won't take you seriously," Lanie finishes.

Nina groans but doesn't even bother to fight with her. "Even more important, you need to figure out what and how you're going to break this news to him. You have to get him on board, so what you say is crucial." Nina's gaze is fixed on me, and I have a hard time not shrinking under the weight of it.

I take a deep breath, thinking about all that's been said. "What do you suggest?"

Nina and Lanie consider this question for several moments. It's Nina who finally offers an idea.

"I'd suggest you tell him you have a tip about several accidents being connected. He'll ask who your tip is from, and you'll maintain that your source has to remain anonymous."

"He won't like that, but he'll agree in order to get the information," Lanie adds.

Nina nods in agreement. "Explain that you and Billy were run off the road by a red truck."

"I can't prove that, though."

"True." Nina taps her chin. "Can Billy offer anything more than it was a red truck?"

"You mean I have to talk to him?"

She shrugs. "If you want him gone."

No question. I'll have this conversation now if it means he'll be out of my hair ASAP.

"What about Jackson? Jenna?"

"I think you should slowly unroll all of this."

I sigh. "It doesn't seem fair to Jenna's family. They don't know she's dead."

"Then start there. But that means you'll be stuck with Billy a little longer."

I groan, teeth clanking together as I war with moral obligations and self-preservation. "I can't keep running to Nick every time something else pops up. He'll get suspicious."

"Nah. Men love to help. Detectives thrive on solving puzzles. You're just pushing the pieces in front of him. Pulling the strings that he doesn't even see. Get crafty with your delivery."

I'm not sure I believe it will work, but at this point, I'll try anything. I may not love Billy, and there's no doubt I want him out of my space, but it's also more than that. Having lost one of the most important people in my life, I understand the need for closure and justice. Billy, Jackson, and Jenna deserve that.

"When the time comes, we'll be right here waiting for a play-by-play of events," Nina says, offering her placating smile.

"Or for the squad car to come for you." Lanie doesn't even bother to look at me when she says it, and I choose to ignore her.

The thought of telling Nick any of this makes my skin crawl. He's the one person who could give me salvation or doom me to a life with Billy Garet.

"First things first," Lanie says, waggling her eyebrows. "More gin."

Two of Pentacles

WARM BREATH TICKLES the back of my neck, causing shivers to race over my body in the most delicious way. The tender kisses that follow have me moaning into my pillow.

I need this.

"I missed you," I whisper into the quiet space reserved for our most intimate moments.

An arm wraps around me, pulling me taut against a firm chest. The kisses to my neck grow more sensual, extending to just below my earlobe. The sensation is tantalizing, toying with the last of my composure.

My head tilts, opening myself for more of everything he's offering, and he makes good on it, running his teeth up my neck to my ear, pulling the lobe between them and biting down lightly.

"Ah," I cry out. "More."

His hand crawls up my belly, stopping at the base of my breast. One finger moves across the bottom, creating a sensation that curls my toes. But it's when his fingers grasp one nipple between them and squeeze that I just about lose my mind.

The smell of mint and leather washes over me, and I nestle into it. I'm about to beg for him to take me when he finally flips me toward him. My eyelids flutter as I smile seductively at Nick lying next to me.

My eyes fly open, and my body jerks to the side, as if trying to get out of dream Nick's arms. I manage to get myself tangled in the sheets, and plummet from the side of the bed, falling to the floor with a loud thud.

"Ouch," I say, making circles with my arm to work out the pain in my shoulder.

Lanie's head peers over the side, her mouth stuck in an O, and her eyes narrowed in on me.

"What the heck? Are you all right?"

I blink several times, trying to formulate words. None come. My mind is too preoccupied with replays of that dream.

Holy hell. What was that?

"You plan to stay down there? I have no intentions of discussing your sex dream, if that's what you're avoiding," she says, raising an eyebrow.

Oh dear god. Of all the times for Lanie to have a sleepover.

"What are you talking about? I wasn't having any dream."

She smirks, rolling her eyes. "Just admit it. I know a sexy dream when I hear one."

I huff, working to untangle myself from the offending sheets.

"Go back to bed. You're delusional."

Lanie yawns, stretching her arms above her head. "Can't. I have class in less than an hour."

My head swivels to locate the clock. 5:45 a.m. Too damn early to be dealing with illicit dreams. I'll need to compartmentalize it as a byproduct of his heroism as of late. Or it could be all the talk of him last night that conjured him.

That's all.

Liar.

I can admit the man is growing on me. But that does not mean I should be dreaming about sleeping with him. That's a bit much, considering I still hardly know him.

When I've managed to pull myself together and usher Lanie out my door, I allow myself to linger over a cup of coffee, enjoying a Billy-free moment. I do my best to push that dream out of my mind, determined to focus on the real issues at hand.

From my perch at the kitchen island, I get a good look at what's become of my once-immaculate home. Dishes in the sink used to give me hives, and empty fast-food containers lying about the counter, heart palpitations. Yet, that's exactly what I'm currently staring at.

I can't even blame the state of the place on Lanie. She's actually thrown her stuff away and even placed her dirty dishes in the dishwasher. It would be too much to ask her to put mine in there as well.

I've allowed my home to resemble a fraternity house after a weekend bender.

Garrett would find this too amusing, considering the tongue-lashing he'd get for leaving his stuff lying around. Apparently with the development that I can see ghosts, my give-a-damn has thoroughly busted.

I take a stroll around my first floor, inspecting the damage. So far, the kitchen is the most disastrous. The office hasn't counted for two years. At some point, I know I need to sift through the boxes and move things around.

Most of the stuff needs to be donated, but I'm not ready for that. I'll hold on to his memory by hoarding all of his things. As long as it's contained to one room, I can justify that it's fine. I'm fine. *Everything* is fine.

In the past, even thinking about parting with his things made me nauseous. Today, that feeling isn't so intense. I'm getting closer to that day, but it's not here yet.

"Are you going to clean this place up or just think about it?" Billy chirps from behind me.

I don't even flinch this time. He's becoming a fixture—one I'd like to remove, like every single piece of gold that was to be found in this home when we bought it. It was an ugly phase when all the knobs and faucets were that putrid shade.

Thinking about those days further reminds me of Garrett, and my chest tightens. "Billy, can I ask you a very personal question?"

He pulls his lip to the side. "Is this going to hurt my brain? Make me dumb?"

"Too late."

He crosses his eyes like a toddler. "You know, for a forty-year-old, your insults and basic demeanor are that of a small child."

"I've never been in forced proximity to anyone who brings out the immaturity in me quite like you do, sport." I offer the most saccharine smile I can muster.

He groans. "Get on with it so I can go do something less painful."

I almost tell him to forget it, but the need for answers is too intense to allow my ego to get in the way.

"What happened when you died?"

Billy looks off into the distance, appearing lost to his memories. For a moment, I wonder if my question is insensitive. I might not like him, but there are boundaries I won't cross even with him. I can razz him. I can even despise the guy. But I won't purposefully hurt someone, and I can imagine reliving the moment you died is painful.

"I wasn't scared or confused. It felt like I was going home." As he's explaining this, his eyes mist, and I feel wholly uncomfortable with that. This is Billy. The ghost I love to hate. He's making it very difficult to maintain my opinion of him when he looks vulnerable.

"I felt at peace, until the light that was shining down on me disappeared and I ended up here."

"I'm sorry, Billy. Truly. I can't imagine how hard that must've been."

He makes a face. "Don't patronize me."

I throw my hands into the air. "Good grief. I meant it, idiot."

"Why are you asking this anyway? You plan to kick off soon?"

My head lowers and I stare at my shoes, not wanting to meet his eyes. "I wanted to know what Garrett might have experienced when he . . ." My voice cracks. I shake my head, trying to clear away the emotion. "Died."

Billy clears his throat, turning his back on me and walking toward the front room. "He likely was beamed up and taken straight to paradise." Resentment is thick in his tone and words, and I can't blame him.

Except I'm not sure he's right. If our accidents are what link us, then Garrett might be stuck somewhere too. I can only hope whoever he's connected with treats him well.

"I was stuck in some gray haze, roaming aimlessly with nobody to talk to until I ended up here." Billy stares off into the corner, lost to his thoughts.

I stuff down the sadness creeping in and decide to distract myself with what always does the trick. Cleaning.

I grab my earbuds off the counter, popping one into each ear and pulling up my music app, shuffling my recently played songs, drowning out Billy and everything else.

I clean for what feels like hours, dancing around each room as I collect trash and stuff it into my large black bag. Billy has been noticeably absent, and I can't say that doesn't make me joyful.

When I'm done and the place is spotless, I jump onto a barstool and pull a notepad and pen toward me. If I'm going to the police about Jenna, I need to have a plan. Recalling all the visions I had,

I try to map out where her remains could be; that's the key. They already found the car, and the cause of her death can be determined with an autopsy. If I want to help Jenna, I need to lead them to her remains.

Closing my eyes, I concentrate on that last image, and that's when I see the shack off in the distance. It's hard to tell how big the building is, but it's at the very least the size of a shed. If there's a building, there's likely a house nearby.

I pull up Google Earth and start my search at Olt Forest, where the car was located. Putting myself in the mind of a murderer, it occurs to me that I would separate the body from the car. I also wouldn't bury the body close to where the abduction happened. I move my mouse away from Knox Harbor, looking for another large plot of wooded land.

It's starting to feel hopeless with the number of wooded areas in that location. I slump back into my chair, placing my arm over my head, and try to draw any additional details into my head. Nothing happens.

"I could use some help, Jenna."

I'm about to shut the laptop down when the cursor begins to move on its own, stopping over a wooded location the next town over from Silverton. I lean in to get a good look and the arrow goes haywire, circling around one spot just off County Road A, in the middle of nowhere.

There's no doubt in my mind—that's where Jenna's buried.

I break into breathing exercises, preparing to face Nick. There's no more waiting around for a stroke of genius to strike, handing me the manual on how to approach my neighbor about tips I've received from beyond the grave.

You've got this.

I repeat that phrase, acting as my own hype girl.

The walk next door to Nick's is excruciatingly long despite the short distance. It's a rather pleasant night, warm for this time of year, and I use that excuse to take my sweet time traipsing across the yard.

If anyone is witnessing this, they probably think I've lost it. My feet can't possibly shuffle any slower. I might as well have a walker, because even Mrs. Craft moves quicker than this.

I've gone over the story so many times that it almost feels like truth. Still, I can't help but worry that Nick will see right through me, uncovering the parts I'm *not* saying.

He's a detective. It's his job to identify and dispel bullshit. He's heard larger tales from better liars, to be sure. That truth has my legs shaking and perspiration building at my hairline. I stop at the base of his steps, not quite ready to knock on the door.

I contemplate aborting the mission and dealing with a surly ghost for eternity, but I know that isn't an option.

I can do this.

My hand rises, but before I can make contact with the white wood, the door swings in and I fall forward, landing right into Nick's strong arms. My right hand is plastered against his washboard stomach. I attempt to remove it, but due to my current position, I only manage to run my palm downward. If the waist of his jeans didn't slow my roving hand, it would keep heading south to dangerous territory.

My eyes trail up his long torso, and I can't help but gawk. He's so tall, easily six foot four, dwarfing me. How have I never realized this before? The false memory of his lips on my neck and hand toying with my nipple infiltrates my mind at the worst moment possible, and I warm from the top of my head to the tips of my toes.

When my gaze lands on Nick's face, I find him smirking down at me in pure amusement.

For shit's sake, what am I doing?

"Alyssa," Nick greets, seemingly unsurprised to find me a limp noodle in his grasp.

I'm a grown woman, not some lovesick teenager. I'm more than capable of not being awkward. I'm here for a very important reason and I need to concentrate on that.

"Embarrassing myself in front of you is becoming a habit," I say, allowing him to help me to standing. "I can assure you I'm not typically this much of a klutz."

He chuckles. "That's not what I've heard."

I run my hands down my black joggers partially to smooth out the material, but mostly to wipe the perspiration from my palms.

"Well, whoever you're talking to seems to have thrown me right under the bus."

He laughs and I follow suit, finally relaxing.

"Were you heading somewhere?"

"No. I saw you on the camera," he explains, pointing toward the device I hadn't noticed.

Wonderful. How much of my stalling did he see?

"Alyssa, look at me," he commands. "No need to be embarrassed. I swung the door open on you."

He might have the reasoning behind my current unease incorrect, but the fact he can read me so well has anxiety rearing its ugly head, considering I'm here to semi-dupe him into helping me send a ghost on to the afterlife.

I take a deep breath, fold my hands together, and squeeze, hoping to produce a modicum of bravery. He steps back, giving me space that I desperately need.

It doesn't help, as my eyes make another perusal of the man, jean-clad and barefoot. My inspection stops on his gray T-shirt pulled taut across his muscular chest.

I clear my throat, hoping to whatever god is looking down on me that he didn't notice my blatant staring at his pecs.

"Wanna come in?"

When my chin lifts, I don't find any indication he's onto my prowling eyes.

I offer a tight-lipped smile, nodding briskly. "Thank you."

As I make my way past him, the pleasant aroma of pine and leather washes over me. Tingles spread across the back of my neck, and I lift my arm to rub at the spot. I wouldn't have thought leather to be an appealing scent, but dear god, is it ever.

My word. *Focus, Alyssa.*

I work to bring myself back to center, concentrating on the task at hand. Swinging around, I nearly bump into Nick, adding one more check mark to my list of blunders.

"I'm sorry. I—"

His hands lift to stop my apology. "It's all good." He continues walking toward the back of his house, and I follow on his heels. "Can I get you something to drink?" he calls over his shoulder.

"No, thank you. I don't want to take up too much of your time."

"Not like I have anything going on." He smiles and now it's his dimples stealing the show.

How have I not noticed how handsome he is before now?

"Please, have a seat," he suggests, motioning toward a chair at his dining room table.

The place is as orderly as I remember from the dreaded night that Billy poofed into my life. It almost rivals mine for tidiness, which Garrett would say is a miracle. I'm one step short of OCD. At least, I was.

Knowing a bit about his fiancée and when she passed, I decide she couldn't have had a hand in his decor. He moved here after her death. It has a feminine touch, which produces an excess of questions. The place isn't at all what I would expect for a bachelor.

"My sister," he says, and I scrunch my nose in confusion. "You said it isn't what you expected." He motions around the room. "Jackie, my sister, decorated the place."

Had I said that out loud? I've lost all my sense, apparently.

"I've never seen your sister around."

He bobs his head. "She used to be here a lot, but she had Zoey almost a year ago. I have to visit her now."

It's so strange how unaware I've been about what happens around me. I've never seen a woman come or go from his place in all the years he's lived here. Was I that unneighborly? He must think I'm such a witch.

He scoots his chair back from the table, creating a noise as it glides across the gray wood floors. It does the trick of bringing me back to why I'm here.

"I have some information to share with you." He doesn't say a word, allowing me to lead the conversation, and I appreciate his thoughtfulness. "I have a source."

His teeth run across his bottom lip, drawing my attention to his mouth. "Anonymous?"

"Huh?" I gnash my teeth together, eyes rising to meet his. "Yes?"

I swear if I don't pull myself together around this man, I'm going to have to move.

"All right. First, let's discuss what happened at Gloria's."

The blood drains from my face and goose bumps rise on my arms.

Here it goes. An interrogation by Nick West. I knew it was coming, but now that the questions are here, I'm freezing up.

"How did you know about that box? And why did you insinuate that Ollie was there?"

I force a phony laugh, trying to downplay what he's saying.

"I only meant in spirit. It was stupid because I wasn't sure what words of comfort to give." I make a show of schooling my face to appear sad, aiming for compassion. Pity is better than Nick running roughshod right through my white lies.

"I can't recall your exact words, but you told Gloria he was there. You even pointed."

"I was nervous, Nick. When I'm uncomfortable, I have a habit of saying things incorrectly."

He takes a deep breath, and for a moment, I think it worked and he's going to drop it. "But the box . . ."

Nick is a pit bull, and I'm rethinking this entire night. But running isn't fair to Jenna.

I'm internally cursing myself for caring too much about the dead and not being prepared for this. I should've worked out what I was going to say when this time came, but here we are, and I'm as clueless as ever.

Keep it simple.

"Corinne . . . the woman who was with me," I say, waiting for him to give me some indication he remembers her.

"The pretty brunette?"

I roll my tongue, instantly annoyed that *that's* how he remembers her.

"Alyssa?" Nick's voice pulls me from my train of thought. "Where did you just go?"

This man sees too much, and it's disarming.

"Did I say something that bothered you?" He chews on his cheek, and I have to wonder if it's to prevent himself from smiling.

Is he onto my feelings? That would be a major problem. I'm sending signals I have no business sending.

"No. Of course not," I say, offering a smile to sell the lie.

"Okay, so if it's not that . . ."

"Corinne is a medium and she told me about the box." I spit out the lie.

His nose scrunches and his lips purse. "A medium? As in psychic?"

"Yes." I take a deep breath and go with it. "I didn't believe her, but she wouldn't leave me alone unless I helped deliver some messages."

For several awkward moments, neither of us speaks. I allow Nick time to contemplate what I've said, and in the end, it's obvious he isn't sold on my story.

"You don't believe me." It's not a question. He's making it clear by his posture and lack of words that he doesn't.

Nick steeples his fingers over his mouth, eyes never wavering from mine. I refuse to look away, because that would be a dead giveaway that my pants are on fire.

"It's not that. I'm just not sure I buy into the whole psychic thing. It's hard for me—"

"You deal in facts," I finish, cutting him off.

He nods, lowering his hands to his lap. "I'm not saying my stance is correct, but it's all that I know."

There was never a time I thought someone like Nick would be easily convinced of the supernatural. Even still, I feel my hackles rising out of pure indignation, because even though he doesn't realize it's me who's seeing ghosts, I'm taking this far too personally.

"I understand. But tell me, how do you think she knew about the box?" I prop my elbow on the arm of the chair and lean against it, likely giving the impression of being haughty.

"I dunno. Maybe she knew Ollie? Or perhaps someone who was close to Ollie knows her. It could be any number of reasons," he says, pulling his shirt away from his chest.

"I see."

I'm trying to not show my offense at his rebuff, but it's hard. This is a situation I've never found myself in before. Trying to convince someone to side with a cause I'm not even admitting I believe in is proving impossible.

"Don't do that," he says, leaning forward, eyes crinkling at the corners.

"Do what?"

"Get defensive. This isn't me discounting *you*. I'm only trying to work through this on my own, and looking at the facts, it seems more likely that the woman is trying to dupe you into doing her dirty work."

"She isn't," I say, placing my hands on top of the table, but never breaking eye contact with Nick.

"How well do you know her, Alyssa? I've never seen her around you before."

I huff a laugh. "How well do you know *me*? We've lived next door to each other for years and you've said more words to me in the last two weeks than you have since you've moved in."

His eyes close and he blows out a breath. "I'm just looking out for you."

"Why?"

"We're neighbors, for one. Then there's the whole break-in situation."

I lift my hands to stop him, needing to get to the important stuff.

"Listen, that's why I'm here. I know that you and your department are extremely busy, so I've been looking into my break-in myself."

His eyes widen fractionally. "That so?"

He doesn't say it in a condescending tone or anything that suggests he's put off by my words. He mostly seems surprised.

"It is," I confirm. Now to pack on the lies. "I understand that Billy Garet is dead, but the likeness between him and my intruder had me curious about the man."

"Alyssa, I'm really sorry it's taken so—"

I shake my head to stop him. "Please let me finish. I understand that you were unable to prove that a break-in occurred, but I know what I experienced, Nick. I need you to trust me."

His mouth drops open before he slams it closed and rushes to correct my assumption. "Of course. I never meant to suggest . . ." His words trail off and he shakes his head. "Sorry. Please continue."

I offer a small smile, hoping to convey that I'm not angry. "I started asking around town and stumbled across some information I thought might be of interest to you."

His eyes narrow and his demeanor shifts from concerned neighbor to Detective West in an instant. "Go on."

"I got a tip from an eyewitness to Billy's accident."

I'm not sure that jumping right into Jenna being dead and pointing him in the exact location of her body is something I'm ready to dive into just yet anyway. I need to slowly feel my way into things with Nick and find a way to circle back to her.

Nick's back straightens and eyes darken. "An eyewitness? I don't have any record of an eyewitness."

"I know. That's why I'm here." I inhale, giving myself some time to work up the courage to lie with a straight face. "Before you ask, I gave my word to my source they'd remain anonymous."

He licks his bottom lip. "I understand."

Something about his posture tells me he plans to attempt to get it out of me either way.

"You see, the night of the accident they'd been drinking heavily, and had no business being on the road. A DUI would've resulted in the loss of their job. They did the cowardly thing and left the scene."

Nick rubs at the back of his head. "Why didn't they come forward once the alcohol had worn off?"

Good lord, lying is so much harder than I thought it would be. "I asked the same thing. Again, it comes down to being more concerned about themselves. They were unsure of what their repercussions would be for not coming forward sooner. They were afraid that they would be charged with obstructing justice, so they remained silent."

He sucks his teeth and taps the table with a closed fist. I wonder what's going through his head, but realize it's not important because there is no anonymous source that's alive and able to corroborate my story.

I can tell by the look on Nick's face that he's trying to maintain a sense of cool. I'm sure it's difficult to hear that a person would be so shallow. He doesn't know that they exist solely in my imagination.

"What did they tell you about the accident?"

"A red truck ran him off the road. They also mentioned that you should look into similarities between the accidents of Billy Garet and someone by the name of Jackson Moore."

His head jerks back slightly and his posture stiffens. "Jackson Moore? How does he figure into this?"

"They said that the night of both their murders—" I clear my throat and shake my head, catching my blunder. "I mean deaths, they were both at Clementine's. My source says both accidents were caused by someone in a red truck."

He takes a deep breath, head tilting to the side, which seems to be a habit for Nick when he's considering what's been said. "Both of those deaths were ruled accidents."

I move my head around, shrugging my shoulders, attempting to play oblivious. "No idea. I was just told that this person doesn't believe they were accidents."

He remains quiet for a few tense seconds, but eventually nods. Another motion he does quite often.

"Does the source think their accidents might've been caused by someone who was also at that bar on both those nights?"

There's the detective I need. Never once did I consider that, and in a matter of minutes, Nick has some additional leads.

"They didn't mention that, but it sounds like something worth following up on."

He runs his hands back through his hair. "Why would someone bring this up now?"

He stands and paces the room, appearing to contemplate all that I've laid on him. After several minutes of watching this play out, he finally addresses me.

"I really wish I was able to know how you came across this information. There are people who say things for no other reason but to cause issues."

My shoulders shake. "Are you saying you don't believe my source? Don't you see the uncanny similarities? Not only with Jackson and Billy but with my accident?"

His eyes close to mere slits. "What are you saying?"

"Spooky Hollow Road is where every one of these crashes occurred, and it was dark every time."

"Your source tell you all that?"

I slump back in my chair, defeat washing over me.

Nick walks to the sink, grabs a cup from the cupboard to his right and pours a glass of water. He's yet to answer my question, and the longer he remains quiet, the more my body shakes.

He makes his way back to the table, taking the seat across from me again, and slides the glass across to my hands that are folded and quaking on top of the table.

I recognize it as a peace offering—one I didn't ask for but appreciate nonetheless.

"Thank you, Nick." I take a sip, hoping it does the trick to calm my nerves.

"I want to make it clear that in no way am I saying I don't believe you. All I'm suggesting is that your source might have ulterior motives."

"They don't." My tone is even and my face is stone, which is a feat considering my current state of terrified.

Nick doesn't scare me; the truth does. I'm sitting in his home, lying to him, because the reality is even less believable. My source is a dead man.

"I wouldn't have come here if I wasn't absolutely sure."

"Between you and me, I'd let this one go, Alyssa. The case was closed by the family, and they're good friends with the mayor. He insisted we drop the case."

Richard Dunbar is a sleazy quack. The fact he was sworn into office is nothing short of criminal. It's a prime example of Knox Harbor politics.

"His family deserves to know he didn't die the way they think he did."

"We don't know that to be true," he says, ever the pragmatic one.

My eyes close when the pounding in my head intensifies.

"Are you okay?" he asks, voice soft and kinder than necessary.

"Fine," I answer, rubbing between my eyes, hoping it passes quickly. "I understand your predicament, but Nick, my source isn't lying. They saw the red truck cause both Billy's and Jackson's accidents."

"I'll look into it, but in the meantime, no more digging on your own. If someone did cause these accidents and they get word you're dragging up the past and they're at risk of being caught, it could put you in danger."

I hadn't considered that piece. Not that I'm running around town sharing this with anyone. The story I've just sold him is entirely made up. But I do my part by looking worried and eager to follow his directives.

I nod, standing up and making my way to the door when that inner voice reminds me about Jenna. She needs the help more than Billy and Jackson at this point.

I twist back toward him, taking a deep breath.

"There's one more thing my source told me you'd be interested in."

He closes his eyes. "Okay."

"They believe a body was buried out in Ansley in another wooded area, just off the road. County Road A."

He groans. "Alyssa, I say this with all the respect in the world . . . please distance yourself from this source. For your own safety."

Standing here in his house, knowing how he's gone out of his way for me these past weeks, and how obvious it is that he truly is concerned for me, I feel it's time I extend a proper olive branch. I've not exactly been the friendliest to him the past couple years.

"I promise, Nick. Thank you for listening."

He offers me one of those rare smiles that reaches all the way up to his bright blue eyes. "Anytime."

"And thank you for taking my trash down these past two years. I really appreciate it."

His head moves back slightly, giving me the impression I've shocked him in some way, but he quickly recovers. "Whatever you need. I'll always be here."

19

Nine of Wands . . . Reversed

Nick

I PULL MY gray T-shirt over my head and discard it on top of my overflowing laundry pile. This week has been exhausting. I've hardly had time for anything other than sleep, and the state of this room shows it.

My bed was haphazardly made, and it's evident from the rumpled gray mess that's calling my name. For a bachelor, my place is spotless. My family likes to call me OCD. I'm not. I just prefer a clean space to come home to. The organization has everything to do with my sister.

Falling back onto my bed, I grab my black-covered pillow and place it over my face, groaning into the soft material. I should shower. I should eat something. All I wanna do is sleep.

It's unlikely, because my mind will be racing most of the night, analyzing all that Alyssa said and my less-than-diplomatic responses.

The way her face paled before hardening into stone will stick with me.

"Dumbass," I mutter, closing my eyes. In my defense, it's a lot to unpack, but I'm going to attempt to think of anything else.

As soon as she left, I put a call in to the station alerting the guys on duty to the tip about the body. It's likely nothing, but I told her I'd follow up on it, and I'm a man of my word.

My mind wanders with all the possibilities. Was Corinne her source for all of this? I make a mental note to look into the woman, because while I don't know Alyssa that well, I believe that she believes what she was told.

Everything I know about Alyssa Mann came from Garrett. He and I bonded taking out the trash on Sunday evenings. We started up a friendly camaraderie, mostly conversations surrounding sports and his family. The way he would talk about his girls was a clear indicator that he had a life most men would love to have. He'd tell me all the funny shit that occurred the day before, typically involving a very clumsy Alyssa. He'd brag about their artistically gifted daughter, Ava. Through his stories, I feel like I know them.

But really, I don't.

When Garrett died, it rocked me. It typically does when a healthy man is tragically killed. A freak accident could happen to any of us. Life is unfair that way. One minute you can have everything, and the next it's pulled out from under you like a rug missing the gripper.

And now, someone has Alyssa believing it wasn't an accident.

Of everything she said, what really stood out was her linking the Garet and Moore accidents to her own. Is this Corinne woman playing with Alyssa's head? What would the motive be?

I'll do everything in my power to help Alyssa get closure because she deserves that much. Having lost Isla, I can't imagine questions surrounding her death hanging over my head. In her case, we knew what went wrong. Having someone play with Alyssa's mind about Garrett's death pisses me off beyond reason.

You like her.

I sigh heavily, recognizing the truth even when I try to push it aside. I do like her. What's not to like?

But that's not why I'm going to help her. Despite how much work I have ahead of me, I'll do it to give her peace.

I'm just getting comfortable when my phone rings from my jeans pocket. For a moment, I think about just letting it go to voicemail. With my luck, it would be Captain, and I'd catch major shit for ignoring a call from him. Grudgingly, I remove myself from the comfort of my king-sized bed and root around for the buried phone.

When I finally locate it, it's my sister's name lighting up the screen.

"What's wrong?"

It's the first thing I say, because it's after twelve o'clock and she's calling me. Which is highly unusual.

My baby niece wails in the background, putting me on high alert.

"Jaclyn. What the hell is wrong?"

"Nothing's *wrong*, idiot. I've been calling you all day and you haven't returned any of them." She coos at Zoey before returning to our conversation. "Zo woke up. She's teething. Thought I'd give you one more chance to answer before I called the station."

I let out an exasperated breath, running my hand back through my hair. Being a detective, I'm more than adept at remaining calm, but when it comes to my family, all bets are off. I've learned to keep my cool where they're concerned, but at this time of night, it's tough not to be worried. Especially with her husband, Joe, working nights on the force.

"Sorry, Jack. It's been a day."

She sighs. "I figured. How you holding up lately?"

I've avoided her calls for this exact reason. I don't wanna talk about it, and I sure as hell don't want to hear her morose tone. It's so unlike her. She's a bubble of energy that has the ability to bulldoze right over the hardest asshole. Tonight, she sounds sullen and pathetic. I'm sure she's expecting the same from me.

I've buried that shit so deep, there's no way it's coming back to the surface.

You'd think that six years later, I'd be able to handle a simple conversation, if only to assure my little sis that I'm all right. Not when it comes to this. Avoidance has been my coping mechanism.

"I'm fine. I was busy."

It's silent on her end for several seconds—aside from Zoey's cries—but I don't say another word. The next to speak loses, and tonight, I'm in no mood to play this game with her.

"She wouldn't want you to grieve alone, Nick. She'd want you to get back out there."

My eyes close, the pain duller every year, but still there. Still haunting me.

"I wasn't alone. My neighbor was here."

The second I admit that to her, I regret it. Jaclyn West-Olsson is the female cupid, ready to ensure the arrow strikes its target. I'm not even sure she'd take the time to confirm I was truly ensnared before audaciously forcing a union.

"Your elderly neighbor or the single woman?" Her tone makes it clear she's only fishing because she wants to hear me say it. She knows damn well who it was.

"Jesus, Jack, she's not single. She's widowed." She squeals as though I just told her I'm officially off the market and buying a ring. "Slow down, Andretti. We had some business to discuss."

She tsks like that's ridiculous. "What business could you possibly have with her? You're an exceptional neighbor who keeps his side of the yard pristine."

She's not wrong, but I've learned to just get to the point with her, or else I'll be on the phone all night.

"There was an incident at Gloria's involving Alyssa."

"Spill."

There isn't a choice. She'll show up on my front door to demand an answer if I hang up on her. So I fill her in on everything. She's the only person in this world outside the department that I share information with, because I trust her implicitly.

"You should listen to her source and look into things. And then ask her on a date."

My mouth drops open and some strange sound escapes me. Dumbfounded is my current state.

"You're unreal."

She huffs. "I know you, Nick. The second that woman said psychic, you tuned her out. If it doesn't fit in your limited idea of possibility, you don't believe it."

"That's not true."

"It is. And let me tell you, many police forces partner with psychics to solve cold cases."

"How would you know?" I pull the phone away from my ear, checking the time. Twelve fifty. Way past my bedtime. I put the phone on speaker and lay it next to my head.

I wonder if she'd notice if I fell asleep on her.

"Don't you remember mom watching Montel Williams every time Sylvia Browne was a guest?"

"Who?"

"Just look it up and stop being a skeptic." She clicks her tongue, a habit she's had since childhood. "You know everyone is rooting for you to fall in love again, right? Why not the gorgeous neighbor next door?"

My hands knead my temples, a headache brewing. "I can't talk about this, Jack. I need sleep."

I hear her intake of breath and know she wants to argue, but thankfully, she doesn't push.

"Fine Captain Cranky. I'll call you tomorrow."

"Lieutenant Cranky," I correct.

"More like Lieutenant Smartass." She chuckles, sounding more like herself. "Call me if you need anything."

"Will do. Get some sleep. Give Zozo a kiss from her favorite uncle."

"Only uncle. Love you, skippy."

I internally groan at my childhood nickname, which our father called me because when I was young, I walked on my toes. I was so traumatized by the nickname that I learned to not do it, but the name stuck.

The line goes dead, and man, am I thankful for that small miracle.

Jackie could talk all night about whatever you'll indulge her in. She's fifteen years younger than me, but some days it feels like forty.

The shit I see every day ages a man. How can it not?

She's still young and naive. Not that she believes that. At thirty, married and with baby number one, she somehow thinks she's veteran enough to offer advice on everything regarding relationships and life in general. It makes her an epic pain in my ass most days. Tonight, I can't even indulge her like I typically would.

I'm just relieved that my change of topic stopped her from prying into my feelings. This month represents the single worst time of my life.

Pain.

Heartache.

Loss.

Six years ago, Isla died. She was thirty-five years old. A call came over the scanner while I was out in the field that assistance was needed at Knox Harbor Elementary School, where she taught third grade. I was already promoted to Detective Lieutenant, but that wasn't going to stop me from hauling ass to the school. When I got there, my former partner was already on the scene. He tried to distract me while they wheeled out a stretcher, and that's when I knew.

It was her on that gurney.

A ruptured aortic aneurysm.

She didn't even make it to the hospital.

That day changed my life in so many ways. The strength I thought I possessed abandoned me and I collapsed in on myself. I couldn't handle any reminder of her for a long time. Her personal items were dropped off to her mother. The house we owned together was sold. I've always been surrounded by death, but hers, I would never have been prepared for. It took almost a year before I could even visit her grave.

Time hasn't healed my wounds, but it has made it easier to cope. But I have no plans to put myself in the position to feel loss like that again.

Garrett's death made those feelings so raw. I knew what Alyssa was going through only a few feet away, and there was nothing I could do for her.

Her remark tonight about hardly knowing her is true. But something has shifted in the past two weeks and the urge to get to know her increases every time I'm in her presence.

There's just something about her that draws me in. Beauty aside, she's witty and easy to be around. I don't know if our shared grief is any factor, but having someone who gets it without having to discuss the specifics is somehow comforting.

Some deep knowing tells me that having and losing someone like Alyssa would truly kill me, and that's reason enough to keep my distance.

I won't cross a line, but I will keep her safe from whatever motives her source has.

Jackie's comment about departments using psychics comes back to mind and curiosity gets the better of me. I grab my laptop and queue up Google. The search results are mind-blowing. Over ten million results in an instant. I type in *Sylvia Browne cold case files* and a *Newsweek* article jumps out at me. Apparently, Jackie was on to something.

Not that I buy into this stuff. It's impossible.

Right?

Thunder cracks and the house rattles as a storm rages outside. It's supposed to be like this all night as a line of strong storms blows through New England. I shut down my computer and fall back into bed. For most, this would be yet another obstacle in the way of sleep. Not for me. It's just what I need to finally pull me under, chasing away all thoughts of psychics knowing things they shouldn't. But it doesn't stop the dreams of strawberry-blond hair splayed over my pillow, the beautiful woman wrapped in my arms fitting perfectly against me.

+ + +

I'VE BEEN SITTING at my desk for the past two hours, searching through what information I can find on Jackson Moore's accident. It's not typical for me to work on a Saturday, but Captain strongly suggested I be here with him until the Cruz case is closed. It's seven o'clock when I look up from the computer, and all the hours I've spent researching have provided exactly zero signs pointing to foul play.

My mind continues to wander to the events of last night and all that I've learned today about psychic abilities. On my lunch break, I continued my investigation into this phenomenon, and despite my skepticism, there are thousands of accounts that psychic visions have led to cold cases being solved. I'm not about to admit I'm a converted believer, but it does raise some questions.

Jesus, West. Knock it off.

I rub at my temple, trying to stave off an impending headache from staring at this screen for too long.

"West. You're up," Captain yells from the doorway leading to his office.

I lift my chin in confirmation that I heard him and will be there shortly. If there's one thing you don't do, it's keep the captain waiting.

I shut down the ancient desktop, close my notebook containing all the information I found, and make my way to Captain's office.

"Close the door."

Nothing good typically comes after those words, but I'm not nervous. I asked for this meeting.

He's typing away on his own computer, an upgrade from the one I'm forced to use. He lifts one finger into the air, signaling he needs a moment.

I kill the time by taking in the small space that I hope will one day be mine. File cabinets line every gray wall, holding important case files. Many are just waiting to be cracked back open and finally closed for good. Sitting in a display case hanging behind Captain's head is his Medal of Valor, a representation of the man he is.

Fifteen years ago, Captain almost lost his life trying to protect a woman being kidnapped by armed men. His quick thinking and action saved them both, and that medal represents his bravery.

Captain Tyler Grayson is one of the best men I've ever known, and I'm proud to serve under him.

He finishes typing and looks up at me.

"You wanted an audience?"

"Yes, sir. I recently was presented with some information regarding the Garet case."

His eyes narrow as he likely tries to recall the details of that specific file. "You mean the accident the mayor himself made a *pointed* request to close?"

I was wrong.

The captain's tight features were the first sign I was about to get my ass handed to me, but I promised Alyssa I'd attempt to get the case reopened, and I'm not backing down.

"The very one, sir."

He murmurs something unintelligibly, lips forming a thin line. Captain's not a fan of the mayor and his requests. There's no love lost between the two men, and I have to side with Captain. The mayor sticks his nose in cases he has no business messing with. But it's above my pay grade, and I know better than to comment on it.

"What was this tip and who was it from?"

Captain doesn't have time for games. If you want his attention, you get to the point fast.

"I filed a report recently about a break-in that occurred next door to me. The intruder claimed to be Billy Garet."

Captain rubs at his chin. "Now that you mention it, I do remember that. What's this got to do with the tip about his case?"

"The woman who gave the account said the intruder claimed to be Billy Garet, and stranger still, she described Billy to a tee when giving the description of the suspect."

He twists his mouth. "Very strange." He shakes his head but doesn't comment further. He's likely wondering why I'm bothering.

Break-ins are something the local sheriff's office deals with, not the homicide unit.

"I bring that part up because that same woman gave me an additional tip. Her source told her to have the department look into Clementine's the night of both Garet's death and another death, Jackson Moore. They claim the person responsible for both accidents was there both nights."

I fabricate a tad, hoping it'll be enough to get the green light to investigate the tip.

"Did she give you the name of this source?"

"No, sir. She refused."

He chews on his cheek, mulling things over. "Mayor Dunbar asked that we permanently close that case because his family found a suicide note. On top of that, Jackson Moore was the person the family originally blamed. I can't see how dragging up those cases now would do any good."

"With all due respect, sir, with this new information, I think we have enough to reopen both cases. I'd think the families would want to know about this."

He tips his head to the side, giving me a look that would chill most men to their bones.

"You telling me how to do my job, West?"

I straighten my back, sitting up taller. "Course not, sir. I'm only suggesting that I'd be happy to work the cases if the order was given to reopen it."

His stone-cold glare fades away, and he shifts his gaze to a file on his desk, flopping it open and signaling our time is almost up.

"Doubtful, West. The mayor was very adamant that the family wanted closure and closing the case provided that. It's unlikely he'll want to open old wounds."

So much about how this town works doesn't sit well with me, but aside from not keeping Captain waiting, you don't question him either. Knox Harbor politics is beyond his control, as much as he'd like to say otherwise.

Old money holds the power here, and Mayor Dunbar's family has been at the top of that chain since the founding of the town.

"Leave this alone, West. Hear me?"

"Yes, sir." I stand, readying to get back to work when Captain speaks. "There's something else I want to speak with you about."

"Sir?"

He folds his hands on top of his desk and leans forward. "You holding up okay? I know this time of year brings up a lot of . . . demons."

A chill races down my spine and goose bumps pebble across my arms at the turn this conversation has taken.

By demons, he's referencing my penchant for hitting up the local watering hole to shove down my feelings with a half bottle of Jack Daniel's. It almost cost me my job. I quit cold turkey and haven't had a drink in three years.

"I'm fine, sir. It's been six years."

He grunts. "That doesn't mean jack shit and you know it. Time doesn't make the hurt any less painful on the anniversary. I know that better than anyone."

He does. He's lost many in the line of duty throughout the years. Most of them were blood. He comes from a long line of law enforcement and men too brave for their own good.

"I'm fine. Seriously, Cap."

He clears his throat, waving his hand in the air to shoo me off. Captain is as uneasy with emotion as I am, which makes this whole conversation even more perplexing. It goes to show he might be a hard ass, but he cares.

"Good. Now get back to work, West."

I nod, hoping to convey that I appreciate his concern and the fact that he doesn't press. "Thank you, sir."

My hand's on the knob when he calls out. "I almost forgot. Nice work on the tip out in Ansley. They found tracks right where you said. They're digging today."

My chest tightens and my ears buzz. That was the last thing I expected to hear and possibly the only piece of information that would force me to go against Captain's order and dig into the other cases myself.

If a body is found, I have to give serious consideration to everything else Alyssa told me.

Things just got a whole lot more interesting.

20

Nine of Pentacles

IT'S BEEN THREE days since I involved Nick. I wouldn't be surprised at all if the moment I left, Nick got to work investigating Corinne. He hadn't bothered to hide his skepticism of her and her motives.

Today is a day of self-care, which has been high on the priority list. Lucky for me, people are always owing Lanie favors. She cashed in big for the sake of this restoration and was able to arrange a spa day for the two of us. It meant that Nina couldn't join, but she didn't seem the least upset about it.

Nina doesn't get caught up in the girlie frills. You'll rarely see her nails painted, and aside from the highlights she gets every eight months, she doesn't trip over missing a hair appointment like Lanie would. She's miserably married and yet perfectly content the way she is. It pisses Richard off to high hell, which is a huge bonus. She doesn't fit his ideal image for the mayor's wife, which only fuels her resolve to remain uninterested in beauty routines.

Once upon a time, I actually did care. Before Ava was born, I drove into Boston to work for one of the largest advertising firms on the East Coast. My clients were high-end brands that loved to shower me in gifts. Now, I'm a widow living off my dead husband's life insurance, barely getting dressed on the daily.

No more.

Lanie and I walk into Luxe Lavou, an upscale salon and spa in the heart of Knox Harbor. It opened two years ago and has a wait list months in advance. Whatever Lanie did for the owner must've been huge. I'd ask, but some things are better unknown where Lanie is concerned.

"Ladies, welcome," a tall brunette coos, coming out from behind a large mahogany counter to meet us. She's wearing a black smock over black leggings, and her hair is twisted into a fancy knot at the base of her neck.

"Thank you, Katrina."

The woman bows her head to Lanie, grabbing two menus from the top of the bar.

A bulky, medium-height man, wearing a Yankees hat, walks into the salon, heading directly to the desk. His biceps are so built, his veins protrude.

"Hi, Marcus."

The man looks up, offering a wicked grin to Lanie. There's something menacing there—a hidden secret only they share—and I'm not sure I want to know it.

"Lanie. Glad to see you took me up on my offer." He turns to Katrina. "Make sure they receive the best."

"Thank you, Marcus. We appreciate the hospitality."

"We have a private room ready for you to relax and unwind while our staff prepares your treatments."

The woman pulls my attention to her, momentarily distracting me from my suspicious thoughts surrounding Marcus. I shake off the unease and try to focus.

Katrina takes a step toward the back, looking over her shoulder to ensure we're following. "First, allow us to get you into something more comfortable."

Lanie slides toward me, pulling my arm under hers and giving it a good squeeze. My excitement mounts, and I'm more than ready to begin the pampering I've been promised.

We follow her through a door into a hall where the natural light filtering into the lobby is snuffed out. Chandeliers adorn the ceiling, giving off a warm glow that's just bright enough to illuminate the walkway.

"There are robes waiting for you," she says, arms rising out to the side to point at two doors opposite each other. "You may change and leave your belongings in one of the lockers. Your resting room is this door here." She motions with both hands to the room three doors down. "Would you like something to drink? Water? Mimosa?"

"Wa—"

"Mimosa," Lanie cuts in, drowning out my request.

The girl has never turned down a mimosa and I'm not at all surprised that today is no different.

The woman looks to me with raised brows.

"I'll have a mimosa as well. Thank you."

She nods, bowing slightly before taking her leave.

"Meet you in the room in five," Lanie calls over her shoulder as she pushes through her door.

I take my time, examining the large changing room. A double vanity is stocked with all the products a girl could ever need. Shampoo, conditioner, lotions . . . you name it, it's there. A walk-in shower lines the back wall, and there's a door leading to a private toilet. Along the opposite wall from the private commode is a row of lockers with a long leather bench situated underneath.

The lockers are all currently open, so I take the middle one, stuffing my clothes and purse inside. I'm ready for that mimosa and relaxation, which reminds me that it's been more than five minutes, and Lanie is likely wondering if I've bailed.

I chuckle just thinking about how ardently I opposed coming here. What was I thinking? This place is magic, and I haven't even had one treatment.

Shaking my head, I shut the locker door and blink at the figure standing beside me.

"Holy Mary. Where did you come from?"

A young woman, mid-twenties if I had to guess, with large sapphire eyes and a short blond bob, is staring at me in awe.

"You can see me." It's not a question. She claps like a kid on Christmas morning, excited to receive her top wish-list item.

Another freaking spirit.

With my hand to my heart, I close my eyes and breathe.

"Don't sneak up on people like that. You about gave me a heart attack."

"But you can see me." Her excitement is growing by the minute. "You don't know how long I've been trying to contact my sister. I need your help."

My head shakes and I lift my hands to stop her from continuing. "No. No. No. I'm here to escape ghosts, not work for them. This is my pamper day. Please go away."

Her hands rise to a praying position and her face falls. "Help me."

I click the lock and grab the key, turning away and rushing from the room. When I make it to the hallway, Lanie is leaning up against the wall, pretending to look at a watch she's not wearing.

"Took you long enough," she snips. "I about stormed the room to drag you out."

I turn back toward the changing room, expecting to see the ghost girl, but she's not there.

Thank god.

Hopefully she got the message and skedaddled.

"What's wrong?" Lanie searches my face, eyes narrowed and lips pursed.

"Just need that mimosa," I say, hoping the reminder of alcohol is enough to distract my boozy friend.

It works.

A smile spreads across her face and she nods, wiggling her eyebrows. "Let's go."

She pulls me toward the resting room, and I must admit, this place gets more fabulous with every room.

"Wow," I breathe out.

"Right? I asked them to give us a full thirty minutes, minimum, in here. It's so relaxing."

She heads toward one of the cream chaise longue chairs. The small table next to each has a mimosa waiting for us, and the first thing Lanie does is take a sip, moaning around the effervescent drink.

I'm too caught up in the details of the room. It's a scene right out of a Hallmark movie. Dimmed lights, cozy blankets, a fire blazing . . . serenity.

I don't waste time, curling up and pulling the plush, heated blanket over me, sighing in contentment. "This is wonderful, Lanie. Thank you."

She sighs. "I'm happy to have an excuse to cash in on this."

We talk in hushed tones, both trying to maintain the peacefulness of the moment. Lanie fills me in on our schedule for the day, and I don't understand what half of it means.

"We start out with a ninety-minute full-body relaxation massage. I've already asked them not to talk."

"I'll probably fall asleep," I admit.

"That's the point of relaxation, Ally."

I shrug. Not going to fight her on that. "What's next?"

"A vitamin C anti-aging facial. I've already instructed them to give you any add-on treatment you need based on your skin. Then salt glow body scrub and Vichy shower, and then we'll break for lunch."

"Do we leave?"

She shakes her head. "No, they bring it in. We have our choice of a few options. They'll likely give you the menu when you're back in here between treatments."

"This is pretty cool," I admit, and she grins.

"That's just the start. After lunch, we have collagen-infused whirlpool pedicures, manicures, hair treatments, haircuts and styling, and we finish the day with makeup application."

Holy hell, she really went all out.

"Alyssa?" A tall raven-haired beauty calls from the doorway. "Are you ready to begin?"

I've never been more ready.

+ + +

THE FIRST HALF of the day breezed by. I'm relaxed, rejuvenated, and ready to see what they're able to do with this hair. I twirl a piece around my finger, inspecting the ends.

They have their work cut out for them.

I'm seated in a massage chair with a pink-haired woman at my feet, scrubbing at a callus I didn't even realize I had.

"When was the last time you had a pedicure?" Lanie asks from the chair next to mine.

I shrug. "I don't know."

"It shows," she says, scrunching her nose. "The poor girl's gonna have back problems."

To the pedicurist's credit, she doesn't comment either way, remaining focused with a stony expression.

A prickling sensation sweeps through me the longer I stare at the woman. There's something detached and sad about her.

"There were things left unsaid that she wishes she would've

told me." The ghost is back, but I refuse to allow her words to tug at my heartstrings.

Why do spirits suddenly think it all right to ambush me in the middle of my day? Furthermore, since when do I see ghosts that I'm not connected to in some way? I loose a breath, not sure how this works. Once she makes contact with me, does it mean she's also attached to me?

No, thank you. I already have a ghost problem. I'm not looking to add another to the roster.

I make a mental note to call Corinne as soon as I leave to uncover the cause of this unwelcome phenomenon.

"If you just relay my message, I *will* go away."

I ignore her, turning my head to Lanie. "What color did you go with?"

"I already showed you. Pink Flamenco." She points toward the bottle of OPI polish sitting next to her pedicurist.

"Please," the spirit begs, annoying as ever. "Can't you see she's hurting?"

I chew on my bottom lip, realizing I had noticed that. *But what can I do?*

Having heard my internal thoughts, the girl storms forward with her request, her eyes lighting up.

"You can relay things to her that only she and I know."

The woman working on my feet, glances up at me, but her expression is still lifeless.

Damn it.

"Is there any way I could choose a different color? I'm not loving my original choice," I lie, needing a reason to get away from the others.

If there's one thing I've learned since acquiring this curse, it's that others don't need to be made aware of it. People don't appreciate things they can't understand.

"Sure. You can slide these on," she says, positioning a pair of disposable slippers for me to slide my feet into.

I'm walking toward the next room where the wall of polish is located and realize the woman isn't following me.

"Would you mind helping me?" I ask my pedicurist, earning a pinched look from Lanie. "I'm so indecisive today."

The woman nods, stands, and makes her way toward me. When we're out of earshot, I turn to the ghost girl, ready for her to speak her request. She doesn't waste time, diving right in.

"Please remind Tasha that she promised me not to mope. This new brooding attitude is for the birds. She knew I was dying, and we lived those last few months in a way I hadn't ever dreamed. She's supposed to be hunting. Carpe all day."

I pull a face. "Hunting what? And do you mean carpe diem?"

"What?" Tasha asks, assuming I'm talking to her.

"It's an inside joke. She'll get it," the ghost explains. "Make her believe I'm here."

"Tasha," I say, and she looks over at me with narrowed eyes.

She's not wearing a name tag and she never gave me her name. I'm sure she is wondering how I know it. Especially since I was informed that they use aliases here. There were too many employees with the same name, and it became a scheduling nightmare.

"I have someone named . . ." I glance at the girl.

"Savanna."

Meeting Tasha's eyes, I continue, "Savanna here with us. She wants you to be hunting?"

Her breath hitches and she stumbles backward. "W-what did you say?"

I rush on. "You're supposed to stop moping and get to hunting. Carpe all day."

She blinks several times as tears well in her eyes. "Savanna?"

she whispers into the air, searching the area for her invisible sister. The upside is she appears to believe me.

"You can't see her, but I can," I explain. "She looks happy. Healthy."

I'm not sure why I feel the need to stress this. Maybe because it's something I'd want to know. Especially if I lost someone to illness, which is what Savanna heavily implied.

"Tell her I'm hanging with Grandpa Jerry." She smiles, looking at Tasha with fondness.

"She wants you to know she's with Grandpa Jerry."

Tasha bobs her head several times but remains silent.

"Explain to her that I can hear anything she wants to say," Savanna instructs. "That should do the trick, and I'll be on my way."

I relay the message and Tasha swallows. "She's really here?"

"Yes, and no offense to you or your sister, but I'd like to get back to my pamper day. Can you say what you need to say, so she can go to the light?"

She sucks her top lip into her mouth, shoulders slumping. "Is that what she wants? To leave?"

"Yes." It's Savanna who speaks, but Tasha doesn't hear.

I nod in confirmation and the pink-haired girl sighs heavily, eyes closing.

"I slept with Ryker the Rake two years ago. I regret it every day."

Savanna gasps, hands flying to cover her mouth. "She didn't. Good lort."

"She says good lort."

Tasha snorts, eyes lifting skyward. "Please tell her to lose that word in the afterlife."

The ghost girl chuckles, moving to her sister's side. "Noted."

Tasha's expression morphs from playful to sad. I swallow,

readying myself for whatever emotional goodbye is to come. I've turned into a giant sap these days.

She takes a deep breath and looks down at her feet. "Tell her she was the best sister and that I wish it had been me who got leukemia."

Savanna's head shakes back and forth, eyes wide in something resembling horror. "Not a chance. She needs to finish that song and head to Nashville. If she doesn't, I'll find a way back to earth to haunt her ass."

This ghost isn't too bad. If she wasn't determined to head toward her next chapter, I wouldn't mind her sticking around. I'd take her over Billy any day.

"Savanna says to finish the song and go to Nashville or else she'll haunt you."

Tasha's entire face lights up and a smile I didn't think she was capable of appears. "On it."

The relief that washes over Savanna is tangible. The air feels lighter, and I'm able to breathe easier.

"Thank you," Savanna says, offering me one last smile before she blips out of existence.

"She's gone," I tell Tasha, who continues to smile as if this brief interaction has changed her life.

It probably has. Goodbyes aren't given to everyone.

We head back into the room and I take my seat next to Lanie, offering her a tight-lipped smile as I level Tasha with a look that threatens maiming if she speaks a word of what just happened, and she nods, signaling she got the hint.

She jumps back into her job, talking animatedly to the other pedicurist. The entire vibe of the room has shifted. Tasha's demeanor is light and carefree, and the other woman appears taken aback by the change but rolls with it. I might've complained about having my day interrupted by Savanna, but in truth, it feels good to help.

I feel lighter too.

Speaking with ghosts no longer feels like a curse. Not after seeing what it can do for others.

I've been thinking that I need to get back out there and find something to fill my time. I can't live off Garrett's life insurance forever, and I wouldn't want to. I need purpose in my life. That thing that lights me up inside.

Maybe I could find a way to use my gift of communicating with the dead?

That's a contemplation for another day.

21

Eight of Cups . . . Reversed

"I GOTTA SAY, you don't look horrible," Billy muses. "You might actually be considered pretty now."

"You're still annoying," I singsong, unwilling to allow Billy to get to me anymore.

I don't care what his opinion of me is. I feel better than ever. Forty feels like a fresh start and I'm about to make this next decade the best one yet.

"Love that yellow sweater, and those jeans actually complement your figure. Who dressed you? Was it Lanie?" He continues to attempt to grate on my last nerve, pretending he cares about my outfit. It's just another way for him to insult me, but it doesn't work.

Not today, jackass.

"You're all set to march next door and declare your love to Detective Dreamboat."

He bats his lashes and puckers his lips, making kissing noises, which manages to flip my switch and pull the desired ire from me.

The glare I shoot in his direction has zero effect on the irksome ghost. If anything, my reaction to that comment has him beyond thrilled with himself.

"Why are you glaring into space?" Corinne asks as she types away on the computer.

She's been browsing the website Crime Solvers, an amateur sleuth site where the participants solve crimes and present their cases to local authorities. Corinne thinks it could help us build a case to pitch to Nick.

I think she's wasting her time.

These online sleuths fastidiously study recent crimes, uncovering things based on a plethora of evidence. Billy's case has been closed for almost two years. We've got little to nothing.

"Let's go over this again," I address Billy, ignoring Corinne's earlier question. "What can you remember?"

He bites down on his tongue, squinting his eyes in concentration. After a few minutes, a rush of air expels from his lungs. "Not a damn thing."

My hands run roughly down my face.

"Don't smear your makeup," Lanie scolds, batting my hands away. "Now you've gone and done it. I'm going to have to fix your right eye before you head to Nick's."

"I'm not going to Nick's until I'm thoroughly prepared."

Lanie's head lolls back on her shoulders. "We've been over this. You have to. Besides, you look smoking hot. It's the perfect night. You might even get a date out of it."

Lanie and her matchmaking know no bounds.

"Why is everyone talking about declarations of love and dates? I'm not in the market for any of that."

"Who said anything about love? I was simply suggesting a good romp."

"Who even says 'romp'?"

"Leave her alone, Lane. She's not trying to seduce him," Nina chastises.

Lanie smacks her lips together. "Maybe she should."

I shake my head and close my eyes to ward off a headache. "There will be no seduction. Ever. I'm not interested in men."

Billy's eyes widen, and a mischievous grin spreads across his smarmy face. "You switched teams? That could go a long way in changing my opinion of you."

"You're a pig," I snap, crossing my arms over my chest. "I'm not interested in *anyone*. I'm perfectly content being single."

"I really wish I could hear what he says," Corinne muses, still searching the sleuth sites. "Seems to have a knack for getting a rise out of you."

"He's a menace." I gnash my teeth together, giving myself an internal pep talk to woosah and ignore them all.

It's no use; Lanie won't be deterred easily.

"Regardless, you need to speed up the process of getting these ghosts gone. It won't happen with you sitting on your hands over here."

"She's not ready. Let's move on."

I nod, offering my most brilliant smile to my supportive bestie. "Thank you, Nina."

She turns on me quickly. "I didn't say I agreed with you." She levels me with a look that warns that I won't like what she's about to say. "All the talk of dates aside, you should be having this conversation with him. Tonight." I make a face, somewhere between a grimace and glower. "Don't look at me like that," she scolds. "If it were Garrett stuck on earth, needing someone's help, would you want them to do differently?"

I grind my teeth, hating it when Nina gets all wise. Next, she's going to be spouting off that it's my moral obligation to assist the dead.

"The sooner we uncover something of use, the sooner we can usher Billy off to hell," Lanie says, earning a wide smile from me.

Billy huffs an annoyed laugh, launching into a diatribe on the subject of hell and his insistence he won't be heading anywhere but north.

"Is he almost done with his babbling?" Jackson groans.

"Doubtful." I glance over Corinne's shoulder. "Anything of use?"

She taps her fingers on the table, leaning closer to the monitor. "Did the truck happen to hit him at all?"

I glance over to Billy in question. His eyelids lower and his tongue sticks out as he thinks. The moment he lands on something useful is obvious with the gloating grin that spreads over his face. "Yeah. His fender hit my front driver side when he sideswiped me."

My eyes go wide in disbelief. "His?"

He blinks, mouth dropping open. He's coming to the same conclusion as me. There are things he's forgotten. "I guess I got a quick glimpse of the driver. It was a man."

"This information is critical, Billy. What else are you forgetting?"

His arms fly up. "I didn't even realize I knew that. I'm not purposefully keeping secrets, you dementor."

I don't miss his reference to the soul-sucking demons from *Harry Potter*. Ava was obsessed with that franchise, so I'm very familiar. Lifting my hands into a meditative position, I close my eyes and focus on deep breathing. I will not allow this unalive asshole to get to me anymore.

When I'm well and calm, I relay the information to Corinne, and she dives back into her research. Ten minutes later, she yells, "Bingo."

"What did you find?" I say, crowding over her to get a look.

"Personal space." She swats at the air, but I don't back away. "There is likely paint transfer, from which a forensic investigator should be capable of, at the very least, identifying the make of the vehicle." I nod, allowing her to continue. "Chances are, whoever caused the accident is local. We rarely get out-of-towners in Knox Harbor."

"Which means it should be fairly easy to narrow down the suspects. Especially knowing the driver was male."

"Correct." Her words garner hoots from Lanie and Nina.

"Good. Okay . . . Billy, anything else?" I call over my shoulder, refusing to look in his direction.

"No. I was too busy clutching the wheel, trying not to die."

I roll my eyes at his annoying sarcasm. "I sometimes wonder why I even try with you."

"You want me gone."

Truer words have never been spoken.

"How do I explain this sudden tip from my anonymous source without Nick thinking I'm up to no good?"

"Oh, you're up to no good, but only where he's concerned. Everybody knows you're tripping over yourself to bang the guy."

I growl at Billy, drawing the attention of the three women in the room.

"I won't even ask," Lanie says, lifting her eyebrows into her hairline.

"Seriously, girls. Help me figure this out."

Nina taps her chin, Lanie bites her bottom lip, and Corinne picks at her long, black-painted fingernails. For a moment, I think they're going to leave me hanging.

Lanie clears her throat. "I call to order the first official meeting of the Gin and Tarot Club. Today's mystery . . . the Sideswiper of Spooky Hollow."

I choke, glancing around to find Nina excessively blinking and Corinne's left eyebrow peaked into a perfect point, her nose crinkled and lips pursed.

"The what club?"

She motions around to our glasses, each filled with gin. With the heaviness surrounding us, we've all graduated from wine to the stronger alcohol. Corinne gets all the credit for the newly acquired taste of Tanqueray. Unlike hers, mine needs a mixer. Tonight, it's tonic in my glass.

"With your new abilities, Corinne's use of the internet and tarot talents, Nina's access to the mayor, and my . . . well . . . drinking skills, we have an opportunity to make a difference in people's—and ghost's—lives. We can't squander that."

"I'm not following," Nina says, looking around the room for anyone to come to her aid.

"Of course you aren't." Lanie rolls her eyes. "We should start a club that utilizes these assets to solve crimes."

"Gin is an asset?" I attempt to tamp down my amusement.

Lanie doesn't need any encouragement. She's seconds away from going all Girl Scout leader on us. Give her any power and she'll run with it.

"Come on, guys. Admit it, it's a good idea."

We all look at one another. I'm waiting for someone else to step up to stomp out her flame.

No such luck.

Corinne's eyes twinkle, and I know we've lost her to Lanie's dark side. She's sold. Hook. Line. Sinker.

"Nina . . . ?" I draw out her name, hoping she'll be the voice of reason like she typically is.

She shrugs.

Damn. Lanie got to her too.

I sigh, knowing when to throw in the towel. I've been overruled. "What exactly is the goal of this club?"

Lanie's face lights up when she realizes that she got the green light. She claps her hands together and leans in as though we're about to make a circle and sing kumbaya.

"Keep it simple. We enlist the help of the spirits on hand and inspect the details of crimes to solve them."

"We utilize our resources to gather evidence and make arrests when necessary," Nina suggests, sounding sure about whatever she's been working out in her head.

"Yes," Lanie jumps in. "Every meeting, Corinne will read her cards pertaining to our mission of the night."

They had me hooked until that last part.

"This is an ongoing club? As in, once we find a way to send Billy and Jackson on, we're going to actually open ourselves for more ghosts?"

Ollie scared the bejesus out of me. He turned out to not be so bad, but what if the next one is? Will I never feel safe in my own home again?

"I see the panic, and I'll remind you that there are ways to protect yourself, Alyssa. We'll work on it with the help of my mom." Corinne's eyes hold mine, and I see that she fully intends to keep her word on this.

I take a deep breath. "What is the mission tonight?"

"Corinne, take notes," Lanie instructs. "Alyssa, call to the room Jackson Moore and Billy Garet."

My lips smack together. "Will we always treat this club like an official hearing?"

She narrows her eyes at me, pulling an irritated face. I don't say another word, crossing my arms over my chest and getting comfortable. This is Lanie's show.

"Tonight, we've learned that Billy was run off the road by a man." She turns toward me. "Could you please ask him if he can be sure what the make and color of the vehicle driven by the man was? Also, can he recall if the driver stopped after causing the accident?"

"He can hear you, you know."

She shrugs. "I'm only trying to include you in this task. Don't want you to feel worthless."

I roll my eyes. "News flash—I'm the one who can actually hear the spirits."

It's Corinne who grumbles at that, still not thrilled that she can't communicate with them too.

"It was a red Ford truck. F-250. It was big. I can't be sure if he stopped, but I don't think he did. I vaguely remember as my car veered off the brim, the truck disappeared around the curve. He left the scene. I'm almost positive, but not one hundred percent."

I relay that information to the group. Corinne jots everything down, while Lanie and Nina stare into space.

"Jackson, you're up," I call out, assuming his debriefing is about to begin.

"It was the same asshole who killed me," he bites out through his teeth, hands balling into fists in front of his chest, looking ready to fight. "Except there were three people involved with my accident."

"Three? This is the first I'm hearing of this."

"Yeah, well, things aren't exactly clear, toots. It's taken me a while to work it out."

"Just . . . keep going." I rub at my forehead, trying not to lose my cool.

I sympathize with the not-remembering part, considering I've had my own blockages, but the longer it takes to work this all out, the longer I have to be stuck in this perpetual state of Billyxiety.

"There was someone driving. Never got a look at who it was. Coulda been female for all I know. But there were two goons in the bed of the truck. One looked like a white Gumby. Super tall and oddly thin for a man. The other was built like a brick shithouse. Not quite as big as me, but bulky. And bald."

Now we're getting somewhere. These descriptions are *gold*!

I share the details with the group and the girls get a bit giddy over the descriptions.

"With those specifics, it shouldn't be hard to ID our guys," Corinne says, turning back toward the computer and typing faster than I thought possible. "But what did he say happened?"

I glance at Jackson, who's currently picking at something on Billy's hoodie. Billy slaps his hand away and Jackson lunges forward, baring his teeth. Billy jerks back with a very unmanly whimper.

"You're dead, Billy. You shouldn't be such a coward." I smother my smile under my fist.

He ignores me.

"Can you tell me what happened? What caused your accident?"

"Yeah. The douche canoes threw a branch out the back of the truck into the road."

"A branch? Did they see you?"

He compresses his lips. "I was on a Harley. The lights and purr of the motor would've made it impossible for them not to."

"What's this about a branch?" Lanie asks, eyes darting toward the corner where the guys are situated.

"Those men threw a branch onto the road right in front of him."

Corinne's finger flies up into the air. "Another great detail. The online report of Jackson's accident doesn't mention a branch. Which is highly suspicious."

"Why is that suspicious?"

"If they didn't name that a possible cause of the accident, it's because it wasn't there. The men must've moved it."

"Sons of bitches," Jackson grumbles.

"Holy shit, guys." Nina's dramatic tone draws all our attention toward her. Her eyes are on her phone. "They found that girl, Jenna Cruz's body. It hasn't been released to the public yet, so keep that between us."

"How do you know?" Lanie questions, leaning toward Nina's phone to try to get a look at the screen.

"Richard texted he wouldn't be home tonight because he needs to prepare damage control to keep people from freaking out."

That's all I needed to hear to feel confident that Nick West won't doubt me anymore.

More importantly, Jenna can finally rest in peace. If her body was found, that hopefully means she's well on her way to the afterlife and no longer seeking revenge against the people who did this to her.

Tingles race through me and goose bumps rise to the surface of my arms. Despite my earlier reservations, there might be something to this Gin and Tarot Club. If my gift can help people, I shouldn't turn my back on that. It's important work and it's not the first time I've thought about using it for good.

Not only do I feel empowered, but I also feel I might've found my purpose.

22

Four of Swords . . . Reversed

Nick

I PULL MY car into the gravel parking lot of Clementine's. For years, this bar was my unhealthy escape—the place I'd spend hours working to numb the pain. I'd end my shift, head straight here, and not leave until last call.

After my three years of sobriety, the place hasn't changed one bit. The sun set hours ago, but I know that the blue aluminum siding needs to be replaced. It's so dull it looks more gray than blue. The letter *O* on the *Open* sign doesn't illuminate, and the rest of the word blinks rapidly, likely from a weak power source. The only two windows along the front have been boarded up for ages, making it look more like a biker bar than a town institution.

Whether it's day or night, the place is a black hole, void of light. The walls are paneled in cherry throughout, which doesn't help the lighting situation. Not that it matters. Most people who spend any amount of time at Clementine's aren't there for the ambiance.

They're there to forget.

Every local regular has their own sordid story and reason for needing escape. If you're there long enough, you'll learn many of them the further into the bottle they get. I'd still be among those regulars if not for Shirley Clementine, the owner.

She gave me a verbal slap upside the head and told me to get my shit together. She might own a bar, but the woman hasn't had a drop of alcohol in forty years. She said she watched so many others ruin their lives on booze that she put her whiskey on the shelf and never looked back. When she told me I should do the same, I listened. One does not argue with Shirley's logic.

Now, I don't even come here for the food.

Tonight, I don't have a choice.

The body that Alyssa spoke about was Jenna Cruz's. She was found right where Alyssa said she would be. I have so many questions about the validity of this supposed psychic, but I have to move on the information she gave me, despite Captain's warnings.

The hard part is going to be pretending I don't know anything. I have a personal history with Jenna. She was a good girl. Didn't deserve what happened to her.

The dickhead mayor insisted we keep a lid on the findings until his team is able to pull together a PR strategy.

"Nick," Amanda calls from the bar. "Long time no see. How ya been?"

She's worked here for the past ten years and has had to deal with my drunk ass on more occasions than I'm proud of.

"Amanda," I say, lifting my chin as I move toward the lacquered bar top. "Things are good. Placed an order."

"Double cheeseburger with extra pickles and a side of fries?"

I grin. "That's it."

It's what I ordered damn near daily when I used to frequent the joint. It's the only edible thing in the place, as far as I'm concerned.

"Should be right up," she says, turning toward the wall of liquor and pulling a bottle of bourbon from the shelf. Her yellow

Clementine's T-shirt rides up her body, revealing skin and a pink thong peeking out from the top of her blue jeans. I turn my gaze away quickly, only to find several of the other patrons staring like the perverts they are. I shoot a look that warns them to knock it off, and it's met with grunts and mumbled curses, but they all go back to what they were doing.

I wasn't sure what to expect when I walked in here tonight. My fear was that I'd be itching for one drink. One would turn to two, and before I knew it, I'd be drunk off my ass with no way to get home.

Like it used to be.

It was always Amanda or Jenna that would help my bombed ass to their car and go out of their way to drop me at home.

Pathetic.

That need for a drink is absent. There's not a part of me that wants that life again. I'm here to play chicken with my job by looking into Alyssa's other tip. Glancing around the bar, the one person I hoped to see is absent.

Might not be getting anywhere tonight with my investigation.

"How's it been?" I call to Amanda.

When she turns to face me, I see the tears welling in her eyes.

"Have you heard anything about Jenna? We're all really worried."

I swallow down the lump forming at the base of my throat, putting on my best face of stone.

"Nothin'. Sorry."

"It doesn't make sense, Nick. She just up and left. No call or nothin' to Shirley. The woman's distraught." She shakes her head. "At first, I didn't question it. She was always talkin' about skippin' town. Figured she finally did it and we'd hear from her once she got settled."

"I'm sure everyone wants answers," I say, trying to decide how to change the subject, but Amanda plows ahead.

"As soon as we saw her car on the news, we knew somethin' ain't right."

I lick my bottom lip, trying to hold in my own emotions. Shirley has to be beside herself with worry. She was like a mother to the girl. "How's the place holding up?"

She huffs. "We're managing, but she left us in a bind for sure. We had to hire some young college girl who ain't worth shit." She grabs a frosted mug and pulls the tap handle, allowing Busch Light to flow into the glass. "Jenna didn't take a freakin' thing with her." She shakes her head, mumbling under her breath. "You ask me, something ain't right."

"Tim, this is your last one. I'm cutting you off after," Amanda calls down the bar to a local, who's obviously overstayed his welcome.

She slides the mug down the bar, and he catches it without looking. A sure sign he spends far too much time in this place.

Amanda goes about pouring two fingers into a glass and slides that one down toward Butch Sutter, a white-haired man in his early sixties. He looks up and catches my eye, lifting the glass into the air. "Cheers, sons of bitches."

My head shakes at the crass remark, recalling the days I'd have been sitting right beside him, lifting my own glass.

Thank god for Shirley's intervention.

"Some things never change, huh?" Amanda drawls, passing the bag of food across the bar to me.

"And some things do."

She offers a crooked smile, knowing I'm referencing my own sobriety.

"You're different, Nick. Always have been."

"I'm not so sure about that," I say, pulling my wallet from my back pocket. "But I appreciate that you think so."

Her smile falls and she toys with the soda hose. "You just needed to grieve."

My back straightens and I clear my throat, not wanting to go down that road. It's too raw, considering the time of year. Amanda doesn't seem to notice.

"That'll be five fifty," she says, grabbing an Old Mill Light from the cooler and passing it to Charlie Dunbar.

Charlie is the mayor's black sheep son, who spends his father's money on cheap beer and prostitutes, if the rumors are to be believed. I don't care to know. Not my jurisdiction.

"That's your last one too, Charlie."

He mumbles something unintelligible, signaling he's well past drunk.

"Sure he should even have that one?" I ask, leaning over the bar and handing Amanda a ten.

She smirks. "Should be, but he actually has a ride home from daddy tonight." She shrugs. "I'm gonna let Charlie be *his* problem."

I chuckle. "Good luck with that."

She widens her eyes in an expression that says *I need all the good luck I can get* before she turns toward the cash register.

"Keep the change," I say to her back, and she lifts her hand in thanks.

I glance at Charlie once, hoping to convey he'd better not give Amanda any trouble. He's notorious for causing issues. Mayor Dunbar has gotten good at covering up for him, so he doesn't face public backlash for not getting Charlie the help that he needs. He looks away quickly, avoiding my glare.

Piece of shit coward.

He has the world at his fingertips, yet he wastes away in this place, too lazy to get a job and contribute to society. Bravery and purpose are two things his dad can't buy him.

I'm halfway to the door when Shirley calls my name from the back hallway that leads to the coolers and kegs.

"Shirley. Didn't think you were here tonight."

Shirley is far too old to still be working the bar, but she stops by on a daily basis to check in on things. She's a micromanager even pushing eighty, and it drives the bartenders nuts. Her thick bifocals signal that she's half-blind and has no business driving, but until she manages to kill herself or someone else, I guess the local DMV will keep giving her a license.

"Good to see ya, Nicky. What's new at the station?"

"I'm a steel trap, Shirley. I'll never tell."

It's something she always asks, and my reply is always the same, except this time, it's not playful banter on her part. It's desperation.

"Well . . . glad to hear you guys caught that murdering hitchhiker. The people were on edge. This place was a ghost town."

"Wasn't my case, but I'll pass on the thanks."

She blows out a breath. "Now if you could only figure out what happened to Jenna."

My eyes avoid the five-foot-nothing woman because she's got a seasoned bullshit meter. "You think the hitchhiker had something to do with it?"

She nods and with that simple move, tingles work their way down my spine. The last thing I wanted when I entered this shithole tonight was to get bombarded with questions about Jenna. I should've known, but it's not why I'm here.

"Did something happen? Anything that would lead you to believe it's more than her simply wanting to get out of here?" I ask, hoping to put a list of suspects together.

"Nothing concrete." She shakes her head, looking sullen. "She was actin' strange a couple days leading up to the night she didn't show for her shift, but I couldn't get her to talk to me. You know Jenna. She listens to everyone else's problems but refuses to talk about her own." She glances down at her feet, wringing her hands together. "She wouldn't have just not shown up. She knew how much I depended on her. She was like family, Nicky."

I nod, knowing she speaks the truth. There isn't much that makes sense about Jenna's death. She was well liked among the patrons of Clementine's.

"Keep your chin up."

It's such a stupid thing to say, knowing what she's about to learn any minute now. It will rock her world. It'll change the dynamics of Clementine's for sure.

She smiles up at me with her crooked, yellowed teeth.

"I actually came in here tonight to see you," I admit. "Need your confidentiality about what I'm about to share with you."

Her face lights up. This is the first—and only—time I've ever spoken to Shirley about a case. Even in my drunken stupor, I knew better.

"I'm looking into the death of Billy Garet. Remember him?"

She bobs her head, puckering her chapped lips. "Sure. I'm in a book club with his momma. She's still torn up about it. Wants answers, like all of us would."

My eyes narrow in on the diminutive woman, thinking back on my conversation with Captain. Her words contradict the mayor's. Not that I can share that information with her.

"What was that look for?"

"What look?" I say, trying to deflect.

She places both hands on her hips, leveling me with a closed-mouth frown. "Nick West, I might have thick glasses, but that doesn't mean I can't see."

Doesn't it, though?

"I was just thinking about the case. Wasn't Billy here that night?"

Her face turns grim. "He was. Jenna and Amanda said he didn't leave the pool table all night."

I consider what I know about his case and this note that implied he took his own life.

"Did either of them mention if he acted strange?"

She shakes her head. "Not that I can recall, but you can ask Amanda." She waves a wrinkled hand in the air. "I'm outta here. Good to see ya, Nicky."

"Wait." My hand snaps out, landing on Shirley's frail shoulder. "Before you go, I have a huge favor to ask." Her head tilts to the side, waiting for the ask. "Could you pull the footage from the night of Billy Garet's death and also the night of Jackson Moore's? I'll call tomorrow with the exact dates."

"Now, why would you need that, Nicky?"

"You're just gonna have to take my word that it's important and you'd be helping out the families of both men."

She smashes her lips together, apparently not satiated. "Fine. Get me the details and I'll see what I can do."

"Thank you, Shirley." She waves her hand in the air as she turns and makes her way back toward the kitchen, grumbling the whole way about how everyone always wants something from her.

I shouldn't press my luck poking around here for more information on Billy. I've already asked a lot of Shirley, and the mayor claims the family wanted the case closed. If I were smart, I'd obey Captain's direct order.

Apparently, I'm not.

My feet are carrying me back toward the bar before I can think twice about it.

"What's up, Nick? Food okay?"

"Food's fine, Amanda. I have a question for you. Got a minute?"

She sweeps her eyes over the bar. Every man in the joint is either involved in conversation or watching the television.

"I have a couple minutes."

I jerk my head toward a vacant high top in the corner, and her eyes narrow. She follows reluctantly, probably running through all the reasons I might wanna talk to her in private.

"I have a quick question for you, but I need it to stay between us. Okay?"

She bobs her head, worrying at her bottom lip.

"The night of Billy Garet's death, was he acting out of character? Doing anything that seemed off to you?"

She purses her lips, appearing to think back on that night.

"Billy didn't come in much. Not sure I'd know if anything was off per se."

"What was his demeanor like?"

She shrugs. "He was laughing and having a good time with Marcus."

"Marcus?"

"Marcus Wells. They were running the table all night. Seemed to be having a great time."

"Not the sort of behavior that would lead a person to run themselves off the road and into a tree."

Her eyes widen. "He wasn't drunk, Nick. I wouldn't have let him drive out of here if he was."

"I'm not implying that," I say, to ease her mind.

"Am I in some sort of trouble?"

I shake my head. "Of course not. Between you and me, I'm looking into Billy's death, and I'm really not supposed to be."

Her mouth falls open and she bobs her head. She leans in conspiratorially and whispers, "I won't tell."

I smother a laugh with my fist. "Thank you, Amanda."

She straightens up. "He only had two or three beers that whole night. He was too busy winning."

The toxicology report said as much. He wasn't drunk, and according to Amanda, he was acting fine.

Something is off here.

"I appreciate the information."

She smiles wide. "I'm always happy to help. Anytime, Nick."

I head toward the door, ready to get home and eat my food, which is likely cold at this point.

Not that I'm even hungry. My stomach is in knots for reasons I can't exactly pinpoint.

My intuition tells me that the Garet case shouldn't have been closed, but who am I to argue with the captain? He says the family wants it closed, and despite what Shirley said, she's known for sticking her nose where it doesn't concern her. Owning a bar and acting as an unpaid therapist for years will do that to a person. She could have it all wrong.

Maybe.

Ten of Swords

FOR THE FIRST night in over a week, I sent Lanie home, perfectly content to have some time to myself. With my earbuds in, I got to work cleaning up the house. I was determined not to let things get as bad as they had lately.

My head's spinning with all the details I've uncovered, and I've been finding ways to keep busy while I sort through it all.

I head out to the trash bin to dump a full bag of trash left over from the junk food binge that occurred tonight, not paying attention to my surroundings at all. When I turn, a tall, dark figure stands in my path. I yelp, practically jumping out of my slides. My eyes close, and when they open, I breathe a sigh of relief that it's only Nick.

His mouth moves, but I can't hear him over Snow Patrol. I put a finger in the air, grab my phone from my back pocket, and shut off the music.

"Sorry, I didn't know you were behind me."

He smiles. "You seemed a little distracted. Anything good?" He motions to my ears.

"'Chasing Cars.' I've been cleaning."

"Listen, I don't want to bombard you on the street, but we need to talk."

I smile internally, relishing the fact that he's forced to admit that my source might just know a thing or two.

He places his hands in his pockets, rocking back and forth on his feet. He looks younger in the dim lighting provided by my motion sensor, and I have to bite my cheek to stop myself from smiling.

"Do you wanna come in?" I ask, motioning toward my house. "It's probably better if we don't have this conversation out here."

He ceases the rocking and removes his hands from his pockets, tapping the sides of both legs. Is he nervous?

"That works."

Nick follows me into my front room, and I motion for him to take a seat on the chair across from the ancient floral disaster of a couch. I've never been embarrassed by the outdated furniture, but having him in the space, I suddenly wish I'd sprung for a new set a long time ago.

"Can I get you something to drink? Coke? A beer?"

"I'll take a coke."

I nod and briskly make my way out of the room as quickly as I can, only to find Billy holding his stomach, bent over laughing, while Jackson glares into the side of his head.

"What's so funny?" I cross my arms over my chest, popping out my hip.

"Jackson just about had a coronary," he says, wheezing. "His face was priceless."

"About?" I drawl, looking between the two.

Jackson attempts to land a smack to the side of Billy's head, but it's no use. His hand goes right through, only managing to make Billy laugh harder.

"Will you tell me what's going on?" I say to Jackson since he's the mature one of the two.

"West is a recovering alcoholic. Saw it myself at Clementine's. He's been sober for years, but you don't wanna be offerin' him alcohol, toots."

My stomach twists. I recall that Garrett had once mentioned Nick was on the sober path, but I'd hardly paid attention, and now I'm kicking myself for it.

"There's nothing funny about that, jackass," I snap at Billy.

"I'm not laughing about that. I'm laughing at this goon's reaction. He was choking on air."

"We're supposed to be helping her get closer to the detective, not run him off, you insensitive dickhead," Jackson says, leaning against the wall. "He has serious issues," he says to me, nodding his head toward Billy.

I pull a face, having so many questions about what Jackson's just said. But I've been out here too long already, so I push them to the side for now.

"Go away," I whisper-yell, grabbing two Coke cans from the refrigerator, leaving Billy to his theatrics and Jackson to continue glowering at him.

There's no way I'd bring it up, but considering he asked for a Coke, knowing the subject we're about to embark on, it's likely true.

I practically shove the soda in Nick's face, popping the top and half draining my can before I've even sat down. I'm preoccupied thinking about all this man has been through and I haven't had caffeine since this morning. I'm in dire need.

Nick's eyes widen as he watches me chug my drink. "Thirsty?"

I gulp down one more sip, propping my legs up on the couch. "It's been a long life."

"I've gotta admit, I've never seen someone take down a Coke so quickly. Good thing it's only soda or else I might be carrying you to bed tonight."

My mind goes right down the gutter at the thought of Nick taking me to bed—in any fashion. He must recognize his semi-blunder because his face flushes and his mouth slams shut.

Thank god it's him feeling awkward this time.

I place my can on the table, hoping to steer the conversation, and my perverse thoughts, to something a bit safer. Anything to get my mind off Nick's firm chest pressed against me.

Stop it!

"It's probably better that I stick to this. With the events of late, I'm not sure I'd know when enough is enough," I say, apparently hurdling right over safe, deep diving into another muck-filled pool of chitchat.

The topic is potentially heavy, but it gives him an opening to confide in me, and I'd be lying if I said I didn't hope for that. I want to know more about Nick and that surprises me more every day.

"You're probably right," he says, taking a drink and cutting off that possible discussion.

A part of me is disappointed, but why would he? We're still merely strangers, dealing with a host of odd occurrences that I've managed to pull him in to, and I must remind myself that's why he's here.

"Like I said, long life."

He chuckles, but quickly smothers it. "Not the whole life . . . I hope."

I shrug. "No, but the good times are a little clouded under the crap of the past few years."

He nods, eyes darkening slightly. "I understand."

"I know you do." The words come out a little too breathy considering the topic.

I attempt to take another sip of my drink, only to find it is empty.

For a minute, I contemplate what to say. Should I jump into the whole Jenna thing or dive right into the new information I have on the guys? Instead, I veer off topic.

"I'm sorry about your fiancée. I had no idea."

Of course I'd move from a brutal topic to an even worse one.

"Didn't expect you to. We're neighbors, but we practically live in separate universes."

He isn't wrong, but my stomach drops at his words. I don't like the way we've ignored each other. Neighbors should be friendly. Neighbors should know who lives next to them. Otherwise, you're living next door to Boone Helm, none the wiser and marked as his next filet.

"But that does bring me to what I wanted to talk to you about." Nick cuts in, halting the scene playing out in my head involving me, a hatchet, and a hillbilly serial killer.

I really need to cut back on true crime.

"You were right about the body."

I bob my head, sucking in my cheeks. What do I even say? Duh? Obviously? Told you so?

Mature, Alyssa.

"I'm sorry to hear that. The last thing I wanted was for her to be dead."

He pulls his bottom lip into his mouth. It makes a popping sound when he releases it.

"From what I've heard, it sounds like it was a brutal end for her," I say, hoping he'll share any details that might help me uncover more from my visions.

"I'm not at liberty to share any details of the case."

I huff, falling back into the couch. "Why? I shared information with you."

He rolls his tongue, appearing to consider his next words.

"I swore an oath when I took this position, and it's not something

I take lightly. My job depends on my protection of confidential information and the details of the case."

There's nothing rude about his explanation. If anything, I get the sense that he wants to convey that if he could share with me, he would.

"Being bludgeoned in the head would be a rather horrific death. Especially since the guy didn't kill her right away."

He tilts his head to the side, narrowing his eyes on me. "What aren't you telling me?"

I shrug. "We're not at liberty to discuss the case."

He fidgets, turning the can in his hands. "I've upset you."

"You haven't. You have your duties and I have mine."

Nick sits back, arms propped up on the chair, eyes trained on the ceiling. "Listen, Alyssa, I'm a man of few words for good reason. My dad always said, 'If you don't speak, you don't say stupid shit.'" His head dips and our eyes connect. "It stuck with me. But sometimes, I forget that sage advice and say stupid shit anyway."

I can't help it—I laugh. I'm not sure if that was his intention, but based on the mischievous grin he's aiming my way, he totally meant to break the tension.

Well played, sir.

"Is that why you've never said more than two words to me?"

"I talked to you," he says, looking surprised by my accusation.

I smile, recalling the few times we did talk. It was never anything more than *Hi* or *How's it going*. He would barely make eye contact with me. I'm glad those days appear to be over.

"You talked to Garrett. Not me."

He bites the inside of his cheek, eyes narrowed in on the ratty couch. "What was there to say? Garrett and I had guy stuff to talk about. You and me . . ." His words trail off.

"Guy stuff?" I chuckle.

"You know what I mean." He goes silent for several seconds, picking at something on his jeans. "Let me repeat, if you don't speak, you don't say stupid shit. I was comfortable with Garrett."

"And you weren't with me."

He shrugs. "It's not exactly that."

There's no need to keep going down that path. I get it and he isn't wrong. Simple greetings were enough for me back then too.

"For the record, I've never heard you say anything that could be deemed stupid."

He levels me with a look of challenge.

"I swear."

"Maybe so, but if I'm being honest . . ." Nick's demeanor shifts, and I grow nervous about what's coming. He seems to be thinking it over, which only furthers my discomfort. "When Garrett died, I refrained from offering my condolences because my dad's words were always in the back of my mind. The last thing I wanted to do was upset you."

Not what I was expecting.

"You wouldn't have, Nick."

He grunts, dipping his chin. "One would think that due to my own . . . situation, I could manage to speak words of comfort, but having been in those shoes, I know there are no words that do justice for grief like that."

His words sober me because he's right. So many people meant well when they called or texted, but no words truly comforted me. Only Ava had that ability, because at that time, she was the only person I felt could possibly hurt as much as I did.

We're quiet for a few minutes, each lost to our own thoughts and memories.

"Want another? Maybe water?" I ask again, jumping up from the couch. I need an escape from the emotional awkwardness that's suffocating the room.

"Sure. I'll have another Coke."

An hour later, we're sitting on the floor next to each other, chatting about life. I haven't had this much fun in years, and it feels good. I'm not ready to call it a night, which is surprising considering the late hour.

We've veered far from topics of death and have been sharing stories from our past that have us both belly laughing. Who would've thought that I'd share a moment like this with my surly neighbor?

"I can't believe Mrs. Hampson said that to you. I mean, I know she's eccentric, but the stuff that comes out of her mouth sometimes." My hand lands over my mouth as the cackles continue.

"You think that's good? Once, I was called out to break up an argument between her and Nan Jenkins. She was angry because Nan had told her it wasn't a good idea to burn full moon intentions on the lawn when it's dry." He lifts his eyes into his hairline. "When I agreed with Nan, she turned to the other Red Hatters and proclaimed that explaining something to an ignorant person is harder than making a camel jump over a ditch."

I can picture the scene perfectly in my head, and it brings up a host of questions. Just what are those Red Hatters getting up to? Burning intentions on the full moon sounds more like something Corinne and Lanie would do. Not the likes of the Red Hatters. What on earth do they have in those cups I see them drinking from?

"She then turns to me and says, 'Turkish proverb, dear. It simply means you're a fool.'" He laughs, chest heaving. "The woman's ruthless."

I wipe a tear from under my eye. "I've been on the receiving end of Mrs. Hampson's affinity for Turkish proverbs. At least yours didn't include a rat and balls."

He chokes on his Coke, eyes widening. "Do I even wanna know?"

"Doubtful."

We both laugh before a yawn escapes me.

"I should get going," Nick says, rounding up his cans.

"Don't worry about that," I say, placing my hand on top of his.

We share a look and the air in the room shifts. Nick's pupils widen and my body instinctively leans toward him. His gaze falls to my lips and my eyes half close, waiting for him to step across that line.

"I should go." He says the words again, voice thick and heady.

My eyes fly open and my stomach rolls.

Oh god. I'd practically begged him to kiss me. I might not have uttered the words, but my body spoke volumes.

I jump to my feet, grabbing the cans one by one and smashing them in the middle so I can carry more. "I'll take care of this."

He follows me into the kitchen with the trash I couldn't manage, neither one of us speaking. When I turn around, he's right there. In my space, sucking all the oxygen from the room.

I take several steps away from him and he follows, until my back hits the counter and I'm caged in on either side by his arms. "Don't do that," he says, voice low and gruff.

"Do what?" I say, looking into his eyes with a challenge I'm praying he accepts.

I'm not sure I've blinked in the past minute.

"Pretend we didn't have a moment." He leans in until our lips are mere inches from each other. "I want to, Alyssa. God, do I want to." His eyes close and his features pinch. "But not like this. Not now."

I swallow, unable to react, let alone form words. I'm completely content to allow him to run the show.

"Say something," he commands, forcing me to join the conversation.

I take a deep breath. "What do you want me to say? That I want it? That I don't want you to be chivalrous?"

"Yes. That's exactly what I want you to say."

A small smile spreads across my face. "I want you to kiss me. But you're right. Now isn't the time."

The second the words leave my mouth, I'm internally kicking my own ass.

Nick's expression morphs from desire to disappointment, and I want to melt into the floor.

He pushes off the table, putting far too much space between us, leaving me cold and needy. "Good night, Alyssa."

He leans in and places a chaste kiss on my cheek before turning around and leaving. I stand still for a minute, palm pressed to my cheek where his lips touched my skin. My body aches for more, but my mind screams for me to be content with where things are.

There's so much more for Nick to discover, and it wouldn't be good to mix personal and business before he knows all the facts. He gave me a reprieve tonight, but the tough conversations are coming.

I rush to the door just before he's about to shut it. My foot kicks out, stopping it from closing.

"Thank you, Nick." The words rush out because I'm desperate for the night not to end like this. Not after what just almost happened.

His head tilts. "What for?"

"Everything? Humoring me the other night. Not making me feel like too much of a crazy person." I lean against the doorframe, arms crossed over my chest, attempting to keep out the chill from the night air.

"It was a good night." He looks uncomfortable, eyes darting off to the side.

I take a step forward, reach out, and lay my hand on his shoulder. He glances at where I'm touching him but doesn't move away or say a word.

"It was. Thank you."

He clears his throat, taking a step back. "Get some rest."

My hand drops away and for reasons I have no intention of analyzing, I regret the moment is over.

I go to shut the door to find Billy waiting there. "Why are you letting him leave? He's the only one who can help us. Get out there and tell him the rest." He points, stomping his foot.

"No," I whisper. "I'm tired."

I don't want to ruin things by bringing up morbid topics again.

"Move it, or I'll bring friends to haunt your ass all night. You think *I'm* annoying." He whistles. "Just you wait."

I don't know if he's bluffing, but I'm not willing to chance it. One aggravating ghost is more than enough.

I rush through the door, running down the steps and after Nick. "Wait."

He turns around, eyes wide in question. "You okay?"

I nod several times, hunched over with my hands on my knees, trying to get my breathing under control. For Pete's sake, I ran twenty feet, not a mile. I need to hit the gym pronto.

"A red truck that was driven by a man had two guys in the bed; they threw a large branch into the road, causing Jackson's accident. That same vehicle sideswiped Billy's Jeep on the front driver side. Billy lost control and went off the road. He overcorrected and his vehicle flipped into the ravine. The man in the truck never even hit his brakes." The words rush from me like blood from an open wound.

His hands raise to his temples, kneading before sliding down to form a steeple at his lips. "A man? Is your source positive?"

"Yes. The driver of the *red truck* was a man." I emphasize the details, needing him to investigate this claim.

He takes a deep breath. "Not to be repeated . . ." He gives me a look that signals he's waiting for my agreement to remain silent on whatever he's about to say. My head bobs in confirmation. "They said they found a note that proved Billy caused the accident himself."

The sudden shift in the air is palpable and it doesn't take long to figure out why.

"No way," Billy says, appearing behind Nick. "There was no fucking note. I'd never do that."

"What's wrong?" Nick asks, looking back to see what I'm staring at.

"Make him understand there was no note," Billy barks.

I can't do that. Without evidence, he won't believe me.

"What?" Nick drags the word out. "What aren't you saying?"

I gulp, knowing I have to lay it all on the line. My eyes close as I try to figure out how best to come clean.

"Tell him," Billy demands, severing the last string holding my sanity together.

"It's me, all right? I'm the source. I speak to the dead."

The moment I speak those last five words, I know I've lost Nick's help.

He blinks several times, his face a mask. "Thanks for the tip. If you hear anything else, let me know."

"You don't believe me."

He opens his mouth, then shuts it. "I don't know what to believe, Alyssa. You've given me different stories every time we've talked." He takes a deep breath, likely trying to remain calm. "Tonight was great and now . . ." he kicks the ground. "Now I don't know what to think."

"Nick, I—"

He cuts me off. "I suggest you get some rest and leave the investigation in the hands of the police. This amateur sleuthing needs to end. For your safety."

He's done helping me. He won't say the words because we live next to each other, but that's exactly what he's saying with his posture, his cold expression, and the way he's taking small steps back to put distance between us.

"Good night, Nick."

I don't say anything else, turning on my heels and stalking back to my house.

Our easy camaraderie had been too good to be true. I'm on my own now.

"Alyssa, wait," he says in a commanding voice, one I've never heard from him.

It's enough to stop me in my tracks. I turn around, crossing my arms over my chest. I won't back down. I refuse to backpedal. The truth is out and if he can't handle it, that's his problem.

"Why are you angry with me?" He truly appears puzzled and that manages to annoy me.

"I'm offering you information that you'd never be able to uncover on your own, because the evidence has been hidden for years."

"And I appreciate it. But you have to understand that without physical evidence, there's not much I can do with it. Running around dragging up accidents from the past and pointing fingers at every guy driving around town in a red truck is dangerous, Alyssa. Don't you see that?"

"So start looking for the physical evidence. I'll tell you where to look when I get downloads of information."

He huffs, running his hand through his hair, stopping to pull at the roots. Frustration is oozing off him.

"Do you want me to lose my job?"

I shake my head back and forth. "No. Of course not. I'm only asking you to look into things."

He takes several steps toward me until we're toe-to-toe. His hand reaches out, running back through my hair, placing a loose strand behind my ear. "If I could follow up on these leads, I would."

But I can't. He might not say it, but it's clearly written all over his face.

If he wants to walk away from this because of his pride and unwillingness to be open-minded, that's on him.

"I understand."

I don't, but I'm not going to drag this dead-end conversation on.

He leans in and kisses my cheek again. My breath hitches and my eyes close.

"Good night, Alyssa."

With that, our talk is done and I'm left with butterflies and anger warring to take center stage.

24

Seven of Cups . . . Reversed

DOWNTOWN IS BURSTING with activity due to the annual fall festival. It's the biggest event of the year, and people come from all over to join in. Tents are set up in a horseshoe in the square, sheltering artisans from around the state selling their goods. Local restaurants offer samples of their gourmet dishes, while food trucks line Main Street with typical fair treats. All the usual offerings are here, including just about anything that can be fried, cotton candy, and my personal favorite, elephant ears.

The green is set up with a handful of rides sure to twist your guts and make you puke. At least, that's what it would do to me. About the only ride I could be convinced to get on is the Ferris wheel, and I'd still have to be dragged onto it.

Even with all the hustle and bustle going on around me, my attention is solely focused on the girl at my side. Having Ava back home beats a day at the festival any time.

"What should we do first?" Ava asks, sounding much younger than she is.

Her excitement is palpable, filling my cup and warming me from the inside out.

"We can grab some food?"

The smell of charred meat turns my stomach and I almost rescind that idea, but Ava beats me to it.

"Not before we ride the rides. I'll get sick."

"I will not be getting on a single one of those death traps." I eye the Tilt-A-Whirl with contempt. Just watching it spin in circles is enough to make my stomach turn. "I'd prefer that you stayed away from them too."

I'm only half-serious. There's no way I'd deprive my girl of her childhood right to fun.

"Mom," she chides. "It's happening. I'm riding them all."

"Go for it, but I'm gonna sit this one out."

"Hey, Ava." An adorable girl with bleach-blond hair braided over her shoulder calls out, waving to grab her attention.

"Carly," Ava squeals. "Momma, can I?"

Her ice-blue eyes twinkle as she waits for me to give her the go-ahead. She'd brush off her friends because she doesn't want to leave me by myself. My sweet girl. She's always thinking about me, but I don't want that.

I offer a small smile. "Go have fun." Leaning down, I place a small kiss on her cheek. "Maybe they'll ride the rides with you."

She giggles, and it's music to my ears. "I'll text you later. We can meet up for dinner?"

"Sure. Now go."

She runs off and I watch as she rushes into the arms of the blonde and another girl with ashy hair. They all look so happy to see each other, and I'm glad. The last year she spent at Knox Harbor High was rough. She was depressed and missing her daddy something fierce. Today, all signs of that sad girl are absent, and I couldn't be happier.

"Alyssa, dear, how are you enjoying the festival?" Nan Jenkins strolls up wearing a bright red suit with gaudy gold buttons. Her hair is pulled into a tight French twist, putting her overly Botoxed forehead on full display.

"It's incredible," I say, glancing around, taking it all in. "Just like every year." She does her own sweep of the area, pride shining brightly on her faux-tan face. The woman missed the memo on graceful aging.

"You and the rest of the committee always knock it out of the park."

She beams, grabbing my hands in hers. "You should really join us next year. We could use some fresh ideas."

We both know she doesn't mean it. Women like Nan Jenkins don't like new ideas. They're set in their ways, constantly insisting on tradition.

A few younger residents in town have attempted to join the committee in the past and were run off. The only person I know who's ever gone head-to-head with them and come out alive is Lanie. And that's because she just doesn't care about ruffling feathers. In fact, I think she gets some sick pleasure out of it.

"I'll think about it," I lie. Otherwise, Nan will sit here and tell me all the reasons why I should reconsider.

"Sorry to rush off, but word has it that the hunky detective just took the ladder."

I have literally no idea what that means, and she must see the look on my face, because she doesn't leave me on tenterhooks.

"Nick West is up at the dunk tank." She leans in conspiratorially, glancing around to ensure she's not overheard. "That man without a shirt is a sight to behold. I'll hold the memory in my mind for the rest of the year."

It takes everything in me not to react to those words. The laughter bubbles up in my chest and I stuff it down. Nobody laughs at Nan Jenkins and lives to show their face in town again. She's known for causing scenes.

"Have fun," I reply, but she's already well on her way to join all the other thirsty women vying for a peek at Nick West's perfection.

I will not be one of them, especially after last night.

"I wondered when you were going to get here," Lanie says, sliding up next to me and bumping my hip with hers.

"Ava only got into town forty-five minutes ago. She wanted to jump right in the car as soon as she pulled into the driveway, but I refused. I'm not going to share her without getting at least ten minutes of her to myself."

"Did you sleep all right? I was worried leaving you alone."

I wave a hand. "I was fine. Until Nick about scared the hair off my head, almost kissed me, and then proceeded to lecture me on my sleuthing."

She lifts both hands out in front of her. "Whoa. Slow down and spill the details."

I tell her the shortened version and watch as her face contorts from giddiness to anger.

"You gave him solid proof. How dare he. I'll kick his ass next time I see him."

I chuckle. "That won't be necessary. I won't be involving him in any of this, and hopefully we'll go back to the way things were. Two neighbors who almost had a thing but missed the opportunity."

It's not what I want, but how can things be any different? If he can't believe that I communicate with the dead, it will be hard to progress into anything more than neighbors.

Lanie doesn't appear to be listening anymore. Her eyes are trained on something in the distance. I can't make out what has her so enthralled.

"Let's go," she says, linking my arm with hers and pulling me forward.

At five feet eleven inches, Lanie and her praying mantis legs make it darn near impossible for me to keep up. I'm practically falling over as I futilely attempt to anchor my feet in my sandals, trying desperately not to lose one in the process.

"Hold up, Lanie. Why are you in such a hurry?"

"We're going to miss it," she practically screeches directly into my ear. "And today of all days, he's getting his comeuppance."

Up ahead there's a wall of women, and I don't even have to see what's on the other side. A crowd of mostly female gawkers can only mean one thing. Nick West is shirtless and dripping wet.

Lord have mercy. What is Lanie up to?

The crowd parts like the Red Sea as Lanie drags me ahead. I dig in my heels and try to halt her progress, but the woman is stronger than she looks.

"Make way," she shouts over the clucking and chirping of the women griping about being interrupted. "Alyssa is here for revenge."

My head snaps to her. "What on earth?"

Nick chokes out a laugh. "Revenge? Dare I ask what I did?" He doesn't meet my eyes, because the guy knows exactly what he did.

Nick places a hand over his heart as his pecs shift with every movement.

Look away from the thirst trap.

"No matter. Give it your best shot, Alyssa."

There's a challenge in his words, and I can't help but gape at the man in response.

"Are you insinuating that I can't hit that massive target?"

The big black circle with a red dot in the middle is the size of Ava's head. If I can't hit that, I'll give up ice cream.

He shrugs, biting his lip in an attempt to not smile.

"Oh my god! He's flirting with you," Lanie whispers out of the side of her mouth.

"No, he's not. He's mocking me." I twist to the side, holding out my hand to the busty brunette with the lowest V-cut shirt I've seen. "The ball, Harley."

"No," she snaps. "I only got to throw one ball. I paid for five."

Lanie reaches around me and grabs the ball from her hands. "Too bad. Beat it, hussy. I mean, Harley. You can finish your turn after Alyssa drowns him." She glances up at Nick. "I mean, dunks him." She offers a sugary-sweet smile to Nick, who can't contain his laughter.

"I'm so sorry. Do you mind if I just throw this one?" I ask, to be kind. I may not like her, but I don't subscribe to being rude.

She rolls her eyes. "Just throw the freaking ball, Sally."

"Oh, it's actually Alyssa."

She blinks. "I don't care." She waves her hand in front of her nose as if she's smelling something foul.

I turn back toward the dunk tank. Nick looks smug atop his watery throne, and I can't wait to swipe that arrogant grin from his handsome face.

"You are so going down."

"Let me make a deal with you, blondie. You dunk me with one shot, I'll make things right and buy you an elephant ear."

Game on.

I make a show of stretching, sticking my tongue out the side of my mouth, eyes never leaving Nick's. Mischievousness shines brightly back at me. He's enjoying this.

"Are you gonna throw the ball or stall all day?"

"Yeah, throw the ball already," someone yells from the crowd.

I take my stance, cock my arm back, eyes now trained on the target, and let it rip. The whole crowd is silent as the ball whizzes toward the target. I wait with bated breath until the ball hits square in the center of the target.

I don't miss the surprise on Nick's face as he plummets into the ice-cold water.

I turn to Harley, brush off my shoulder, and say, "Tell him I don't want his elephant ear, or anything else for that matter."

Lanie cackles as she follows behind me.

This festival is already turning out to be a blast.

+ + +

"I'M SORRY. FOR whatever I said that made you feel this way, I apologize. I never intended to hurt you."

Nick found me despite my every attempt at avoiding him. He coaxed me into giving him a few minutes to make things right. Since we live next to each other, I thought it best to repair things a tad.

"It's fine, Nick. We've been over this. You believe what you believe. I'm not trying to convince you of anything."

"This is only for your safety, Alyssa. I'm done chasing these leads until my captain tells me otherwise. My job depends on it."

I'm not mad anymore. I understand his stance. Nick's an honorable man, and I can't fault him for that. He didn't call me names to my face, and he wasn't rude. He may have insinuated that I was lying, but who wouldn't have that knee-jerk reaction? The least I can do is drop it and move on. The only thing that changes is that I lose my help on the inside, which will likely delay Billy's exit.

I lift my shoulders. "Fine. Can we talk about anything else? I'd rather forget about that and focus on being friendly neighbors."

He smiles, but it doesn't reach his eyes. "I still cannot believe you hit that target on your first try."

"What? Why?" I place my hand over my chest, feigning offense. "I'm athletic."

Nick turns to look at me, and those adorable dimples make an appearance. "I've seen you dance."

I rack my brain to uncover when he could've possibly seen me dancing. Did he look in my window? Because inside my house is the only place I'd be brave enough to let loose. I'm a crap dancer. *How embarrassing.* I have to do my best not to flush right in front of his face.

"Since when does dancing equate to athleticism?" I grumble, picking off a piece of fried pastry dough and shoving it into my mouth.

"Fair point." He grabs for a chunk of the elephant ear, and I level him with a mock glare that he completely ignores. "Have you had a good time today?"

"I have. Ava, Nina, Lanie, and I all had dinner together."

"What did you eat?"

I cock an eyebrow, wondering at his curiosity surrounding my fair food choice.

"What? It's a fair question. You can tell a lot about a person based on what they eat at a festival."

"Can you?" I drawl, smashing my lips together so that I don't smile. "I had a corn dog."

"With mustard or ketchup?"

"Both." I tear off more of the treat and take a bite. "I also had meat on a stick, complete with fries drenched in vinegar."

His eyes bug out. "You ate all of that?"

I shrug. "Like it's hard."

His lips tip up at the corners as he chews our apparently shared dessert. I'm not sure what it is about the act of chewing, but Nick makes it look like an art form. Sensual. Seductive.

Get a grip.

"What did you do after you gorged yourself on fried food?"

I cringe, knowing the effects of that binge will plague me later.

"We shopped at the vendor tents, and I bought Ava a hand-crafted metal bracelet that she insisted on having."

"Yeah, I saw that."

Nick found me at the checkout, claiming to be bound to his word. Now we're seated on a bench on the outskirts of the hoopla, sharing an elephant ear.

"Thank you," I say, lifting the plate just a bit. "You didn't have to do this."

"Apparently, I did. Wouldn't want you seeking revenge." He flashes a grin that I'm sure has melted a few hearts throughout the years. I swallow, twisting my head in the opposite direction.

"I've gotta ask . . . what exactly are you seeking revenge for?"

"Lanie's just being Lanie. She's overprotective." I shove the last piece of fried dough I can stomach into my mouth.

"That's good. You need friends that have your back." He continues to stare at the side of my head, so I turn back toward him. "But you didn't answer my question."

"Who knows what Lanie was talking about. She's random."

He purses his lips and I know he isn't going to allow me to skirt around the answer.

I pull my hair over one shoulder, tugging at the ends. "It was just me being overly sensitive. I got my feelings hurt, which isn't your problem."

He chews slowly, eyes sweeping over my face and pausing just for a fraction of a second on my scar.

I lift my hand to my temple, running over the raised mark. With the help of an incredible doctor and persistent care on my part, it's hardly noticeable, but it's there. For the longest time I thought of it as a reminder of all that I've lost, but not anymore. It's a reminder of all that I've endured.

I'm stronger because of the trauma I've experienced.

"Is it because I wouldn't kiss you?" The way his husky voice delivers the question has my toes tingling.

I run my tongue across my bottom lip, wiping away the sugar that's clung to it.

"That was . . . disappointing," I admit. "But I understood why you didn't. Lanie was referencing your refusal to believe in my gift."

He lowers his head. "Alyssa, it's not that. I've learned in this job to remain levelheaded. I was going down a path that would cost me my job."

It's not hard to see that Nick takes his job seriously, and it's not hard to believe that not solving a case would haunt him. He's too good of a man. Having to walk away from these tips can't be easy for him.

"For the record, I did follow up on Clementine's."

My head snaps to him. "You did?"

"I asked the owner to pull up the recordings from their security cameras on the nights of both accidents. I haven't heard back from her yet, but I know she'll come through."

"Thank you, Nick." My eyes close, hope pouring into me. I might have a chance of ridding myself of Billy after all. "I appreciate that."

"I'm not sure what I'll do with it, but I did follow up." His eyes bore into me, silently pleading to hear the truth in his words. "Every single case I've ever worked has kept me up at night until I was able to close it. The ones that went cold still bother me," he says, echoing my thoughts. "If I find something on them and go to the captain with it, I'll likely be reprimanded for going against orders."

"I don't want that."

He wipes off his mouth, dragging his hands down his scruffy chin. "I also want you safe. I've said it before, but it's worth repeating. When people are running around claiming that accidents could actually be murder and there's truth in it, the person responsible will panic. That would not be good for you."

I'm not trying to put myself in harm's way. Not that I don't want to help these spirits. I do. But not at the cost of my and my friends' safety.

"Thank you for caring."

My phone vibrates, and I pull it out to see I've gotten a text from Ava.

> **AVA**
> Can I hang w/ Carly and Simone for the night?
> We're having fun and I don't wanna leave.
> Carly said I could crash at her house.
> Pleeeeease.

Typically, I would insist that she make it home at some point, but considering she needs to live a normal teenage life, it would be best if she stayed with her friends.

> **ALYSSA**
> Sure! Have fun.

> **AVA**
> We still have tomorrow night.
> Oh. OK. Thanks mom! Love you.
> I'll text you when at her house safe.

> **ALYSSA**
> Thank you. Love you too.

"Everything okay?"

"Yeah," I say, rereading the text. "It's just Ava. She's growing up so fast, and I don't know how to handle it at times." Locking my phone, I see the time flash on the screen. It's getting late, and since I'm not waiting on Ava anymore, there's little reason for me to stay at the festival. "I gotta get going. I'm exhausted."

"Do you want me to walk you to your car?"

I stand up, heading toward the nearest garbage can, and toss the paper plate in. "That's not necessary. I can manage."

He's quiet for a moment before he stands and takes a step toward me. His sheer presence is enough to intimidate me.

"I want to. This festival might be in New England's safest town, but it draws in characters from all parts of the country. Better to be safe than sorry."

"Ever the detective," I bemoan teasingly.

He shrugs. "It *is* my job." He grabs my hand, intertwining our fingers and all words escape me. "And, if I'm being honest, I want more time with you."

I'm floating on a cloud, my feet just barely touching the ground. His words have me warm and dare I say hopeful. For what, I haven't quite worked out yet. My mind is full of so many possibilities. Things I probably have no business thinking at this stage.

When we make it to my Volvo, I open the door and turn too quickly, nearly bumping right into Nick's chest. Not for the first time. We're inches apart, and I feel my entire body flush from the proximity.

"Sorry," he says, but he doesn't back up.

"All good. I just wanted to thank you again."

He grins down at me, pulling me into an embrace that I melt into before I remember I'm supposed to be keeping my distance. "Be careful," he says into my ear, causing a riot of tingles that remain well after he ends the hug. "Too many people leave this festival intoxicated. There are extra patrols tonight. You'll wanna drive slow to avoid a ticket."

I'm about to say something quippy when a commotion in the

distance catches my eye. A red truck is what initially draws my attention, but it's the three men in what appears to be a heated conversation that holds it.

Nick twists around to get a look at what I'm seeing. "What do we have here?" he says under his breath.

Richard Dunbar has his finger pointed into the chest of a stocky man, who looks like he could smash Richard to pieces if he wanted. A third man stands off to the side, arms crossed, looking down at the other two. I can't make out much more because the only light in the area comes from one telephone pole. It's enough for me to make out the mayor, but the other man's face is hidden in shadow.

"What is Mayor Dunbar doing with Marcus Wells?"

"Who's Marcus Wells?" I ask, looking up at Nick.

"He's a local criminal with his hands in many of the businesses in town. Extortion, bribery, money laundering—his rap sheet is extensive. But somehow, he's always getting off with a slap on the wrist." He takes one more look. "Curious that the mayor of all people appears to be well acquainted with him."

The scary man pulls what appears to be a case of liquor from the back of the truck, and hands it over to Richard.

"The man's dirty," I say offhandedly. "I just wish it could be proven, so Nina would have an excuse to leave his ass."

Nick's hand lands on mine, gripping the top of the door. "If he is, it'll come out at some point. It always does."

I huff. "Not for men like Richard Dunbar. Men like him always seem to sneak under the radar. Besides, the most you'd find out about him is that he's a philanderer who can't keep his tiny toad in his pants."

I look back over toward the truck and watch as Richard stalks off in the opposite direction, box in hand. The tall man gets into the passenger seat, and the truck turns around, heading toward us.

As it slowly rolls past us, heading toward the exit, my eyes collide with the man's black orbs. A demonic smile spreads across the driver's face as he gets a look at me.

My skin crawls from his unwanted attention. There's something evil about him, but also familiar. I'm trying to place what but am coming up short. As the truck continues on, I see Jenna, pointing her finger in the direction of the truck.

A warning. A sign.

I can feel it.

That's when it hits me, and the air whooshes from my lungs.

Marcus Wells. The man from the spa.

Who happens to be beefy and bald.

Jackson had described his killers as a tall, abnormally skinny man and a beefy bald guy.

Could I have just come face-to-face with the murders?

I grab Nick's shoulder, shaking it. "It's him. That's the guy."

Nick twists me so that we're face-to-face. "Who? What are you talking about?"

"You saw that man, he looked evil. And the red truck. It has to be those men that are behind all the murders."

His eyes close and I wonder what's going through his head. I don't have to wait long.

"Please keep that between you and me. That man is dangerous."

"I will. I promise," I say, willing to give him that much reassurance. For now.

I smile up at him, but I can't get the creepy grin or the darkness of that man's eyes out of my head. It'll be a miracle if I don't have nightmares about him.

"Hey. Look at me," he says, placing a finger under my chin and tilting my head up to look into his eyes. "He can't get to you. I'll be right next door. *I* promise, you're safe."

His words cascade over me like the balm I so desperately needed.

"Okay." It's all I say, because I'm tired and calmed by his promise of protection.

"Get home and get some rest, Lyss."

Lyss.

It might only be a nickname, but it's something that furthers the shift between us. And I like it. A lot.

Five of Pentacles

UNLIKE EVERY OTHER year, I skipped the rest of the festival, not in the mood to see happy families going about life like people aren't dying all around them.

The non-dramatic part of me simply had no interest in running into that man in the red truck.

I have bigger issues currently, anyway.

Ava ditched me most of the weekend to hang with friends, leaving bright and early Sunday to get back to school so that she could . . . hang with friends. I'm not bitter at all.

More importantly, I'm struggling with my next move. I've hit a dead end with Billy and Jackson. They haven't been able to remember anything else that could help. Not that their accounts are what I need. At this point, it's physical evidence that needs to be uncovered and the one person who could help in that department I've sworn not to involve.

"I called this emergency meeting of the Gin and Tarot Club to get to the bottom of Alyssa's current state of depression."

My eyes practically cross as I stare at Lanie with something just a skip away from contempt.

"The last thing I need is this meeting. I'm not depressed." I look around the room at Nina and Corinne—who is apparently an official member of our group—and find concern and agitation.

The agitation is clearly a Corinne staple, so I don't take offense at it.

"You can all leave." I pull my cardigan tight across my chest, shivering from the cold draft floating through the place.

This morning the wind picked up, and it's been pouring rain all afternoon. The temperature has dropped at least fifteen degrees. Not good for the eve of Halloween. Tomorrow is going to be a chilly, muddy mess.

Not that it matters. My child has left the nest for bluer skies and a flock that doesn't include me.

"What's going on in there?" Lanie says, tapping my forehead.

I'd been so lost to my pity party of one that I hadn't noticed she'd barged right into my personal space.

I swat at her hands. "Go away."

"Sorry, that doesn't work for the living . . . or the dead." She glances at Corinne. "The Moradi grimoire is defunct."

Corinne rolls her eyes, not at all affected by Lanie's ribbing.

"Why were we called here on a Monday? What's"—she motions to me—"all this about?"

I lift the side of my lip, baring my teeth like a wild animal.

"Alyssa, love, talk to us." Nina's therapist voice grates on me, and I have to bite my tongue to give me time to think through my response so as not to be offensive.

Their go-to assumption is always depression and I'm ready to turn the page on those days. This is desperation.

I feel like the clock's ticking and I'm running out of time to solve this before someone else pops up murdered.

"I don't need your counsel, Nina. Go home to your sterile

mansion on the hill and ask your worthless husband why he's meeting up with the town criminal."

Not any less offensive.

She blinks, purses her lips, and goes all angry Nina on me, which is something I've seen twice in my life.

"You don't get to do that. Just because you're having a hard time, it doesn't mean that none of us have our own issues. You and I both know I can't accuse Richard."

"And why is that, Nina? We all share everything with you, but you won't confide in us about what he has on you."

Her mouth falls open. "You know I can't tell you that. I'm trying to protect you."

"I don't want your protection! I want the truth."

Nina's bottom lip quivers.

Holy Mary, I've gone and done it.

"I'm sorry, Nina, I didn't mean to attack you. It was unfair."

A tear drops from her eye, and now I really feel like a jerk.

She swipes it away, turning her head to look out the window.

Rain pounds against the glass as the wind whips the remaining leaves and dead branches from the trees. The crap weather reflects my mood to a tee.

"You're not the only one who's having a hard time." Her voice shakes and I want to hug her. "You and I both know Richard's hands aren't clean, but my hands are tied."

Nina is never like this. She's strong, too much for her own good at times. Things must be really bad at home, because outside of that place, Nina has always been happy.

"What's going on, Nina?" I practically whisper, for fear that my words will cause a full-on sob fest and I'll be joining right along with her.

She shakes her head. "I didn't come here to talk about me. We all came here to help you and you're acting selfish."

My head jerks back. She might as well have popped me in the nose. Nina never speaks to me like this.

"Selfish? How?"

She stands and starts to pace, hands balled into fists, placed on her hips.

"Great. Now we have two members losing their shit." Corinne stands. "I'm not going to be a witness to mental breaks without the gin in hand."

She walks into the kitchen, leaving the three of us alone.

Nina spins on me. "You've made zero progress with ridding this house of ghosts. What are you waiting for?"

"Nick asked me to stop. I don't think he entirely believes me about the ghosts."

"So what if Nick doesn't believe you? That shouldn't come as a shock considering the man is a detective and you've provided him little in the way of evidence."

"I told him where to find the body!" I practically shout. "What more evidence does the man need?"

"To believe you speak to ghosts?" She laughs maniacally.

Dear god. Nina is losing it and I really need to figure out why.

"You'll need a damn miracle to convince that man of that. Get off your ass and find the physical evidence."

I'm speechless. Nina is the soft-spoken friend. The supportive, help you navigate the issues friend. She's not whatever this is.

"Okay, guys," Lanie says, trying for soothing. "This isn't helping. And if I'm honest, I don't like you two fighting. That relationship belongs to Nina and me. You don't get to be the favorite and the antagonist."

Nina and I both look at Lanie with equal expressions to convey she's also lost it.

"All I'm saying is we need to work together to give Nick a solid case." She looks to me. "Assuming that's possible?"

I sigh, making my way back to my spot on the hideous couch. "It has to be. I'm just trying to figure out how."

Nina sits next to me. "How what?"

I take a breath, meeting her blue eyes. "Find the evidence. Help these spirits. Figure out who's behind their deaths before someone else dies."

Nina places her hand on my lap. "You're putting too much pressure on yourself. These are serious crimes and you're no detective. This isn't something you can do on your own."

A complete one-eighty from her comments minutes ago, but I'm done trying to pry Nina's truths from her. That day will come, but we have bigger fish to fry at the moment.

"That's why we're here," Lanie says, taking a seat on the floor at our feet. "Let's build this case."

For two hours the four of us research the dates of all the deaths and worked on the timeline and commonalities, jotting it down onto a yellow piece of paper.

Death Timeline
Billy Garet—August 17, 2021
Garrett Mann—September 23, 2021
Jackson Moore—April 13, 2022
Jenna Cruz—August 10, 2023

"Every death, apart from Jenna's, occurred on Spooky Hollow Road and a red truck driven by a man is thought to be involved. Billy, Jackson, and Jenna all have Clementine's in common and knew who each other were." Lanie runs down the information, waiting for us to chime in if she's missing anything.

"Okay, Billy," I call out. "I need you to run down everything that happened from the time you left Clementine's until your accident."

He inhales long and hard, half rolling his eyes, apparently done with his portion of solving his own death.

"I argued with Jackhole." Jackson growls, baring his teeth, and for Billy's part, he doesn't cower.

Jackson could break the likes of Billy over his knees, but I suppose there isn't a need to fear that when you're already dead.

"Decided it was probably a good idea to cut the night short, since I had already made a fortune. Went to the bar to close out my tab with Jenna. Talked to Charlie Dunbar, who was seated at the bar. Offered to buy him a drink. Then I left."

I relay what he's said to the collective, and everybody seems to feel the same way as I do . . . we're at a dead end. Except for Nina. She's worrying at her bottom lip and wringing her hands together.

"What's wrong, Nina?" I ask, watching as her demeanor continues to take a shift toward uncomfortable.

"Could you ask Billy what all happened with Charlie?"

My eyes narrow in on my friend, questions mounting about her sudden interest in her stepson. I turn to Billy.

"Jenna said he was cut off and needed to get himself a ride home because she couldn't take him that night. He said he already had a ride home. I left and that was the end of it." He shrugs, like it's not relevant, but looking at Nina's face, I'm not so sure.

She takes a deep breath. "I think Charlie might've had something to do with this."

"What?" all of us say at once.

"I'm pretty sure that's the night that Charlie wrecked his truck. The next morning, Richard was livid, throwing things around and screaming at Charlie about how stupid he was driving around town drunk. Richard got the truck fixed and that was the end of it. We weren't to talk about it because that would harm Richard's political career."

"Did you say he wrecked his truck? What color is it, Nina?" I ask, practically whispering.

"Red."

"Can you provide evidence of the damaged truck and where Richard had it fixed?"

She chews on the inside of her cheek. "I don't have access to our bank accounts to pull up the charges, but Richard always uses Santos in Silverton for repairs."

"Do you think you could get the information from them?" I ask Lanie, keeping my fingers crossed that we'll have something of value to add to this case.

"Hell yes she can," Lanie chimes in. "I'll make sure of it."

✦ ✦ ✦

WE WERE IN the parking lot of Santos ten minutes before they opened, determined to get in and out with everything we needed. It's your typical auto body shop. Plain white brick building with multiple service bay doors.

We've been sitting in silence while I sip on my latte, Nina rests her eyes, and Lanie surfs through social media.

I lean into the driver's side door, watching Lanie as she laughs at various posts and makes faces at others.

"Please explain this," I say, motioning toward Lanie's cropped tank top that shows the bottom swells of her ample breasts.

She doesn't look up, but I see her glance at me out of the corner of her eye. "Chill, Mother Teresa. It never hurts to use your assets to get what you want."

Lanie is a gorgeous girl, but she's also smart, charismatic, and loyal to a fault. My hope is that one day, she'll know her worth. The girl could get anything she wants wearing a potato sack.

A brown-skinned man with a medium build wearing a green

boilersuit makes his way to the door of the front office, unlocking it and stepping inside.

"That's him. Leon Santos," Nina whispers, as though he can hear her. "He owns the place."

"It's go time, ladies." Lanie says it like we're about to take to the track to cheer on the local football team. "Nina and I will go in, and Alyssa, you keep watch."

I pull a face. "Keep watch for what exactly? This isn't a heist, Lanie."

She shrugs. "If he doesn't cooperate, it might become that. I'm not opposed to grabbing the computer and running."

"Hey Zeus, Chris. Please don't let her turn this into a crime," I beseech our more levelheaded friend. "On second thought, I'm coming to help."

Nina smiles. "It's best if you stay out here, Ally. If too many of us bombard the man, he might not be as accommodating." Her smile turns to a grin. "For the record, it's Jesús Cristo."

Huh? I shake my head, not in the mood to deal with Nina's insistence on correcting me at every turn. It's not important.

I'm not sure I agree that one extra woman will result in a guy not being accommodating, but I'm not going to argue. I'm perfectly content sitting my hind end in this car and allowing them to shoulder the load this time.

"Don't worry, Ally. I did not call off work today to be arrested. I assure you, there will be no theft involved." She turns toward Lanie. "Got it?"

Lanie rolls her eyes. "Let's go."

Twenty minutes later, both girls are rushing back to the car, looking triumphant.

Lanie is carrying a piece of plastic, and Nina's waving her phone in the air.

Nina motions for me to pop the trunk, so I do, watching as

Lanie rushes to the back, placing the piece of aluminum she was carrying inside.

They hop into the car, chatting animatedly.

"What happened?" I ask, but neither one stops to answer me, continuing to talk in gibberish I can't follow. "What happened?" I yell, garnering looks of shock from both my friends, because I rarely get loud.

"Apparently, Richard convinced Leon to total the truck. In exchange, Santos got to keep the truck for scrap. It's still sitting behind the shop two years later." Nina smiles wide, pointing toward the trunk. "Leon had one of his guys cut off a piece of the fender, where there is still black paint from another vehicle."

I gasp. Corinne had mentioned that they could match paint from transfers. "You guys . . . that's huge."

Lanie bobs her head. "Best part—Nina was correct on the dates. The truck was brought in on August eighteenth."

The day after Billy's accident.

"I thought you said he had the truck fixed?" I say to Nina.

"That's what I was told. But the more I think about it, the truck he drives now is slightly different. It would appear he bought him a new one, practically the same."

"Billy," I call out, needing him to confirm what I already suspect. "What color was your Jeep?"

Billy's seated next to Nina in the back, smiling like a clown. "Black, baby."

I start the car and put it in drive, ready to present our case.

"Where we off to?" Nina asks, but her green complexion tells me she already knows.

"Nina, I'm sorry, but we have to give this to Nick."

Her eyes close as she breathes in and out a few times. "I know. It's just going to make life a bit difficult."

My stomach plummets thinking about how Nina will fare

when the news breaks that her stepson is being tried for vehicular homicide and fleeing the scene along with who knows what else. It'll ruin Richard's perfect reputation, right at a crucial time for reelection.

Will she be safe?

"You need to leave him, Nina," I say, glancing at her through the rearview. "You can stay with me. I'll help you."

She shakes her head, lowering her eyes to her lap. "I can't even think about that right now. We just need to hurry. Lanie paid off Leon, but I don't trust him."

She doesn't need to say anything else. I put the pedal to the metal and haul ass toward Nick.

I pull into the police station on two wheels, because there's no doubt in my mind that Leon Santos has already tipped off Richard to our visit. Men like Santos don't poo where they eat, and Richard Dunbar has probably lined his pockets far better than Lanie ever could.

"Lanie, grab the fender," I order, turning back to look at Nina. "I think it's best if you stay out of this part. I don't want your life to be any more difficult because you were involved in uncovering Charlie's crime."

She nods. "Agree. I'm going to sit this one out."

I offer her a tight-lipped smile and jump from the car, rushing to catch up to Lanie. We burst through the doors, headed toward the receptionist.

"May I help you?" the white-haired woman with hard eyes, almost black in color, asks from behind the desk.

"We need to see Nick West immediately, please. We have evidence of a major crime," Lanie explains, voice even and leaving no room for argument.

"Let me see if he's available."

"If he's here, he's available," Lanie says, drumming her claw like nails on the desk.

The woman shoots her an annoyed glare before calling Nick. "He'll be out shortly."

She turns her chair, giving us her back. A clear dismissal, no doubt a result of Lanie's directness.

Less than two minutes later, Nick saunters out, looking every bit the calm and collected man I've grown to view him as.

"Alyssa?" he says, when he sees it's me and Lanie. "What's going on?" When he asks this, his gaze is fixed on the fender in Lanie's hand.

"Evidence," she says, lifting it up.

"Come with me," he orders, turning on his heels and stalking toward the back.

His body language isn't exactly screaming that he's glad to see us.

He steers us into what appears to be an interrogation room.

"What's with this?" Lanie asks, dropping the fender on a desk and popping her fists on her hips. "We aren't suspects. Certainly, you can find better accommodations for us."

He takes a deep breath. "I think it's best if we have this conversation in here. Somewhere we won't be overheard in case what you're carrying there was obtained any other way than legally."

"Nick, you know we wouldn't do anything that wasn't above board. We simply asked and a nice gentleman provided us with some proof we need for you to start up the investigation."

He closes his eyes. "I said I was done with the cloak and dagger stuff. I can't be running around trying to solve cases that don't concern the department."

"We understand. That's why we did our own investigation."

He groans. "Alyssa, you promised me you wouldn't."

"My promise was null and void the moment I told you physical evidence might exist."

His hands rise to his temples, and he rubs at them hard. "I can't do this today. Please go home and stop this."

"No, because we know who's responsible for, at the very least, Billy Garet's death."

His head lolls back on his shoulders. "This I've gotta hear."

"Charlie Dunbar."

His eyes snap to mine. "Charlie?" His head shakes back and forth. "No, Alyssa. You can't go around accusing men, especially the mayor's son, of crimes without solid evidence."

"Did you not hear her when she said we have it?" Lanie's hand shoots out toward the fender. "Let me break it down for you, Nick. Charlie left the bar at the same time as Billy. That should check out if you watch the tapes that Alyssa claims you already requested. Then the idiot drives down Spooky Hollow and sideswipes Billy's black Jeep, transferring paint to the fender of his red truck that was taken to Santos auto body on August eighteenth, the day after Billy's accident."

"Like she said, all very easy to confirm." I take a step toward him. "Look at the evidence, Nick. You'll see we're right. Charlie Dunbar caused that accident, likely because he was drunk, according to Billy."

Nick huffs a humorless laugh. "The only evidence you have that Charlie was intoxicated comes from a ghost?" He shakes his head. "Please go home and don't mention this to another person. I'll repeat . . . for your safety."

He turns his back on us and walks out, leaving Lanie and I standing there speechless.

"He isn't going to listen," Lanie says, sounding dejected for the first time ever.

"We'll make him," Billy says, appearing next to Lanie.

"How are you going to do that?"

Lanie's eyes narrow in on me. "Who you talking to in the middle of the precinct?" she whispers out of the corner of her mouth. "Please stop."

I ignore her, giving Billy my full attention. Nobody's around and she's more than clued in to my ability.

"According to Harry, we can haunt someone other than you if you're nearby. That might speed up his belief in us." He shrugs, picking invisible lint from his gray hoodie. "Jackson's already on board."

I smile wide. "Do your best work."

Nine of Swords

Nick

TURNING MY BACK on Alyssa was hard. I care what happens to her, and this insistence that she's seeing ghosts has me worried. Even more concerning is the fact that the people she's closest to seem to be feeding into the delusions instead of getting her help.

"Was that Lanie Anderson?" Eric asks, strutting toward me as if she's still around to see him.

"Yes."

He lifts his eyebrows, eyes darting around. "Care to tell me what she wanted?"

"No."

"So we're at *that* stage. One-word answers?"

For the first time ever, Marsha comes to the rescue, waddling up, holding the fender out toward me. "This was left at the front. Not sure what to do with it."

I grab it from her hands, not sure myself. I give it a quick once-over, my eyes staying rooted on the black paint marring the red, and my gut knots. Could I be wrong?

No.

And even if I am, things will have to unravel in due time, when Captain gives the okay. Otherwise, I'll be up shit creek without a paddle.

What the hell was Alyssa thinking? I warned her multiple times about the danger in running around insisting that accidents were homicides. Now she's claiming it's the mayor's son. Her best friend's stepson? She has no idea what shitstorm she could stir up making that claim.

"What is that?" Eric asks, looking at the fender and then to me.

I walk around him, car part in hand, dropping it onto my desk. "Why all the questions, Malone? You're giving me a headache."

"Who pissed in your coffee?" he says, walking up behind me. "I'm curious, man. It's not every day you see Lanie and Standoffish Widow in the precinct, bearing gifts of . . . sawed-off plastic?"

My fingers massage at my temples. "Stop calling her that."

"I'm just repeating what you've always called her," he says, puckering his lips. "I keep forgetting you caught feelings."

"Drop it, Malone. We're done talking about this."

He raises both hands. "All right. All right. Captain wants us in his office. He expects a debriefing on the Cruz case."

Captain's timing can't be worse. The last thing I need is a grilling about a case I've hit a dead end with. My brain is fried from Alyssa's claims. "This conversation will go down like a cup of cold sick."

"Huh?" Eric glances around as if someone can shed some light. "What does that even mean?"

"You're about to find out," I say, dragging my feet all the way to the captain's office, with him hot on my heels.

I'm about eight feet from the door when something in my path trips me. I attempt to right myself and end up slamming into Captain's door, creating a sound that rivals a brick being tossed at the wood.

"Shit. You okay, West?"

I spin around, searching for whatever caused my fall but find nothing.

"There was something . . ." My words trail off as I continue to search for an apparently invisible object. "Where did it go?"

"Are you gonna bust down my door or get your asses in here?" Captain yells from the other side.

I share a look with Eric before pushing it open and heading straight into the fire.

"Care to explain that?" Captain says, looking at Eric and then me.

"He tripped over his own feet," Eric says, smothering a laugh.

Captain grunts, steely gaze trained on me. "Take a seat, boys. What do ya got for me?"

I make to sit and somehow miss completely, falling straight on my ass.

"Jesus Christ, West. What the hell's the matter with ya?"

I pop up like a jack-in-the-box, looking to Malone with a scowl meant to shake him to his bones. He bites his bottom lip, trying desperately not to burst into laughter in front of Captain, but I know he didn't do it. He wouldn't clown around in Captain's office.

"Try it again," Captain commands, looking at me like I've lost it. "And someone better start talking. I have the feds breathing down my neck, and Silverton all over our ass for info about the missing persons report. I need something to get them to piss off."

I pat the chair, sitting down slower than a geriatric man, feeling about two feet high in front of my colleague and mentor.

I'm shaken from the confrontation with Alyssa. That has to be it.

"The car was wiped clean and there was no additional evidence to be found," Eric starts, and Captain cuts him off before he can continue.

"What about a murder weapon? It had to have been something large based on the crack to her skull."

"Nothing that matches, and no blood was found at the scene. She was likely killed somewhere else and taken to that location to dump," I say, rubbing my leg anxiously. Anything to get rid of this pent-up energy coursing through me.

My hairs are sticking up on end, and I swear to god the vent is blowing directly on my neck, giving the sensation of a whispered breath. A very uneasy feeling is creeping over me, and the need to get the hell out of this office before I make a further fool of myself is intense.

Captain's phone rings, distracting me momentarily from my unease. "Get outta here and find me something useful," he barks, waving his hand in the air.

He does not have to tell me twice.

I'm out of my chair, going hell for leather to my desk.

"Dude . . . what is going on with you today?" Eric stares at me like I've sprouted a third eye, and maybe I have.

Something is off, and I can't put my finger on it.

"I'm not feeling right today," I say, swiping the back of my hand over my forehead, feeling for a high temperature.

Eric looks around and leans in. "Go home, man. I'll cover for you."

The last thing I need is to go home. I don't want to be anywhere near Alyssa. It was my conversation with her that sent this day spiraling into one disaster after another. Now I don't know where we stand and that has me bothered.

"No. I'll be okay. We've got work to do."

His eyes widen as if to say *Yeah, right.*

I take a seat at my desk with Eric right across from me, pulling up a file to look over my notes. I make a mental list of all the people and places we still need to speak to. Shirley comes to mind, and I wonder for a moment why.

Maybe I should ask her for the tapes leading up to Jenna's disappearance. She has to have the others I requested ready to go by now.

I grab a pen, preparing to write down all the questions I have for her pertaining to Jenna. I'm writing out my list when some unseen force pushes my hand across the paper, the ball of the pen scraping against the wood and creating a screech that hurts my ears.

Eric jumps back, mouth hanging open, eyes darting left to right. I have absolutely no justification for what just occurred. Not only am I losing my grip on reality, but now I'm losing control of my motor ability.

"I think I'm just gonna go," I say, thrusting my thumb over my shoulder.

Malone's head bobs animatedly up and down. "I think that's best." He glances to the fender. "What do you want me to do with that?"

Taking a deep breath, I say something completely against my better judgment. "Have forensics see what they can make of the paint transfer."

Like the reliable partner he is, Eric doesn't even question my ask. "On it," he says, grabbing the plastic and heading out.

Within five minutes, I'm in my car heading home, trying to make sense of all the strangeness from today. I contemplate calling a doctor, afraid this is the start of a serious medical condition. My balance is off, my whole body is tingling . . . something must be wrong.

I pull up Jackie's number, trying to decide whether to tell her what's going on but decide better of it. She has her hands full with Zoey, and I don't want her to panic. Which she would.

I've just placed my phone in the cup holder when my wheel jerks left, narrowly missing an oncoming vehicle before screeching to a halt at the entrance of Clementine's.

My chest heaves with each ragged intake of breath, while my heart practically pounds out of my chest.

What the fuck is happening?

I no more than think it, and my horn begins to blare, right along with my radio. I grab my hair at the roots and pull, losing the last grip on my sanity. The car door flies open, and my feet are moving without conscious thought, carrying me toward the building. I attempt to dig in my heels and stop this madness, but my entire body is stiff and tingling.

A bright light shines in my peripheral vision, and I turn to see that it's illuminating a red truck.

Charlie Dunbar's truck.

"What voodoo is this?"

I have no way to explain these bizarre occurrences, other than it's something beyond this world.

What are the chances that Alyssa would accuse Charlie Dunbar of vehicular homicide, I'd rebuff her claims, and my possessed car would force me here? The very place he's likely been since it opened this morning.

I might find that I've gone and truly lost my mind, but I'm here, so I might as well see where this day takes me. What more do I have to lose at this point?

As soon as I enter the dingy building, my eyes land on Amanda. Based on the way she's staring at me, she thinks I'm here to relapse. Her lips are turned down into a frown, and the disappointment aimed at me stings, even if it's misguided.

"Nick?" she says it like a question, but I'm not paying any attention to her.

I'm focused on the man hunched over the bar, sipping something stronger than his usual beer. Instinct tells me not to approach Charlie without more to go on.

"Is Shirley here?"

Her shoulders relax and she yanks on her yellow shirt, offering a tight-lipped smile. "Yeah, she's in the office. She won't mind if you head on back."

I nod before making my way toward Shirley's office. The door is open when I get there, and she spins around in her chair when she hears me approach.

"Nicky. Glad you're here." She doesn't smile, turning back toward her computer monitor that's currently playing the recordings from the bar camera. "Do you have any update on what happened to Jenna?" Her voice wavers, thick with emotion.

I have no doubt that's why she turned her back on me. She's strong, having grown up in the school of hard knocks.

"We're still investigating."

She sighs. "I don't have your tapes yet. Lazy son of a bitch hasn't shown up to attempt to fix this. All I'm getting is static, on every single recording. I have to be doing something wrong." She turns to look at me. "You're more than welcome to take a look yourself if you have time."

"That would be great. Thanks, Shirley."

She moves from the chair, motioning for me to take her vacated seat.

"I tried to view the night before Jenna went missing and that's when I found the recordings are all wonky."

"Has this happened before?"

"I've only checked a recording once before. There was a fight and I needed to provide evidence to the police because one of the guys filed assault charges. That recording was perfect. But that was months ago." She grabs money from a drawer and stashes it in her purse. "If you figure it out, you'll have to do some toggling if you want to check different cameras."

This is news to me; the only one I was aware of is the visible camera over the bar.

"Where are the other cameras?" I ask, getting comfortable in the chair.

"I have one in the back alley for safety purposes. Can't have my girls or the kitchen staff getting mugged in the middle of the night when they're leaving here." She purses her lips. "There's also one hidden in the front lot; that way, if there are fights after hours, we have the details on what went down. You should be able to access back to the spring of 2019."

She goes about showing me how to search for specific dates.

"Pretty straightforward. Need anything else?" she asks, hand still over the mouse.

I'm about to tell her I'm good to go when the computer goes haywire, shifting from one camera to the other, finally settling on the one over the bar. A man is leaning down, saying something into Charlie Dunbar's ear. I move closer to the screen and when the guy turns, I get a good look at him.

"What is Marcus Wells doing here?" I ask, looking over my shoulder at Shirley.

"Marcus? He's Amanda's boyfriend. He's always here."

My eyes widen with that knowledge. Does Amanda know she's in bed with a criminal?

"What the hell?" Shirley says, eyes narrowed in on the screen. "The cameras have all gone to shit." I turn around to see the screen flick on and off before a video pops up. "What is happening?"

Shirley asks. "I tried to pull that up for a week straight and just got static."

I check the date on that particular recording and the blood drains from my face. August 10, 2023. The day Jenna went missing.

I shrug because I have no explanation. It seems to be working now. The whys hardly matter. I click the play button and watch what unfolds.

Jenna walks out the door at 3:15 a.m. according to the time-stamp. Aside from Jenna's Volvo, a black Yukon with blackout windows is in the back, right next to Jenna's car.

"Any idea whose car that is?" I ask Shirley, who practically puts her nose to the screen to get a look.

"No clue. Never seen it."

Jenna's eyes are on her phone, and I watch as someone with a black ski mask exits the Yukon and approaches her. There isn't sound on this camera, but the man is pointing toward the phone, and it looks like he's instructing Jenna to take some action. Then he grabs it from her hand, and she takes off running. She doesn't get far, because a second man exits from the passenger side and grabs her from behind, placing her in the back of the Yukon.

"Oh my god. She was taken right from the parking lot?" Shirley's voice breaks on a sob.

Within a minute, the man who threw Jenna in the back of the Yukon gets into her car and both vehicles drive off. I write down the time, and I rewind the video and take some stills to send off to try to get a positive ID on the plates.

"This whole time I had evidence. I could've saved her." The fragile woman is falling apart.

I spin around in my chair and grab her hands. "You did the best you could. This isn't your fault." Another sob rips through her chest, shaking her frail frame. "We'll get them, Shirley. I promise."

She wipes her face, working to pull herself together.

"For the time being, I need you to keep this information to yourself. If it gets out that we have this, the people involved could run."

Her eyes grow hard, and I know on this she'll be a steel trap. "I won't breathe a word."

I continue to play and rewind the tape, taking in every detail I can manage, including the description of the masked men. Based on their size and bulk, there's no question that they are men. One is extremely tall and lanky, while the other is built like a brick shithouse.

"Holy shit. I know who one of them is," I say out loud.

He's currently in this bar. Seems highly suspicious that he's my primary suspect in Jenna's death and he just so happens to be here talking to a man that Alyssa is accusing of vehicular homicide. Not that they're connected. But still.

I rewind the tape and watch it again. The other has the same build as the second guy who was talking to Mayor Dunbar at the festival. But what could their motive be for killing Jenna? I make a quick phone call to Malone and relay all the information, instructing him to get eyes on Marcus Wells and a subpoena to access Jenna's phone records, including her texts, videos, and access to her iCloud, because I know she had an iPhone. We had extensive conversations over the years about her opinion that Apple was superior.

I get Amanda to arrange for a ride for Shirley, unwilling to allow the woman to drive in the state she's in. The unwarranted guilt that Jenna was taken from the Clementine's parking lot will be something that haunts her for the rest of her life, and that kills me. She doesn't deserve that.

Shirley sits silently beside me, waiting for her ride, while I jot down notes. A nudge tells me to check the tapes from the night of

Billy's accident too. I pull up August seventeenth but can't see Billy for most of the video, as the camera doesn't reach as far as the pool tables. I'm about to skip forward, when Billy saunters out from where the pool tables are located to the bar.

The video continues to play until Billy pays his tab and leaves the building. Charlie Dunbar leaves a mere minute behind him. I skip to the front parking lot camera and rewind to see Billy talking in the parking lot with some dark-haired girl, long enough for Charlie to come staggering out. The girl says something to Charlie, who appears to completely ignore her. She shrugs her shoulders, gives Billy a hug, and heads to her car. Billy gets into his black Jeep and takes off. Charlie leaves moments after him, heading in the same direction. In his red truck.

Shit. Alyssa might be right.

Anger courses through me. This entire time Billy's family has been made to believe that he caused his own accident, when it's becoming more likely that he was an innocent victim of a drunk driver.

Before I know it, I'm on my feet and heading toward the bar. I grab Charlie's arm, yanking him out of his chair.

Amanda gasps. "Stop, Nick. What are you doing?"

I lean in to Charlie. "I know what you did."

He doesn't even fight me when I pull him toward the back. This is not a conversation we're gonna have in the middle of Clementine's with a worked-up Amanda hovering around. When we're out the back door and alone in the alley, I let go of Charlie.

"I want you to tell me what happened the night of August seventeenth, 2021."

His shoulders hunch over and his chin dips. "How did you find out?"

He doesn't even try to deny he did something.

"Video evidence is pretty damning. Not to mention I have a part of your truck with the paint transfer from Billy's Jeep."

He nods. Not quite a confession, but enough for me to know he did it.

"It was an accident. I never meant to hurt anybody." The blubbering idiot starts crying right in front of me, a broken man who's been living with this guilt for years.

"Did you have anything to do with Garrett Mann's accident? Or Jackson Moore's?"

Charlie's head shakes. "No, I had nothing to do with any of that."

Out of nowhere, a buzzing in my ear makes my head spin. I press my cheek against my shoulder, turning away from Charlie. I know better than to turn my back on a suspect, but I can't help it. The pain in my ear is excruciating.

The buzzing dies down and I shake my head to rid myself of the last of the pesky noise. I lift my head, and my eyes connect with a woman's in a car at the farthest spot from me in the parking lot. Her eyes bug out and her head snaps away. But I already saw her.

Lanie Anderson, in the passenger seat of Alyssa's Volvo.

What the hell are those two up to now?

Completely forgetting about the crying Charlie, I make my way toward the car, determined to unearth what game they're playing at.

A loud pop sounds, piercing my ears again, and before I have a chance to identify the source of the shot, Charlie falls forward. I draw my gun as more shots are fired, ricocheting off the dumpsters. I catch a glimpse of blond hair as someone moves around the corner, but I don't see anything else.

"Get out of here," I scream, running toward the car. They need to get far away from here.

By the time I reach the street, the gunfire has stopped and the girls are safely out of the parking lot. I pull my phone out of my back pocket and dial the station.

"I need backup and an ambulance in the back parking lot of Clementine's. Stat. Shots were fired, and I have a man down."

Despite my asking for an ambulance, I fear it's pointless.

Charlie's dying.

27

Ace of Swords

NOT ONE OF us said a word the entire way to my house.

We're all in shock.

I didn't leave until I was sure that Nick was going to be all right. After the first shots rang out, no more came, and Lanie insisted he was safe. It's not easing my worry.

He has to be okay.

"I think I need to go home," Nina says, back hunched and makeup smeared down her cheeks.

She's been in the bathroom for the last twenty minutes. We knew she needed space and gave it to her.

"Do you think it's a good idea for you to be driving in this state?" Lanie asks. "We'll be worried about you."

"I'll be fine, but I really need to be home to find out what's going on with Charlie." She sniffles, wiping her nose with the sleeve of her shirt. "I know he's been involved in some bad things due to his alcoholism, but the guy's had a rough life. His parents are narcissists who pushed him aside his entire life for their own careers."

A stray tear falls down her cheek. "I don't agree with half of the things he's done, but I've always felt sorry for him."

I offer a tight smile. "I understand. Just text us when you get home."

She nods, not saying another word as she makes her way toward the door. She pauses with her hand on the knob and turns back. "Is it just me, or did you see the woman with the gun?"

My mouth drops open. I hadn't seen a thing. I was too focused on being caught by Nick and what he was going to do when he reached my car.

"A woman?"

"A blonde, wearing a yellow tee."

"I'll make sure Nick gets those details."

She doesn't say anything else, leaving us alone, lost in our own thoughts.

"Do you think he's dead?" I ask Lanie.

She takes a deep breath. "I don't know. The way he fell, and that blank look on his face . . ." She bites her bottom lip. "We were too far away for me to be sure."

Exhaustion washes over me, and I can barely keep my eyes open. Lanie and I are both curled up on my couch in the bonus room, too tired to move upstairs. I grab a blanket and throw it at her, getting one for myself too. It doesn't take long before my eyelids grow heavy and my eyes close. The last image my brain conjures before I nod off is Nick running toward my car.

Please let him be safe.

✦ ✦ ✦

A HARD KNOCKING has me shooting straight up, head swinging from side to side. The sun is out, and I've been blessed with another day.

Unlike some people.

A quick glance at the clock tells me I've slept well past breakfast and halfway through lunch.

The knocking sound begins again, and that's when I realize someone's at my front door. At first, I consider ignoring it, but the incessant pounding is enough to give me a headache.

"I'm coming," I yell out, managing to stir Lanie.

"What's going on?" Her voice is full of sleep and her eyes aren't even open.

"Someone's at the door. Go back to sleep."

She pulls the blanket up over her as she twists to her other side. You never have to tell Lanie to sleep more than once.

I yank the door open, ready to give a tongue-lashing to whoever finds it necessary to practically punch through my door, only to find Nick, fist raised and wearing the same clothes as yesterday.

There are bags under his tired eyes and his hair is good and mussed, looking like he's been running his hands through it all night.

My breath hitches and without thinking, I launch myself into his arms.

"Nick," I cry out, tears welling in my eyes. "I'm so glad you're okay." The words are whispered into the crook of his neck, and I feel his entire body shiver in response.

His arms wrap around me, pulling me flush to his chest.

"I have so many questions," he says into the top of my head. "I'm sorry for not listening sooner." His fingers run through my hair, while his other hand remains wrapped around my back. The moment is incredibly intimate, and I don't dare move. "You could've been hurt."

I swallow, thinking about how close to danger he'd been.

Pulling away, I stare into his eyes. "I was worried sick. Don't ever d—"

My words are cut off when Nick's lips crash against mine,

swallowing my choked cry of relief. When his tongue begs entrance, I open willingly. The kiss isn't gentle. It's a dominating kiss. A claim stemming from fear and desperation.

I claw at his shirt, gripping it tightly against my palms, needing to feel each beat of his heart. Each labored breath he takes.

Our tongues tangle in a dance that's ours alone. It lights up every piece of me, sending tingles down my spine and chills across my neck. This is unlike anything I've experienced before, and despite everything, there isn't sadness with that truth.

It's different, but that doesn't take away from what I had with Garrett. If anything, my life with him taught me to not settle for less than anything that makes your soul light up. He gave that to me during his short life here on earth, and I know without a doubt he'd want that for me again.

I push all thoughts of that life away as I allow myself to melt into Nick. To allow this growing need to bloom. I'm not sure how long we stay like this, front door wide open for the world to see. Neither of us cares. Let people talk. In this moment, it's just us.

My body is flush against him when he pulls away, breath ragged.

"I'm sorry." His thick, smoky voice makes my feet tingle and belly flip-flop.

I almost don't want to ask, because if he says he regrets kissing me, I might die.

"For what?"

"For kissing you." My mood plummets, and he must see it because his eyes widen fractionally, and he rushes to explain. "I'm not sorry I did it. I'm sorry I didn't ask."

The corners of my lips tip up into a wide grin. "I thought it was hot."

He chuckles, pulling me in to him and placing a chaste kiss on my lips. "It was a long time coming, if I'm honest."

My head bobs like a broken doll head. "It was."

That dimpled grin I'm growing to crave greets me. "There will be plenty more of that if you want, but I have questions and I need answers."

I gulp, stepping aside and motioning for him to come in, shutting the door and steering him toward the front room, as far from Lanie as possible. As ridiculous as it is, I want to keep him to myself for a bit.

"Why were you at Clementine's?" he blurts out, not even waiting for me to sit.

I grimace, thinking about our part in putting Nick in the line of fire and really questioning if now's a good time to bring up ghosts.

"Do you really want the truth? Or should I lie to you?"

He stares at me intently, and I can't make out what's going through his mind. "The truth, Alyssa."

I roll my tongue, savoring the hint of mint still on my breath. All the various ways to stall filter through my mind, and for a split second I consider denying what happened. One quick look at Nick tells me that won't work.

I take a deep breath and exhale for a ten count.

"We kinda . . . sorta . . ." My eyes dart around the room, avoiding him.

"Alyssa," he drawls, knowing damn well that I'm hedging.

"We recruited Billy and Jackson into haunting you."

His head jerks back, eyes bugging out of their sockets. "You what?"

"We needed to make you believe in their existence. So they agreed to find ways to make you second-guess your stance."

He takes a menacing step toward me, and I back up in response. We're doing a dance. One step forward. Two steps back.

"As in tripping me and moving my chair?" he grits through his teeth.

I shrug, gnashing my own teeth together. "No clue. They didn't exactly give me details."

Nick grunts, running his hand back through his hair. "A man is in a coma, and we have no leads on who shot him. I'm exhausted and I just need a straight answer. What were you doing at the bar?"

My hands lift. "First, you do have a lead."

His head tilts. "Is this coming from ghosts?"

I shake my head. "An eyewitness. Nina saw a blond woman wearing a yellow shirt fire the gun."

Nick's breath hitches. "Is she positive?"

"Yes. One hundred percent."

"Shit." He starts to pace. "Shirley said she's dating Marcus."

"You know who it is?"

He turns to me. "Yes."

He pulls his phone out of his pocket and makes a call.

"Malone. Get an APB on Amanda Hersch. She's wanted in the attempted murder of Charlie Dunbar."

My stomach tumbles at the news that Charlie is fighting for his life. I suspected that he was dead, but I'm relieved that's not the case. He deserves to be brought to justice in another way.

"Now tell me why you were at Clementine's," Nick says, crossing his arms over his chest.

"In order for them to connect with you, I have to be close by. We followed you because it didn't seem like the ghosts were making headway and I needed them to continue the quest."

He groans, head falling back. Nick's focus remains on the ceiling for several minutes while I sit here twiddling my thumbs and questioning whether I've just ruined any and all chance of experiencing that kiss again.

I break the silence. "Why would someone want to kill him? Did someone from Billy's or Jackson's family figure out he was behind their deaths?"

"No. It was the bartender, Amanda. She watched me drag Charlie out. Word around town is that she's dating Marcus Wells, who I suspect had a hand in helping Richard cover up the accident, and more."

"You believe that he killed Billy?"

Nick sighs. "He admitted to being the cause of Billy's death, but he denied having anything to do with the others."

"That doesn't make sense. He has to be connected. Otherwise, I'm back to square one on how to get rid of these ghosts."

Nick glosses right over my panic, but what he says next revives my hope. "I got the sense he might've had an idea who did." He tilts his head, fingers steepled at his lips. "What I'm about to ask, I wanna make perfectly clear is only because I have had a day from hell, and I am at my wit's end."

"Okay. What do you need?"

"If you can talk to the dead, do you think you could speak to someone straddling both worlds?"

"You mean Charlie?"

"Yeah. I mean, I'm not exactly sure how these things work, but if it's a possibility, now would be a great time to use your skills."

I clamp down on my cheek to refrain from grinning. Now would not be a good time to rub it in that he was wrong.

"I'm not saying I believe in all of this, but I believe in you, Alyssa. I'm willing to keep an open mind if it helps solve these cases."

That he believes in me is everything. I smile wide. "Let me make some calls. I'm not sure if it's possible. I'll need some help."

+ + +

AS SOON AS I called Corinne and filled her in on what went down, she rushed over here and started preparing. Lanie and I ran out to check on Nina and tell her our plan. She decided she wanted to come along, and I wasn't about to deny her the front-row seat to what I hope is the beginning of the end for Project Ghosts Begone.

Walking into my formal dining room, the first thing I notice is the vintage candelabra in the middle of the table. Five candles glow in the otherwise dark room, throwing shadows to bounce off the walls of the shoebox space. Corinne has hung towels over the windows, blocking out the light. At any other point in my life, I'd be running for the hills. Nowadays, it feels status quo.

When you see actual ghosts on the daily, you tend to get over your fear of shadows.

"What's happening here?" I ask Corinne, who appears to be meditating in her seat at the head of the table.

"Shh," she hisses. "I'm preparing."

"How long do you need? I have to call Nick, and then we're ready to go."

She inhales, pursing her lips, and exhales through her nose. "Make the call."

Less than ten minutes later, we're gathered around my dining room table, holding hands. Corinne and I are at opposite ends at the heads of the table. Nina and Nick are on either side of me, and Lanie is between Nina and Corinne.

"Be prepared for bizarre changes from that one," I whisper to Nick, nodding my head in Corinne's direction. He grins, squeezing my hand.

I lean toward Nina. "Pay attention this time. I can't be the only one who witnesses the possession." Her head shakes and she lowers her head to hide the smile.

"I've already seen my share of crazy," she says.

"During this séance, remain in your seat and holding the hands of the person to your right and left. Do not, under any circumstances, break the sacred circle. Do you understand?"

Yeses ring out around the table as we all agree to Corinne's terms.

"Bow your heads and pray," Corinne commands. "God. Goddess. Mother Earth. We beseech you to connect us to the imprisoned spirit of Charlie Dunbar of Knox Harbor."

I concentrate on Charlie, running his features over and over in my mind, willing his spirit to present itself.

Nina's hold on my hand tightens, but I don't chance a glance her way. I know this has to be difficult for her, so I offer the only comfort I can in the form of a hand hug.

The table trembles under our arms, and even behind my closed eyelids, I can tell the candlelight is flickering faster than normal, until the flames are snuffed out entirely. A chill works down my spine, alerting me to a spirit's presence.

I pop one eye open, trying to adjust my eyes to the dark. All I see is black until a flare of light streaks across the room.

The tiny hairs on my arms rise like they normally do.

The overhead light flips on, and in the corner is a very confused Charlie. His arms are crossed, and his eyebrows are folded in. My body sags with relief that it's him and not some other stranded spirit.

"Charlie," I coo, in an attempt not to startle him.

He's not dead, but his spirit is in a sort of limbo. According to Natalia, that comes with a lot of haze surrounding their memories and surely a barrel of trepidation. He might be in so much shock that this entire experiment will result in nothing helpful.

"He's in shock," Billy whispers into my ear, confirming my suspicion. "Be gentle with him. You've got this."

Billy's reassurance is unexpected and dare I say a bit heartwarming. All this time, he's been an epic pain in my rear, but in this moment, he looks tired and anxious. Maybe his crankiness has everything to do with being stuck in limbo. In another time and place, maybe he wasn't so bad.

Ugh. Am I really giving the dunderhead a pass?

Nope. I refuse to soften my heart toward him until he's on his way to the afterlife.

"Go on," Billy urges. "Make him listen."

I glance around the room, and everyone offers smiles and nods of encouragement. Except Nina, who hasn't raised her chin. She's staring at the table, tears streaming down her face.

I want to wrap her in a hug, but that's not what's important right now. Nothing will be right in Nina's or any of our worlds until these cases are solved and these ghosts are at peace.

"Charlie, I'm Alyssa Mann. I was at Clementine's when you were shot."

His eyes bulge, and I immediately wish I'd skipped the whole shot part. Or at the very least eased into it. His teeth chatter so hard, I fear they'd all break off if he weren't a spirit who has no actual teeth.

"I want to help you. But before I can do that, I need you to answer some questions for me. Can you do that?"

"Y-you'll help me?" he stammers.

"That's the plan. I might be able to help guide you back to your body."

Corinne pops one eye open, and I can see the reprimand she's holding back in that one eyeball. She's thinking I shouldn't be promising stuff I have no clue I can make good on.

She's not wrong, but we'll be here all day if I don't lead this conversation and give him a reason to calm down.

It seems to do the trick. He's no longer shaking and his shoulders have straightened, so I push forward.

"You admitted today that you were involved in the death of Billy Garet. What can you tell me about that night?"

He squints, looking at something in the opposite corner. "I don't remember anything about that night. But I remember the next morning. My truck was smashed to hell, and I told my dad I'd run someone off the road." His mouth presses together. "We heard that some guy was in an accident leaving Clementine's the night before. It happened on Spooky Hollow, which was my typical route. Dad pieced things together and told me not to tell anyone. He'd take care of it."

"Richard covered up the accident for you?" I press, needing him to say that part.

Nina groans. "We already know this."

I don't address Nina, knowing I have to continue working with Charlie while he's being cooperative.

"Yes. Got a new truck out of the deal." Something shifts and his face contorts. "Not like it mattered. I was never good enough. Always a disappointment. He didn't help to save me. He did it for his political career."

Hatred oozes from every word he speaks, and I get the sense he'd like nothing more than to see his father suffer. Which gives me an idea.

"He told you not to tell anyone, but you did, didn't you, Charlie?"

He doesn't even hesitate. "Spilled my guts to the bartender a month later. She was always cozying up to him when he came to the bar to get me. I wanted her to know what a scumbag he was. Couldn't keep it in." His sadistic smile says it all. He told what happened to take down his father, with no care in the world that it would incriminate him too.

I relay all this to the group, leaving out the bit about the bartender and Richard, for Nina's sake, and know immediately that Nick is putting together ways to prove all of this.

"Ask him which bartender he told."

I raise a brow at Nick, wondering why that matters.

"I heard him," he says, saving me from repeating it. "Jenna."

"He says he told Jenna."

Nick's eyes widen. Just a hair, but enough for me to know that prompted some clue that's vital in his case.

"Tell Charlie to use me to communicate with the group," Corinne says.

My face screws up. "No. That's . . . got to be dangerous."

She rolls her eyes. "It only works for a few minutes, but it'll be long enough if you hurry that everyone will hear the details, which could lead to more theories. I'll be fine."

Charlie rubs his hands together like this is the one thing he's been waiting for and without another prompt, he practically leaps across the table, merging his spirit with Corinne's like something out of a nineties movie.

"Hurry," Nick encourages. "She said it won't last long."

"Did you have anything to do with my accident? Or Jackson Moore's?"

"Nah. That wasn't me. Dad made sure I had a ride home after Billy's accident to prevent another." He grunts. "I'm not sure what happened to you, but I know he was likely involved in Jackson's."

"How do you know that?" Nick asks.

"He was there the night I told Jenna. He's the only other person who knew." He chuckles darkly, and it sounds deranged coming from Corinne's mouth. "My old man was livid. Threatened to kill me if it got out and his career was sunk. He didn't even give a shit about the possibility of prison."

"You think he could've had something to do with Jackson's death?" Nina asks, voice pitching. "As in . . . he murdered someone in cold blood?"

Corinne's one shoulder shrugs. "Wouldn't put it past him to take out Jenna and Jackson since they knew. Anything to ensure his reputation remained intact. I'm pretty sure he tried to take out Jenna, but it went south." He laughs bitterly. "Not that he'd get his hands dirty. He'd have his two stooges do it."

"It went south . . . how? What do you know about that?" I press, needing to hurry this up.

He shakes his head. "Not much, and I can't provide you any solid evidence. I just overheard a conversation a couple years back. About a month after the accident, he was reaming out one of his goons for missing his chance. Andy was blubbing about following the wrong Volvo. Jenna drove a Volvo, so I assumed they were after her. I did my best to shield her after that."

Nick's head snaps to Corinne. "What did you just say?"

She purses her lips but repeats the last part.

"Fuck," Nick says under his breath. "That's how you're connected."

"What are you talking about?" I ask, looking back and forth between Corinne and Nick.

"Billy's accident was August 17, 2021. Your accident was September 23, 2021. A little over a month apart."

"Okay?" I draw out, not seeing the parallel.

"He said his dad might have attempted to take out Jenna a month after the accident, which lines up with yours. Jenna drives a Volvo and you . . ."

The color leaches from Nina's face, and my stomach tumbles down to the depths of my body. "Drive a Volvo." The words come out as a whisper as I digest what he's suggesting.

"Holy shit," Lanie spits. "Richard was behind your accident."

Wheel of Fortune

NINA MOANS, SLUMPING forward onto the table but never breaking the circle. "This can't be happening."

I'm numb from head to toe, barely noticing the way everyone around the table is staring at me in various expressions of sadness and concern. My hands shake, and Nick squeezes the one he holds in support. Still, my teeth chatter and bile rises up the back of my throat.

Garrett is dead because my car coincidentally is the same as the intended target. It was wrong place, wrong time.

A sob rips through me and I try to lift my hands to my mouth. Nina and Nick hold my hands in place, ensuring the circle isn't broken.

"You have to finish questioning him, Alyssa." My head turns toward my best friend, and I see nothing but pain and sorrow. She mouths the words *I'm sorry*, and I want to fall apart.

For Garrett. For me. For Nina.

We're all victims of Richard Dunbar's actions and he will pay.

The time will come for me to process, but she's right, I need to finish this.

"Who were your dad's men?" I ask Corinne, while Lanie coos words of encouragement to Nina.

"Andy Bernas and Marcus Wells."

"Is there anything else you can tell us, Charlie?"

Corinne is quiet for a few minutes, peering over my shoulder toward the window.

"My dad's dirty. He's got his hands in a lot of criminal activity. I want to see him rot in a prison. Get him on anything you can."

"I'd love nothing more than that, but without proof or something more to go on, I'm not sure that's possible."

"Look into Luxe Lavou. I'm positive you'll find he's been laundering money through the place."

I share a glance with Lanie, and I'm a little unnerved to find not a hint of surprise. What does she know?

"And the shipyard at the docks. He's running drugs or something from there. He's always talking about important cargo."

"Thanks, Charlie. I'll do my best to ensure he goes away."

Our time's up, as indicated by Charlie being catapulted from Corinne. She's bent over the table, heaving in air, all the while Charlie looks perfectly fine. Bored, even.

"Can I go now? Some guy named Harry is trying to talk to me. He says I need to stick around in limbo for a while longer. I'm gonna fight him."

Oh, thank god. Harry can guide him back.

"You should probably listen to him. He'll help you."

He doesn't waste time, disappearing without another word.

I glance around the table, meeting everyone's eyes. "He's gone."

Nick pulls his phone from his pocket and begins to type. "I'm trying to write down all that was said before I forget."

"Why am I still here?" Billy groans. "He admitted to my death. Shouldn't I be well on my way to paradise?"

He should. At least, one would think so.

"I don't know, Billy. It looks like there's more to uncover."

I slump back into my chair, feeling utter defeat.

"I need some fresh air," Nina says, jumping up from the table and rushing from the room.

I go to stand, but Nick pulls my arm down. "She'll be okay. She's innocent in all this. Just give her some time."

"He's right," Lanie chimes in. "Thankfully, she never had access to their accounts. She's in the dark, and that's the best news tonight."

Lanie closes her eyes and breathes, Corinne moving to her side and grabbing her hand. *Comforting* is not a word I'd typically associate with Corinne, but maybe I've been too hard on her. Her head lifts and our eyes meet.

"If Richard was trying to get rid of the people who knew Charlie's secret, and he attempted with Jenna, then he had to have been involved with Jackson's," Corinne adds to the conversation, getting us back on track.

"The two men in the back of the car were Andy and Marcus. There's no doubt in my mind," Jackson says. "I was acquainted with Marcus from pool at Clementine's. The stockier man in the bed of the truck always looked familiar, but I couldn't put a name to the face. As soon as she said it, I knew."

I relay the info to Nick, and he scowls.

"This is all well and good, but without solid proof, we've got nothing." He scratches his head. "We need evidence to pin Richard, Andy, and Marcus to murder. The fender with the paint should help prove that Charlie caused Billy's accident and that Richard at the very least attempted to cover it up, but outside of that . . . we've got nothing."

"I can help with that," Jackson says, coming into the conversation. "I got hard up for money and started blackmailing Dunbar around December of 2021."

My hand slaps my forehead. "Where was this information weeks ago, Jackson?"

"Forgot."

My lips smack together, and I shake my head, but I share this news with Nick, who whistles.

"There will be a paper trail for that. We just have to uncover it." He taps his chin. "Ask him where he had the money sent."

"Right into my bank account. It came from an account owned by a Carrhid Durban."

I rush to the kitchen and grab a notepad and pen, practically running back into the dining room. "How do you spell that, Jackson?"

He relays the spelling and I push the paper over to Nick to see if he's familiar with the name. He grabs the pen from my hand and starts rearranging the letters.

Not two minutes go by before Nick bursts into laughter. "Thank god the man's an egomaniac. Carrhid Durban is an anagram for Richard Dunbar."

"We'll get the evidence we need."

He types something into his phone, and when he looks back up, I lift a brow.

"Sent a text to Malone with some details. I need him to get on this. Too many people know." He looks around the table. "This must stay between us."

Corinne mumbles and Lanie flips Nick the bird, but he doesn't care.

"How do we prove that Andy and Marcus were involved?" I ask, tapping my fingers on the table. "Richard must've been driving. Why use a recognizable vehicle?" I'm thinking out loud, trying to sort through all the thoughts floating through my mind.

"In the event they were seen, people would look at Charlie," Nick says, shaking his head. "The bastard was willing to let his son take the fall."

What a sick man. That's one thing I'll never understand. How anyone would throw their own child down the river to save themselves.

"Why the length of time between my accident and Jackson's death? And Jenna's?"

"It took him some time to find a way to make my death look like an accident," Jackson offers as a reason. "With the first attempt at taking out Jenna failed, he must've thought he could control her if he stayed with her. Buy her pretty things and promise her the world and she'll comply."

I choke on air. "What?"

Jackson gives me a look that screams *You all right*? "Jenna and Dunbar were fucking." I wince at the crude word, but more than that, at the knowledge that Richard was having an affair with Jenna Cruz.

"How do you know this?" I question, needing proof.

Proof to help solve her case and proof for Nina to get some closure about the scumbag she married.

"It was common knowledge. Jenna was always gushing at the bar about the gifts he gave her. The Volvo was a gift from him."

"Richard was having an affair with Jenna. He bought her the Volvo." I tell the collective, but it's Nick I look to.

"We'll be able to find records of that. I've already put in a request for her phone records, including texts and videos. Hopefully we'll find something incriminating there." He yawns. "It might take a while, but Richard Dunbar is going down for murder."

"I might have something that could help," Lanie says, eyes on the table. "It won't necessarily put them away for murder, but it might lead to more."

My body shakes with worry at how Lanie got caught up with Marcus. It was clear a few times that she knew more than she was letting on. I should've pushed, but I didn't want to think the worst of my best friend.

"Marcus came to me recently and asked to buy my studio. He told me I could run it and keep one hundred percent of the profits. He said in exchange, he'd need me to create customer profiles for dummy accounts who will pay in cash. I'd only have to deposit that money to a separate account. He handed me a box of booze, except inside it was filled with cash."

"Money laundering," Nick grates.

"I'm not an idiot. I knew what he was up to." She shrugs one shoulder. "I told him that my dad's an underboss in the Scottish mafia and he'd kill him if he found out. I promised to keep his secret and even suggested he speak to Milly instead. She's hard up for cash."

I bark a laugh. "Scottish mafia? He believed you?"

"I'm very persuasive. He even threw in an offer for me to use every facility he's involved with. He's a chickenshit."

The sound of a train blares through the room, shaking the walls and causing the lights to flicker.

"What now?" Lanie cries.

"Harry," Billy scolds. "What the hell?"

"Harry?" I ask, head bouncing back and forth between Jackson and Billy.

They're too busy high-fiving and bouncing around like children. That's when I know.

They're finally ready to move on.

"We're going home, Karen." Billy's smile is contagious.

I roll my eyes, but I can't help but smile back, because despite everything, I'm going to miss his smart ass.

"What do I need to do?" I ask, jumping up from my chair.

"Harry said you have to give our spirits permission to move on."

I nod. "Sure you don't wanna stay?"

"Are you nuts?" Lanie yells. "Send them packing."

Billy chews on his bottom lip, pretending to consider it. "No. I've had plenty of time with you."

Jackson bobs his head. "I'm with him. Time to go, toots."

"Jeez, guys. You sure know how to make a woman feel special."

"It's no offense to you, toots. Paradise just sounds like my kinda place."

I smile at Jackson, happy for him. "I'm sure it will be wonderful. No need to swindle people out of money." I look between both. Neither are innocent of that.

Jackson has the good sense to appear contrite.

I rock back on my heels, feeling awkward. I've spent a lot of time with these two. Some good, some bad, but either way, they deserve something nice from me as a farewell.

I turn to Jackson first. "Jackson, I'm sorry you got an unfair shake for simply being in the wrong place at the wrong time."

He punches his fist into his palm. "I was right where I was supposed to be. The money I took from Dunbar paid for my baby mama's house."

I didn't even know he had a kid. Wow, I was a horrible host.

"What's your kid's name?" I ask, determined to help his child out however I can. It's the least I can do.

"Ashley. She has her mother Heather's last name, Miller."

"I'll make sure she's cared for. I hope paradise is everything you could imagine."

He offers a toothy grin. "Right on, toots."

"You have my permission to move on, Jackson."

He smiles, pointing toward the sky before blinking out of existence, hopefully on his way to somewhere better.

I'm left with Billy. My first ghost and the biggest pain in my ass I've ever encountered.

"You better not smite me by forcing me to stay here," he says, waving a finger at me. "I've got plans for the other side."

I roll my eyes. "Pestering some other poor soul?"

"Likely." He grins. "Listen, I wanna thank you for closing my case. I'm sure my mother will be more at peace knowing I didn't harm myself. For that, I'll always be grateful."

"I'm happy to have helped. Truly. You deserve peace and so does she."

I take a deep breath, preparing to ask the one question I've been waiting to have answered.

"Billy, before you go, can you tell me anything about Garrett? Where he is or how he's doing?"

He sighs. "He's someplace better." His one eye closes while the opposite eyebrow lifts into his hairline. "He told Harry, who told me to tell you that even if he could, he refused to be involved in anything cliché like the movies you used to force him to watch."

I burst into laughter, recalling movies we've watched over the years and how it always irked him and Ava that those people got to see their loved ones when nobody else gets to. It was entirely ridiculous, but just one of those things, and it brings a smile to my face.

"We wouldn't want that." I smile, but inside I'm crushed I don't get to say goodbye to him.

"Don't do that," Billy chastises, pointing a finger at me.

I catch a tear falling from my eye.

"He was never here to begin with, Alyssa. He was pulling strings with the help of someone big upstairs. He didn't choose not to see you. He lived a life without regrets and for that, he never got stuck here."

"Why? His accident wasn't solved just like yours. Why did you get stuck, and he didn't?"

He shrugs. "Maybe Garrett was a better man than me. Look at it as my punishment for a life that was less than straight."

I hiccup, wiping away more tears. Nick pulls me in to his side, offering me comfort I desperately need.

"Now you've gone and messed up your makeup. Nick will not be impressed." Billy grins. "You two look good together. Don't fuck it up."

I pull a face, glancing up at Nick. He smiles down at me, not seeming to give one iota about my smeared appearance.

"I'll miss you, Billy."

"Me too, Karen. Me too."

My arm lifts and I give the command. "You're free to move on."

He offers me one last smile and makes his way to the afterlife.

Justice

TWO WEEKS LATER

"OH MY GOD. Look at this one," Lanie says, holding a 4x6 photo in the air. "What's happening here?"

I make my way to Lanie, who's sitting cross-legged on the floor in front of a box of old photos she found in the bottom drawer of Garrett's desk.

We've been working for three hours to clear out the office. Corinne and Nina left twenty minutes ago to take one carload of items to donate to the local shelter. One more trip and all the boxes will be gone.

Going through Garrett's things hasn't been as hard as I'd thought it would be. It's the memories I have of our life together that mean more than a holey pair of jeans and trophies from high school he planned to throw out but never got around to.

It helps that I had my village here to keep me focused on the good times that each of the items I'm parting with were part of.

"Lemme see," I say, grabbing the picture and inspecting every aspect. "Ugh. That was the road trip from hell. We were visiting

Garrett's aunt in Cincinnati and Ava ended up with the stomach bug. She threw up until we reached the Pennsylvania and New York line."

"You're smiling," Lanie muses, inspecting the photo closer.

"Garrett had made some remark about my insistence on leather seats turning into a lifesaver." I chuckle. "That's a smile that reeks of *I told you so*."

"I can't even imagine what a mess that would've been with the stomach bug, a child, and cloth seats. Yuck." Lanie shudders.

"Exactly my point."

"That's the last one," she says, dropping the photo into the box and getting up off the floor. "It's all done."

"We're back," Nina calls out, joining us in the office, with Corinne hot on her heels.

I look around the space and smile, thinking about all the things I plan to use it for.

"What's that grin about?" Lanie asks.

I make my way out of the office toward the kitchen and the three of them follow me, nobody saying a word. "I've been thinking a lot about how I can use my gift in a bigger way. To help more people." I grab the folder of research I've been doing, open it, and slide it across the counter to Lanie and Nina.

They browse through the paperwork, and a wide smile slowly stretches across Nina's face.

"Seriously? This is amazing, Ally."

I nod. "I'm going to put that prelaw degree to good use. Finally."

"What exactly does that entail?" Lanie doesn't look up at me as she continues to shift through the paperwork.

"I'll likely need to work for another agency and get my three years of experience. Nick put me in touch with a guy who I'm meeting next week to discuss the various paths I could take."

"White Knight Nick swooping in to help his fair maiden. So cute."

My nose screws up. "You're ridiculous."

"And you're falling in love," Lanie singsongs.

My head snaps to her in surprise. "Love? Are you crazy? We haven't even been on a date, Lanie. Love does not factor in." I shrug. "We're just flirting."

"Stop flirting and get to fu—"

My phone beeps, thankfully cutting off what was sure to be Lanie at her most inappropriate.

> NICK
>
> Are you home?
> I have something I wanna tell you . . .

> ALYSSA
>
> Everything okay?

> NICK
>
> Fine. More than. Today we got the break
> we needed.

> ALYSSA
>
> I'm here. The crew is too, FYI.

> NICK
>
> See you ladies soon.

"What are you grinning about?" Corinne asks, glancing at the phone I have in my hand.

"That was Nick. Something big must've happened today with the case. He's on his way here to tell us."

Nina's shoulders straighten. "Good."

Lanie claps her hands and opens a cabinet, pulling down four shot glasses.

"What are you up to?" I ask, watching as she keeps busy pulling a bottle of liquor from the top of the refrigerator.

"We need a toast before he gets here. Can't drink in front of him, but I'll need the shot to take off the edge."

I roll my eyes. "You're a boozehound."

"I thought we discussed this," Corinne grumbles. "You're forty, not eighty. Lose your grandmother's vocabulary and start calling her a lush. That I'll accept."

"You're impossible."

She shrugs, grabbing her shot of gin that Lanie poured.

"Why gin? It's not exactly a good choice for a shot," Nina interjects.

"It's what we have. It'll do."

Lanie lifts her shot glass. "To Nick and his team. May they have the information they need to put those assholes away for life."

"I'll drink to that," I say, lifting my glass.

The other two follow suit.

"Cheers," we say in unison, slugging back the liquor.

✦ ✦ ✦

"WE HIT THE jackpot with Jenna's phone records," Nick says, leg bouncing from adrenaline. "It'll be hard for any of them to enter a not-guilty plea. Jenna's cell phone and iCloud were packed with incriminating evidence. Especially for Richard." He glances at Nina, but she doesn't react.

She's sat stone-faced and quiet through Nick's news. I wonder what's going through her head, but right now, I just want to hear everything Nick has to say.

"She had videos of Charlie admitting what he did and Richard alluding to collusion among other things. She was clearly documenting everything."

"Why?" I ask, confused since she was supposedly in a relationship with Richard.

"According to a string of text messages exchanged between the two, she was trying to get him to leave Nina and he refused."

Nina huffs a humorless laugh. "Of course he did. God forbid the man does me a favor."

"A scorned woman looking for revenge," Lanie chimes in and Nick shrugs one shoulder.

"He told her she could keep the items he purchased, but they were over."

I chance a glance at Nina, but again, she doesn't give anything away.

"That's when she started threatening to expose him."

"Motive," Corinne muses. "She was going to expose him, so he took her out first."

"It would seem so." Nick sighs. "We have a team on their way to Jenna's. Her mom gave permission for us to search the place." He turns toward Nina. "They're in the process of obtaining a search warrant for your home too. I shouldn't be telling you this, but since I know you have nothing to hide, I'm giving you a heads-up. They'll have it in hand by the end of the day."

She nods. "I have nothing to hide. Let 'em search."

Nick offers a tight-lipped smile.

"What about Jackson's case? Any progress there?" I ask, thinking about the burly biker I came to adore.

"I shared the tip about the branch. We have our team looking into the details of the accident. I hope that forensics can analyze the crime scene notes and work with a crash reconstruction expert to determine that the damage to the motorcycle could've been because of a branch."

"How will that prove it was Bernas and Wells?" Corinne asks, parroting my thoughts.

"Unfortunately, it won't. I just hope that it will aid in one of them offering up details for a plea deal. The prosecution is prepared to offer deals in exchange for closure for the families, from what I've been told."

"Did my tip help?" Lanie asks.

"It will," he says. "We have a team already on scene at Lux. I'm sure we'll have evidence within the hour. Marcus is cocky. Thinks he's above the law."

"When you have the mayor covering your tracks, I guess you can be arrogant," Nina remarks, and we all nod in agreement.

"We talked to Milly. She admits that he approached her, but she maintains she turned him down. She gave us permission to access whatever we needed to prove her innocence."

I'm relieved to hear that. It would've been horrible if Milly and the diner went down because she was hard up for cash.

"I think we should do something to help drum up business for her." I'll do whatever it takes to not lose a Knox Harbor staple like Milly's.

"From what she said, someone approached her about investing in the diner. She's negotiating a partnership as we speak." Nick glances down at his phone.

"That's fantastic. Any idea who?" As soon as I ask the question, my eyes land on Lanie.

Her head is lowered and she's playing with her fingers. A giveaway that she might have an idea. I want to ask, but Nick speaks, drawing my attention away from Lanie.

"Nah. She wouldn't say. Said they prefer to remain anonymous, but that we'd uncover it if we started digging." He glances around the room. "These are all details I should not be sharing with any of you. It goes against my better judgment and could cost me my job. But if not for you four, these cases would've remained closed or cold. But I need all of this to stay in this room. My job depends on it."

"I won't say a word," I promise, and the other girls offer their own vows of silence.

He nods. "I've gotta get going. They've got something at Lux. I have to head that way."

He eyes the empty shot glasses that none of us remembered to put away. "You ladies have fun."

My face warms, but he doesn't see. He's already headed toward the front of the house.

"I'll walk him out," I say to the group.

Lanie waggles her eyebrows, earning a scowl from Corinne, but I don't catch whatever's said. I'm too focused on catching up to Nick.

When we reach the front door, he steps through and I shut it behind us, shutting out the chatter from inside.

"I'm sorry about . . ." My words trail off and Nick's lips form a thin line.

"Sorry about what?"

"The alcohol. I . . . well . . ." I sigh. "I know that you're sober."

He nods. "That doesn't mean you can't drink. I didn't know when to stop, Alyssa. I was using it as a crutch to forget my pain." He offers a sad smile. "Those days are behind me. I'm better now."

"I know you are."

I hope he knows I mean that with my whole heart.

"What are you troublemakers up to today?" he says, grinning wide and breaking the tension.

"We've been working in the office. It's my turn to cope with my grief in healthy ways."

He grabs my hand and pulls me toward him. "Day by day, Lyss. I'm here for you. Whenever you need to talk."

I lean up on my tippy toes and place a kiss on his cheek. "Thank you, Nick. For everything."

He lets out a breath. "We have a long way to go to close this case, but all the steps are in place, and I feel good about things."

"Me too."

A large white truck pulls up, drawing our attention to the street.

"What's this?" he asks, motioning toward the truck.

"New furniture." I shrug. "It's all part of the moving forward phase."

He pulls me into a hug, placing a kiss on top of my head. "I'm proud of you."

I sigh into his embrace, not wanting him to leave. I could stay out here like this all day.

When he releases me, stepping back, I miss his touch instantly.

"I'm going to be busy for the next few weeks, working with the force to close these cases."

I nod.

"When it's all over with, I want to take you out."

He lifts his hand, running it over my scar. At one point, that would've been enough to send me spiraling, but not anymore. I know that he sees it like I do. A warrior's mark. A reminder that I've been through hell and survived. It's a representation of my strength.

I lick my lips, grinning up at him. "Take me out where, exactly?"

"On a date. Somewhere nice."

"Will that date end in a kiss? Maybe more?"

I'm flirting something fierce, which is new. Nick brings out a playful side in me. One that's entirely new. Based on the way he's smiling and shaking his head, he likes it.

"I'd plan on it." He smirks.

"Well . . . you better get busy, wrapping this case up."

He leans in and places a chaste kiss to my lips. "I'll see you later." He basically jumps off the porch, forgoing the stairs entirely. I have to cover my goofy grin with my fist. He's only a few feet away when he turns back over his shoulder. "You four stay out of trouble. No sleuthing for a bit."

I offer a three-fingered salute, which earns an eye roll and smile in return.

There's no doubt that things are about to get interesting between me and the sexy detective next door. And I'm here for it.

Epilogue

Ten of Cups

ONE MONTH LATER

TODAY IS A day for celebration, and I'm doing that by going on my first official date with Nick. We've hung out several nights, but this will be the first time out on the town, where other people will see us together. The rumor mills will be buzzing by tomorrow.

The entire town has been jonesing for new gossip. Apparently, talk of murder is growing old.

Rumor has it the prosecution offered Richard a plea deal if he'd testify against Bernas and Wells. There's no doubt in my mind he took it. Several pieces of jewelry were recovered from Jenna's home that were insured by Richard. Not to mention the apartment itself and her car were both in Richard's false name, Carrhid Durban.

Santos is set to testify that Richard brought in the truck and paid him off to total it and discard the evidence, incriminating him further. A handwriting expert confirmed that the note found by Mrs. Garet, which was supposedly written by Billy, was in fact not. There was DNA pointing to Richard. And that's just the tip of the iceberg on what the DA has from Jenna's phone.

Nick spoke on behalf of Charlie, asking for a reduced sentence for his help in solving the case. He left off that alcohol played a major part in his admission. Either way, he'll serve time for vehicular manslaughter.

Wells offered the DA details on where Amanda could be hiding, and when she's brought in, she'll face attempted murder charges at the very least. He also supplied information on Jenna's murder weapon and details on how Bernas killed her, for his own deal. They're all sinking their own cases, and it couldn't be sweeter to watch.

Not for everyone. The Red Hatters were hoping for a trial worthy of a Netflix documentary and are very public with their disappointment on how quickly it's being wrapped up.

As if the details of the crimes aren't juicy enough.

I'm just happy to have my house free of trapped spirits and their crazy hijinks.

Tonight, I refuse to think about any of that. I'm moving forward with my life and this date is just the start.

I took special care getting ready for tonight, blowing out my hair and working some light curls into the mix. My makeup took some time, choosing colors that complement my green eyes. Shaky hands, a symptom of nerves, made it difficult to line my eyes with charcoal liner, but I managed. A simple shiny gloss over my lips finishes the look. Makeup isn't something I typically care to perfect, but tonight I hope to knock Nick's socks off.

Stepping up to the floor-length mirror I take a look at the end result and smile. Lanie helped me pick out my outfit yesterday. When she first offered her assistance, I was nervous. My style typically differs from hers, greatly, but I must admit, she nailed it.

She chose an off-white sweater that she suggested I tuck a portion of into my light skinny jeans. It's accessorized with nude pumps and gold jewelry.

I glance down at my hand, staring at the ring I've worn for almost seventeen years. There will never come a day that I don't cherish the memories associated with this token of Garrett's love, and no part of me that believes Nick would mind if I kept it on my finger.

A tapping noise sounds on my window, but I ignore it, snapping a picture and sending it off to my friends and Ava for validation that I look as good as I feel.

The sound continues and I grow curious. Making my way to the window, I peek around the curtain to find a small cardinal tapping its beak against the glass. I recall Garrett's mom's insistence that cardinals are a sign of your loved ones who've died being present. I bend down, eye level with the bird, who's perched on the small ledge. It doesn't fly away, and I have to wonder if there's some truth in the myth.

"Hi, Garrett," I whisper, holding on to the hope that maybe this little guy is the spirit of my late husband, coming to give his blessing.

He taps his beak against the window once more before flying off into the night. A sense of peace washes over me and I close my eyes to bask in it.

I find myself slipping off my wedding ring and placing it on the opposite hand. I'm not sure what possesses me to do it other than a deep knowing I've learned to trust.

I doubt a day will come when it's permanently removed, because my love for Garrett I'll carry until my last breath. Nick or whomever else I decide to give my heart to in the future will have to understand that for us to work.

My phone pings, and I look down to see a text from Lanie.

LANIE
Holy Hotness! I did good . . .

ALYSSA
I think so! Thanks for your help!

LANIE
Have fun tonight! Wear protection.

I gasp at the audacity of my friend. Not that I'm surprised. The girl wouldn't consider it a date if it didn't end with sex.

The thought of being with Nick makes my stomach flutter and tingles spread across my body.

I've never been so nervous in my life. Well . . . maybe one night, under the stars with a man who changed my life. But I know this will be different. Not better or worse, just . . . different.

Nick and Garrett are two entirely different men.

Nick is gruff and alpha, things I never thought I'd want, but it turns out, it's exactly what I need. The way he stares at me turns my belly to molten lava and my legs to mush.

I don't usually rush into things, but a man like Nick West has been hard to resist. Tonight, I might not. To hell with waiting. Life's too short and I want to be wrapped around Nick until the sun rises.

Hopefully he won't take much convincing.

I grab my long, camel coat and head downstairs just in time to hear a knock on my door.

My entire body burns, knowing who's on the other side.

Here goes nothing.

I swing it open and my breath hitches as I get a look at the man. His hair is artfully mussed, giving him an air of *I don't give a flying F*, but his nervous smile tells a different story. He's wearing a black round-neck sweater that molds to his slim, fit torso perfectly. It's paired with dark jeans and black boots that make the whole package something straight out of my dreams.

"You look beautiful, Alyssa."

I grin, thinking about how freaking hot he looks with the moon shining down around him, illuminating him like a Greek god. I'm going to throw caution to the wind and shoot my shot by pulling him into my house and making him mine.

Grabbing his arm, I pull him in, not at all gentle. I barely have the door closed before his mouth is on mine and I'm throwing my coat to the floor.

Sweet Jesus can this man kiss a girl senseless.

Every night we've spent together since the case was solved has gotten progressively more intense, but right here in this moment, you'd need a foghorn and fire hose to separate me from him. Even then . . . good luck.

His arms wrap around my body, pulling me flush against him. I moan into his mouth as proof of his attraction presses against me. My core tightens with need and my kisses grow feral. Our tongues twirl around each other in between nips at my bottom lip. The mewling noises coming from me would be embarrassing if I wasn't so lost in him.

I slide my hands down his sides until they hit the top of his jeans, moving toward the button. My fingers fumble with the thing, attempting to make my intentions known.

Nick groans, pulling away and leaning his forehead against mine. His breathing is labored and when I place my hand on his arms, which are pressed against the wall encasing me, I feel them quiver under my touch.

He clearly found it hard to pull away . . . so why did he?

Mint and sandalwood wash over me until Nick presses off the wall and puts distance between us, leaving me panting with need.

"That . . . was some greeting." His husky voice settles over me and the tingles from before magnify.

I step back into him, pushing up on to my toes, grabbing him by his sweater to pull him closer still. "It doesn't have to stop there."

I press my lips to his, resulting in a lingering kiss that I hope conveys *I'm ready for more.*

"We'd better go," he chuckles against my lips, pulling away again and grinning down at me.

I don't need him to tell me he can read me like a book. He's been able to since the day we first spoke. Right now, my body is screaming *Come hither* and he sees it. So why stop?

"Do we have to?" I bite my bottom lip, trying at seduction.

"Yes," he says, hauling me into him once more and placing a soft kiss to my forehead. "I'm doing this right. Food first and then we'll see where this night goes." He winks and fireworks explode in my gut. "You look too gorgeous not to show you off. I want everyone in town to know you're mine."

Well, when he puts it like that . . .

There's no doubt in my mind that dating Nick will be an adventure. One that begins tonight.

I grab my coat off the floor and follow Nick into the cold Massachusetts night. I close the door and lock it, but when we turn to go, Nina is standing in the dark, blocking our path.

She looks haggard and sick.

"Nina? What's wrong?" I ask, rushing to her side, pulling her arm under mine to ensure she doesn't fall over.

"I . . . I saw what Richard did." Her voice wobbles so much I almost miss the words.

"What do you mean? Are you saying you didn't know this whole time?"

That would change everything. Nina always told us she was protecting us by not sharing the details. If she didn't know, why was she so scared? What has she been hiding?

She shakes her head violently. "I knew he was aware of my past, but he promised he wouldn't interfere if I stayed. I just saw what Richard did today when I visited the prison to serve him divorce papers."

My mouth drops open and I'm unsure what to make of this.

"How did you see it?" I manage to get out.

"When I touched him, I saw the measures he's taken in case I left. It was like watching a horrible movie. He lied to me, Alyssa." Her bottom lip quivers and I take a step toward her.

I'm not surprised to hear that Richard lied to her. He's lied to everyone. She doesn't need to be reminded of that right now.

I glance at Nick, whose eyes are narrowed in on Nina.

"Did you find anything during the search warrant that could be used against Nina?" I ask Nick, wanting to get as much information as I can to try to understand this development.

"No," he says, shaking his head. "There wasn't anything incriminating for her. What does he have on you, Nina?"

As curious as I am to finally uncover her secrets, I want to protect her more. I trust Nick implicitly, but I think this is something we should discuss when she's not distraught. Right now, the bigger question for me is how she acquired the information.

"We'll get to all that," I say to Nick, but my eyes never stray from Nina. "But right now, I need to understand *how* you found this out."

She swallows. "I think something is wrong with me. Ever since your birthday. The night we first saw Corinne, I've been seeing strange things when I touch someone. Personal stuff I don't want to see." I blink several times, trying to process what Nina's saying. "I thought I was going crazy. It wasn't until I saw Richard's thoughts that I realized how messed up I am." She grabs my arm. "Help me."

I gulp. This can only mean one thing . . .

Nina has a gift too.

Acknowledgments

First and foremost, thank you for reading this book. I hope it provided a fun escape with a few laughs along the way.

A huge thank-you to my agent, Carrie Pestritto. You're an absolute rock star and I'm so grateful to have you in my corner.

Thank you to my editor, Esi Sogah, for taking a chance on this debut author. You'll never know how your decision to help publish this book changed my life in so many amazing ways. Thank you isn't enough.

Thank you to the entire Berkley team. You've been incredible to work with. This experience has been a dream and I give you all the credit.

Many thanks to Amy, for encouraging me to write this story. If not for our phone chats about my woo happenings, this story wouldn't be here today. Thank you for always having my back and being the sounding board I need. You've been a constant in my life, and I value our friendship immensely.

Thank you to Sharon, for posting that branding question back in the day. That one event changed so much in the best way. You pushed me to publish my first book and I'm eternally grateful. You knew my hopes and dreams in publishing before I did.

Thank you to my "West" aunts whose influence throughout life helped me to see that I am good enough.

Thank you to the "Holtz" aunts for talking books with me. I appreciate you so much.

To my grandma, Shirley, your tender heart and caring ways were a comfort growing up. I'll always remember that it was the field behind your trailer where I first found my knack for daydreaming. Thank you for the years of pancakes, cuddles, and support.

Thank you to all the bloggers, influencers, Paper Myths, and Graceley for your help in getting the word out about this book. Your support is much appreciated.

Thank you to my mom, Theresa, for all the times you took care of the kids so that I could finish this book. You and bonus dad were lifesavers on numerous occasions. Mostly, thank you for instilling in me that I could do anything I set my mind to. I hope I've made you proud.

Thank you to S and C, for everything. This project took a village. I appreciate you two beyond measure. Save a room for me in Florida. I'm ready for some relaxation and nightly sunset cheers.

Finally, thank you to my family, #14, Z, A, and G. Your love and support throughout all of this got me through the longest days. I write because I love to, but I publish for you and the dreams we have for the future.

MELISSA HOLTZ is a former publicist and marketing expert in the romance genre. Now in an advisory role to several bestselling authors, she consults on industry marketing trends. *An Enchanting Case of Spirits* is her debut novel.

Visit Melissa Holtz Online

MelissaHoltz.com

⊙ AuthorMelissaHoltz

♪ AuthorMelissaHoltz